Portia Da Costa is one of the most internationally renowned authors of erotica.

She is the author of seventeen *Black Lace* novels, as well as being a contributing author to a number of short story collections.

Also by Portia Da Costa

The Accidental Series:
The Accidental Call Girl
The Accidental Mistress
The Accidental Bride

Gothic Series:
Gothic Blue
Gothic Heat
Gemini Heat

Novels:
Hotbed
Shadowplay
The Tutor
Entertaining Mr Stone
Continuum
The Devil Inside
Hotbed
Gemini Heat
The Stranger
In Too Deep
The Gift

Short Stories:
The Red Collection

Suite Seventeen

PORTIA DA COSTA

BLACK
LACE

13 5 7 9 10 8 6 4 2

First published in 2007 by Black Lace, an imprint of Virgin Publishing
This edition published in 2014 by Black Lace, an imprint of Ebury Publishing
A Random House Group Company

The Random House Group Limited Reg. No. 954009

Addresses for companies within the Random House Group can be
found at: www.randomhouse.co.uk

A CIP catalogue record for this book is
available from the British Library

The Random House Group Limited supports The Forest Stewardship
Council® (FSC®), the leading international forest-certification organisation.
Our books carrying the FSC label are printed on FSC® -certified paper.
FSC is the only forest-certification scheme supported by the
leading environmental organisations, including Greenpeace.
Our paper procurement policy can be found at:
www.randomhouse.co.uk/environment

Printed and bound by CPI Group (UK) Ltd, Croydon, CR0 4YY

ISBN 9780352347817

This one is for Boy,
a beloved friend who is sorely missed.

Suite Seventeen

Prologue

The taxi drops me outside the familiar rambling, ivy-covered building and, as I pay the man and step out on to the gravel, my heart gives a thud and starts to race.

Calm down. Breathe. There's nothing to be afraid of.

Well, maybe there is, but it's a good kind of fear.

Waverley Grange, it says on the sign, and the logo's discreet, elegant, and conservative.

Conservative? You must be kidding!

The Waverley might well be the acme of discretion and elegance on the outside, but it's the last place on earth you'd call conservative. At least, not if you know what to ask for.

The lobby is unusually quiet. The subdued décor purrs money. Wood panelling gleams softly with a loving sheen. Understated prints hang on the walls. A few old but treasured pieces of furniture adorn the hushed space. A low table. An ornate coat-stand. A couple of squashy leather chesterfields in a deep bay window.

All so comforting. So welcoming. So innocuous.

I drag in a deep breath, my breasts lifting beneath the tailored jacket of my suit, and walk briskly and determinedly towards the reception desk.

Behind it stands a tall rather striking woman, writing in a ledger. As I approach, she looks up and I admire the way her long dark hair is wound into a complex knot at the base of her shapely skull. Her statuesque bosom is encased in a plain immaculate white blouse and I admire that too, sneaking glances at it but hoping she doesn't notice.

'Good evening, Mrs Conroy. How nice to see you again.'

The engraved nameplate on the desk says 'Saskia Woodville – Assistant Manager' and her smile is as elegant and deceptive as our surroundings. Her expression is warm, yet at the same time strangely cool and assessing. It's not something you could put your finger on, but it's there, because I know what I'm looking for.

'Good evening. It's nice to be here again,' I answer, trying to ignore the quivers and shivers in my stomach and my crotch. I definitely need to brush up on my thespian skills. They're developing, but they could be a good deal more accomplished in scenarios like these.

The assistant manager consults her register, even though we both know she certainly doesn't need to. 'Ah, yes, Suite Seventeen ... It's all ready for you, Mrs Conroy. Do you have a bag?'

All I have is a smallish shoulder bag. I don't need anything else. Everything I'll ever really need – now and forever – is up there in that suite. But I still tap the bag and nod, as if it were an extensive matched set of Louis Vuitton that I couldn't possibly manage all on my own.

Saskia the manager smiles, a sly glint in her dark eyes. 'Of course. I'll get Maria to carry that up for you.'

She dings a bell on the desk and almost immediately a slightly dizzy-looking young blonde woman comes scooting through a door behind the desk and rushes forward to assist me.

She isn't doing nearly as good an acting job as either Saskia or I. She's even biting her soft pink lips in an attempt to stop herself from laughing. As well she might, given the clichéd pantomime silliness of her get-up.

Maria is wearing a full-on, full-blown fetish French

maid's outfit, complete with four-inch stiletto heels, starched lace cap and white apron. Her saucy black skirt floats on a soufflé of soft net petticoats and barely covers the tops of her shapely thighs. My God, how I wish I were that young with legs that long and curvy!

'Good evening, Ma'am,' she coos, bobbing me a curtsey and reaching for my near nothing of a burden.

I allow her to take it because, for the moment, I'm the one who's in charge and here to be waited on.

'Show Mrs Conroy to Suite Seventeen, will you, Maria?' Saskia says in a cool loaded tone, and naughty Maria's face straightens immediately. I hide my own smile now, knowing what might – or most probably *will* – happen if young Maria doesn't behave with a bit more decorum.

Maria bobs another curtsey, takes the room key-card and says, 'Please come this way,' in a bright, 'must please the clientele' voice.

I flash Saskia a smile, and she nods gravely. She looks serious, formal and professionally courteous, but I can see that, beneath her composed act, she's really smiling too. Even laughing.

In the lift, I have a tough time not grinning at Maria the maid. Just as tough a time as she's having not smiling at me. In the end, she has to look downwards and study the highly polished toes of her patent leather high heels.

In the floor-to-ceiling glass on the back wall of the lift, I find something else to look at that makes my insides quiver.

The exposed backs of Maria's pretty thighs are all red.

The sight of that simmering skin makes my sex clench with anticipation and longing. I flick through a short mental list of people who might have perpetrated that fiery glow. There's one blindingly obvious candidate, of course, and I wonder if he too is here in the hotel tonight. Obviously, not in Suite Seventeen though.

As I surreptitiously study Maria's luscious thighs, my mind also flicks through a catalogue of devices. Strap? Cane? Hand? What did that to her, I wonder, feeling an intense urge to touch my own thighs through the smoothly woven cloth of my skirt. The compulsion is like a hunger and, trying not to draw attention to myself, I press my palm against my own flesh. It's not as firm and resilient as young Maria's, but it's not bad. In fact, it's pretty damn perky for a woman who won't see forty again.

As the lift doors slide smoothly open, Maria totters ahead of me, and I wonder if the soreness makes it difficult for her to walk. And I also wonder if she's wearing any underwear beneath that snowy froth of petticoats.

I'm wearing knickers myself but only because tonight they've been specified. I drag in a long deep breath at the sight of the brass numberplate on the door in front of us.

I don't really know why it's called Suite Seventeen. It's not actually a suite, but simply a large fairly luxurious room with a bathroom. But it does offer so many more facilities than any normal bedroom does.

Tucking my bag under her arm for a moment, Maria deftly slips the key-card into the slot and opens the door, before stepping back to allow me to precede her into the softly lit interior.

My heart thumps hard again.

As expected, a familiar dark-clad figure is sitting in one of the large overstuffed chintz-covered chairs. His body is still and utterly relaxed, almost as if he's been meditating while he was waiting for my arrival.

'Will that be all, Ma'am?' Maria asks, keeping her gaze lowered as she pops my bag on the sideboard, then skitters backwards respectfully towards the door.

Before I can answer, my fellow 'guest' speaks softly. 'No, stay a few moments if you would.'

His voice is deep and beautifully accented. It's the sort of voice that seems to play upon nerve ends in sensitive intimate places and induce pleasure even without the benefit of physical touch. It's certainly doing diabolical things to me.

Maria half-steps towards the door and then falters. She bites her soft pink lower lip, in a quandary. She's been refused permission to leave, but probably needs the permission of another to stay. Her eyes flit swiftly around the room, and she suddenly shrugs, almost apologetically ... but not to me and not to the man in the chintz chair.

I don't think she'll be in any real trouble, but I suspect her thighs might get even pinker before the night is out.

But it's not really Maria's thighs I should be worrying about. It's my own. Growing more and more excited, I press them together, and clench my buttocks and my sex. Anything to get some stimulation. I'm so turned on now that I swear I could scream ... and I don't think he's even looked at me yet.

For several moments, he just sits there in silence. Utterly motionless, he stares out of the window at what really is a very beautiful night. The heavy velvet curtains are open and light from the high-riding full moon adds to the glow of illumination provided by several carefully arranged antique lamps.

The tension in the room is thick enough to slice. I'm the one who's biting her lips now, and I'm clenching my fists too, while Maria is clearly fighting hard not to fidget and dance about. She wants to get back to her own man, I know that, and, even though he's not specifically my type, I can understand why she dotes on him.

But what of *my* man?

My heart flutters. Can I really call him that? Can a man so dominant and so alpha be claimed that way? He's a force of nature, and that's difficult to possess.

Suddenly I have to gasp. I didn't realise I'd been holding my breath. The small sound finally attracts the attention of the long figure lounging amongst the chintz.

His eyes are lustrous in the warm light, mesmerising and slanted and the colour of beaten copper. They look almost alien somehow. He favours me with a narrow perusal, taking in everything about me in a single long quantifying look. His body is possessed of an uncanny, almost reptilian stillness and, if it wasn't for the slow even lifting of his deep broad chest, I could almost imagine he was a graven image. A lifelike representation of some ancient Mediterranean god.

The seconds and moments string out and I imagine my nerves being stretched like elastic bands. But, just when I think I really am going to scream, he blinks once, in a sweep of thick black lashes and tilts his dark head a little.

Oh, God, let me move. Let me speak. I'm going crazy.

But of course, I can't speak. Or move. Not without his permission.

'So ... Here we are,' he says quietly, and the soft words seem to bounce off the delicately patterned paper on the walls.

I curl my toes inside my shoes and seriously wonder if I'm going to pass out.

The words also seem to unlock something inside him. He relaxes even more in his chair, stretching out his long, long legs in front of him. He's wearing leather trousers, which should be a ridiculous macho-stud cliché, but actually just look wonderful encasing his lean powerful thighs. The fine hide gleams too, just like his eyes.

'Undress her,' he says in a level ordinary voice as if his request was entirely normal and usual.

We both know who has to undress whom and, diligently, Maria springs into action – while it's my turn to act the graven image.

She's excited too. I can see it in her eyes as she begins to unbutton my jacket. I detect slightly less of that anxiousness to get away now, as if she's decided that she likes this scene and wants to play in it. She licks her soft pink lips as she works on the buttons, really putting on a show, and, as she slides the jacket off my shoulders, her fingers brush against me far more lingeringly than they need to.

Suddenly, and so shockingly that I sway on my heels, a phone rings, and our master picks up a mobile from the dressing table beside him.

'*Pronto?*' he says, his voice more musical in his native tongue, and Maria and I freeze in our tableau, even though we both know we're not supposed to eavesdrop.

It's impossible to hear who he's speaking to, but it's clearly a friend, and I think both Maria and I have a shrewd idea which one. Our master laughs softly, and looks slyly our way as if responding to some appealing suggestion. His dark eyebrows lift, and he answers, 'Why, yes, I'd be happy to ... That would be my pleasure. *Ciao!*'

As if to confirm my suspicions, he winks at Maria as he snaps his phone shut and she, in turn, smiles – a slow, sly smile – then glances around the room. She speaks not a word, but I can see she's communicating.

Which leaves me, standing here, waiting. My nipples are startlingly prominent beneath the silk of my blouse and my lightweight lace bra, and without warning Maria touches a fingertip to one of them, and flicks at it. I catch my breath and my master laughs with delight.

He laughs even louder when Maria grabs hold of me, messily kisses my lips and gropes my bottom.

I want to kiss back, because she's pretty and sexy and I'm very fond of her, but I haven't been given permission to do anything yet. Unlike Maria. By unspoken agreement she's now a free agent. She's changed sides. She's not quite my mistress but she's got the upper hand.

Despite this, she continues to undress me. After a fashion . . .

First, she half unfastens my blouse and pushes it off my shoulders. Then she flicks down the straps of my bra and shoves that down too, exposing my breasts.

Part of me wishes she'd undress me properly, but another part of me – some deep dark slut right at the centre of my psyche – just glories in being exhibited. My nipples harden even more, almost to the point of pain, and I can feel myself anointing my panties.

Maria steps back, and casts a glance towards my master, who nods approvingly. With lazy grace, he gets to his feet, and I tense every muscle in my body, hoping he'll come over and fondle me. But instead, and to my surprise, he peels off his own shirt. He strips it off quickly, flings it on the floor and just stands there like the male model he once was, posing. As he eyes me, assessing and critiquing my bare breasts, he idly fondles his own flat male nipple.

My God, you don't half love yourself, don't you?

In all my life I've never met a more unrepentant

narcissist than this tall dark beautiful man. But who can blame him for being entranced with his own appearance? *I'd* be entranced by *my* own appearance if my face and body were as sensational as his.

The chest he's touching so lovingly is broad and sculpted. He's a cliché of male catwalk pulchritude – a woman's sex fantasy of silky tanned skin, ripped musculature, imposing height and elegance. He patently adores himself – and I adore him too.

His copper eyes challenge me and taunt me. *You want this body, don't you?* they seem to say, and I have to grit my teeth to stop myself from nodding.

Well, if you want me, those gleaming eyes tell me, *you'll have to do something to deserve me.*

It's a long moment, a multilayered communication, and beneath the surface of our game something else entirely different stirs. His lips soften for an instant, he blinks just once and almost smiles. And then the momentary reveal is gone again; his head comes up imperiously, and I tremble.

My arms hang down by my sides, framing my bared breasts and my stiff nipples, but my curving fingers tingle and prickle. I want to either touch him, or touch myself. I cast a brief, pleading glance towards Maria, begging her to reach between my legs and give me ease, but her expression is arch and taunting too. I'm *her* toy now, just as much as his.

Maria gives me a stern look. Well, as stern as she can while wearing her cartoon outfit. 'She's a bit insolent, isn't she, this one?' she observes to my master, but, before he can answer, she's touching me again. Pulling at my nipples. Tweaking them. My toes curl again in my shoes as I fight the small pain, and deep in my crotch I feel a heavy clenching pulse of raw desire. A blush of hot excitement stains my face.

'She has no discipline,' my master comments, moving closer, allowing me a better view of his perfection as he observes me, his strange eyes critical.

I hunger for him. I yearn to touch that strong smooth jaw and those lush sexy lips. I want to slide my fingers around the shape of his proud skull, and then release his long black hair from the leather thong that contains it at the nape of his neck. I can almost feel the satin caress of it against my belly and my thighs as he deigns to consider my pleasure and kiss my sex.

Which probably won't happen for a while yet, but you never know.

As I look up at him, drinking in the fire and the mock disdain in his eyes, he speaks again. To Maria once more, not me, his slave. 'I'd like to see her cunt,' he remarks bluntly.

'So would I,' intones Maria with a bright smile.

And, with that, she pushes me back towards the bed, groping my breast again as we go. She shoves me back against the patterned duvet cover, and then manhandles me right across it until my feet are off the floor. My master follows and settles gracefully beside me while Maria quickly unfastens my skirt and peels it off, then tugs off my panties too.

'Knees up! Open yourself!' she commands, and meekly I obey, assuming a position that both humiliates and glorifies me.

On my back, with my stocking-clad knees clasped against my breasts and my feet in the air, the entire topography of my sex and bottom is crudely on show for the pleasure and edification of my master and his associate.

I close my eyes, the thrill in them too intense to reveal, but that low accented voice says, 'No, no, no ...' And then he's in my face, looking down at me, his own eyes dark as night, and pagan. He inserts a finger inside me and slowly pumps it in and out while I gasp for air like a beached fish.

'Filthy girl,' he whispers, while I fight the orgasm that I know I'm destined to be punished for.

And, all the while, a still, small, grown-up and detached part of me smiles and counts the years since I could genuinely be called a girl.

But, do you know, as I start to come, I just don't care!

1 Bar Hopping

I imagine everybody's looking at me as I walk into the bar, but if I'm honest with myself I don't particularly know why they should.

The elegant Lawns Bar at the Waverley Grange Hotel is full and buzzing tonight, and there are plenty of stunning young women in here. Why should heads turn for a rather ordinary widow in her forties, even if she is pretty well preserved and not really showing her years?

It was a daft idea to arrange to meet Charles here, really. I should have done what I always did when I was dating Stan, back when the dinosaurs roamed and allowed myself to be picked up, treated like a lady and driven to the restaurant, the pub or wherever we were meeting.

But something's got into me lately and I've started doing mad things now and again. Well, to be honest, I'm doing them pretty often.

It all really started when I sold the rambling show-piece of a house that I'd shared with Stan and moved to something far more modest. A nice little detached in Lavender Court – light on upkeep and with a small easy-to-manage garden.

So far so good ... until I started watching my neighbours.

Gathering my nerve, I walk up to the bar and choose a stool down at the quietest end, and away from the main throng. I don't want to get mistaken for a woman who's trying to pick up a man.

The instant the idea prances through my head, I feel a shuddering kick of excitement, deep in my belly.

What *would* it be like to pick up a stranger here? Then take a room, drag him up there and have great sex?

Sex. Again.

I can't stop thinking about it. I haven't had any for far too long and, up until I moved into Lavender Court, I honestly hadn't missed it all that much. But one night I happened to look out of my bedroom window . . . and what I saw in the moonlight has been in my thoughts ever since.

A rather sweet-looking young barman approaches and asks me what I'd like. He has the most gorgeous eyes and, for a moment, he's the one I've picked up and lured to my room. I get a dirty little frisson as I wonder what his cock is like, and he has to ask me again about the drink before I can gather my wits and order a gin and tonic.

I didn't mean to order a real drink this early. I was planning to stay on mineral water until Charles arrives. But the clean bite of the gin is welcome and bracing when the barman proves to be as efficient as he is pretty and my drink arrives in double quick time.

'Would you like to open a tab?' he enquires, while I gulp down my first sip like a lush.

Tab? I've never opened a tab in my life. I haven't even bought my own drinks in quite a while. But in for a penny, in for a pound. 'Yes, that'd be great!'

He nods and gives me a delicious smile, and like a daft old bat I smile back, as if I'm flirting. Maybe I am. Yummy young barman humours me with a naughty little wink.

As he moves away to serve someone else, I feel ridiculously keyed up. It's as if I've already swigged down two or three gins instead of just a few sips of one. My heart is racing, and my skin is warm and seems hypersensitive inside my clothes. I look down and nearly spill my drink ... because my nipples are actually poking visibly against the dark-red velvet material of my dress.

My God, I'm turning into a dirty old woman!

My thoughts immediately turn to Charles, my date. I'd seen this as just a pleasant evening out with a very personable, slightly younger man who just happens to be my new investment manager. A chance to get out of the house. Nothing more ... Although I must admit I was quite flattered when he suggested a chat over dinner instead of at the office because it would be more 'relaxed'.

Now, with my nipples on red alert and other bits of me feeling distinctly roused, I begin cautiously to speculate that there might be more than just my portfolio on the table

Charles is cute. Very cute indeed. Thirties, crisply cut dark hair, quite lean, but with what looks like a pretty good body beneath his smart trendy suits. And he does seem to be a bit on the flirtatious side with me. I'd put that down to just him buttering up a good customer, but who knows ... There might be something real to it if I were to indicate my willingness.

Tonight could be the night. If I wanted it.

And right now, with a bit of Dutch courage and a lot of pent-up frustration fizzing through my veins, I *do* want it.

I signal for another drink, wondering how much of a mistake it was to get here so early. And when the cute barman delivers it, and I take my first sip, I sense a subtle change in the atmosphere in the bar. One or two people nearby turn around and, when curiosity gets the better of me, I too turn to check out whoever it is who's just entered ...

And I get the surprise of my life.

It's one of my neighbours! The ones I watch . . .

Her name is Maria Lewis. I know that much because we've chatted quite a bit over the garden fence or when our paths have crossed while coming and going. In fact, she was the one who reminded me about the Waverley. She's mentioned it once or twice, come to think of it, although for the life of me I can't remember in what context.

Maria is really pretty. A genuine stunner. She has shiny, wheat-blonde hair styled in a flirty, retro shag cut – and she's always smiling as if she knows an exciting secret.

Which she probably does . . . And it'll be something to do with the big burly, rather imposing man that she lives with. He's about twenty years older than she is, and he's her boss as well as her lover. They both work for the local borough, and he has a high-powered job as the Director of Finance. Robert Stone always looks as if he's thinking about that same exciting secret that Maria is, and it's obvious from the way they carry on that they're both sex mad. Not to mention completely besotted with one another.

Gosh, she looks awesome tonight.

Here I was, thinking I'd pulled out all the stops with one of my Christmas cocktail dresses . . . But I look like a frump compared to beautiful young Maria in her short tight black dress, her sheer smoky tights and her killer heels. Her look is 'high-class hooker', but, seeing all the admiring and frankly lustful glances she's getting, I suddenly wish that I looked a bit tartier myself.

She approaches with all the sass and grace of a supermodel, and all the sensuality of a woman who's getting masses of fantastic sex. I wonder whether to wave and try to attract her attention. She's always warm and friendly when we meet putting our dustbins out for collection, or to chat about the weather and the soaps, but tonight she looks as if she has an agenda.

In which case, where's her beloved Robert? Despite their bizarre sexual antics, I've never seen a couple more obviously in love, and it seems odd that he's nowhere to be seen.

But, before I can even start to dither, she looks straight at me, beams and then sashays in my direction. 'Hi, Annie, how goes it?'

There's a genuine pleasure in her voice, as if she's really delighted to see me here, and this quite shocks me after the plastic way some of my so-called friends have started greeting me nowadays. It seems that my former circle from the golf club and the Townswomen's Guild and elsewhere see me as an inconvenient 'spare' or a threat to their marriages because I'm on my own. So the invitations are so thin on the ground these days they're virtually non-existent.

But that's by the by because, instead of the expected air kiss, Maria leans right in and gives me an enthusiastic smacker on the cheek, followed by a tight close perfumed hug. While I'm still absorbing this, she pulls up a stool next to mine and perches her beautiful little bottom neatly on it.

'I'm so glad to see you here,' she says with a sparkling, but decidedly mischievous smile. 'I told you you'd like the Waverley and you're looking very sexy tonight.' She eyes me up and down in a way that does strange, strange things to my innards, then gestures cheerfully around the long softly lit room. 'It's great, isn't it? I just love this place!'

Following her gaze along the bar, I remember the way her eyes lit up when I told her, just yesterday, that I'd decided to come here. What is it about this place that she knows and I don't? When she glances back my way, she touches my arm, and my innards do that weird thing again, only more so this time.

'Let me get you a drink. What are you having?'

'I'm fine thank you. But let me get you one instead,' I answer quickly, wondering if it's the gin that's making me react so peculiarly.

She smiles sunnily, says 'OK!' and, before I can signal, the yummy barman is in front of us, also grinning hugely.

'Hi, Greg,' purrs Maria, leaning forwards and exhibiting her luscious breasts to him as if she knows him intimately, 'moonlighting again, are we?' With that, she gives him an outrageous wink and licks her pink-painted lips.

'Well, until you get your bloke to sort me out a decent salary increase, I need the extra cash,' he says, without rancour. And the knowing expression in his eyes only strengthens my feeling that these two are more than close.

They exchange a bit of chit-chat about Borough Hall, and I gather that 'Greg' works there too in the daytime. A few moments later, Maria is sipping a mineral water courtesy of my new 'tab'.

Now I've got a drinking companion, I don't really know what to say. I don't really know anything about Maria except superficial stuff ... and the fact that she and her lover are rampant exhibitionists and appear to be into robust and kinky sex. One night I saw them go out in the car ... and she was blindfolded and in handcuffs! And later, in the back garden, I watched – hidden behind the curtains and with my hand in my knickers – while the apparently oh-so respectable and upstanding borough director of finance spanked her bottom and then fucked her over their garden bench.

And when you've seen *that*, it's pretty difficult to discuss the weather or current affairs without your imagination wandering wildly off topic ...

Still, I have to try. 'Where's Robert tonight?'

This brings an almost beatific smile to Maria's face. Her eyes close for a moment, and she takes a slow sip of her water, managing to make it look as if she's imbibing some ecstatic concoction of absinthe, opium, chocolate and rampant aphrodisiacs. 'Oh, he's around,' she murmurs, licking her lips again.

My God, whatever she's getting with the man – over and above what I've already seen – I want some! But I have a sinking suspicion that, despite my mad fancies and misguided hopes, I'm not really going to get it from Charles. When he eventually arrives, that is. I check my watch and see that he's already fifteen minutes late.

'What about you? Where's your date?' Maria enquires. 'It's very rash of him to keep you waiting here alone, isn't it? I would imagine that there are droves of men just falling over themselves to spend time with a beautiful woman like you.'

Er ... I beg your pardon? I glance in the mirror behind the bar and, in between the various inverted bottles of spirits, I see myself. And it's a surprise ... Not a beauty, certainly, but still, somehow, almost a different person. My eyes are bright, and there's a flush to my cheeks that's not so much matronly as young and fresh and sexy. I look excited, and sort of interesting, as if I'm expecting something magical to happen ...

Maybe it will.

'I told you, it's not a date, not really. Just a business dinner to do with investments,' I point out, although I am flattered, and quite turned on in a weird sort of way that she persists in thinking it could be otherwise. There was a note in Maria's voice that suggests she might be seeing that 'interesting' look too, and, even more bizarrely, that she almost might want to fall over me herself.

Suddenly, I wish I hadn't said that Charles is my investment manager. It makes this night out sound far more mundane than it should and it also suggests that I'm rolling in money. Although I am, in a modest way, I suppose, it's not something I particularly want to brag about. I'd much rather she thought I had a *real* date!

'So, this investment bloke of yours, does he fancy you? I bet he does.'

'He's a friend.'

'Oh, yeah, like Robert is *my* "friend"?' she says pertly, her fine blue eyes glinting.

Does she know I've been watching them? It certainly seems that way. She's grinning broadly and, a second later, she winks again.

Then she slips off her stool. 'Come on. Let's go to the cloakroom. Girl talk,' she says, grabbing my arm and tucking her hand around it to pull me along after her.

After just managing to snatch up my bag, I fall into step, feeling a little bit befuddled.

'So, this guy you're waiting for, do you think he'll be a good fuck?'

I tip half the contents of my bag out on to the vanity counter in surprise. I can't deny that I *have* been wondering, but it sounds so blunt the way Maria just blurts it out like that. I watch myself blush even more in the mirror while she blithely tops up her lip-gloss.

As I scrabble my bits and pieces together, she gives me a sly look via the glass. 'Surely I haven't embarrassed you, have I?'

She caps her gloss and helps me retrieve my stuff. My perfume atomiser takes her fancy and, before I can stop her, she's plucking at the neckline of my dress, pulling it away from my skin, and squirting scent down my front.

'There, that's better. A woman should always smell of lots of scent, or lots of sex! That's what men like.'

I blink in the mirror at this brazen and beautiful woman beside me as she slides an arm around my shoulder and pulls our heads close together. I could be twenty years older than she is and, even though I don't quite look my age, a marked difference between us does show. And yet I know in my gut that she's the one with the most experience when it comes to men and sex.

But I don't mind that. I just want to learn. I want to know the things Maria knows. And do the things she does too.

'So?' she persists, giving my shoulders a squeeze. 'Your chap? What's he like in the sack?'

'I haven't slept with him!' I protest, biting my lip.

'*Yet*,' she corrects with authority. 'So what's he like generally then? Is he hunky? Old? Young? Pervy? Straight? What?'

'Youngish. In his thirties. Good looking. But, beyond that, I don't know . . .' I feel a bit pathetic, but Maria just smiles.

'Obviously, you're keeping him waiting . . .' She nods sagely. 'That's a good strategy. Make him beg for it. Make him grovel. They like that really.'

'Do you ever make Robert grovel?' It's out almost before I can think about it, but even as the last word leaves my lips I get a flash vision of that tall strapping Robert Stone of hers on his knees, kissing her feet, stark naked.

'Oh, yes! Sometimes,' she says brightly, releasing my shoulders only to start fluffing and flicking at my hair. She tucks some behind my ears, then teases a few tendrils forward again in a way that looks much cuter and flirtier than the way I'd done it. I make a mental note to book myself in for restyle in the very near future.

'But not usually in the garden,' she adds airily, reaching for her lip-gloss and taking my face by the chin and making me look at her so she can apply some on me.

I probably couldn't reply even if she wasn't painting my lips, but I know my face must be a picture.

'It's all right. We know you watch us,' she says, and then presses her own lips together, prompting me to do the same. Like a robot, I copy her. 'We like it. It's one of our biggest kinks!'

Suddenly, it's all too much and I sway on my feet but, with a strength unexpected in such a trim girl, Maria catches me and manhandles me on to a padded sofa in the corner of the room – presumably there expressly for swooning middle-aged ladies to subside on to!

A second or two later, she's holding a glass of cold water to my lips. 'Hey, don't get upset!' She strokes my cheek. 'We're all friends here. Nothing's wrong.'

I give her a wan look. I'm unconvinced. For all my sexy thoughts and my attempts at boldness, when it comes to it, I'm way out of my depth.

'I was like you once,' Maria says kindly, sliding her arm around my shoulder again. She smells nice. 'I didn't realise all this sex stuff was going on around me, and I was completely wet behind the ears.' She gives me a squeeze, and it feels lovely, and reassuring, but also scary. 'Until one day, it all sort of dawned on me ... and I met Robert ... and I saw it all. It was like stepping through a magic mirror somehow.' She glances towards the glass, and gives me a strange dreamy look ... 'And suddenly you're in another world, and it's *all* sex. And it's *all* right. And it's *all* good.'

I sip my water, wishing it was more gin, but, weirdly,

I get what she's saying. I can somehow see that magic mirror, and I sense that it's right in front of me. I just need the courage to step through.

Maria cocks her blonde head on one side, as if she's read my thoughts. 'You're already halfway there, Annie. You can take that step. When your date comes, just seduce him. Take what you want. He won't be able to resist you. You're gorgeous.'

It *is* seductive. The idea itself ... She makes it sound so easy. And yet it looks as if Charles isn't even going to bother to turn up.

'Yes, so gorgeous I think I've been stood up,' I observe. But I'm not upset somehow. Charles isn't the only fish in the sea. He's not even the only financial expert.

At that moment, my mobile chooses to ring, and Maria dashes for my bag, fishes out the handset and passes it to me.

'Oh Annie, I'm so sorry,' says a regretful Charles when I put the phone to my ear, 'I can't begin to apologise. A panicking client rang right as I was about to set off. He's flapping unnecessarily, but I had to calm him down.' In his charming, slightly middle-class voice, he launches into a sleekly plausible spiel about the nervous client.

It all sounds perfectly believable, even though the cynic in me does start to wonder if he's had a better offer from someone younger and prettier. But, just as I examine those qualms, an astonishing thing happens.

Maria unzips the back of my dress, and then pushes the bodice a little way down my shoulders so she can reach my breast. Her fingers slide inside my bra and she gently begins to fondle me.

I gasp, and Charles interprets it as exasperation and introduces another round of smooth apologies.

But I couldn't care less. The touch of Maria's fingers

is completely entrancing. I don't really care that she's a woman and I barely know her. I just melt against her, and press my free hand over hers, through my clothing. It seems perfectly natural, and she smiles sweetly and breathes 'Good girl!' into my ear.

My other nipple peaks and stiffens against the lace fabric of my bra, and a tingle of sensation tumbles through me, settling in my crotch. I feel heavy and tense there suddenly, and get this crazy urge to work my hips. It's almost as if Maria were touching me down there too. And as Charles purrs on, I really, really want her to.

But, alas, the sound of other nearer voices suddenly shatters the magic mirror, and returns Maria and me to the real world. With a swiftness and aplomb that suggests this is far from the first time she's fooled about in this cloakroom, Maria zips me up and adjusts my dress. And, by the time two other women enter the room, bitching to each other about some third party, I'm looking as prim and unfiddled with as a Reverend Mother.

'Annie? Annie? Are you there?'

I zone back into the world of Charles and his honey-dipped apologies, as my companion smirks at me and then runs her tongue around her pink-painted lips.

'Yes! What is it?' I say sharply, suddenly wishing he'd just shut up.

At last, he seems a little taken aback, but I just say, 'No problem. Don't worry about it. We'll do this some other night.'

'Shall I arrange a taxi to collect you and take you home?'

Maria is still looking at me, her eyes sparkling with challenge.

'No, it's OK, I'm going to stay here. I think I'll have

another drink at the bar, and then I'll get my own taxi home. Don't worry, I'm a big girl, I can take care of myself.' Before he can protest further, I just say, 'Goodnight, Charles,' and snap shut my phone.

'Good for you!' says Maria firmly, and starts fluffing my hair again.

'I think I will go home though.'

Her periwinkle blue eyes go narrow. 'You don't have to,' she says, in a low measured tone, her eyes dancing. 'You could always join Robert and I.' She pauses, giving me that slow sly wink again. 'See how the other half lives.'

I feel as if I need to pant. As if I might hyperventilate. I think about some of the things I've seen them do – and I know I'm not ready.

Maria cocks her pretty head on one side, and seems to do that mind reading thing again. 'That's fine. All in good time. But do have that drink. You never know what might happen. Or who you might meet.'

Five minutes later, we're out in the bar again, but I'm on my own. When we entered the room, I noticed Maria's man, my neighbour, Robert Stone, seated alone down at the far end. I was just about to smile and wave, when she touched my arm. 'Uh oh, it's a game, Annie. I don't know him tonight. We're strangers ... hooker and john.'

And now I'm watching the play unfold.

Two minutes after she took a seat, a short way away from him, he moved in. Now they're chatting. Flirting. There's a wicked light in his dark eyes, but he appears to be playing things straight. As I observe, he writes something on a piece of paper, and places it beside Maria's drink. She reads it, gives him a cool look and then shakes her head. Stone does a passable impression of looking flummoxed, and then writes again, and the process is repeated. After four attempts, he obviously gets it right and Maria smiles archly, pats him on the arm and slides off her seat.

As she walks out of the bar, she gives me that wink again.

As Robert Stone follows her, a moment later, he shrugs and winks too.

And that leaves me here alone, watching the ordinary folk. Or at least I think they're ordinary. Maybe everyone's playing sex games here but me.

I decide to sip this gin slowly, keep my nose down and observe for a while, then leave. Being felt up by my pretty and obviously bi-sexual neighbour is a promising start to my new life as a sex maniac, but probably excitement enough for one evening.

Don't be greedy, Annie, I think, swirling my ice, and glancing along the length of the bar.

Cute barman is polishing glasses and chatting with other customers. How would it be to seduce him? I wonder. Does he have a break soon? Obviously this new appetite of mine isn't that easily suppressed.

A moment later, a figure appears in the doorway at the far end of the bar, then slides behind the counter and begins talking in hushed tones to the cutie.

It's a woman. A towering, unnaturally tall woman in a short body-skimming long-sleeved dress made of a shimmering, dark-crimson material, lamé or something. She's astonishingly big-boned, but she has the most beautiful long black hair that hangs around her face like curtains of silk, and her legs are amazing. They seem to go on for miles, encased in glossy black tights, and on her large but elegant feet she's wearing black velvet stilettos.

I can't hear what they're saying, but the woman's voice is husky and slightly accented and does weird things to the region of my solar plexus, even at this distance. And the barman is staring at her with the strangest expression on his face.

It's a combination of awe, downright fear and confused lust.

And I don't blame him because I think *I* fancy her too! What's happening to me? Am I a lesbian?

I'm about to down my drink and get the hell out of the bar when the tall woman seems to dismiss the barman, who promptly scuttles away, presumably on a break. A second later, she scans the entire room with a narrow imperious look … and to my surprise – and horrified excitement – her gaze settles on me.

There's a long beat, and then, as if in a movie, she's gliding slowly the length of the bar, in my direction.

In the strange attenuated moments of her approach, I realise two significant things. One, that she's even more beautiful and exotic than I imagined. And two, that, despite this undeniable beauty, and the smooth graceful way of moving, 'she' is almost certainly a man dressed in very superior drag!

2 **Valentina**

I simply gape at the vision before me.

Because make no mistake, he *is* a vision. He's far more beautiful than most of the women I know and, despite broad shoulders and a deep but apparently unpadded chest, he looks a damn sight more feminine than a lot of them too!

His face is perfectly made up, but the paint is subtle and done with a light skilful hand. His lips are red, but it's a soft red and slightly pearly, and his striking copper-coloured eyes are ringed with smoky gun-metal grey rather than panda rings of thickly painted black. Even his eyelashes look real rather than false.

I cannot see a single hint of any kind of beard shadow, but whether that's from a hyper-close shave or clever foundation it's impossible to tell.

'May I get you another drink?'

Oh, God, that accent! I've always had a thing about Latin lovers in romance novels, especially Italians, and Mr Beautiful here has the most gorgeous continental lilt to his voice. It's all such a killer combination that I'm in danger of slipping off my stool at any moment. I suddenly wish Maria were here to help me cope with the sensory overload.

'Um ... er, yes, please,' I stammer, aware that I simply could not stop staring at him if my next breath depended on it.

He gives me a strange slow, deeply complex smile and my mouth goes dry. Hurry up with that drink, I think, although I know that somehow I would never

28

ever attempt to give orders to this man, regardless of whether he was here to serve me or not. Those odd metallic eyes alone could forbid me anything . . .

With a swift nod, he turns away and prepares another gin and tonic without asking me what I want. He's quicker and even more efficient than cutie boy Greg, fingers tipped with nail polish the exact colour of his dress moving deftly and with absolute confidence. Within seconds, what looks like a generous double is set before me.

'I h–have a tab.'

Oh, God, I'm still stammering! I *must* pull myself together and speak normally. But there's something about this man/woman's challenging expression that turns my head as much as it intimidates me.

'This one is on the house,' he says pleasantly, that soft accent doing the weirdest things to the parts gin could never reach.

I open my mouth to protest, but somehow he quells me with just a glance. It's as if I'm hypnotised. Under a spell. I can't look away.

'Am I your first?'

I blink, but despite my desire to converse normally, all the words dance insanely in my head and I can't marshal them into a question that would make any kind of sense.

'Your first transvestite,' he prompts, and the amusement in his eyes is almost alien.

'Yes. Yes, you are,' I manage, downing the last of my old drink and almost gritting my teeth in my efforts not to grab the new one and sink it in one.

Never, ever, has anyone – man, woman or beast – had this intense an effect on me. Not even wickedly wonderful Maria, a short while ago.

'So? What do you think?' He makes an elegant gesture, his hands palm upwards, as if presenting himself for my approval. 'What do you think of "Valentina"?'

I don't know what I think. It's more a case of *feeling*. And I feel confused, attracted, surprised. Turned on.

'I don't know. I'm still trying to work that one out.'

My voice is level but my hand shakes wildly as I lift my glass and some of the diluted gin spills out over it. Before I can scrabble for a tissue, Valentina takes the glass in one hand and sets it down and, with the other, raises my gin-splashed fingers to his lips and slowly sucks them clean of the aromatic liquor.

His mouth is hot, and his tongue ferociously mobile, moving evocatively over my skin. Those parts that the gin couldn't reach feel as if they're being licked and laved and tantalised. I've never experienced anything quite like it. It's a perfect transference from my fingers to my sex.

He releases me, and only now does he reach for a cocktail napkin from a nearby dispenser.

I am panting, I realise, because I feel as if I've just been thoroughly ravished.

And I liked it.

'Now what do you think?' The silky accent seems to play across my clitoris like electricity arcing over a damp surface.

I blurt out the first words my grey matter can latch on to. 'You're not gay then?'

I nearly rock off my seat when he laughs. A full, deep and very masculine laugh that causes one or two people close by to look at us.

'No, I'm not gay. I love women ... although I do sample men occasionally.'

Suddenly, I realise that I'm well and truly through that magic mirror now, and as I accept that, things become easier. I'm in a realm where questions that were once unthinkable are now common and intriguing topics of conversation.

'So, wearing a dress – is that a sex thing for you?' I take a swig of gin, trying out the new sexually curious me.

Valentina smiles, and seems quite impressed. Pleased with me somehow. I notice that, despite the bizarre perfection of his looks, one of his front teeth is ever so slightly crooked. It's a flaw, but somehow, because of it, his androgynous beauty suddenly seems infinitely more human.

'Yes. Naturally . . . Or why would I do it?'

Why indeed? In this mirror world, I get the impression that almost everything is probably to do with sex.

'Right . . . Good.' The words are inane but I still feel as if I'm on track.

I essay a glance at his crotch. Surely, if wearing makeup, tights and a frock is a turn-on, there should be evidence.

He gives me that narrow smile again but, this time, it's thrilling rather than vaguely mocking. 'One doesn't have to be rampant to be aroused.' He shrugs his broad lamé-clad shoulders. 'Which is useful when wearing a slim skirt.'

I take another sip of gin. I'm still not sure what's going on here. I'm sexually excited. I'm turned on. But I don't exactly know what by.

His gleaming eyes narrow and he tilts his head a little, making his silky black hair swing. I would put good money on it not being a wig and most women I know would kill for locks as luxuriant and beautifully conditioned.

'So, have you decided? Me wearing a dress . . . Is that a sex thing for *you*?' He leans on the counter, his beautifully manicured fingers spread, challenging me. It's as if my thoughts are writ large all over my face.

'I don't know...' I wrack my befuddled brain and, suddenly, the perfect answer comes to me. 'Sort of ... It's like I'm getting a message, but it's scrambled. It doesn't quite make sense.'

Again, he favours me with that look that suggests he's impressed with me.

He opens his painted lips to answer, but, at that moment, Greg the cute barman shoots out of the door at the end of the bar almost as if he's been fired out of a cannon. He looks flustered, and his hair's a bit awry. I get the definite impression that he's overrun on his break, and the flush on his fresh young face suggests that it's not just a quick cup of coffee and a fag he's partaken of.

Valentina's smooth brow puckers and he shrugs expressively as Greg hurries up and starts to burble excuses. 'Enough! Forget it!' The transvestite's voice is crisp and dismissive and Greg looks seriously alarmed. 'You can take over again now, and I want you to take especially good care of this lady.' He turns to me and gives me a small, strange and even more complicated smile that does beautiful things to his rosy mouth. 'Alas, I have to go now ...' A pause. 'But I look forward to clearing up that signal for you soon.'

For a moment, I have no idea on earth what he's talking about, and I must look incredibly dense.

'The scrambled message,' he says softly. Then, after taking my hand in his so briefly that I'm not really sure it's happened at all, he's walking away, calling, 'Ciao' over his shoulder.

'Crikey, he is really something else, isn't he?' I say to the still flustered Greg.

'You can say that again.'

There's real feeling in his voice, and I'd like to engage him in conversation about our dear departed frock-wearing friend, but suddenly there's an influx of punters into the bar. Looks like a party of some kind has just broken up in the dining room and they've all adjourned here to continue their festivities.

So I'm left with my thoughts. And a jumbled mish-mash they are too. I'm still not entirely over my encounter with Maria, much less my confrontation with my first ever transvestite.

What did I feel just now? Attraction? Revulsion? A bit of both? I don't know if it's the gin, or just because this is one of the strangest nights of my life, but suddenly I find myself wondering what it's like to have sex with a man in a dress.

'Valentina' was very beautiful . . . but as I'm not even sure I like women that's not exactly the most reliable yardstick. And I can't take any of the usual things I like about a man seriously if they're tricked out in the accoutrements of a woman.

Broad shoulders – in crimson lamé?

Long muscular legs – in sheer tights?

A big cock?

Yes, let's face it, women like those. And presumably Valentina's is nestling in lace or silk underwear if what's beneath is consistent with what's on top.

I down half my drink in one. This is just too confusing. I can't take any more. I'm going home.

Probably the best place for me too. The woman on duty at the reception desk gives me an odd look when I collect my wrap from the cloakroom and ask if she could call a taxi for me.

'Of course. Straight away,' she murmurs. Her face is pale and rather serious, and her tightly coiled dark hair gives her quite a stern look, but behind her black-rimmed glasses her eyes are dancing. They're full of almost the same strange indefinable challenge that was in Valentina's.

'I'll ... um ... wait outside.'

Irrationally flummoxed, I almost scuttle out on to the forecourt.

The Waverley used to be a grand old country mansion house before it was made into a hotel, and it's surrounded by extensive formal gardens. You can't get the full effect of them at night, of course, but the moon's up, so there's the impression of their beauty to be seen. And smelt. Some night-perfumed species fills the air with an intoxicating fragrance.

I stare down the drive towards the gates, where the taxi will appear. I'll be able to see it arrive long before it reaches the building, so I allow myself a little wander along a path that threads its way amongst the flowerbeds.

I stare up at the moon. Looking for answers, I suppose. Although I'm not quite sure what the questions are.

I still can't stop thinking about Valentina and, to a lesser extent, Maria and her consort, Robert Stone. I suppose those two are still in the hotel somewhere, doing Lord alone knows what to each other. I cast a glance towards some of the lighted windows, picturing my neighbours behind one of them ... in bed.

Are they playing with handcuffs and blindfolds? Indulging in spanking games? Or just plain fucking, for a change?

Movement catches the corner of my eye, and at first I think it's my taxi that I've seen in my peripheral vision. But then it dawns on me that whatever it was came from the wrong direction. I glance towards the corner of the building and see a figure heading away along one of the less defined paths, towards the woods that more or less surround the main garden.

My breath stills inside me.

It's someone tall. Someone with long black hair, but *not* wearing a dress.

No, strangely, it's a man wearing jeans, but no shirt. As he disappears into the copse, I catch a fleeting glimpse of a bare chest gleaming in the moonlight.

It's her.

It's *him*.

And, before I can allow myself to think, I set off towards the same dark gap between the trees.

My heels crunch on the gravel, but somehow I know that he meant me to see him so I don't bother to disguise my pursuit.

Once in amongst the trees, the path is rough and gloomy. I can barely see my footing and I could easily trip or tread on something I hardly dare think about. There could be anything in here. Creepy crawlies, foxes, even snakes! And yet I soldier on, peering through the murk and bushes, tracking my quarry. I think . . . I can't actually see him any more, and I'm seriously beginning to wonder if I might just have conjured him from a fevered imagination.

'Fuck!' I growl, as my heels start to sink into softer earth with an ominous squelch. It's not a word I'd generally use in politer company, but this isn't polite company and I'm not the Annie of old. And out here, in the grove of total insanity, the word is deliciously apposite.

'Is that what you want?' a soft familiar voice enquires as I suddenly burst through into an area of slightly less dense undergrowth, tripping as I go.

As I find my feet, I see my companion, leaning against a tree and smoking.

It's Valentina, of course. Or should I perhaps say 'Valentino' now?

I see the same imposing height. I see the same heavy black silk fall of hair. Still the same incredible face. He's scrubbed off some of the makeup he was wearing in the bar but not quite all of it. His eyes are still circled by a faint shadowed line.

But I see his body now – and the shape of his shoulders, his chest and his torso. All of which, along with long lean legs clad in ripped and torn denims, adds up to the quintessence of a full-on red-blooded, almost stereotypically macho male.

He might have been plucked straight from a women's beefcake calendar, and, as he takes a pull on his thin black cigar and blows the smoke to one side, his eyes remain on me, studying me narrowly. 'So, what do the signals say now?' He taps away ash, motionless in every other aspect. Especially his eyes.

I'm out of my depth. In fact, I think I'm probably in the wrong ocean. But somehow I can't help but snipe back at him. 'The signals say "what the hell is this man doing prancing about in the woods, half-naked?" ... That's what they say!'

'The hotel has a strict no-smoking policy –' he takes a long slow, indolent drag '– and this is one vice I don't care to inflict on other people.'

Fair enough, but still, why the he-man bare chest?

'And sometimes, I like to strip off the layers, the masks and the transformations and just be me.'

It's as if I've spoken. Or he's read my thoughts. It scares me and I think I need to run, run, run and get away from here. 'Well, I won't disturb you then. Good night.'

I make as if to turn and backtrack along the path, but, before I can, he pinches out his cigar in a lightning gesture, flings it into the undergrowth and launches himself forwards. The messages from my brain to my muscles are hijacked somehow, and he has me by the arm before I've even moved an inch.

'If you didn't want to disturb me, why did you follow me?'

His eyes shimmer in the faint light that breaks through the tree canopy, and his face appears hard, yet amused. Now, when he looks so unambiguously male, he confuses me far more than he did when he was in a dress.

'I don't know . . .'

It's the truth on one level, but on another it's a total lie. No matter what warnings my brain is shrieking at me, every cell in my body just wants to get next to the cells in his. I knew it the moment I saw him in that red dress. Even before I actually sussed out he was a man.

Unable to articulate my feelings, I reach out and touch his chest. His skin is warm, with a faint veil of perspiration. It's a sultry night, but not so hot that he'd be sweating out here in the dankness of the copse. So maybe it's me who's getting to *him*, despite his aura of primal male confidence. The mask he's still wearing even if he says he's got rid of them all.

I can feel his heartbeat though, and it's so unnaturally even and steady that I wonder if he's indifferent to me after all.

And then he kisses me.

In another of his pre-emptive strikes, he sweeps me into his arms with a bizarrely romantic flourish, and presses his sensuous, mobile and still vaguely pink-tinted mouth down on mine. I expect him to play the ravishing predator with me, and dive in immediately with his tongue, but instead his lips just rest lightly against mine. And that's more intoxicating, really, for the delicacy of the pressure than any amount of brute demanding force could ever be.

He's the first man I've been kissed by since Stan, apart from perfunctory kisses of comfort, from relatives, at the funeral. I thought I might be kissing Charles tonight, but, hey, how wrong can you be?

Acting purely on instinct, I coil my arms around him. I can't believe this is happening and I can't believe what I'm doing. This new different, impatient me takes the initiative and presses her tongue against his lips, demanding entrance.

He laughs – the sound deep and rough in his chest – and he admits me. Then a second later, it's like he throws a switch and takes total control. Now, his tongue does invade. The action is graphic, blatant and obvious. Thrust, thrust, thrust, just like sex. My sex quickens exactly as if it is.

Everything comes together. My long months of celibacy. The bizarre erotic antics of my neighbours and my recent run-in with Maria. The vague fancyings I've been experiencing for men like Charles and Greg. And finally the appearance of this man, dressed as Valentina the beautiful transvestite.

I've never wanted to fuck more in my life.

As if reading my every emotional and physical reaction, he cups my bottom with his long elegant hand and kneads my buttock as he presses my crotch against his groin. He's hard as iron in his worse-for-wear denim, and, as if possessed by the spirit of an entirely new and different version of myself, I grind my pelvis against him with enthusiasm.

He laughs again, increasing his efforts, fingertips curving lewdly and almost poking at my sex from behind. I can barely believe it when I seem to automatically adjust myself so he can get in closer. He's pressing against my furrow now, squeezing rhythmically and tauntingly.

'*Now* do you know?'

I daren't look into those strange metallic eyes of his, but, inexplicably, I answer with a nod instead of breaking free and running for my life. Or at least running for the sane steady, normal respectable life I've led until now.

'Good. Now you're being honest,' he murmurs, his slight accent more noticeable all of a sudden, as if excitement has stripped him of his polish. 'Show yourself to me.'

Suddenly, I feel light-headed. I'm in Wonderland, but at the same time it's real. I step back, not sure what I'm doing, and strike some sort of pose. My pashmina starts to slip off and I grab for it, dropping my bag in the process and spoiling the effect entirely.

He shakes his dark head and his amazing hair ripples like a heavy shot-silk curtain.

'Not like that,' he instructs, pulling a slim silver case and matching lighter from his back pocket. 'Show me your body.' Illuminated by a narrow plume of flame, his face looks satanic as he lights another cigar.

What does he want me to do? Strip off? I cast him a pleading questioning look, and he nods.

I glance around. There's nowhere to put my things, so I just let my bag and my wrap fall, and reach for my zip. I feel ungainly and lacking in grace, but he watches with interest and what might be appreciation as I wriggle free of my dress. Grateful that I chose fake tan instead of tights tonight, I step precariously out of it and fling it in the general direction of the other stuff.

This pretty lingerie I have on was chosen as a confidence booster more than anything, with only the very remote chance that Charles might see it. I can't tell what effect it's having on my watcher. He's probably seen far more daring and far more seductively filled ensembles in his time, and I feel a bit silly displaying my middle-aged body like a vamp.

Yet he purrs something indistinct in Italian that sounds generally encouraging, and I take heart from that, and begin to heel off one of my shoes.

'No, leave them. I like shoes.'

Instead, I reach around and unhook my bra, acutely conscious that my breasts aren't quite as pert without the benefit of its underwires and subtle shaping and moulding. When I hesitate, he clicks his tongue and shakes his head again.

I whip off the bra and fling that down too, resisting the almost overwhelming urge to cover myself.

He says nothing. He just watches.

Obviously, it's an all-off situation. And I'm scared. Stan was the last man to see me naked and, before that, just two or three boyfriends, and, years and years ago, my dad, when he bathed me as a baby. I've just never done this sort of thing before. I've never even *thought* of doing this sort of thing before. And, here I am, stepping out of my knickers for a gorgeous but very peculiar man who I only set eyes on for the first time about an hour ago.

I feel as if I might faint. But some unforeseen sense of wickedness, and daring, and downright perverted lust keeps me upright. It might be *his* lust, but I think it's more my own. I don't know quite how to stand but, in a moment of bravado, I throw back my shoulders, lifting my breasts.

His gleaming eyes cruise all my hot zones. Thighs. Pubis. Breasts. He's assessing me, rating me ... awarding marks out of ten? I probably stack up as rather average compared to the sort of younger sexier women he's used to, but I don't care. And he doesn't seem to either. I guess he's a past master of masks, but there's a light in his odd eyes that's unmistakable.

'Turn around.'

I comply, unsteady on my heels, but determined to keep it together. After a few moments of his intense scrutiny, I nearly leap out of my skin when his hands cup my naked buttocks. I never even heard him approach.

He palpates my flesh as if he enjoys the texture. Obviously, I pass muster because he drops a swift kiss on the back of my neck.

'Do you touch yourself?'

As he asks, *he* touches me. One hand remains cupped around my bottom, fingers sliding rudely into my groove from behind. The other one slides over my hip, and then across my belly before plunging without further ado into my bush. In an instant, he's dabbling in my wetness from the rear and flicking my clitoris from the front, and I cry out.

'No!' he says in my ear, sharply. 'Stay quiet. As quiet as you can ... Let me work you.'

I suppress my cries, but I can't keep myself from panting.

Let me work you.

The words seem to intensify the sensations, and also objectify me, elevating my arousal to an astonishing new level. The idea of being just a thing for him makes my sex lurch and flutter and slick arousal slide tellingly down my leg. When he takes my clitoris between his finger and thumb, I groan, despite his embargo. And, when he pushes a finger inside me at the same time, I yelp and come.

My pelvis lurches, jerking and jerking, but he doesn't miss a beat. I grab onto him wherever I can reach – arm, hip – to stop myself falling as my crotch seems to implode in a delicious ball of pleasure.

And it goes on! He works me to not one climax, but two, three, while I cling on to him, the nails I so carefully manicured to impress Charles digging into the flesh of this half-naked stranger. I ignore his command of silence now, unable to prevent myself making hoarse uncouth sounds.

Just when I'm convinced I'm going to fall over, he abandons my sex and manhandles me bodily to the ground. I'm like a rag doll, limp from my wrenching orgasms, and I just go where he directs as he sets me on hands and knees, nudges apart my thighs and adjusts the tilt of my pelvis.

At the rasp of his zip, I have a sudden moment of abject terror, stunned by the thought of potential disease, and the fact that, even at my age, I could still get pregnant. But then there's the tiny ripping sound of a condom wrapper being torn open. A few seconds later, I feel the large blunt, but mercifully latex-clad head of his cock nudging insistently at my entrance. He grabs me firmly by the hips and shoves me on to him, and then I'm filled up, jammed up, stuffed up, my body stretching as never before to accommodate him.

'Touch yourself,' he commands and, still holding my hips, he begins to thrust in long hard, steady, rhythmic pushes.

When I obey him, my one remaining hand isn't enough to keep me aloft and I find the side of my face pressed into the crumpled heap of my clothing.

Sex has never been so demeaning, but never ever quite this hot. I rub furiously at myself as he fucks and fucks me.

It barely takes a moment and I'm coming again, grunting and drooling against my own abandoned dress while my lover pumps away at me like some kind of sex machine. My sex clutches and grasps at him, clenching hard, but still he goes on and on, stroking remorselessly. I continue to climax, totally lost, no longer in a position to even care what happens with him.

But then, he cries out. Something unintelligible, but quite possibly beautiful in Italian ... and I do care. The sound of his voice is masculine, but also strangely sweet and plaintive, and I push back against him, abandoning the knot of nerves that no longer needs my attention and reaching between our legs to very gently cup his balls. They're tight and I feel them lurch as he ejaculates.

Seconds later, it's all over and he lets out another musical shout as we collapse in a heap on top of my dress and underwear. At least, I'm a heap. He probably looks like some graceful ballet dancer or ice-dance champion at the end of a dramatic routine.

We lie in silence. I can't speak. He just doesn't. But then, eventually, he eases himself off me, sits on the ground at my side and lays his long gentle hand on my back.

'Are you all right?' The hand moves, stroking and soothing as if I'm a skittish filly.

I take a few deep breaths. Am I all right? I'm too flabbergasted to tell. I've just had my first ever quickie. In the woods, and with a total stranger. How weird and sleazy and dangerous is that?

And yet it felt perfectly natural to me. And somehow it doesn't feel sleazy, even now. And it only feels dangerous in a way that makes my blood sing.

'Yes, I'm fine. Thank you,' I murmur, sitting up. Nevertheless, I blush like a teenager.

He strokes my face this time, with what feels like real fondness, then hands me my underwear.

I dress in double quick time while he disposes of the condom I know not where. But by the time I'm decent again, he's smoking another cigar.

Unexpectedly, he offers me the case as if it's quite normal for a woman to smoke thin black cigars. Maybe it is amongst the sort of women he knows.

'No, sorry, I don't smoke.'

'Good for you,' he says with a shrug. 'Far better to stick to the healthier vices.' He gives me a roguish wink, which makes his dark metallic eyes twinkle.

It seems that's as far as it goes in terms of us

discussing what's just happened. He nips off his half-smoked cigar, flings it away, then, almost companionably, he takes my hand and leads me back along the path towards the Waverley. Neither of us speaks, but, to my surprise, I'm not too troubled by this. I feel bizarrely comfortable with this odd man that I only know in the biblical sense.

When we reach our destination, I'm amazed to see that my taxi is waiting. My erstwhile lover speaks quickly to the driver, then opens the back of the cab and gently bundles me inside. 'Don't worry, it's on the Waverley's account. It's the least I could do.'

I flash a small grin in his direction as he stands there just looking at me, hand on the cab door. 'Well, it's been ... um ... interesting ... That is, if I didn't just dream it all.'

He laughs softly. But the smile he gives me is another extraordinarily complex one, a mosaic of emotions. I see flirtatiousness and sexual challenge, but also gentleness and undeniable kindness. And there are other feelings too, far more fugitive.

He's wary. Perplexed. And, if I didn't know better, I'd say he's worried too, on some very deep level. But then it all clears again, and he's just heart-stoppingly sexy.

'It's been wonderful.' He reaches in, takes my hand and, as he gives it a quick light kiss, I notice for the first time that his short but elegantly shaped nails are still painted with rosy polish. 'And I'll see you again soon.'

With that, he releases me, swings shut the cab door and slaps the side of the vehicle to indicate to the driver to pull away.

As we speed off into the night, I twist around and look back through the rear window ... but he's gone.

Did I actually dream it after all?

3 **Girl Talk**

If this was a film or a hard-hitting television drama, I'd be in the shower now, scrubbing at my private parts with carbolic soap, trying to scour away the shame and degradation of having indulged in casual sex with a man I barely know.

But it isn't the telly, it's real life, and I don't feel ashamed and degraded at all. Here I am, lolling in a hot scented bath and I can't remember when I last felt better. And I can admit that without feeling the slightest bit of disloyalty to Stan. I really believe that he'd be as pleased for me as I am for myself.

I feel as if I'm fizzing somehow. Glowing with excitement at what I've done and what I felt. I understand what that secret is now that Maria and Robert Stone are always quietly smiling about. Or at least I understand some of it. I'm sure there's a lot more to learn.

On the rack stretched across the bath in front of me, I've got a large glass of wine and a box of Hotel Chocolat truffles. All I need to create the totally hedonistic scenario would be a giant spliff, but, as I don't even smoke ordinary tobacco, a head full of Technicolor memories will have to do instead.

I can still hardly believe what I did.

I bonked an off-duty transvestite in the woods in the middle of the night, and I'd do it again in a heartbeat if I got half a chance. How wild is that?

Of course, there's still a tiny voice inside me suggesting that what happened was so 'out there' that I really might have imagined it all.

But I did it. I really did it.

Closing my eyes, I let the pictures flood in again. I see a broad bare chest gleaming in dappled moonlight. Eyes like beaten copper glinting at me, daring me to action. And a sheet of black silk hair that sweeps across my skin as he fucks me.

Down in the water between my legs, my wetness blends with ordinary wetness. I'm aroused again and I can't keep the smile off my face.

Valentino was huge, and he knew what to do with it too. Not having an extensive roster of lovers to compare and contrast, I've never really pondered the question of whether 'size matters' or not, but now I know that, even if big isn't always best, in my case, last night big was amazing!

I try to imagine him inside me again. And maybe this time, face to face, on more or less equal terms. Conveniently putting aside the fact that his face is smoother and younger than mine, I imagine him staring down at me with those amazing hooded eyes filled with passion and lust. Lust for me.

The wine tastes as strong and fruity as my nocturnal adventures. I take a last swig, and then slither down further into the water. Sliding my knees apart and bracing myself as best I can against the sides of the tub, I just hope my heels won't slip at the critical moment. This would be the perfect time for one of those deluxe waterproof vibrators I saw featured in a magazine the other day, but, as I didn't act on my impulses and actually order one, I've just got to make do with my fingers.

I get down to business, rubbing my clitoris and loving it. It's surprisingly easy to believe that it's Valentino's larger and defter forefinger that's circling and teasing. It seems bizarre that a total stranger knew better how to pleasure me than I do myself but, until recently, I haven't masturbated much. I've never really felt the urge. Never needed it.

But now it's as necessary as breathing.

I continue to fondle my clitoris. Not expertly, but it still feels nice, very nice. I slip a couple of fingers from my other hand inside myself to sweeten the sensation.

Closing my eyes, I imagine Valentino here in the bath with me. It's not that big a tub and I've no idea how he'd arrange those long powerful legs of his and manage to thrust at the same time, but in fantasyland everything is possible. In my daydream, he's managing beautifully, really giving me his all, while at the same time massaging my clitoris with those light but devilish strokes.

And he's looking at me too. He's staring right down into my face, with fire in those incredible eyes and a smile on his full sensual lips.

I'm close, perilously close, even without the benefit of a waterproof vibrator. I'm lost, irrevocably lost, deep in my inner mind-movie of me being fucked by the most beautiful, most athletic and most exotic man I've ever met in my life. I feel myself about to climax and the craziest thing happens.

Suddenly, the incredible eyes are ringed with smoky dark eyeliner and the sumptuous lips are immaculately painted with frosted rose-red gloss. Valentino is Valentina now, and she's wearing her crimson lamé dress as she fucks me.

But it's still all right.

I cry out and jerk, and, around my fingers, my flesh clenches hard. Wine and luxury chocolates as well as the soap-dish and the loofah all cascade into the bath in a mad chaotic mess.

But I'm coming like an express train, and I don't give a damn!

* * *

Next morning, I do give a damn because the inside of my bath is covered in disgusting smears of melted chocolate. Shame about those truffles, because they're my favourites. But I can always get more. What I can't get is myself, the way I was before the events of last night.

My life has changed. In a big way.

And not only because I fucked Valentino. I also have to deal with the consequences of what happened with Maria in the cloakroom. My face burns at the thought of seeing her again. It'd probably be easier to contend with Valentino. At least with him I have the option of simply never ever going back to the Waverley again.

But I can't ignore my next-door neighbour forever, can I? Not unless I move again, and I don't want to do that.

By the time both me and the bath are cleaned up, though, I've got things back in proportion. And that strange sense of wonder has returned to me.

Valentino said, 'I'll see you again soon.' What does that mean? I wonder. Does he mean see as in dating? I don't really think so. I have the distinct feeling that someone like him doesn't progress along the normal 'relationship' route. Lunch, drinks, dinner, all that malarkey. And then the delicately negotiated path to bed and something more serious.

How on earth do these things work when you start with the sex?

'Don't be a silly old mare, Annie,' I tell myself, which causes my cat Boy to look at me as if I'm demented. 'Whatever it was that happened last night, it *wasn't* a "relationship", it was a . . .'

One night stand? Quick shag? I don't know *what* it was, to be honest!

Boy continues to eye me as if I've lost my marbles

and, as I turn out a Whiskas pouch on to his dish, I tend to think he might be right. When he's done, he swirls briefly and sympathetically around my legs, and then prowls off again. He has his own life and routines, and he likes to keep to them, despite the fact that mine have suddenly gone to hell on a handcart.

Once upon a time, I would have been gardening by now. Or baking. Or perhaps making preparations to meet a Townswomen's Guild friend for lunch. I might even have been playing a round of extremely bad golf.

But now all I want to do is jump in my car and drive to the Waverley – to find out if there really is a tall beautiful transvestite called Valentina, who presumably works there. Either that, or find the next-door neighbour I dallied with last night, and drill her with a million and one questions about the 'magic mirror' and what lies beyond it.

Robert Stone's black Mercedes was gone by the usual time this morning, even after God knows what sort of rollicking and frolicking he and Maria got up to last night. They seem to be able to indulge in all sorts of bizarre sexual antics and yet still function as more or less normal human beings with jobs, in the daytime. Whereas I'm finding the transition from one to the other distinctly bumpy. Maria and her Robert will both be at their desks now, doing whatever they do on their different levels of the bureaucratic local government hierarchy.

I mooch out into the garden, wishing I could summon up some enthusiasm for weeding and dead-heading instead of the ever present nagging urge to go back upstairs, draw the curtains and play with myself while fantasising about Valentino.

As I drift towards the fence, the sound of a vintage 80s radio channel drifts over it – and my heart lifts like a kite on the wind. Feeling like a twittery overgrown schoolgirl, I run to the fence, peer over and there she is. Maria.

She's lying face down under a parasol on a garden recliner and wearing only the skimpiest pair of bikini bottoms.

'Hi! Taking a day's holiday?' I call out to her, unable to think of anything less inane for the moment.

But this was the woman who touched me last night. Something that would have been pretty life-changing if I hadn't run into Valentino afterwards. My heart thuds and my palms are damp as I rub them against my shorts.

But Maria just turns over and smiles at me, and, suddenly, I know everything's going to be all right between us. I even get the impression that her beautiful naked breasts are smiling too.

'Nope, just pulling a sickie.' Cheerful and unconcerned, she rises gracefully and strolls across the grass towards me. 'There'll be hell to pay from the boss.' She winks broadly. 'But, hey, that's one of the perks of living with him, isn't it?'

I can well imagine. My mind flicks to the time I saw him spanking her with his belt, right here in their garden. It looked awfully painful, but afterwards they were all over each other like a pair of sex-starved minks, and from the way she cheered him on it was patently obvious that she loved it.

I wonder what perks like that actually feel like?

Not quite knowing what to do, I just smile.

'Why don't you come round? I was just going to make some tea. Or maybe we could have a glass of wine instead? It must be about that time.'

It's such a normal suggestion, even from a topless girl twenty years my junior, but the way Maria's blue eyes glint seems to hint at something more.

'I'd love to!' I say, quashing the last of my qualms. 'Let me bring a bottle though. Which do you prefer? Red or white?'

'I'm easy, whatever you fancy. I'll get the glasses.'

My heart is fluttering a bit. I dash back into the house, thinking about the way she just winked at me. It was exactly the same way she did when she was flirting.

I grab a bottle of Shiraz and, as an afterthought, one of Chenin Blanc too. Half out the door, I catch sight of myself in the hall mirror and frown. How 'straight' I look this morning. No sign now of the middle-aged but sexy raver of last night. Just ordinary me in my summer slumming-around 'uniform' of baggy cotton shorts, sleeveless top and comfy flatties.

Boring! Boring! Boring!

I ought to be wearing a skimpy boob tube and a thong bikini. My figure would just about stand it. But maybe it's safer to stay covered up for the time being.

Round in next door's back garden, Maria has pushed aside her lounger and spread out a giant tartan blanket and a heap of cushions under the parasol. She's also set out jumbo wineglasses, a cooler and several family-sized bags of Kettle Chips.

'I thought we'd have a picnic.' Maria is sitting with her smooth legs elegantly folded and is already munching. I watch her lick crisp grease off her fingers, keeping her eyes locked with mine as she sucks each one.

If I were a man, I'm sure this little performance would have induced a hard-on in seconds and, even though I'm not, I have to admit that it stirs me.

I open the red and pour us both an extra generous measure.

'So, what happened last night?' Cutting right to the chase, Maria downs a hefty belt of Shiraz, and then waits for my answer.

'How do you know anything happened?' Now it's come to it, I don't know where to start, so I prevaricate by sipping from my own glass. The warming fruitiness of the strong wine is revivifying. 'In fact, I was just going to ask the very same question of you.

Maria draws in a deep breath and her eyes flutter closed for a second. The way her gorgeous bosom lifts is pretty warming and fruity too.

'Oh, something *always* happens when Robert and I go to the Waverley.' She aims a sly glance at me from beneath her thick lashes. 'But, you ... something happened to you too, you've got the look of it all over you. Sort of shell-shocked but smug at the same time. Come on, spill the details! Enquiring minds need to know!'

I nearly point out that being caressed by a woman for the very first time in my life could qualify as my 'something' but somehow I know she isn't going to buy that.

I swig more wine. It's supermarket stuff, but it's pretty beefy, and I only had a slice of toast for breakfast. Almost immediately, I start to feel pleasantly swimmy and far more relaxed.

'Well, after you and your Robert disappeared to play your games, I had another drink and a very interesting chat with one of the bar staff.'

She cocks her blonde head on one side, her eyes narrowing. 'Young Greg? Oh, way to go, girl! He's very tasty ... and he has a gorgeous dick.'

That I don't doubt, but I still go on. 'No, not Greg ... er ... another person.'

'Really? Who might that be?' Her pink tongue flicks out, and licks a drop of Shiraz from her lip. I'm almost certain she knows exactly who I'm talking about. But, suddenly, I feel like having some fun.

'Well, it was a woman, actually. A very tall and beautiful one, with gorgeous long black hair. She had on this stunning short red lamé dress and she had fabulous legs. Do you know who I mean?'

Maria's laugh is a low sexy ripple that makes her lush breasts shake like firm jelly. 'Now don't be naughty, Annie,' she purrs, 'we both know that Valentina is a drag queen, gorgeousness and fabulous legs notwithstanding. For a man, he's the most beautiful woman I know.'

I giggle. The wine's really getting to me and, rashly, I knock back almost half a glass at one swallow. 'Oh, God, yes, I wish I was half as good looking as he is . . . and I'd kill for a pair of pins like his!'

Before I can stop her, Maria swoops out a hand and runs her fingertips up my calf to my knee, making me shiver involuntarily. 'Oh, I don't know, Annie,' she says, giving me an arch creamy smile, 'you've got sensational pins yourself. Nothing at all to worry about there.' She squeezes my knee, makes a little foray further and then withdraws her hand again.

My heart's thudding, and it's not entirely due to thoughts of what Valentino did, either in or out of his red lamé dress.

'So, you talked to Valentina. What else? Don't try and kid me there isn't more.'

How to answer her? I know what I felt, but describing it to someone else could end up making me sound either too stupid to live or just a rather sad old middle-aged letch.

I glance furtively at Maria, and suddenly realise she'll probably think I'm an idiot if I *didn't* fuck Valentino. And being a letch is probably a good point in her book.

'I met her again later . . . I mean, I met *him*.'

'Really?' Her eyes widen, and I get the feeling that I've surprised her somehow. She leans forward again, as if every inch of her naked skin wants me to go on.

'I was waiting for my taxi ... and I saw him. He was ... um ... well, just going for a walk, I think. So I decided to follow him.'

'Where did he go? What happened?'

Is it my imagination, or is Maria even closer now? Our bare knees are touching and her skin feels deliciously warm and slightly moist with the heat. It reminds me of the touch of Valentino's chest.

'Into the woods. You know, in the grounds at the Waverley. I saw him disappear amongst the trees and I just had to follow. I couldn't help myself. It was like a compulsion, do you know?'

Maria studies me intently, her brow slightly puckered. She looks avidly interested, yet there's still that faint element of disbelief. As if she's not hearing quite what she expected. I feel a bit aggrieved. Doesn't she think I can pull a beautiful man like Valentino? I'm not completely past it, after all.

Then she shakes her head as if she's suddenly understood what I'm thinking. 'I know ... God, yes, I know ... That's exactly how I feel with Robert. It seems totally insane, and yet you can no sooner not do it than you can stop breathing.' Her eyes look dreamy and distant for a moment, and I sense her heart has flown elsewhere ... to Borough Hall, probably, and her lover's office. But almost immediately, she's back again and more assertive. 'Go on. What happened next?'

'I caught him up and we had a chat.'

Maria lets out a hoot of laughter, and it's obvious from the mischievous expression on her face that she's not underestimating me at all now. 'Now, now, Annie, we both know that's a naughty little fib. Tell me the truth. The *whole* truth.' She laughs again. 'And don't be afraid to embellish it.'

Now it comes to it, I'm afraid to speak. I feel as if I want to breathe hard, to gasp. My head feels light, just the way it did in the woods with Valentino, and it's as if I'm pushing against some kind of membrane, and just the tiniest bit more pressure will propel me through it and into that mysterious other world.

'We did talk ... but then suddenly we were kissing. I've never just kissed a man out of the blue like that before. Without even knowing him. But it felt natural. Right. Exactly as if that was the way I ought to behave. Does that make sense?'

'Of course it does,' murmurs Maria. 'Welcome to the world of "seize the day", Annie – the world of grabbing what you want when you want it.'

But, if that was the right thing to do, why does she still look as if in some ways she doesn't quite believe what she's hearing?

'So what happened next?' she prompts.

'He told me to strip.'

'Oh my God!'

Suddenly, I'm cross with her, and it must show because her face looks suddenly guilty. But before I can launch into a spiel about how it's perfectly possible for older women to have fun too, she forestalls me.

'Look, Annie, I'm sorry. It's not that I don't think you're fanciable or anything...' For a moment, her lips quirk in a totally impish way. 'Because you *are*. Very much so. I certainly fancy you...' She doesn't quite wink, but the twinkle in her eye is near enough. 'It's just that Valentino has certain preferences.'

'What preferences? Other than wearing dresses and lipstick and a fondness for indulging in outdoor sex?'

'Oh, wow, so you *did* fuck him?'

'Yes, I did ... but you were talking about *preferences*. And why do you seem so surprised that he'd actually fuck me?'

Maria looks embarrassed, and blushes prettily. Despite my desperation to know what's going on, I feel a distinct frisson pass through me. With her lovely face all flushed like this, and her nipples as hard as two little plum stones, she really is the sexiest woman I've ever met, and I get this bizarre urge to touch her the way she touched me last night.

'Well ... er ... I don't know how to say this without causing offence.'

'Oh, come on! I'm a big girl, I can take it.'

'Right. OK ... The thing is that Valentino doesn't normally go with women as old as you.' She snags her lip with her white teeth and grimaces. 'Not that you *are* old or anything. It's just that Saskia says he had a very bad experience with an older woman once. He was insanely in love with her, and she dumped him, and now he only fucks and plays with women younger than he is. Twenties, early thirties, you know?'

I nod. I understand her surprise now, but it's still sobering to be reminded that you're middle-aged. And just when you've started to feel younger than you've felt in years and years.

'It's not *you*, Annie. It's *him*! You're gorgeous ...'

I laugh wildly. It's nerves more than anything. Suddenly, the madness of all this is brought home to me. What am I doing? I should get myself off back to the golf club and my Townswomen's Guild cronies and forget all about this crazy mirror world of kinkiness and transvestites and dangerous *al fresco* sex and pretty half-naked women who claim to fancy me.

'Don't laugh! It's true,' she goes on, reaching out and laying her hand lightly on my thigh, just below the edge of my shorts, 'you're clever and elegant and beautiful ... and you're very, very sexy. What does it matter if you're over forty, or whatever? You're an eminently fuckable woman, Annie, and Valentino would have to be blind, deaf or mad, or all three not to want you. Hang-ups from his past or otherwise.'

'If you say so . . .'

Can I believe her? She seems honest enough, and always has done, despite her sexual quirks.

'So, you fucked him then?' she goes, her blue eyes round with expectation, 'How was it? Was he amazing? I'll bet he was . . .'

It's just like being back at school. Two best friends holed up in the girls' loos, comparing notes on their boyfriends and their first forays into furtive sexual fumbling. Maria is so enthusiastic and so excited that it feels quite natural to answer her now. A moment ago, I felt middle-aged and wanted to run, but now I feel as young as that girl who once shared naughty secrets, crammed into a cubicle with her confidante.

'Yes. Yes, he was . . . or it was more a case of *him* fucking *me*. He was definitely the one in charge.' I try to analyse what I felt, but it's difficult. I certainly can't put into words that strange compulsion to obey a man against all reason. 'But I liked it that way.'

'Valentino always takes charge. He's a natural dominant. I'm not sure if he ever bottoms.'

I shouldn't really quite understand what she's on about, because this is all so new to me. But somehow I do. I get the drift, and a horrible suspicion forms. It forms into the shape of a green-eyed monster.

'Do you know him well?' I ask, doing a very poor job of feigning only the most casual of interests.

I want to ask if she's had sex with him, but I can't quite blurt out the question. Obviously, I've still got a way to go yet in this new world of being frank and uninhibited.

'Not very well. Not really . . . And, obviously, not in the biblical sense.' She gives me a very straight intense look over the rim of her glass, and I feel as if I have to brace myself for something. 'But I've done one or two scenes with him, of course. With Robert. In Suite

Seventeen.' She sips her wine again, and then grins at me, obviously slyly pleased with the impact of her bombshell.

'Scenes?'

'You know, sex games ... like the one Robert and I were playing last night. Fantasies. Scenarios. Sexual role-playing.'

My mind runs riot. I've seen these scenes of theirs, right here in this garden. Spanking. Bondage. Dominance and submission that even a born-again ingenue like me could comprehend.

'So what happens in this Suite Seventeen then? Is it some kind of torture chamber?'

'Oh no, no, no. It's just a perfectly good luxury hotel room –' she quirks her neatly groomed eyebrows at me '– with a variety of extra accoutrements, so to speak. You'll see.'

I let that one pass, although the seed is sown now. I imagine what it would be like to spend a night in that room. Playing scenes ... with Valentino. For a moment I fantasise about being tied to a wide white bed, naked, while he looms over me, a riding crop in his hand and his glorious cock poking out of the front of his jeans.

'Er, what sorts of things? Whips and chains? Handcuffs and stuff?'

'Yes, amongst other things ... and of course there's the CCTV.'

'CCTV?'

She grins suddenly, looking inordinately pleased with herself for some reason, while I absorb the import of a room with hidden cameras that observe people at their most intimate moments.

'Yes, and that was partly my idea in a roundabout way. It's a long story ... I'll tell you it one of these days, but, basically, there's an array of webcams set up in

Suite Seventeen. To cater for the voyeurs –' she drops another of her outrageous pantomime winks '– and of course the exhibitionists like Robert and me.'

Voyeurism. Exhibitionism. Two sides of the same coin.

I already know that I like watching, but what about *being watched*? Would that be just as much of a turn-on?

'Oh, you'd love it, Annie,' Maria says slyly, as if she's read my mind again. 'It's an unbelievable high, knowing that horny people are watching you and envying you. Knowing that the men wish they were the ones fucking you, and the women just wish that they *were* you.'

I close my eyes, and suddenly I'm in the woods again, on my knees being serviced, only this time with dozens of eyes observing Valentino and me from the cover of the trees. Men masturbating as they watch, excited by the way I groan and writhe. Women too, caressing themselves and feeling envious of my pleasure at the hands of such a powerful exotic lover.

'Do you want to watch now?'

Maria's voice is sultry, and she stretches like a sleepy sun-warmed cat amongst her heap of cushions. As if it's the most natural thing in the world, she begins to touch herself, playing lightly with her nipple while her other hand slides beneath the abbreviated triangle of her bikini bottom.

'Or maybe we could pretend we're *being watched*,' she offers, all seduction as her fingers move and flex beneath the thin fabric, and her hips begin to lift.

I know what she's suggesting. I think I want it, but, just as I'm about to move towards her, a long shadow falls across us.

'There's no need to pretend, you outrageous little

hussy,' interjects a stern, yet familiar voice from some-where behind me, 'you *are* being watched.'

Heart thudding, I roll over, and meet the gleaming brown eyes of Robert Stone.

4 Demo

My mouth drops open. How the devil did he get here?

Robert Stone is a large man, in every sense. He's both tall and stocky and he takes up a lot of space. How can it be possible that we didn't hear his footsteps? And yet, somehow, it doesn't surprise me. Even from what relatively little I've seen of him, it's evident he moves as lightly as a cat.

The imposing Mr Stone favours me with a warm smile, and his lustrous brown eyes flick momentarily to my bare legs and then to my cleavage. He's standing over us so he can see right down my top, and the way his mouth curves appreciatively gives me quite a boost. Especially with Maria's younger, far perkier and completely naked breasts just feet away.

'Good afternoon, Mrs Conroy,' he says, eyes on my face again, his smile wide and white. 'Beautiful day, isn't it?'

'Um ... yes, it is. Glorious. Best day we've had so far.'

Those eagle eyes cruise my frontage again for a second, and my confidence just soars.

'But please do call me "Annie", won't you?'

'Of course ... Annie.' His eyes glint, and he looms over me then hunkers down between Maria and me.

For a moment I speculate on what might have happened if I'd moved in next door and he *hadn't* been living with a beautiful young woman who he's obviously completely dotty about.

'And call me "Robert". It's about time we all got to know each other better.'

All manner of insane images flood my brain, and I speculate on just exactly how a threesome might work, and what would go where. But then Robert favours me with a little tilt of his head, and a shrug of his shoulders that seems to draw a line under our interaction for the moment.

Both of us return our attention to Maria, who, amazingly, is still enthusiastically playing with herself.

'What on earth do you think you're doing, Miss Lewis?' he says, his voice quiet and even, and threaded with an authority that makes my belly quiver. God alone knows what it does to Maria's. 'When I left, you told me you were too ill to go to work, and now, when I return for lunch to check on your health, I find you out here in the garden, lounging about virtually naked and behaving in a lewd and inappropriate manner in front of our neighbour.'

Maria looks as if she might faint at any second. Her lovely face is lit from within by total adoration. I experience a tick of envy, a longing to feel that same emotion for a man of my own. Then another face flicks across the screen of my mind, a quick impression of dark eyes, rosy lips, and black silk hair ... and I get a strange sinking yet fluttering sensation in my mid-section.

I think I already feel it, never mind longing for it.

'I – I started to feel better,' Maria says in a small voice. She's still got her hand in her pants, though, almost as if she simply can't stop touching herself. Maybe she can't because the baleful presence of her lord and master turns her on so much she just *has* to masturbate? I can easily see now how that would happen.

'So I see,' he counters, not appearing to notice the fondling fingers. He's looking directly into her eyes, holding her with his. 'But if you felt better, did it not occur to you to get dressed and come into work like a normal person?'

'No, Mr Stone, I'm sorry. It was just such a nice day. It seemed a shame to be indoors.'

Robert Stone rises to his feet, stepping away from the parasol and heaving a mock sigh. Like a displeased schoolmaster, he crosses his arms over his solid chest and shakes his greying head.

'I see that we're going to have to do something about this. What do you think, Annie? Miss Lewis has a distressing habit of irresponsibility and laziness and she really needs to be encouraged to shape up.'

I don't know about Maria, but I suddenly feel faint again too. I'm suspended across three worlds somehow. My old mundane life. The bizarre almost theatrical scenario playing out here in this garden. And another world of possibilities and potential, a domain ruled by a strange charismatic man who I know even less about than the one standing here beside me. Despite this disorientating sense of trilocation, it suddenly seems perfectly easy to answer.

'Yes. Definitely. You should certainly do something about it.' The firmness in my own voice astonishes me. I sound as if I know exactly what I'm talking about and I really mean it, even though I'm probably the one here who's most guilty of irresponsibility.

Robert Stone gives me a strange breathtaking, almost layered look. Top layer, righteous approval. Beneath it, pure perfect devilment. 'I'm so glad you think so, Annie. It's so refreshing to meet someone who understands traditional values.' He beams, and then turns back to Maria, his middle-aged 'Mr Average' face suddenly almost beautiful in its stern composure. 'Kindly remove your hand from there, Miss Lewis, and stand up.'

Maria obeys him, her eyes downcast and submissive as she gets to her feet with as much modest grace as is possible given that she's topless.

'Give me your fingers,' her lover commands, and she holds out her hand, the one fresh from her crotch. He cradles it in his own hand, which is nearly twice its size, and lifts her fragrant fingertips to his face. He sniffs, and tut-tuts, but his eyes close in momentary bliss like a master perfumier who's found the perfect formula. 'Clean them.' He releases her hand and crosses his arms in front of him again, watching.

I won't say I can't believe what I'm seeing, because I'm rapidly discovering that I can believe *anything* of these two, but the reality of what's playing out almost overwhelms me. I'm being given a personal demo of how to play sexual power games. A private tutorial. And the players putting on the show are virtuosi.

Maria slips three fingers into her mouth and sucks on them noisily. Robert Stone gives her an old-fashioned look and she hesitates, and then sucks more daintily. After a moment or two, she slips her fingertips out from between her lips, and when he nods, she proffers them back to him.

His great head tilts, and around the corners of his lips there's the very faintest intimation of a smile. He folds her small hand in his, tastes the very tip of her forefinger, and then nods again. 'That's better.' Approvingly, his eyes lock on hers.

Something tells me I should retreat now, and leave them to it. What's passing between these two people is too intense, too intimate. But I can't go. I can't miss this. It's my education.

'Now then,' Robert Stone says quietly, using the hand that he's still holding to lead Maria across to the sturdy garden bench that's served them so well in the past. 'A dozen should suffice.' He pauses by the bench, and glances my way. 'What do you think, Annie? A dozen? Or maybe more?'

I scramble to my feet. I need to be near to this. 'I – I wouldn't like to say. I'm not an expert in these matters. I'm sure you know best, Robert.'

'Yes. Actually, I do,' he says with a look of unalloyed happiness on his face. With his free hand he gestures graciously to another garden chair, not far from the bench, which offers a prime view of the proceedings. 'Do take a seat.'

'Thanks,' I mutter, blushing now. My nipples are standing out prominently beneath the thin cotton of my top, and Robert Stone's sly glance at them says he's aware of my arousal.

The chair is hard against my bottom and the minute I sit down I suddenly want to wriggle. My sex feels as if it's a yard wide, and I'm more turned on than ever now. Even more so than when Maria was flirting with me. I really want to masturbate.

As I fight with myself, Robert Stone makes preparations. 'Pull down your bikini bottoms,' he instructs Maria softly, 'just down to your knees. No further.'

I like the way that there's no shouting. No stroppy commands, or domineering histrionics. He speaks quietly and calmly to his submissive. His voice is almost kind.

'That's good,' he encourages when she complies.

Next, he removes the jacket of his expensive suit and lays it over the end of the bench. As he takes his seat, he's loosening his tie, and then when he's settled himself, he rolls up the sleeves of his mid-blue cotton shirt.

And, all this time, his eyes are on Maria as she stands before him like some perverted Aphrodite, her skimpy bikini bottoms around her knees and her breasts, belly and pubis on show for his approval.

And mine too.

'Now then, Miss Lewis.' His voice is shot through with genuine affection as he leans forwards and cups Maria's chin in his fingers, making her look at him. 'Time to assume the position.' He releases her and sets his large feet more firmly against the grass-covered earth, his powerful thighs braced.

Maria gives a demure little nod and, with an almost ritualistic grace, she drapes herself face down across her lover's lap. Arms forwards, her hands brush the grass like a ballerina's, and her shaggy blonde hair falls around her face. Her lush rounded bottom is beautifully presented, a perfect target.

How does it feel to do what she's done?

To make oneself so totally exposed and vulnerable? How does it feel to lie there, wondering when the first blow is going to fall, and how much it's going to hurt? I'm fairly stoic myself, and not afraid of a bit of pain, but it's hard to imagine actively wanting to seek it out.

As I listen to the thud of my own heart, I reach dimly towards a kind of understanding. I want what Maria wants, even though I don't quite yet comprehend the mechanism. I know I'd be afraid, yet I want the fear too.

Maybe it's like giving a gift? One that Maria's giving to Robert because she loves him? I sense though, that it's a gift for her too.

This is all too much and too deep. I wish they'd just get on with it.

The whole day around us is frozen. Even the birds in the trees don't seem to be singing, and the faint traffic noises from the main road a few streets away sound as if they're dozens of miles in the distance.

Then, like a master showman, Robert Stone cracks his knuckles and gives me a quick impish glance before returning his attention to Maria. He places his large left hand lightly on her bottom, and it's like he's testing her flesh and calculating angles of impact and degrees of force.

Then, with no further ado, he spanks her.

It's like a gunshot in the scented summer air, and so much louder than I'd expected that I jump an inch out of my seat from the shock of it. Maria yelps plaintively, but stays far stiller across her master's lap than I do in my chair.

'Please try to be quiet, Miss Lewis,' he says quietly. 'Remember we have a guest. You must put on a good show.'

I see Maria's fingers clench against the grass, her whole body taut. I can't see her face but I imagine her biting her pink lips.

'Relax,' instructs Robert, 'you know it always hurts more when you're tense.'

Immediately, she obeys him. So completely it's actually visible. Her body droops across him like a bolt of silk and, as the second blow descends, and the third, she seems to absorb the force of it, and become one with the falling hand that punishes her.

With the fourth and fifth, the sensuality of the display increases exponentially. Rose-red fire burns in Maria's buttocks, a graphic perverted expression of passion and lust. She begins to move against Robert's knees and I can't tell whether it's a squirm of pain or because she's so aroused that she simply can't contain herself.

I suspect it's the latter because I can't contain myself either.

I know I'm only seeing this from the outside, but somehow I'm in it too. My knickers are damp and sticky, and with each blow my heart seems to turn over with a strange dark yearning. For two pins, I'd throw myself out of my chair and abase myself at Robert Stone's feet, begging him to punish me too. But, somehow, I know it's not my place. Not quite yet.

This is just a beginning. I'm a welcome and privileged observer here, but not yet ready to be elevated to participant status.

Despite her master's instruction, Maria is no longer silent. She's emitting little broken whimpers and an occasional low keening sound just after a strike. Her bottom looks so hot now that I almost imagine that Robert's hand sizzles when it makes contact and, if I'm wet from just watching, between her legs she must be running like a river.

And then, as suddenly as it all began, it's over. I've lost the capacity to count – I'm halfway to forgetting my own name – but Robert Stone hasn't, and the dozen is tallied off and complete. His great hand comes down again, but slowly and caressingly, settling like a benediction on the crimson blotchy planes of Maria's bottom. She hisses between her teeth, and then mews slightly when his big fingers flex and the tips of them dig infinitesimally into her flesh. He does this a couple of times, a bland almost assessing expression on his broad face, then his eyes seem to twinkle like two stars and he slides his fingertips down the cleft of her backside and into her sex from behind.

Maria wriggles and coos as he paddles about in there for a few seconds, and her master nods to himself as if making a decision.

'We'll have to do something about this,' he murmurs abstractedly.

In a smooth, beautifully syncopated manoeuvre, he lifts Maria up and sets her on her feet, then stands up himself, and scoops her back up into his arms as if she weighs only a few ounces.

Against all the odds, it's extraordinarily romantic,

and I feel a crazy urge to sigh like a wedding guest when the groom kisses the bride.

Either that or masturbate myself senseless right in front of them.

'You're welcome to join us,' offers Robert, his voice warm and conversational as he turns towards the house with his swooning burden in his arms and glances back at me over his shoulder.

For a split second, I contemplate accepting the invitation, and my mouth opens to say 'yes', but right at the last instant, the few remaining shreds of the normal straight, uninitiated and cautious Annie Conroy hold me back.

And the shreds are right. I'm not quite ready for a threesome yet. Especially as I get a strong sense that, despite his polite offer, the mighty Robert Stone would much rather be alone with the woman he loves.

I dart to my feet, and start to step away. 'Maybe another time perhaps?' I manage to make it sound as if it's just coffee and doughnuts he's just asked me in for. 'It's a nice offer, but I'm ... um ... expecting a phone call, actually. I'd better nip back home.' I start to sidle sideways towards the path, still subconsciously reluctant to leave.

'Of course.' Unoffended, Robert beams. 'We'll look forward to it,' he continues as if it really were just morning coffee. 'Only let's not wait too long.' He gives me a nod and then adjusts his precious armful and strides off purposefully towards their house.

'Talk to you later, Annie!' trills the dangling Maria merrily just as they disappear.

Which leaves me on my own – and wondering if I've just woken from one of those bizarre dreams again.

Once back home, I stagger into the kitchen and get sidetracked from my need for a strong black coffee by the even greater need pounding between my legs. Before I really know what I'm doing, I find myself slumped against the worktop, my hand down my knickers rubbing frantically, as if my life depended on it. Unsurprisingly, resolution comes fast and with a huge pleasurable jolt. How could it be otherwise after the scene I've just witnessed?

When I'm done, though, I feel vaguely melancholy, and I'm grateful when Boy slithers in through the flap and winds around my legs in a figure of eight of affection. I give him a kitty treat to show my appreciation, and he wolfs it down, and then wanders off again, obviously feeling his job's well done.

What Stone and Maria have got, I want. I feel as if I've been waiting my whole life for Sexual Wonderland, even though I never knew it existed. My life with Stan was happy and fulfilling in all sorts of ways, and I don't regret a minute of it. But this is a different me now, with new and different needs, and I've got to shed my inhibitions like an old cocoon or a redundant layer of skin.

Sipping my coffee, I sit in my window seat, staring out not at the garden, but a slowly circling parade of images, speculations and notions. Old parameters of desire and desirability seem to dissolve and be replaced by entirely new ones.

Eventually, it finally dawns on me that what I said about a phone call is actually true. Charles is supposed to be ringing me today and I'd completely forgotten all about it.

The answerphone is flashing and there are several texts and voicemails on my mobile. All to much the same effect – which is that Charles wants to reschedule our date, and go over some documents.

His voice is as smooth and suave as ever, but as if I've acquired a new degree of acuity somehow, I detect a tiny irritated edge. He's trying not to show it, but I can tell there's more riding on this for him than he's letting on, and that makes me vaguely uneasy.

Why is he so anxious to move ahead on this? Before the delights of kinky sex took my life in a stranglehold, I recall Charles saying that Stan's money needed managing more efficiently. We only discussed it in the broadest terms, but suddenly there are 'documents'. I'm not sure I like the sound of that at all.

Then, a new thought occurs and, in spite of my disquiet about the money stuff, I crack a smile. Perhaps I can find a way to distract him from all the financial talk.

Last night, when I set out for the Waverley, I was all fluttery and excited about the prospect of dining with a handsome younger man. Things have changed since then, in more drastic ways than I could ever have imagined. But Charles is still a handsome younger man.

What does his body look like, I wonder, under those sharp super-trendy suits he wears. He's tall and lean and really very handsome with his dark elegantly styled hair and his thin intelligent face. There's nothing particularly exotic, mysterious or dangerous about him, like Valentino. And he has none of that piquant blend of gravitas and mischief that Robert Stone possesses. But still, he's a pretty hot example of metrosexual manhood and, even before last night, I can't deny that I'd wondered what it would be like to go to bed with him.

He rings again while I'm making yet more coffee. 'Annie, where have you been? I've been trying to get in touch with you all morning. I do hope you're not cross with me over last night?'

His voice is all charm, as ever, with that flirty flattering note that he's been developing lately. But, now I'm alerted to it, I hear the distinct thread of impatience beneath the smoothness, and that rubs me up the wrong way.

He's up to something, but, despite my growing irritation with him, I feel a thrill of something that tastes strangely like gamesmanship. Ah hah, this polished young stud thinks he can get the better of a naïve and sexually needy older woman, does he?

Well, think again, Charlie boy! I'm not the Annie Conroy you were dealing with a couple of days ago. I count to ten in my head, and then add another five. I can almost hear his growing frustration down the line.

'Annie? Are you there?'

'Yes, Charles, I'm here. I've just been chilling out in the garden with my next-door neighbour. A few glasses of wine, a spot of girl talk, you know how it is? I just lost track of the time. Was there something you wanted?' I keep my voice soft and low and unconcerned. Let him stew.

'Well, it's a gorgeous day for it. I wish I'd been there. I can just picture you in a bikini, Annie,' he counters, re-establishing his charm offensive. 'Anyway, I was hoping we could, shall we say, reconvene our dinner date tonight and discuss your portfolio? I've lined up a really exciting raft of investments, and we need to get you in now, on the ground floor, so to speak.'

'Really? As exciting as that?'

Twisted as it seems, I try to imagine that I'm Valentina. How would 'she' respond to Charles and his BS? She would probably have seen through him far sooner than I've done and have been ready to act accordingly.

'Yes. Yes, it is, actually . . .' He's beginning to sound ever so slightly rattled now, and the edge in his voice excites me.

It's not half an hour since I was masturbating like a madwoman in my own kitchen, but suddenly I want –

no, I *need* – to do it again. As Charles hesitates, I slip the hand that's not holding the phone into my knickers.

'I thought perhaps that we could try somewhere else tonight. Somewhere a bit more upmarket.' He names a trendy and ludicrously overpriced restaurant in town, but I'm barely listening.

I'm working my bottom against the edge of the kitchen unit, and slicking and flicking at my clitoris. I'm so needy, and so wet, and not far off.

The movie in my mind starts to roll again and, in it, my finger is replaced by Charles's tongue. He's kneeling before me naked, and giving me the most splendid cunnilingus while Valentina, in her red dress, smacks his bottom ferociously with what looks like a riding crop.

She whacks him hard, his tongue goes wild, and so do I!

Bouncing against the marble edge of my expensive kitchen unit, I bite my lip and toss my head as my sex throbs and ripples at my touch. The phone clatters to the floor but luckily it doesn't break. Not that I care right at the moment. As if from outer space, Charles's voice squeaks and protests, repeating my name.

As soon as I've caught my breath and pulled my hand out of my pants again, I scoop up the receiver.

'Annie? Annie? Are you all right?'

'Fine. I just saw a squirrel on the window ledge and it made me jump and drop the phone. Don't fuss.'

What a splendidly creative lie! I feel deliciously proud of myself. I really must be a born-again wicked woman if falsehood comes so easily to my lips.

'What about this evening then?' he persists. I can feel him having to fight to maintain his lightly teasing tone. 'Shall I book a table at La Gavroche? They know me there, I'm sure they'll have something for us.'

'No, I prefer the Waverley Grange. Book a table there. Say it's for Mrs Conroy. I'm sure they'll have something there for *me*.'

But, even as Charles concedes gracefully, and we make arrangements for him to pick me up at eight, I have no idea whether my bold claims are bullshit or not. I can't remember if anyone at the Waverley actually knows my name. And yet, somehow, I have the strangest feeling that they might. At least they might now.

Tonight is not a big deal, and I must play it cool. But even so I think it merits some careful preparation. I need to look my best if I'm going to get the better of Charles.

The City Beauty Rooms can fit me in, and I end up having what amounts to almost their entire 'day of beauty' shoehorned into a couple of hectic hours. Various bits of me are plucked and creamed and pampered, and I indulge myself in an oxygen facial and then a trim and restyle with Serge.

I love the result. Basically it's my existing style, only much bouncier and fluffier and flirtier looking, complete with clever layers and a selection of highlights and lowlights. The latter are mainly designed to mask my few stray greys and provide a softer more flattering foil to my pale complexion. I know I shouldn't pander to the idea of primping myself about just for a man, but, as I smile at the results in the mirror, I'm aware that most of this beautification hasn't a thing to do with meeting my financial adviser.

I might have made dinner arrangements with Charles, but the preening, grooming and restyling session is all about Valentino. If he's there tonight, I'd really like to dazzle him.

On arriving home, I'm stopped in my tracks by a

large white box on my back step. It's the sort that high-end clothes boutiques pack very special dresses in.

I carry it inside and set it on the kitchen table. When I lift the lid, there's a little note resting on top of the multiple leaves of fine silky tissue paper that protect whatever lies beneath.

A little bird tells me you're going back to the Waverley tonight, it says in a crisp bright hand. *Thought you might like to borrow something to wear. See you later.*

It's just signed, *M*.

Cheeky young minx! Doesn't she think I've got any sexy clothes of my own? I've got a whole wardrobe full of dresses, separates, suits and evening wear. Everything a smart woman needs for any social occasion, including some expensive designer items.

And yet, without a doubt, I know I'll wear Maria's choice instead. I just wonder who she's picked out this item in order to impress. And how she knows I'm even going to be at the Waverley tonight. Jungle drums, I suppose. She and her Robert are obviously on intimate terms with people there – someone called Saskia, Greg the barman and Valentino the whatever, to name but three. If Charles has already booked our table, it's obviously got back to Maria by now.

With a sense of fatalism, I dive into the tissue paper, slightly anxious that I might find something that's probably way too young for me.

As I pluck away the last leaf, I soon discover that I needn't have worried.

It's a dress, but not the abbreviated 'fuck-me' body-skimmer that I was afraid of. In fact, I'm irrationally disappointed to find an elegant and extremely tasteful 'little black'. It looks about my size, which is unsurprising because, even though Maria's figure is somewhat tighter, perkier and more toned than mine, we're still basically the same height and shape.

Wrapped in additional layers of tissue is a pair of shoes. They're black velvet, with heels a tad higher than my usual choice, but nothing I can't handle or be comfortable in.

But beneath the dress and shoes, and under yet another sheaf of tissue, I find the real goods. A set of underwear that's as unrestrained and blatantly sexy as the dress and shoes are subtle.

My fingers actually shake as I lift out a plunge-front underwired bra and thong set in aubergine figured satin, encrusted with buttermilk-coloured lace – and my confidence falters slightly as I fondle the beautiful garments.

Naughty lingerie like this belongs on a fearless young woman's body, not that of someone who's middle-aged and still not quite sure of herself. The thin silk slides over my fingers, light as a feather and subtly perfumed by fabric softener and I can't help wondering what happened when Maria herself last wore these beautiful things. Did she display herself to her beloved Robert in them? Then seduce him utterly and temporarily flex her female supremacy in the never-ending game of love and lust they play?

As I return my borrowed finery to the box, my fingers make contact with a second slip of paper, tucked away at the bottom. And, when I unfold it, I find what can only be described as a motivational mantra ... for a seductress.

I am a queen. I am a goddess. I am in charge.

'If you say so, Maria,' I mutter, and then nearly jump out of my skin as the clock chimes the hour and tells me how little time I have.

Grabbing my precious bundle I run for the stairs.

5 In Charge of Charles

I am a queen. I am a goddess. I am in charge.

Silently, I repeat the mantra. I think it's working, despite the fact that it makes me want to giggle. I'm not usually into all this self-affirming feminism and such like, but I must admit that part of me is feeling pretty goddess-like at the moment.

Of course, some of it might be to do with the champagne that Charles and I are drinking, but I prefer to believe in the power of positive thought.

Charles, as ever, looks decidedly sleek and groomed and handsome. He's recovered like a trooper from the shock he got when I opened the door wearing Maria's sexy dress.

Because it is a sexy dress, and there are no two ways about it. It looks quite different on a body, far more seductive than it looked in the box. Elegant and sensual, it's about an inch shorter than I would normally wear, and just a whisker lower cut and closer fitting – but not in a way that would provoke 'mutton dressed as lamb' jibes. The moment Charles set eyes on me in it, I could see him mentally recategorising me.

I've been moved out of the 'quietly attractive widow who needs gentle flattering' section and into the 'mature goer, well preserved and definitely up for it' zone.

This suits me fine ... because I've reclassified myself.

'Perhaps we could discuss your portfolio now?' he suggests lightly, his fingers straying to the briefcase he's insisted on bringing with him into the Lawns Bar.

He's been doing a fine job of not really paying any attention to it, but, with my new awareness, I'm attuned to his body language. I can almost see him calculating precisely how long he has to spend making mildly flirtatious small talk before he can broach the subject of my investing my late husband's assets in a way that will no doubt make *him* a great deal of money too.

I feign nonchalance. Giving him a creamy Maria-like smile, I lean against the back of the banquette we're sitting on and glance around the room. Then I cross my legs in what I hope isn't too obvious a way, reach for my glass of bubbly and turn towards Charles again. Regarding him coolly, I feel as if I'm channelling a combination of Maria, Catherine Tramell from *Basic Instinct* and Valentina – and it's both hilarious and dangerously exciting.

Charles reaches for the briefcase.

'I'd much rather you didn't.'

I recross my legs and take a sip of champers. It's sumptuously delicious and, either by accident or more of the slightly disquieting design that provided tonight's outfit, it's a much better bottle than the one Charles ordered. I make a show of savouring the gorgeous taste, running my tongue over my lower lip to scoop up a stray drop. If I were to stand outside my own skin now and watch this little drama workshop, I'd probably laugh myself silly, but I'm on the inside and, against all the odds, my pantomime vamp act seems to be working.

'You're the one who said we should get to know each other better socially, Charles,' I purr, noting that he's crossed his own legs now. Is he actually getting aroused too? 'So socialise with me.'

Giving me an undeniably seductive smile, he glances around the softly lit room. 'It's not bad here, is it? I was expecting it to be a bit faded. A bit provincial, you know? But it's actually got quite an interesting ambience.'

My eyes drift, inevitably, towards the bar.

No sign of Valentino tonight, alas, in either of his guises, but cute young Greg is on duty again, and he catches my eye with a knowing wink and a cheeky smile. Is he the one who's upgraded us to the deluxe champagne? It's unlikely he has that degree of autonomy, but you never know.

'Yes, interesting,' I answer airily, smiling back at Greg before I return my attention to Charles.

I don't know whether it's the champagne, or the little game I'm playing, but I could swear he's jealous. He follows my glance towards the pretty young barman, and his eyes narrow with suspicion and carefully suppressed resentment.

'And apparently the rooms have an interesting ambience too. My friends tell me that Suite Seventeen is particularly spectacular.'

Charles nearly spills his champagne, but recovers heroically. 'Really?' he murmurs, flashing me what he obviously thinks is his best killer smile.

And it isn't half bad actually. Not so long ago, it would probably have had me fluttering. But that was before last night, in the woods.

'Really,' I affirm, giving him the benefit of a leisurely sweep from my Dior-augmented eyelashes.

I can almost see the cogs of his brain whirring. He's calculating the odds of success of a really heavy pass, knowing that he might ruin his investment plans if it all goes spectacularly wrong.

'Might be a good idea to reserve a room,' he says after a moment, his voice deceptively light, 'better to discuss all this in private, maybe.' He nods towards the briefcase, looking decidedly pleased with his own ploy.

I have to admire the way he thinks on his feet. 'Mmmm ... perhaps you're right.' I keep it non committal, and then change the subject abruptly, hoping to throw him off kilter again. 'Shall we eat? I think I'd prefer a bar meal in here actually, rather than all the bother of the restaurant. Could you get me a menu, please?'

Warring emotions race across Charles's handsome face. This new Annie that he wasn't expecting confuses him, and he's doing his best to hide the fact. I'm playing fast and loose with both his business plans and his dinner arrangements, and he *is* turned on. I can tell because he twitches his jacket across his groin area as he gets to his feet to snag a menu from an adjacent table. Poor lad, he's getting far more than he bargained for tonight, and I've a suspicion that he bargained for quite a lot.

I am a queen. I am a goddess. I am in charge, I chant again inside, determined not to lose my control.

Charles is nothing if not a fighter, though, and his smile is almost sultry when he returns with a menu. He's super-smooth, and he's adaptable, I'll give him that, and we start to discuss our order as if a bar meal had been his idea in the first place.

It's because he wants me to invest, the realist in me mutters subversively. He's got to keep his cool so he can get you to do what he wants.

No, it's because he thinks you're sexy and vibrant for your age and he wants to sleep with you, contradicts the new optimistic erotic fantasist who believes that absolutely anything is possible. I choose to believe the fantasist and the realist slinks away, vanquished.

We chat for a while, and drink some more champagne, and Charles is flirting big-time now, touching my arm every so often, his eyes darting surreptitiously from my cleavage, to my legs, and back up to my face.

I'm excited myself now too, although I manage to hide it and match Charles's silky banter.

What is he like in bed? I wonder. Do I even want him? Even the new sexy me thinks that two different lovers in the space of two days is a bit on the slutty side. And how could this affectedly smooth, but basically uninitiated man compare with Valentino, who was so overwhelming and mysterious in the woods?

'I suppose I'd better let the restaurant know we won't be dining,' Charles says cheerfully. 'Will you excuse me just a moment, Annie? I won't be two ticks.'

He's slipped off his designer jacket by now, and I admire his trim arse as he walks away towards the lobby.

But then, as I return my attention to the room itself, a tall elegant figure unwinds itself from a low chair in the far corner that I've barely registered before ... and my interest in Charles suddenly recedes towards extinction.

How the hell could I not realise he's been here all the time? Does he have super powers? A cloak of invisibility?

Valentina sashays towards me, gliding like a screen siren, copper eyes gleaming in the bar's soft lighting.

She – no, I can't think of him as anything but 'he' now – he is wearing a slim dark-blue dress made of fine stretch velvet. It's daringly short and skims skilfully over a body I know is male beneath the glamorous female trappings. But, just as last night, the illusion and the aura both deceive the eye completely and make him look deliciously and mind-fuddlingly feminine.

He sinks into the place on the banquette that Charles has just vacated and flicks a glance in the direction of the doorway, long black hair swinging like a sheet of heavy silk. 'Very cute, Annie. Very cute indeed. I do hope you're planning to fuck him.'

His blunt words and my confused feelings intersect with a silent big bang and for a moment I'm knocked sideways. In a world without Valentino, yes, I would definitely be making plans to fuck Charles. But here I am, with this gorgeous exotic, almost fairytale creature beside me, and I can't think about sleeping with anybody but him.

And yet, I know, Valentino is outside all the normal parameters of behaviour and emotion. No petty macho jealousy for him. If he feels it might be diverting to see me fuck another man, he'll certainly encourage, nay, compel me to do it!

This is the secret, hidden in plain sight at the Waverley, and anything is possible and doable and desirable.

'It's crossed my mind,' I reply, hypnotised all over again in the presence of this beautiful bewildering man. He's looking at my mouth as if he remembers kissing it, and I can't help but remember what those kisses felt like. His lips are painted with the same soft rosy-red as last night, and I can't imagine a sight more perversely stirring.

Except perhaps a proper glimpse of the majestic and exceptionally large cock that I know is lurking in wait beneath that slim and elegant skirt.

He gives me a long searching look of amusement. 'Still so cautious.' His mouth curves mockingly. 'And yet last night you were prepared to give yourself to me without a second thought, even though we'd only met for barely a few moments, chatting across a bar.'

'That was different!'

I don't really know how. I only know it was.

Part of me still isn't quite sure whether I want to sleep with Charles, but, if Valentino took me by the hand now and led me away to a bedroom, I'd follow him and spread my legs like his sex slave.

'Of course it was,' he murmurs, taking my hand as if he's read my mind. But he doesn't urge me to rise and follow him. He simply circles his long crimson-tipped fingers around my palm, again and again, and it's like he's slipped his hand into my borrowed knickers and is fondling me.

My reaction must be obvious on my blushing face, because Valentino chuckles. It's a deep thoroughly masculine rumble that's totally at odds with his shimmering hair, his perfect makeup and his short, sexy skirt.

'Let me help you with your decision,' he says crisply, lifting my palm to his lips and kissing it, just once. 'I'll make it for you.' He gives a firm nod, and something in his strange eyes turns steely. 'Fuck him tonight. For *my* pleasure ... I'll ensure there's a room available for you.' His lush mouth quirks again as he releases my hand, revealing the minutely crooked tooth that somehow seems to accentuate his beauty rather than mar it. 'But when he's inside you, think of me ... That's an order.'

I'd think about you anyway.

'Do you understand?'

I nod, completely helpless. I feel as if I've been drugged and, in a way, I suppose I have.

'Will you comply?'

My chin bobs like a nodding dog's, and a sensation like warmed honey flowing through my veins descends through my body to my sex. It's like power and powerlessness intermingled, both at once, and it's as sweet as the honey and just as much a delicious temptation to overindulge. Valentino's smile widens and becomes so dazzling that I almost want to faint at the sight of it.

A rather abrupt-sounding cough breaks the spell, and I almost have to shake my head to clear it and allow thought again. Turning around, I discover Charles, who's staring at Valentino with an expression that's almost equal amounts of revulsion and fascination. His mouth opens as if he wants to speak, but then just stays open, as if he's too transfixed to find the appropriate words.

'How do you do? I'm Valentina. Delighted to meet you.' The ambiguous figure at my side holds out his hand. Clearly, he's behaving exactly as a confident beautiful vamp should do, and he isn't about to get up out of his seat to be greeted.

I watch the silent interplay between the two of them, and feel almost afraid that Charles might finally lose his carefully cultivated cool, because it's obvious that Valentino is challenging him to kiss the offered hand.

'Er ... Charles Ferguson. How are you?' Valiantly, he takes the proffered hand and gives it a manly no-nonsense shake.

Valentino grins archly, not bothering to hide his amusement. 'Am I sitting in your seat?' His accent is soft and flirtatious, and he bats his long eyelashes without shame as he looks up at Charles from under them.

'No problem, I'll get another.' I can see Charles trying to work out his responses. Should he go for charm, and treat Valentino as if he really is a woman? Or stick to bog-standard man-to-man bonhomie? He's finding it difficult, a real test of his social skills.

Valentino has mercy though. 'No need. I have to go now.' He rises from the low seat like Venus from the waves, and I see Charles's Adam's apple bob furiously when his imposing height is fully revealed. Valentino might dress and act like a glamorous super-feminine seductress, but there's no getting around the fact that he's tall, even for a man, well over six feet tall even without the benefit of his elegant high heels.

'Wonderful to meet you again, Annie,' he says softly, leaning down to dispense an air kiss. 'Always a pleasure.' Those luscious black eyelashes of his flick down again, and he leans in even closer. 'And don't forget what I said.' His painted lips brush my hot skin, and his husky voice is inaudible to anyone but me. 'Obey me tonight. And when his dick plunges inside you, it's *mine*.'

Yes, master, an entirely new voice murmurs in my mind, and this time I admire Valentino's arse as he slinks away like a goddess. There's nothing burlesque or pantomime about the way he moves. The perfect chameleon, he seems to actually *become* a woman when he inhabits the dress and makeup.

'Do you know that – that creature?'

There's blatant hostility in Charles's voice and I feel a sudden rush of boiling, curdling anger. How dare he insult my god?

'The creature's name is "Valentina",' I shoot back, giving him a quelling look, 'and I'll thank you to be civil about my friends, if you don't mind. Did you sort things out in the restaurant?'

Charles looks taken aback, and blushes furiously in a way I find strangely arousing. He opens his mouth, and then shuts it again, casting a confused glance in the general direction of Valentino's disappearance.

'Yes, all sorted,' he says, his face mobile as he marshals his composure. Then he shakes his head slightly, and gives me a much more confident grin. 'Annie, you do *know* that he's a man, don't you?'

'Of course I do! How stupid do you think I am?' I remain stern, but I'm chuckling inside. 'I *can* tell a drag queen when I see one. I just happen to think he's a very beautiful one. Don't you think so?'

With a discernible shudder, Charles resumes his seat. Does he think that cross-dressing might be a communicable disease and he's going to catch it off the upholstery?

'Well, I suppose so. Drag queens aren't really my scene.' He glances across the room again, even though Valentino has disappeared now. 'But, as trannies go, I have to admit he's pretty glam.'

'Well, I like him,' I say, enunciating the words in a way that I hope indicates the matter is closed.

Charles gets the message and changes the subject. Discussing a recent programme on the television, he seems vaguely uneasy at first, but soon rallies and gets into his natural charming stride again. I let him think I'm succumbing, and maybe I am a little, but inside I'm still dreaming of long black hair, glittering metallic eyes and outrageous whispered words that command me to madness.

I float through the next half-hour or so. Part of me interacts with Charles, genuinely responding to his accomplished advances and enjoying the compliments and the eye contact and more of those carefully measured little arm pats.

But there's another bit of me, standing back, who laughs at him and almost pities him for his lack of understanding of anything that really matters. I don't understand very much myself as yet, but I can feel the touch of something great and very wonderful.

I glance at Greg, and I know he knows.

I think about Maria and Robert, and, oh boy, how *they* know!

I close my eyes momentarily and see Valentino, in both of his provocative guises, one after another repeating and repeating like a hypnotic slide show, and accept the fact that he might know just about *everything*.

Eventually, of course, Charles gently manoeuvres the conversation around to my investments again. Not surprisingly, as it's the primary reason he brought me here.

But I'm not interested in money matters tonight. 'I'd rather not discuss that here, Charles. I don't feel comfortable talking about my finances in a bar. I think we need privacy.'

His eyes light up. Two birds with one stone, I can see him thinking. He gives me his sexiest smile and I can see that he's fully expecting me to melt, and then he does the hand pat thing again. 'Of course, you're quite right. Maybe we could take this back to your place and thrash things out over a nightcap?' His hand closes around mine, warm and encouraging.

I can see he thinks he's got the cat in the bag, and I glance away. He probably thinks I'm shy and nervous – the blushing forty-something flattered by the attentions of a younger and undeniably handsome man. But really I'm laughing. The cat *is* in the bag and he doesn't have the slightest idea that he's the kitty.

I face him again, eyes level. 'What about that room?'

Charles beams. 'Yes, of course, wonderful idea. You wait here and I'll see what's available.'

'Oh, don't be so middle class, Charles.' Snatching up my bag, I rise to my feet and, without pausing to consult him further, I'm on my way to the door. 'Come on, then,' I fling over my shoulder and then stride forwards.

I'm not worried that he won't follow, but my nerves still twinge a little. All this mad impulsive, take-charge behaviour is still new to me, and the quiet living habits of a lifetime are hard to banish completely.

I chant my mantra, and pray that the puckish challenging spirit of Valentino is truly with me. I sense Charles behind me, and let out the breath I hadn't realised I was holding.

At the desk, the elegant dark-haired receptionist I noticed last night is on duty again, and meets my request for a room with perfect discreet equanimity.

'Of course, Mrs Conroy,' she murmurs, a friendly smile on her face, 'we have Suite Seventeen available. Would that suit you?'

'I . . .' begins Charles behind me, but his voice dries when I hold up my hand to silence him.

The receptionist looks me straight in the eye, and we communicate perfectly. She knows too.

'Yes, that's wonderful . . . Suite Seventeen would be perfect.'

She nods her elegantly coiffed head and reaches for a key-card. Then, pausing, she opens a drawer and takes out a second one. 'For the cable TV,' she says softly, not winking, but as good as when her polite efficient smile widens just a little.

'Do I need to sign the register? Or show a credit card?' I ask, fingering the tantalising plastic rectangle of the TV card and imagining the wonders it might disclose.

'Oh no, Mrs Conroy, that won't be necessary. Not for a good friend of the Waverley like you.' She gives me a slight nod, her dark eyes shining. 'You'll find Suite Seventeen on the first floor and to the left out of the lift. Have a good evening.'

'I will,' I answer and I'm sure my eyes are shining too.

Returning my attention to Charles, I sense him attempting to regain the upper hand as we walk towards the lift. He's definitely what the magazines would describe as a babe magnet, and he knows it, but he's just not getting the Annie he expected.

Well, you'd better get used to the new me, young sir, because the old one's gone forever, never to return.

He slips his free hand around my waist and flashes me a smile full of promise. In return, I give him a long unwavering look. This clearly isn't the reaction he was anticipating, and he looks momentarily confused as if he's somehow lost his place.

This is fun!

In the lift he takes the initiative again and, leaning in close, he tries to kiss me. I give him another blast of the intense assessing stare that I've acquired by osmosis from Valentino and he backs off, wondering if he's made a mistake.

Excellent! I smile and lean in myself this time, taking a kiss instead of passively accepting one.

His mouth is nice and still tastes of the champagne we've been drinking. His lips are firm and, ever the comeback kid, he importunes me with his tongue. I allow it to enter my mouth, but I battle it with my own.

Game on, I feel him think. I think the same.

His arms slide around me, but he's hampered by the case he's still clinging on to. It bangs against my back and I retreat, tutting my tongue in disapproval.

'You'll have to lose the case, Charles, if you want to sweep a lady off her feet.' I shake my head chidingly, but leaven the criticism with a smile. Valentino would be so proud of me.

Just as Charles drops the case, and swoops forwards again, the lift door opens and I sashay out of the car, continuing the smile over my shoulder.

Suite Seventeen is easy to find, and its simple wood-panelled door, with brass numerals and door fittings, is perfectly innocuous. Who'd believe that there's a notorious den of iniquity over that threshold?

I let us in, and everything still seems normal. The room is atmospherically lit with antique lamps, and perfumed with a light vaguely spicy pot-pourri. It's all quite homely really, comfortable and chintzy with a generously proportioned brass-railed bed and a couple of plump cushion-heaped armchairs.

I glance around, scanning for the 'accoutrements'. But it's all still normal. No restraints, no whips or chains, and no sex toys. It's a lovely room but it's not very daring.

'I thought this was a suite?' Charles observes, sounding unimpressed. 'And what's with the chintz and the frills and furbelows?'

I follow his eye and I can't deny that the heavy patterned bed hangings are fussy and rather kitsch.

And then, I remember something I really shouldn't have forgotten, and the penny drops with such a clang that I'm amazed Charles doesn't hear it.

There are cameras in here. Webcams watching our every move. And some of the spying electronic eyes are probably hidden in the complicated pleats and flounces of the chintz bed hangings, monitoring sexual ground zero.

How can I do this?

How can I *not* do it?

Suddenly, I feel angry. Angry with Charles for his condescension and for trying to manoeuvre me into his investments, perhaps by sleeping with me, and believing that he can get away with it. And angry with Valentino for warping my mind, giving me impossible orders, casting an irresistible spell on me ... and *knowing* that he can get away with it!

What if tapes are being made? What will happen to my reputation if they get around? I can just imagine the talk at the golf club, at the nineteenth hole ...

But, as I imagine it, I'm suddenly set free. Who cares what those fuddy-duddies think? I'd much rather be whispered about as a notorious scarlet woman than be mildly respected for my golf swing and my good works. I glance around the room again and just imagine the hot hungry watchers hovering over the monitors, anticipating the moment when I start to undress. I feel like stripping off right now, especially when those many watching eyes consolidate into one unforgettable pair. They're as bright as copper and as dark as night, and so full of sin that a woman could drown in them.

The blood in my veins fizzes and I'm ready to tear my clothes off.

'Shall we get this out of the way first and then...' Charles begins smoothly. And then falters when I spin around and glare at him.

'Oh, don't be such a prick, Charles. I didn't come up here to look at boring financial documents and, if that's all you had in mind, you can fuck off right now and I'll just have some fun with the porn channel and the contents of the mini bar.'

Did I just say that? The spirit of Valentino must indeed be moving in me.

Charles's jaw drops open in astonishment and I feel as if I'm halfway to an orgasm already. Shocking the hell out of him is worth an hour of his most diligent foreplay.

Charles sets the briefcase in one of the chairs, and moves towards me. 'Right, of course,' he murmurs, giving me a seductive look. Yet again, I have to admire him for adaptability. 'It's just that I didn't want to rush things, Annie. I know it's not all that long since your husband died and I didn't want to seem presumptuous.'

The spectre of Stan passes momentarily through my mind, but he's laughing with me and saying, 'Go for it, Annie lass!'

'Charles, I loved my husband, but he'd be the first to tell me to get back in the saddle, so to speak. Now, are you going to oblige me or just stand there like a spare part?'

Stan disappears, and I imagine the sultry painted face of my exotic nemesis again. He's smiling, laughing even, but there's admiration in his amazing eyes too.

Charles slides his arms around me, but I whisk quickly out of them and cross to the television set in a rather fine oak cabinet. Switching it on yields the good old BBC, but when I slide the cable card into a slot on the console, a new menu, in red and black, flicks on to the screen, with a list of categories, followed by the cryptic legend 'live feed'.

When I stab the remote and select live feed, all I get is a blank screen, and the word 'unavailable'.

No wonder. We *are* the live feed.

I double back again, choose the 'Something for the Ladies' category, then 'Italian Guy', and press OK.

The film apparently has no story, because the two protagonists are already in a bedroom and locked in a clinch. He's got his back to the camera, and he's peeled down the skimpy top of his partner and is caressing her breasts while he kisses her neck and she writhes against him, head thrown back in mock, or possibly real, ecstasy.

'Do we need this?' enquires Charles. 'We could make our own movie.'

I'm turned away from him, so he can't see my face. Which is a good job, because I have to bite my lips to stop me from laughing out loud. If only you knew, Charlie boy! If only you knew.

'Well, I don't need it, but I certainly want it.'

And I do. There's a certain delicious irony in both watching and being watched, and there's something about the way the tall, dark and handsome stud in the film is standing that suddenly makes the hair on the back of my neck prickle.

My God, it *is* him!

I kick off my shoes, fling myself on to the bed, and lounge against the fluffy pillows, my eyes still on the screen as 'Italian Guy' strips off for his girlfriend and reveals a stunning and intimately familiar physique.

'Come on!' I call imperiously to Charles, who's just standing there in the middle of the room, as if not quite sure what to do. 'You're falling behind.'

'Okey-dokey,' responds Charles with a grin, and I feel a moment of admiration. He's a game one, I have to admit, and the way he sheds his jacket and tie tells me he obviously thinks the guy in the porn flick is no competition.

Wrong, Charles. You are so very wrong that you couldn't possibly be more wrong.

And I lose interest in him completely when the man on the screen finally faces the camera, and not only reveals an enormously rampant penis, but confirms what I'd suspected all along!

Valentino looks young, barely out of his teens, and his black hair is short and crisply styled, but the sculpted face and the phenomenal musculature are unmistakeable.

I smirk as the irony of the situation doubles and redoubles. I'm watching, and being watched ... and so is Valentino.

'Is that your type?' asks Charles archly, whipping off his shirt with panache and coming to the bed to sit down at my side. 'The "Latin lover"?'

'He's OK,' I drawl, purely for Valentino's benefit, 'I suppose ...' I run my tongue along my lower lip, moistening it. I've no idea where the cameras are precisely, so I'll just have to perform to the room in general. 'He's just pretty beefcake. Eye candy. He probably doesn't have two brain cells to rub together. A guy like that probably just gets by on the size of his dick.'

'So you like the intelligent type then?' Charles leans over me, then starts kissing my neck and stroking the bare skin of my arm.

It's quite nice actually, and I feel a definite frisson of response, but still I crane my neck a little sideways so I can watch Valentino in the screen. He's caressing himself now, posing before his paramour fondling his magnificent erection while she reclines on a bed much as I'm doing.

'I don't have a type. I just like men.'

Which is true, I realise with a strange pleasure. My preference would be the gorgeous specimen who's displaying himself so raunchily on the screen, but wanting Valentino doesn't make me indifferent to the charms of other men. Or preclude me from sampling those charms if the opportunities were presented.

One night in the woods seems to have inoculated me against my former adherence to conventional monogamy.

My nipples are stiff and sensitive inside my borrowed bra, and as Charles cups my breast I feel a stab of real desire.

'Mmm, I like that,' purrs the new assertive me.

'Let's get this off then,' mutters Charles, his voice revealingly gruff as he plucks at the neckline of Maria's dress.

Suddenly, I feel irked by him again. It's clear that he thinks I'm a desperate but relatively inexperienced one-man woman who doesn't know all that much about sex, and that he's doing me a bountiful favour by fancying me. 'I'll undress myself in my own good time,' I retort, sitting up and pushing him away from me, my hand flat on his lightly hairy chest. 'I want to see *you*, Charles. Now let's get *these* off, shall we?' I pluck at his elegantly cut designer trousers, in the general area of the crotch and, before he has a chance to protest, I cup his equipment and give it a squeeze.

Charles lets out a grunt that's half shock and half pleasure and he jerks against my grip, trying to reach for me again. I almost let him, because he really is a very decent handful.

'Strip!' I command him, releasing his package and giving him a stern look.

'With pleasure!' With enthusiasm, he heels off his shoes and then tugs at his socks. My guess is that he's wise to the ways of stripping off for women.

The 'Italian guy' is on top of his woman now, his perfect bottom tensing and relaxing as he thrusts himself into her. She in turn is moaning and writhing beneath him, arching back her head as he mouths her exposed throat like a modern vampire. Impaled on one particularly deep thrust, she shouts some impassioned curse or other in Italian, and I can't blame her either because I too know only too well what it's like to be on the receiving end of that particular bounty!

By now, all Charles's clothes are on the floor, and not even the charms of Valentino's high-class porn movie can distract me from the presence of a stark-naked man right here in the bedroom with me.

Everything about Charles tells me he's a gym freak. He's lean, toned, sleek and tanned and, even though it's not quite in Valentino's spectacular league, his cock is lengthy. And it's rising to attention very nicely. A typical man, he gives himself a quick frisk as he advances towards me.

'You're a very beautiful woman, Annie,' he whispers as he slips on to the bed at my side, and places his hand on my thigh, sliding it upwards. A part of my mind appends the words 'for your age', but I ignore it. It's actually possible that he didn't mean to say that.

He starts to kiss me again, and I let him, because it's nice. I relish the feel of his tongue in my mouth, and his hands sliding under my dress, cupping my bottom and kneading it gently. I jiggle my hips a little, moving against him, rubbing myself against his newly available cock.

Yet, all the while, I keep my eyes on the television screen.

Valentino is on his back now, and his lady friend is riding him like a rodeo queen astride a bucking bronco. I can almost feel that rigid awesome bar of flesh pushing up inside me, and the clarity of the sensation invokes a craving.

I stare at that handsome face twisted in genuine pleasure, and decide that, if I can't have that in reality, I'll take a reasonable facsimile.

Giving Charles a firm push on his furry chest, I flip him over neatly on to his back.

'Oh yeah,' he enthuses, grinning up at me, 'I love a woman who takes charge.' The eye in his rampant cock seems to grin too. He reaches for me, and I let him fondle my breasts through my clothes. 'Let me see you, Annie. You're gorgeous. I want to see you. It's only fair. *I've* stripped off.'

Maybe so, young Charlie, but I know something you don't.

I think of the live feed, and the salivating male guests who might be viewing it. Who are they, and Charles, to see what I choose not to show?

Teasingly, I reach around and unzip Maria's chic and sexy dress. Holding it against me, I kneel up, looming over my eager partner, and do a little shimmy that makes the frock slide down my shoulders.

'More! More!' Charles encourages. 'You're killing me, Annie ... you're killing me.' He laughs and catches hold of the dress, tugging lightly.

For my pleasure, I hear echo in my head and, as if possessed by that spirit, I slap Charles hard on the thigh, and rap out, 'Behave yourself!'

This could all go terribly wrong. Charles obviously thinks he's a cocksman, but there's no guaranteeing he'll respond to domination. Much less to domination by a dominatrix who has barely the faintest idea of what she's doing.

But, to my joy, he lets go and flops back down on to the bed, arms at his side, and a penitent grin on his face. 'Yes, mistress,' he chants.

He's probably taking the mickey, but there's a faint hint of awe in his eyes that says at least part of him is taking me seriously. And, when I glance at his cock, and see that it looks even bigger and stiffer and redder than before, it's easy to deduce which particular part that is.

Oh, Valentino, I think dreamily as I peel my borrowed dress over my head and toss it lightly across the room. I make a vague mental note to get it cleaned and pressed for Maria, and then promptly forget it at the sight of hot genuine fire is Charles's blue eyes.

All for me. Desire for me. I *am* a queen. I *am* a goddess. And despite my inexperience I *am* in control!

Take a good look, I tell him silently, speaking not just to Charles, but to anyone else who might be watching. I feel supreme, I feel sexy and I feel ready. For a moment I fondle my own breasts through the rich satin and lace of the shaped and wired bra, and then I cup my crotch through the fragile, lacy G-string.

Glancing to the side, I catch sight of myself in the dressing-table mirror, and everything I've just affirmed to myself is reinforced.

I look amazing! My face is flushed and animated, my eyes are burning bright and my lips look as full and sensual as they would if Valentino had been kissing me for hours. My body is shapely, delicately rounded yet mature, and my skin gleams with life and my own joy in it. The pretty lingerie and the saucy lace-topped stockings only complete the effect of sexy grown-up womanhood.

'You're beautiful, Annie, really beautiful,' gasps

Charles, and I know with absolute certainty that he means it and believes it. 'Please ... please let's make love. If I don't get inside you soon, I'll come all over myself, I swear it.'

I look at his handsome pleading face and decide to have mercy. But only on my terms. The lingerie stays *on*.

And another thing ...

Condoms.

On a hunch, I lean over, open the drawer in the beside table, and there they are. A selection of Mates and Durex in a rainbow of colours and shapes greets my questing fingers, and I pull out the first packet that I touch.

Fluorescent Bright, it says, and, when I rip open the foil, the contents are indeed an exotic jungle turquoise.

I toss the condom to Charles. 'Make yourself useful,' I murmur, turning my attention to the television screen again, and to Valentino, who's still being ridden by his athletic young lover. His severe beautiful face is contorted in an ecstasy that can only be real and, despite the short cropped hair of this younger incarnation, I seem to see sheets of shimmering black silk tossing and rippling against the white pillow.

For my pleasure, I hear again in my head, and for a moment I seriously wonder if I'm going quite mad.

'Hey, I'm here,' pipes up Charles, laying his hand on my thigh, smoothing it over the lace stocking top and my bare skin above it. 'Let's get it on, beautiful lady, let's get it on.'

Importunate youth, I think, but really, his cock does look quite something. It's like an exotic sex toy clad in the hot-turquoise latex.

'Yes, let's get it on,' I answer, reaching out to handle him briefly. God, he's so hot, even through the condom.

I can't wait any more to obey my master's command.

Flinging a leg across Charles, I straddle him and poise myself above him. My thighs flexing, I nudge aside the narrow crotch piece of Maria's racy G-string. So what if dozens of watchers can see that I was too chicken to include a full Brazilian wax in my beauty day? I no longer care. The die is cast. My fate is sealed.

Slowly, slowly, I descend. Slowly, slowly, the fat rubber-enrobed glans nudges into me and starts to invade.

Charles feels good inside, but he's not Valentino. Charles is big, but he's not as big as Valentino. He doesn't fit the same, and he doesn't stretch me the same. He doesn't expand my mind and heart as his flesh expands my body.

I glance across at the real thing in his porn flick and, as if by magic, he opens those great metallic eyes of his and stares straight at the camera. The glaze of lust is gone now, and he's in command again, his gaze focused, challenging, dominant.

It's me inside you, he seems to say. *And it'll always be me, no matter how many men you fuck.*

I moan, and sink lower, even though Charles is forgotten. He's moaning too as I engulf him, but he might as well be on the moon for all I care. It's Valentino that I'm fucking and being fucked by.

When I settle down and let my thighs relax, and my sex is completely filled, two things happen simultaneously.

The porn movie fades to a black screen.

And the house phone on the bedside table rings.

6 **Phone Sex**

'Don't answer it!'

Charles's voice is gruff with irritation and, as if to keep me in the moment, he grabs my hips and tries to jam me down even harder upon his cock. Something I don't object to, even though I've no intention of not answering the phone.

I know who it is, and I want to commune with him, even if I'm not actually fucking him. Leaning over, I snatch up the cordless receiver, despite Charles's squark of protest.

'Annie Conroy, can I help you?' I enquire briskly. 'Who is this?'

A soft spine-tingling laugh issues from the earpiece and seems to wind itself around the cock inside me and expand it to twice its actual size. Unable to stop myself, I groan softly at the sensation.

'Ah, my dear Mrs Conroy, I think you know full well who this is, don't you?' He pauses, and I can see his smile, and his lush sinful mouth. It seems full and red, although maybe not from lipstick. 'And what are you doing right now that makes you moan so delightfully? Are you fucking your handsome yuppie as instructed?'

Beneath me, Charles starts to struggle, although mercifully he stays nice and hard. 'Who is it? Tell them to fuck off!' he orders through gritted teeth, and obviously Valentino hears him because he starts to laugh again.

'What's the matter? Trouble with your stud? Is he inside you?'

'Yes,' I growl at him, sitting down hard on Charles in

a way that temporarily shuts him up and threatens to do the same for me. My eyes are almost popping out of my head at the sensation of being so full. It's like having two rampant cocks inside me instead of just the one. 'As if you didn't know. Now was there anything else?'

'Oh, a million things, Annie, but what makes you think I know what you're up to?'

'Oh, I think *you* know the answer to that one full well.'

'What's going on? Who are you talking to?'

Charles again. And, suddenly, I don't want anything from him but his cock ... because he's not the one I'm really having sex with.

'Will you shut the fuck up,' I hiss at him, and then, before he can protest any more, I fetch a ringing slap across his face with my free hand.

He makes a noise like a prisoner being given the thumbscrews, but if anything his cock hardens and swells even more inside me.

'I'm talking. Don't interrupt me!'

'Nicely done,' Valentino purrs in my ear. 'I love a woman who takes charge ...' he mocks. 'Is he big inside you, this young blade of yours? Does he stretch you? Fill you up until you feel you're almost choking?'

'Not quite ... but not far off,' I gasp, swirling my hips a little, playing with the toy inside me in an attempt to get him to reach the parts that only Valentino can reach.

Charles grunts and gasps, his eyes tightly closed, tears from where I slapped him oozing down his cheeks. He's grabbing on to the brass bed rail, and I really wish I were Catherine Trammell now, and that I had a white silk scarf under the pillow, so I could tie his hands. There are probably restraints aplenty in this room but now isn't the time to start looking for them.

'Touch yourself,' commands Valentino, his voice like dark Byzantine velvet. 'Stroke your clitoris as I stroked you ... as your sadly inept young lover should be stroking you. Do it now. I want to know your pleasure.'

My head feels as if it's full of his words and they're making me dizzy and sending licks and flicks of raw pleasure chasing around my body. My clitoris feels as if I'm already touching it. As if *he's* touching it. Between my legs, it seems to beat like a second heart.

'Ah!' When I do touch myself, it's like being punched in the solar plexus, the jolt of sensation is so breathtaking. My sex flutters precariously, right on the edge, and Charles moans again as the involuntary response caresses him.

'How does that feel? Describe it to me.'

There's pure iron beneath the velvet now, a soft quiet command. The words seem to pulse in my brain, my heart and my veins, stealing all my faculties and leaving only my most basic animal senses.

'I – I can't ... I don't know ...'

And it's true. I could no sooner cage the devil than quantify the unquantifiable.

'Stroke yourself then. Stroke gently, circle slowly. Bring yourself close to the peak, but don't come until I tell you.'

I daren't move my finger. Just resting it lightly upon myself has me trembling over the abyss. Charles shifts uneasily beneath my spread sex, and just the slight movement has me biting my lips, gripping the phone so hard that I might crack the flimsy unit at any moment. My clitoris seems to lurch in a slow deep, heart-wrenching pulse and, before I can lift away my fingertip, it's too late and I'm coming.

'Fuck! Oh, God! Fuck, fuck, fuck!'

Oh, that's really poetic, Annie, a clear, cool totally

detached entity in the corner of my brain observes, while the rest of me just lets go, totally engulfed in the pleasure of my orgasm. My body doubles up as if protecting itself, my hair brushing Charles's chin as I cradle my own centre and clutch the phone – my conduit to Valentino – against my heart as if embracing the man himself.

I hear his soft laughter, almost through my skin rather than my ears, as my sex contracts again and again at his bidding.

But, as the waves die down, I start to tremble for an altogether different reason.

He didn't bid me to come, did he? He bade me to wait. To hold off. To resist.

As if waking from a trance, Charles tries to grab me again, snatching at my hand and the phone. I twist away, clamping the silent receiver to my ear, listening for recriminations, for mockery ... and, worst of all, disappointment.

'I'm sorry,' I whisper and, even though he doesn't speak, I see Valentino smile in my mind, and shake his dark head, silky hair rippling. But he's not disappointed, not even disapproving, just benignly fond, like a kindly master to a beloved but still inept pupil.

'I'm sorry,' I repeat in barely more than a sigh.

For a moment, that cool clear voice of reason tells me I'm crazy, and this whole situation is crazy, but a truer voice just laughs. And a truer ear hear my master's acknowledgement.

A sense of elation that almost matches the physical delights I'm experiencing washes through me. I feel a connection that's more than physical too, a contact with some knowledge that's both great and esoteric.

But, suddenly, my euphoria is ruptured. Charles grabs the phone from me, shouts, 'Fuck off! Leave us alone!' into the mouthpiece, then flings the handset clear across the room. I hear it shatter as it hits the side of the dressing table.

Red mist – really and truly – gathers in front of my eyes, and I draw back my arm to hit him again, but he catches my arm and wrenches me towards him, hooking his other hand behind my head to clamp my mouth down on his.

Fight or flight instinct gathers, and for a fifth of a second I contemplate leaping off him and fleeing the room. But then dark metallic eyes smile in my mind and I laugh in acknowledgement.

For a moment, I relax. I accept Charles's tongue into my mouth and relish his temporary dominance, my body sparked to life again by his aggressive caresses and the rough way his hands rove from my breasts to my bottom, and finally to my sex. He thinks that he's the one who's getting the better of me, and getting what he wants, but I laugh inside, feasting greedily on his lust.

'Who the fuck was that?' he growls, bucking his hips upwards to get into me as deeply as he can.

I bear down, fighting to get more and more from him as he rubs my clitoris in a way that's clumsy but exciting and deliciously primal. He hasn't the faintest idea, but to me those pleasuring fingers have painted nails.

'Nobody you know,' I spit back at him, wrestling for breath as a new orgasm gathers. 'Forget it. He's not here and you are!'

'Too fucking right,' he mutters, all his veneers of slickness, suaveness and flattery gone AWOL. We're combatants brawling for pleasure now, just everyman and everywoman.

He tries to shift his weight, to roll me over and get me on my back, but I'm not having that. I'm still the goddess and I'm still in charge, despite his tantrums. I grip him inside me, flexing to milk him dry and bring his pleasure to my heel.

My efforts undo him, and he shouts out incoherently, his hips rising, again and again, lifting us both clear of the bed. I'm undone too, another wrenching orgasm gripping the very quick of me. As I reach and reach for an even greater pinnacle, an unseen omnipresent hand reaches out and hands me my pleasure on a plate.

Valentino! I scream inside, my body giving its all for my dark mysterious master.

After an indeterminate period of time lying beached on the bed in limbo, it dawns on me that Charles is fast asleep.

Typical male, shagged out after a long squawk, he's sprawled across the bedspread, limbs at all angles with his deflated cock lying forlorn and shrunken in its gaily coloured rubber jacket.

Suddenly, I don't want to be around when he wakes up. I don't want to be involved in any cringingly embarrassing aftermaths, and I certainly don't want to talk about money. I just want to be away from this man I didn't really have sex with.

Glancing around the room, I slither gingerly off the bed and wonder where the cameras are. Is anyone still watching? Nothing to see now, folks, but an old bird in her undies. The main feature's over. Time to leave the theatre and take your paper cups, your lolly sticks and your popcorn boxes with you.

I've got to get out of here!

Charles grunts and chunters in his sleep and I freeze. But he's obviously deep in slumberland and just dreaming because he turns over, tucks up his knees and grasps his cock like a baby cuddling its comfort blanket.

I retrieve Maria's dress and wiggle into it, crinkling

my nose. I feel grungy and sticky and I smell pungently of vigorous sweaty sex. I'd adore a shower right now, but I can't risk it, for fear of giving Sleeping Beauty here time to wake up. Instead, I dash into the rather modern, gleamingly white bathroom for a quick pee. All that bouncing around on top of Charles after several glasses of champagne has taken its toll on my bladder and the relief of emptying it is almost as intense as coming.

Almost.

I glower at my flushed face and my dishevelled hair in the mirror, then pad back out into the bedroom again to write Charles a quick note.

I'll ring you tomorrow, and we'll talk. Don't *ring me*!

I underline the 'don't' although I doubt if he'll obey me and, after leaving the note on top of his briefcase, I grab my bag and my borrowed shoes and prepare to quit the room.

At the door, a sudden notion grabs me, and I step back inside, return to the briefcase and check the lock. To my surprise, it's open, and there, right on the top of its contents, is the investment documentation.

Needless to say, I don't understand most of the legalese and financial gobbledegook but some of the figures look startlingly large.

Frowning, I huff out my breath, and make a snap decision. I need a second opinion on this, and I've a shrewd idea where I might be able to get one. Closing the case as quietly as I can, I rather pointlessly underline 'don't' yet again in the note and replace it on top. With the portfolio under my arm, and clutching the rest of my belongings, I steal my way to the door, and step into my shoes once I'm safely on the landing.

This floor of the hotel seems deserted, with no noise coming from any of the rooms. I can't hear anyone partying and, if anyone *is* indulging in any wild sex inspired by my own recent antics, they're sweating and humping their way to ecstasy in total silence.

I wonder if Valentino is sweating and humping somewhere in the building.

The spasm of jealousy that invokes in me almost makes me stumble. I gasp for breath and stare around me, wondering where he is, and who might be with him. Standing very still, I try to sense him, and get a feeling of his presence.

Where are you, you bastard? What would you do if I burst in on you now, and demanded –

Demanded what?

I have no claim on him, and he's made no promises. All there is between us is a sexual game and physical chemistry.

Nothing more than that.

Feeling deflated, I walk smartly towards the lift, then stab repeatedly at the button to descend.

When I reach the reception desk, I wonder if the tall dark, Madonna-faced receptionist might have been watching the live feed, but I suddenly feel far too tired to worry about it. All I want to do now is to sneak away home, get a shower and take stock. I want comfort, not mind-games. I want to huddle on the sofa, bundled in a wrap and with Boy purring on my lap while I sip hot chocolate and eat Hobnobs.

First, though, I suppose I've got to pay the bill. For what the receptionist will know was a 'quickie' even if she didn't watch it. Oh, and of course, there's the small matter of the smashed-up phone handset.

'Good evening, madam,' she says softly, her face serene and coolly friendly. No hint whatsoever that she's just observed me cavorting like a randy trollop, having phone sex with one man while having real sex with another at the same time.

'Good evening,' I reply cautiously, placing the investments file on the counter while I rummage in my evening bag for my credit card, 'I'd like to pay my bill please. Just the one night, if that's OK?' I swallow. 'And I'm afraid there's been a bit of damage. I knocked the phone off the bedside table and it broke.'

'One moment,' the dark woman says and, as she consults her computer screen, I notice a nameplate on the desk that I can't remember seeing before.

Saskia Woodville, Assistant Manager, it says.

Saskia Woodville, Assistant Manager, taps a key, and a small mysterious smile plays around her mouth for a moment. She turns back to me, and her eyes are level and neutral again.

'That bill has been settled, Mrs Conroy. There are no outstanding charges.'

'I beg your pardon?'

'The bill's been covered, damage included. There's nothing to pay.' She gives me an innocuous corporate smile. 'Would you like me to arrange a taxi for you? I believe there might even be one waiting outside.'

'Er, yes, please.'

While she speaks softly into the phone, I just stand around like a lemon, my thoughts whirling.

Who's paid my bill, as if I didn't know?

'He'll just be a moment,' says the elegant Saskia when she finishes the call.

'Excuse me, but could you tell me who paid my bill? I'd like to thank them, if I may?'

I get the impression that Saskia would be grinning, nay, laughing her head off if her professionalism and dramatic skills weren't as ingrained as they obviously are.

'I'm sorry,' she replies, 'I can't say. I'm afraid it must have been dealt with while I was on my break.'

'Isn't there a credit card slip or anything?'

She taps her keyboard again, scans the screen briefly,

in what I suspect is a slick performance, just for my benefit. 'Sorry. The bill appears to have been settled in cash, with no receipt issued.'

I feel stymied. Frustrated. I'm being given the right royal runaround. I've been manoeuvred into taking part in Valentino's kinky games, and yet somehow I'm still on the outside of it all. I've not yet quite been initiated into the mysteries.

I hesitate. What to do? Charles might 'come to' at any moment. He might already be on his way down in the lift. I've no intention of getting into any kind of wrangle or debate with him tonight, whether about money or otherwise, so I need to show the Waverley a clean pair of heels.

Saskia seems to sense my inner debate. 'Perhaps you'd like to come in tomorrow for a chat with the manager, Signor Guidetti?' He may be able to throw some light on the matter of the bill.'

Signor Guidetti? I can't stop myself grinning all of sudden, and my frustration and indecision disappear like Scotch mist. I don't need a million guesses to know who Signor Guidetti is.

'Yes, I think I'll do that. Could you tell him I'll be in? Around eleven, perhaps?' My confidence is rising. I'm taking control again and I like it.

'I'm sure he'll be delighted to clear things up.'

'Yes, that sounds like an excellent idea,' I say, smiling back at her. Ridiculously, my heart is fluttering at the thought of that meeting.

Suddenly, we both glance at the investments file. And equally suddenly I have a brainwave. 'Do you think you could put this in the hotel's safe for me? It needs to be kept in a secure place and I'd prefer not to take it home.'

'Of course, Mrs Conroy. We'd be glad to keep it safe for you.' She gives me a fleeting beam of approval that lights her rather solemn face and reveals a hitherto unnoticed radiant beauty.

Now I know for certain she's watched me. And she's complicit. She knows that for one reason or another I need to keep this file out of Charles's hands for the time being.

I get the impression that she thinks it's a good idea.

Valentino!

The first thing that comes into my mind when I wake is his face. I see him with makeup, then without, and I try to imagine what new guise I'll encounter today.

I fell asleep on the sofa last night, watching the television. I'd meant to think things through, analyse my feelings and my actions, but instead I just dozed off, lulled into a stupor by a late-night game show.

To my great surprise, though, I feel fresh and rested, but as I unwind myself from my cosy polar fleece throw, Boy gives me a look as if I'm a crazy person – which I probably am – and requests his breakfast in loud and unequivocal terms.

With my cat fed and away about his business, and a cup of fresh coffee in my hand, it's time to wake up properly and attempt to engage my brain. I should apply myself to the matter of the portfolio, but all I can focus on is my forthcoming appointment at the Waverley.

Signor Guidetti, my eye. I'm in no doubt who the manager of the Waverley Grange Country Hotel actually is, even though the enigmatic Saskia made no effort to connect the dots for me last night.

How will this meeting go? My heart lurches in my chest at the thought of it. What the hell can I say to him? I've had sex with the man, but I know nothing about him. I obey his commands when I shouldn't trust him an inch.

And then there's the matter of the live feed...

While I'm considering more coffee, the phone rings. Of course, it was too much to hope that Charles might have obeyed my request, and as his voice issues from the speaker of the answerphone I consider wrenching the jack out of the wall.

He doesn't sound quite as silky smooth this morning. In fact, he sounds ragged and disorientated.

'Hello, Annie, it's Charles, please ring me. We need to talk. Er, I don't quite know where to start. Last night was amazing, but I couldn't believe that you just left like that. After what we shared...' He peters out. He's completely dumbfounded by what's happened. More so even than me. 'Annie, please ring me. I'm in meetings all morning, but call anyway. I need to speak to you.' He hesitates again, as if embarrassed. 'Um ... you did take the portfolio, didn't you? I can't find it in my briefcase this morning. Er ... call me.'

He breaks the connection, and I'm left feeling almost sorry for him. It must be painful to be so confused and unsure of himself when he's used to being cock of the walk.

But I still have no intention of calling him yet.

I'm not doing anything until I've been to the Waverley.

I dress very carefully. For this confrontation, I need to feel as poised and assured as I can under the circumstances, and maybe a little detached from all things sexy and seductive. This is a business meeting, of sorts, with the manager of a prestigious hotel. I need to look elegant, not too attainable, maybe a little bit corporate.

My wardrobe yields up a treasure, perfect for the occasion. It's a Chanel suit. A real one. An anniversary gift from Stan. It's black, classic-style, with the signature braid in white. I team it with a tie-neck white blouse and black bag and court shoes, and I could be set for a Rotary Club ladies' luncheon.

I'm not an enthusiastic driver and, if I can't walk somewhere, I'll take a taxi or even a bus. But, today, I decide to take my car. In case I need to make a quick getaway.

I'm just backing it out of the drive when I see Maria closing the gate next door.

It seems an odd time for her to be around, but maybe she's pulling another of her maverick sick days. No sign of the magnificent Robert today, but that's not to say he won't turn up before long. When I pull the car back up to the kerb, I lean out and call to her. 'Can I give you a lift anywhere?'

Her smile is beatific, and not a little mischievous. Curiously, she's wearing a suit too. Not a Chanel, but it's a good one nevertheless, midnight blue and slim fitting but not tarty. The skirt is a bit on the short side, but that's more or less standard for a pretty young woman like her, and she's wearing a silky shell top in a periwinkle shade that exactly matches her eyes.

'Wow, yes! I'm off to the Waverley. Are you going that way?'

Something in the way those marvellous eyes twinkle tells me that she knows damn well we are both going there.

'Well, yes I am, as a matter of fact.' I give her a 'surprise, surprise' look. 'Hop in!'

Maria slides into the passenger seat, her short skirt slipping up her thighs and exhibiting suspender button and the saucy lace top of her stocking in a way that I suspect is quite intentional.

'You OK?' she enquires, giving me a sly sideways glance.

Cheeky little madam.

'Yes, I'm fine ... and yourself?'

'I'm fine too.' She smirks now.

'Well, that's great. We're both fine.'

There's silence for a few minutes as I negotiate our way out of the suburbs, but it's not long before we're on the lane leading to the Waverley, and I'm compelled to speak. I can tell she's bursting to know what happened with Charles last night, but I decide to get in first with my own questions and distract her.

'How come you're going to the Waverley at this time of day? Shouldn't you be at Borough Hall?'

'Well, it's a long story. But I'm sort of in the process of changing jobs and I'm working at the Waverley part time now.'

'Like your friend Greg?' I say, absorbing my surprise. I know that Maria loves the hotel, and she and her Robert are favoured patrons, but how can she tear herself away from a workplace where she sees her beloved every day?

'Yes, pretty much like Greg.' She smiles, but doesn't elaborate.

'But I thought you were settled at Borough Hall. I thought you liked it because Robert is there.'

She heaves a little sigh. 'Well, yes, it's heavenly to see him during the day as well as being together out of hours. But that's the trouble. It's *too* nice. And too tempting for Robert ...' She hesitates, and I steal a quick glance at her crooked and regretful smile. 'You know what we're like. We find it hard not to play when we both should actually be working and we've had one or two very close calls lately, you know?'

I do know. I've seen the risks they take in their own back garden.

'I mean, it doesn't matter for me,' she goes on, 'I'm just a wage slave there, no glorious career, but I don't want Robert to lose a job that he's very good at and that he's worked long and hard to achieve.'

She cares so much for him. For a moment my heart twists and I yearn to be in love again myself, so much that I'd do anything for the man at the centre of my life.

'Don't you have to give notice or something? You can't just leave a municipal job at the drop of a hat, can you?'

She laughs again, and it's low, and wicked and sexy. 'Well, Robert and I have some, shall we say, *leverage* over the Human Resources Manager, so he's arranged for my period of notice to be waived.'

The way she emphasises 'leverage' makes my imagination run wild in a way that's not really conducive to safe road-craft. More shenanigans in Suite Seventeen? I wonder.

'That's convenient for you,' I murmur pointedly.

'Yes, it's all worked out very nicely. I just love it at the Waverley.' She pauses, appears to gaze out of the window at sheep grazing in the farmers' fields we're passing.

I steal another glance at her and she's looking mischievous now.

'Oh, come on, Annie! Spill it! You might at least tell me what kind of adventure my dress got up to last night! A little bird told me you were in Suite Seventeen.'

'This bird – or birds – of yours, they're very well informed. How is it that you always seem to know more about what's going on in my life than I do?'

'Well, it's just that I like to look out for you, Annie. I care about you and I want you to have fun. *Did* you have fun?'

I don't need to look at her to know that she's smirking, and I can imagine there's a glint in her eye too, a dark, almost wicked one.

'Well, I'm not sure that *fun* is quite the right word for it, to be honest. But, yes, you could say I had an interesting time. But I've a sneaking feeling that you already know that ... and not via this loose-beaked little bird of yours either.' The road rises a little ahead of us and, to my annoyance, I crunch a gear because I'm distracted. 'It wouldn't surprise me at all if you were at the Waverley last night too. Were you?'

'I could have been,' she replies airily. 'So ... the dress? Did it knock him dead?'

'Knock who dead?'

It certainly had an effect on Charles, especially when I took it off and threw it across the room, but it's not really his opinion I'm interested in any more.

'Your date, of course. The cute investment guy.'

'How do you know he's cute? Have you seen him?'

'You said he was cute.'

Hah, she's right, I think I did. So much has happened in such a short space of time. I can hardly believe that it's only two days since she 'initiated' me in the Waverley's powder room.

'So, did everything go according to plan? Did you bonk him?'

'OK, yes, I slept with him. Now are you satisfied?'

'Ooh no! I want details!'

'Yes, I'll bet you do, but we're nearly there now. Oh, and by the way, I really, really do appreciate the loan of the dress and, yes, it did make quite an impression on Charles. I'll get it dry-cleaned for you before I return it though. I hope that's all right?'

'There's no need, you know,' she says, her voice suddenly sultry. 'I'd much prefer to wear it when it smells of you.'

I concentrate hard on the road in an attempt not to think too deeply about that one. The idea of Maria getting off on the smell of my sweat, and my sex, makes me shudder. But, I also feel turned on in rather a reluctant way. I change the subject to avoid the issue.

'That's a nice suit you're wearing now. Very smart. It looks good on you.'

'Yeah, Robert bought it for me,' she says fondly. 'He has wonderful taste in clothes, and he knows how he likes me to look. Today we're doing corporate and professional, but with a twist.'

'And what's the twist? Or shouldn't I ask?'

Suddenly, it's difficult to keep my eyes on the road, and it's a good job there's no traffic around. Maria moves slightly in her seat, scissoring her long slender thighs in her short skirt and making it rise up to show more of her lace-trimmed stocking tops. She wriggles slowly as if an invisible Robert is touching her, and then places her hands flat on her hips, smoothing her skirt upwards as she lifts her bottom in order to slide it from under her.

'The twist is ... I'm not wearing any panties.'

'Maria!'

Thank God I have good reflexes! I correct my swerve and pull the car to a halt at the side of the lane.

Maria leans back in her seat, and for a moment her long lashes descend and she draws in a deep breath. She's off somewhere with her lover, locked in the secret world with him, desire spiralling so far out of control that she doesn't care that she's showing her pubic mound out here on an open road where anyone could pass by at any moment. The old me is shocked, and a bit fearful of what 'people' might think, but the new me wants to pull my skirt up too. I'm wearing panties, but I suddenly wish I wasn't.

I'm a bit surprised that Maria doesn't touch herself though. She doesn't usually show such forbearance.

'I wish Robert was here,' she says, hitching her bottom around in the seat as if there's a fire burning right in the very quick of her. 'He says I can't touch myself today. He says I've got to wait until he can bring me off, or to ask someone else to do it for me.' Her lashes flutter, and she slides me a sly sideways glance. 'But, if I do, I'll be punished, because he wants to be able to think of me at any time during the day and imagine me wet and frustrated and horny.'

She's not the only one. I grip the wheel hard, my fingers tingling. Who do I want to touch? Maria or myself? Or both?

The fantasy grips me and I have to fight the urge to wriggle, just as Maria is doing. I seem to see a familiar pair of dark metallic eyes and the ripple of black hair as he shakes his head in negation.

Beside me, Maria groans, her eyes closed again as she wrangles with her own internal torments. She spreads her legs as wide as she can within the confines of a Renault car seat, and grinds herself against it, bearing down and rocking. I imagine her juiciness being rubbed into my upholstery.

'Oh, God, I need to come,' she keens.

I know I shouldn't, but I'm just about to offer something ... a suggestion, some help, my own hand ... when there's a sudden harsh accelerating, approaching roar. In the rear-view mirror, I see a motorcycle approaching and, beside me, like a flash, Maria is suddenly decent and demurely covered.

'Oops! That was a close one,' she remarks brightly. Her expression is composed and cheery, as if nothing in the slightest bit unusual has happened.

However, I feel decidedly shaken up. Maria might be

able to flip from sex goddess to normal human being in the blink of an eye, but I'm not as used to the changes as she is yet, and it takes much longer for me to transition.

I'm still suspended between the two worlds when Maria shrugs her shoulders, consults her watch and says, 'Yikes, I am so late! Any chance we can get a move on and burn rubber?'

Such irredeemable cheekiness breaks the spell, and I'm able to laugh as I reach for the ignition. I shake my head, flash her a smile, and then we're rolling.

7 Interview with a Vampire

The Waverley Grange looks distinguished, discreet, yet perfectly innocuous in the mid-morning summer sunshine.

The mellow weathered stonework tells no stories, nor does the rambling ivy. The windows glitter and flash and flash with respectability. The mad riot of colours in the flower beds and the soft insidious hum of the hovering bees there are the only intimations of sensuality, but even they're probably lost on the few guests who are taking the air and relaxing.

Do these people know? I wonder.

Maria has disappeared in the direction of the staff entrance, but not without giving me a naughty little pinch on the bottom as she wished me 'good luck'.

Luck with what, I'm not quite sure, but I've a feeling I'll need it anyway. This isn't just a meeting about a hotel bill.

As I walk into the foyer my heart flutters, and my eyes skitter around, searching for signs of the Waverley's secret identity.

But inside it all looks as ordinary and quietly luxurious as it did from the outside. There's a delicious fragrance from the cut flowers placed in vases here and there, all blended with the soft, lavender aroma of the old-fashioned furniture polish that gives the reception desk ahead of me a well-tended gleam.

A few more guests are sitting around reading papers and taking coffee in the morning lounge to one side, and they all look as straight and normal and sexually unadventurous as you could imagine. Some of the women from the golf club and the Townswomen's Guild come here for little tea parties and gatherings now and again, but I'm sure they'd choke on their petits fours if they knew the things I know.

It's a big hotel, with dozens and dozens of guests under its roof at any one time, and it must require quite an army of staff to maintain it.

So just how many of these are aware of the Waverley's racy sexual underbelly? How many play the games and know the secrets?

Well, there's one behind the desk who's certainly in the know.

Saskia is on duty again, and she looks up with a composed smile from the registration ledger. 'Good morning, Mrs Conroy,' she says, her voice deep and pleasant, 'lovely day, isn't it? I'll let Signor Guidetti know you're here.' Her eyes catch mine for a moment, dark and challenging. 'He's really looking forward to meeting you.'

I stare back at her, smiling to let her know that I know she's talking nonsense, because we both know exactly who Signor Guidetti is. 'Thanks. I'm looking forward to meeting him too. His reputation precedes him,' I add. Her serene veneer almost cracks as she picks up the phone, punches a number and then announces me quietly.

'He'll be right down,' she says after a moment, her dark eyes shining.

'Are you always here?' I ask when she picks up a pen and makes a notation in her ledger. 'Every time I've been here, you've been on the desk. Don't they let you have any time off?'

She's unfazed by my enquiry. 'I've been working some additional shifts in the past few weeks. There's been a lot of staff turnover, and the extra money is always welcome.'

I open my mouth to ask her why the staff turnover, but before I can speak she glances up and beyond me, and nods. 'Ah, here he is now ... Signor Guidetti.'

I want to whirl around, because I seem to have been waiting for this moment for longer than actually makes sense, but I contain myself and turn carefully on my heel. Time seems to warp and slow as if I've been translated into a movie moment.

A tall dark figure is descending the stairs, almost upon me. He moves lightly, yet with purpose, his walk, once he reaches the foot of the staircase, fluid yet inimitably masculine.

He smiles the smile of a polite stranger, but somewhere in the copper depths of those eyes, now masked slightly by gold-framed spectacles, the lights of the devil who knows me dance and flirt.

'Mrs Conroy, a pleasure to meet you,' he says, his voice intimately familiar even though he's wearing yet another, and very different mask today. 'I'm the manager of the Waverley. Gianvalentino Giudetti ... at your service.'

I wonder what the hell to do, but, suddenly, as I put out my hand automatically to shake his, our cinematic moment morphs into a scene from a 1960s romantic comedy. Signor Gianvalentino Guidetti, well-known hotel manager, cross-dresser and general all-round sex maniac, lifts my hand to his lips and fleetingly but with impact kisses the back of it.

'And a pleasure to meet you, Signor Guidetti,' I reply when he straightens up to his considerable height, which seems to be even more considerable than usual somehow, due to the fact that he's dressed in sober business-like black. Behind me, although there's silence,

I seem to hear Saskia laughing behind her cool serene façade.

And she isn't the only one.

Valentino's smile is as devilish as it is in his other guises, and he looks every inch the perverted erotic buccaneer he did the other night, in the woods, despite his elegant veneer of continental male chic.

'Do come this way, Mrs Conroy,' he murmurs, gesturing elegantly towards the broad staircase. 'We can talk privately in my office on the first floor.'

'I'll bet we can,' I mutter under my breath as he falls back to allow me to precede him up the stairs.

He doesn't speak as we ascend, but I can feel him scrutinising my bottom beneath the Chanel. It's almost as if his hands were cupping my cheeks, and assessing their firmness and resilience. Mad thoughts race through my brain, and it's a relief when we reach the landing and the temptation to lift my skirt, and show him my thighs and panties is less acute.

Why am I thinking these thoughts? They're outrageous . . . and yet at the same time, they arrive like second nature. As if they've been lurking in the recesses of my psyche for years and years, and are only now rising and bubbling to the surface.

'This way.' Valentino gestures gracefully, and smiles that courteous managerial smile of his again, directing me along a corridor, until we come to the open door to a spacious office.

The room is both old-fashioned and modern, with venerable, glassily polished oak furniture, on which sit all the accoutrements of modern digital life. There's a laptop on the desk, another computer workstation to one side on a long table, and a bank of small screens that appear to be part of the surveillance system. I only get the most fleeting of glimpses of what's playing, but the views are all unequivocally and uninterestingly chaste.

No action in Suite Seventeen this morning then? Or, if there is, it's happening off camera.

'Let's sit here,' suggests Valentino, all genial mine host as he indicates a large and very comfy-looking sofa, set into a bay window. A low table is set before it, festooned with magazines. He guides me with the lightest, almost negligible touch on the small of my back, and, as I sit down as elegantly as I can on the low cushions, I idly register the covers of some of the publications. They're mostly trade glossies. *Hotelier. Leisure Industry News. Accommodation Weekly.*

But there's a corner of another magazine visible, peeking out from under these worthy publications. I can't see the title, but the cover image seems to be of a person in a zippered latex suit with their ankles tied together.

I hide a smile. Obviously, Signor Guidetti believes that all work and no play make Gianvalentino a dull boy, and likes to take a few minutes off to peruse a kinky porn magazine now and again in between stints working on staff rotas and the hotel's catering budget.

Now why does that not surprise me?

He doesn't sit down straightaway, but just stands a few feet away, completely still, watching me for a few moments. The weight of his stare is like a tangible pressure on me, and that in turn creates a dynamic urge to move. My skin prickles and I want to wriggle, just as I did in the car with Maria. He's just looking at me, and yet it feels as if he's touching me between my legs.

The clock on the mantle ticks and the computer hums faintly and, after a lifetime moment, Valentino smiles slightly in a way that's reminiscent of both

Hannibal Lecter and the sexier versions of Count Dracula. The vampire impression is heightened by today's hairstyle choice too. His soot-black mane is drawn back severely and secured at the nape of his neck in a brushed metal clip, exposing a slight but very distinctive widow's peak.

'Would you care for some coffee?'

I stare at him, stunned and not a little disappointed. Is he really going to play things completely straight, and ignore both last night and the one before? I was half-hoping he'd say something jaw-droppingly outrageous.

'Yes, please. That would be nice.'

He crosses to his desk, lifts his phone and stabs a button. 'Hi, Saskia, could you organise some coffee for Mrs Conroy and me? Thanks, you're a star.'

A moment later, he's beside me, sinking with unstudied grace onto the sofa. He leans back and fixes me with that potent gaze again, made all the more focused by those unexpected spectacles.

In this new corporate guise, he's just as stunning as he is in a frock or half-naked. The suit I thought was black is actually the darkest of midnight blues, and both his shirt and tie are a couple of tones lighter. I suppose I should expect this degree of high-concept sartorial elegance from an Italian, but it's still a surprise after what's gone before.

'So, you have a question about a hotel bill? How can I help?'

I can't help myself. I laugh out loud. The man's unbelievable!

He smiles back at me, his metallic eyes twinkling. 'I'm glad you find my question so amusing – care to share the joke?'

I wait for him to crack, but it seems he's set on maintaining the illusion of normality.

'I – I just wondered how long you're going to keep this up. This courteous hotel manager and valued guest charade I mean. It's ridiculous given what's – what's happened between us.'

He leans back against the upholstery, still eyeballing me. With his long hands steepled in front of him against his mid-section, he taps his fingertips slowly together. He's still smiling, but it's hard-edged now, and dangerous, and I get the impression that from this moment on anything I say, or anything I ask, could be the wrong thing.

My breath catches as I imagine the possible consequences. And my heart bashes in my chest, just at the sight of him.

He's a dark prince, elegant, composed and powerful. He commands the very air that hangs around us. I fiddle with my shoulder bag to stop myself reaching out and touching him to convince myself he's real.

Suddenly, his smile quirks and he snags his lower lip with his white teeth. The sight of that oh so very slightly crooked one reminds me that he's not a supernatural being after all. He *is* real, and his hypnotic grip on me is broken.

'Well, aren't you going to say anything?' My chin comes up, and I meet his glinting eyes.

'I was just thinking about games,' he murmurs smoothly, and seems about to enlarge on that when there's a knock on the open door, and a familiar face peers around it.

'Coffee?' enquires Maria cheerfully, stepping into the room bearing a silver tray set with a fine china coffee pot and all the accoutrements.

Valentino makes an imperious gesture and, as Maria sidles quickly forwards, and sets down the tray, a paper napkin wafts up from it and flutters to the carpet.

'Oops,' she murmurs, then swoops down to retrieve

125

it, and we're treated to a display of lace stocking tops, and then her pretty naked bottom.

I stare at the view almost calmly. Valentino might be a flesh and blood man, not a vampire sorcerer, but we are still in the mirror world somehow. The realm where sexy things like this tend to happen.

Maria straightens and whirls around like a ballerina, the napkin crumpled in her fingers. 'Sorry about that,' she pipes, smirking broadly. She hesitates in front of us, her face alight and expectant.

I glance at Valentino and, even though his face is severe, his eyes are brilliant. 'Yes, it was careless, Maria, very careless. I was hoping for much better from you.'

With obvious difficulty, Maria assumes a penitent expression. It's obvious she's bursting with excitement. 'I know, I'm sorry,' she whispers.

He heaves a sigh. 'Well, if it were up to me, I'd incline towards leniency, and let this one go.' He pauses, snags his full red lip again, then shakes his head. 'But my good friend Robert has requested that I be strict with you. He says that you're flighty and irresponsible and that you need a firm hand. Do you understand?'

Maria gnaws her own lip, eyes cast down as she nods.

As I watch all this, I discover that I'm holding my breath and I have to let it out in a sudden gasp. Valentino gives me a quick sharp glance, and then returns his attention to Maria. My stomach flutters again, and I have the strangest feeling that I too have transgressed, just like Maria.

'In that case, assume the position, if you would.'

Maria backs away from the coffee table towards the middle of the room. Then, quickly catching my eye, she sets her legs apart and slowly bends over, making her tight skirt rise again and tighten over her pert bottom.

Valentino rises to his feet, and makes a Caesar-like gesture, bidding me to accompany him. I follow as if in a dream and he walks across to the bending Maria, moving in a leisurely, almost contemplative way.

'Perhaps you could assist us, Mrs Conroy?' He accompanies this with a slow, sly, sideways glance.

'Um . . . yes, what do I have to do?'

His dark head cocks and light glints off the rims of his spectacles and off his slicked-back hair. 'Ah yes, of course, you're new to this.' He considers the Maria tableau a moment, and then nods towards her. 'First, lift her skirt and fold it out of the way, then take hold of her hands, to steady her.'

Still half-dazed, I comply, slipping up Maria's slender skirt and exposing her. The sweet rounded globes of her bottom are pearly and almost luminous in the sunlight slanting in through the window. They're exquisitely framed by an abbreviated white suspender belt. In a mental tableau of my own, I imagine touching her, stroking and soothing her prior to the coming ordeal, but I know I mustn't. Instead, I move around to her head and reach down to take her hands in mine. Her grip is firm, but her palms and her fingers are damp and sweaty. She appears calm enough but underneath she's as strung out with nerves and anticipation as I am.

Valentino studies the palm of his own hand. His left, I notice. He rubs a thumb across it, circling, contemplating. 'Just three, I think, as it's your first day. Does that seem fair?'

He's asking me, I think, but Maria nods. I just stare into those hypnotic copper eyes.

'Very well then, let's get it done with, shall we?'

With that, he touches her, fingertips floating across her bottom as if testing her readiness. A second later he slaps her hard, really hard, across her right buttock.

Maria's nails dig into my palm and I yelp, even though she remains stoically silent. Valentino catches my eye and gives me that stern cool look again.

During the second and third strokes, we all remain silent. The only noise in the room is the ponderous ticking of that old grandfather clock in the corner of the room, and the slap of skin against skin from each blow.

The moment he's finished, Valentino steps back and nods to me. I release Maria's hands. When she straightens up, she's biting her lip in obvious pain, and she's rippling her fingers as if she's desperate to rub her stinging bottom.

'If you touch yourself, you'll get ten more, young lady.'

Valentino's voice is soft and deadly, and makes Maria's spine stiffen and her fluttering fingers still. She stands proud and motionless now, her skirt still rucked up and her bush still on show.

'Better, that's better,' he murmurs. 'Now, off you go ... and, if I find out that you've crept away to the cloakroom to play with yourself, I can guarantee that you'll be in even more trouble. I don't want to have to give an unfavourable report to your master after just one day, do I?'

'No, sir,' affirms Maria, head bowed. Then she bobs a curtsey and makes for the door, skirt still around her waist. He hasn't told her to lower it, so I suppose that's where it stays.

'Close the door, please,' calls out Valentino, just as she's about to disappear.

Obediently, Maria snags it shut behind her.

We're alone again.

Valentino gives me a serene, unconcerned look, as if nothing out of the ordinary has happened.

'Let's have some of that coffee then, shall we? I hope it's not gone cold.'

'Yes, great,' is all I can manage.

He swings from Valentino, Prince of Darkness, to sleek Signor Guidetti of the perfect manners in just one blink of his astonishing copper-clad eyes.

He plays 'mother', and for a few minutes we sip his very good Italian coffee in silence. Valentino seems as cool as the proverbial cucumber but, inside, I'm all over the place. I'm a war-zone of confused emotions and yearnings, even though I think I'm just about holding it together on the surface. It's hard though, and my hands shake, making my cup clatter.

Quietly and calmly, Valentino puts down his own cup, then reaches forwards, takes mine from my nerve-less hands, and sets that aside too. I realise that it's been empty for several minutes.

'So ... games?' he says, soft and low. 'If you don't like "manager and guest", what *do* you want to play?'

'I don't know ... I don't know what the games are. It's all so confusing.'

And that's true. I want to be a part of this. I want to be a player. An initiate. Whatever.

I want to take risks, and understand, and make this beautiful man want me ... and I never want to play bloody golf again!

'Good.' That's all that he says. But his eyes, his body, his cool intent expression are alive with hidden meanings.

'And, anyway, haven't I already started playing?' My pulse skittering, I challenge his predatory stillness. 'Out in the woods, and again, last night, in the suite.'

His long lashes flick down behind the lenses of his spectacles, and he suddenly moves again, stroking the line of his cheek and jaw contemplatively. The action draws my attention to another detail of this new

Valentino, one that's revealed now his hair is confined in a ponytail. He has sideburns – a pair of nattily trimmed, very masculine sideburns that weren't visible when his black silk mane was hanging loose.

'Correct,' he says, crossing one arm across his chest while pressing a knuckle to his smoothly barbered chin. 'And you've made a good start. You show promise.'

And you're making fun of me, aren't you?

I meet his eyes boldly, but it's one of the most difficult things I've ever done. 'I'm glad you think so, because I don't really have any idea what I'm doing ... or what I really want, other than to be a part of this inner world, or whatever it is. And I don't even know *why* I want it – probably wouldn't even if I did know precisely what it is.'

To my horror, my eyes fill with tears. If only I could describe what I feel and then I'd know what I want, but Valentino's presence and his astonishing charisma just make my head spin.

I scrabble for my bag, but before I can grasp it, or open it, Valentino has plucked a snow-white crisply folded handkerchief from his pocket, just like a magician pulling a bunny from a hat. He flicks it open, then leans forwards and ever so gently blots my cheeks.

'Calm yourself, *tesoro*,' he says softly, putting the handkerchief into my hand, then reaching out to stroke my face with a tenderness that takes my breath away, 'it's the same for all of us in the beginning. Even me.'

Him?

I lift my eyes and look at him, the perfect master, so effortlessly in control of himself and of me. I can't imagine him ever being otherwise, but my mind flicks back to Maria's tale of his lost love – the older woman who dumped him.

'You? I find that hard to believe,' I mutter, dabbing cautiously around the edges of my eye makeup.

'It's true.'

The rueful smile that twists his fabulous mouth makes him look a good ten years younger. For a second, I see him as the angelically handsome boy who became such a breathtaking man.

'There was a time when I was naïve. I knew nothing about anything, even though I thought I knew everything about everything. I was pathetic. I had to learn just as you have to learn.'

'Who taught you?'

Oh damn, I didn't mean to ask that! I don't want to hurt him.

'An older woman. My first –' In the pause, he seems to go inwards, deep into his thoughts and far away from this pleasant, elegant room ... and me. 'And she *did* know everything,' he says in a flat voice that makes me shudder with sudden sympathy. 'She made me feel like an insect crawling on a stone, while she was the sun.'

I can almost see his memories circling around him. They seem like black moths, a living presence, and his tanned finely drawn face looks grim and sad. Did he really love her as much as Maria implied? Suddenly I have to know, even if it's not my business and there's a risk of killing the moment and all its possibilities.

'Where is she now? What happened to her?' I have to know how this *other* older woman made Valentino into the conundrum he is today.

His eyes narrow behind his glasses. His sensual mouth thins. 'She got married to a man her own age. She was one of the richest women in Italy when I knew her, but her husband was even richer. She lives in a *palazzo* on the shores of Lake Como these days, and I don't think she plays any more.'

He's bitter. And he *did* love her. And it *still* hurts. Suddenly, I want to embrace him and comfort him, and tell him that whatever happens I'll never flounce off and leave him for greater riches and prestige.

My heart does a strange sideways lurch when I think that. I open my mouth with no idea of what I'm going to say, but he silences me with his cool fingers across my lips.

'Enough talk. Slaves don't ask questions. They just obey.'

The sudden switchback is a shock, but I experience a lift inside like a bird taking flight. I haven't ruined it. I haven't turned him off. He still wants to play with me. The return to the mirror world is such a relief that I feel almost faint.

'Slave?' I gasp under my breath. The word seems extreme and strange on my lips.

'It's just a word. A convenient label in the absence of something more accurate.' He gives me a long intent look. 'Stand up. Show yourself to me.'

Show yourself to me.

Just like in the magic, moonlit grove. Does he want me to strip off, right here and now?

'Lift your skirt. Lower your panties. Show me your cunt.'

I'm shaking like a reed as I pluck at the hem of my skirt. My fingers feel numb, as if they're made out of funny foam or something, and they won't work properly. Valentino taps his lip with one long forefinger, not expressing impatience, but as if he's just filling time until I can get my act together.

Somewhere outside the open window, a bird sings beautifully and plaintively in the summer air. This mirror world is so similar to the sunny world of reality and normality, but more different, and stranger, than I can yet understand.

I haul up my skirt, and show Valentino the tops of my smoke-coloured hold-up stockings and my white lace-trimmed panties. They're not a particularly racy pair, more an elegant, classic style. But he seems to like them and nods his approval.

'Go on, lower them to your knees.'

I obey him, aware that I'm still fumbling and grace-less. As I tug the elastic down my thighs, lubrication floods out of me, so sticky and profuse that I gasp in surprise. There's so much that I can feel it trickling, sliding downwards and wetting the dark band of my stocking top.

Valentino's chiselled nostrils flare immediately, and I know that he can smell me. I feel a delicious rush of shame. My body seems to have escaped my control completely. Hormones and fluids are pumping and flowing. Bundles of nerve-endings are sparking and firing. My clit pulses slowly in my furrow.

The door is closed, but not locked. Anyone could come blundering in at any moment and see me, a woman in her forties, standing with her skirt bundled up, and her knickers at half-mast, and her legs slightly apart to reveal her juices oozing down her inner thigh.

I bite my lip to contain a moan of pure lust.

I don't know how this has happened. The mecha-nisms of my own desire are a mystery to me now. I can surrender myself only to the consequences. And to my master.

Valentino rises gracefully to his feet and stands in front of me, staring straight into my eyes rather than at my crotch. It's as if, now he's made me expose it, he's suddenly lost interest. He reaches out and strokes my cheek again, his fingertips ineffably light against my skin. Smoothing my hair back from my brow, he leans down and kisses me lightly on my forehead, as if he were a benevolent uncle greeting his innocent niece.

With his mouth against my ear, he whispers into it.

'You have no control, slave. You're wilful and horny and I can smell your lust.' His hand slides down my face and he inserts his large thumb into my mouth, pressing down on my lower lip. 'Can you not contain yourself?'

I want to speak, or even shake my head to admit my fault, but my entire body is so uncoordinated and beyond my mastery that the control messages just won't form in my brain. I just give a huge shudder and suck on Valentino's thumb like a child, a wilful child, suckling on its dummy.

And, just like a comforter, it actually seems to soothe me and clear my mind a little. I know what I want now, and I shift my hips a little in an attempt to let him know.

For one touch of his finger on my clitoris I'll risk anything and pay any price.

'What do you want, slave?' he says, reading my mind. 'Be precise.'

'I want you to touch my clitoris.'

The sound of my voice is rendered muffled and ugly, almost brutish by the obstruction in my mouth, and the clumsy sound of it is far, far more shaming than the exposure of my genitals. I suspect this is Valentino's intent.

'And what will you do to earn this privilege?'

This time he's gracious and slides his thumb from between my lips.

'Anything,' I whisper, my head like cotton wool, light and floating, 'I'll do anything ... master.' The word comes quite naturally, as if I've been using it all my life.

Valentino nods in approval, his beautiful mouth curving a little, not quite smiling but close, very close. 'I hope you realise what you're saying? And what I might ask of you?'

I nod, even though I'm still not quite sure. I've performed, in my small way, in Suite Seventeen, and

I've seen some of the games that Maria and Robert play, but I sense there's more, much, much more. And some of it might be way beyond my comfort zone, possibly beyond my comprehension altogether.

'Anything, master,' I repeat.

'Good,' he announces roundly. '*Molto bene.*' That hint of a smile is more than a hint now, and he takes a step away from me, looking so pleased with himself that I almost expect him to clap.

Me, I just stand here, exposed and confused. Terrified yet longing, longing, longing.

'Let's do this properly.' He walks swiftly towards his desk and lifts the phone again. 'Saskia, is Suite Seventeen free at the moment, please?' His look of satisfaction tells me it is. 'Fine, and please hold my calls for the time being, if you will.' A second later he's at my side, gripping my arm, leading me towards the door.

Normality and fears suddenly grip me, and I falter. Valentino stops, surveys me, head tilted questioningly.

Have I disappointed him? My heart dives as if it's on a roller coaster. Why can't I be as brave as I want to be?

But then he smiles again, and he reaches out and strokes my cheek once more, his brilliant eyes strangely gentle behind his spectacles. 'No, you're right, you're not quite ready for that yet.'

How perfectly he understands me. He knows that I'm not bold enough, not experienced enough, and, swooping down, he tugs at my pants, and lets me lean on him while I step out of them. Once they're off, he slips them neatly into his pocket, and then tweaks down my skirt and smoothes it chastely in place over the tops of my stockings.

'Come on now, let's go,' he encourages me, taking my arm again and escorting me to the door. 'We're wasting time and I want to get started.'

So do I. I'm very afraid, but so do I.

8 Suite Sensations

Fine white net curtains are fluttering in the breeze, and the scent of the flowerbeds below fills the sunlit room.

It all looks so innocent, so pleasant and luxurious with a safe provincial glamour. No one would know we're in another darker world.

'So, here we are again,' says Valentino softly, as if we've been in this room together before. Which we have, in a way ... I felt closer to him last night than I ever did to Charles.

And now, Suite Seventeen doesn't hold any echoes of Charles at all. I fucked him on that bed, but it's as if he was just a cipher, or a living sex toy. He wasn't as real to me as Valentino is now.

I turn towards my companion, and he's studying me narrowly. I haven't the faintest idea what to do or say. I've lost the thread during our silent walk along the corridor. But Valentino clearly hasn't. His dark coppery eyes glitter with what could be menace but which I suspect is simply a perverse form of fun.

'That's a rather beautiful suit, Annie,' he says, sidling over and running the back of his hand down the front of my jacket. 'It would be rather a shame to get it crumpled, or perhaps stained. One should always treat Chanel with respect. Take it off, will you? You'll find plenty of hangers in the wardrobe.'

He's right, there are lots of hangers in the wardrobe, and they're all deluxe padded ones worthy of designer suits just like mine. I wriggle out of my jacket and slip it on to the hanger, then place the jacket on the bed while I shuck off my skirt. Valentino's brilliant eyes follow my every move, but I have the weirdest feeling that the latent drag queen in him is at least as interested in my Chanel as my body. My suspicions are proved right when I'm left standing in my blouse while he takes the hanger and its contents from me, and hooks it on to the front of the big oak wardrobe almost like a religious icon that will preside over our proceedings.

There's a slow lingering, decidedly covetous quality to the way he smoothes and adjusts the fine cloth, his long elegant fingertips drifting over the braid and stitching and the signature pockets.

'*Que bella*,' he whispers, '*que bellisima . . .*'

I get a shock, though, when I glance at his face and find that his hot eyes are fixed on me not the suit.

He reaches out and cups my breast through the silk of my blouse, kneading it vigorously. All the time his eyes remain on my face. The caress is rough and, as he squeezes harder, slightly painful. But, even so, it makes me want to rock my hips. I can feel my sex growing congested and uncomfortable, and my juices gathering and overflowing all over again.

He barely has to touch me and I'm all slick and slippery.

'Take off the blouse.'

I obey him quickly, my fingers tripping up over the fine pearl buttons. I hang that up too, but he's nowhere near as interested in it as he is the suit.

And now I'm standing here in bra, hold-up stockings and high heels. I expect him to tell me to take the lot off, but he just wraps an arm across himself, taps his lip with a finger of his other hand, and studies me, long and hard, in total silence.

Slowly, he walks around me, and I feel his scrutiny like the sighting laser of a weapon tracking meticulously over my body. It's as if he's measuring my dimensions, assessing the texture of my skin, and the shape and consistency of the muscle, fat and bone beneath.

I have the most horrible feeling that he might find me lacking. He favours young beauties, Maria says. Women as fresh, lush and juicy as she is herself. I feel as if I need to speak up, to plead my case somehow, but I know I mustn't.

He makes another circuit around me, and we end up standing face to face. Restlessness bubbles up in me like lava in a volcano mouth. Kinetic energy builds in my hips, my limbs, my hands. My fingertips almost begin to creep towards my crotch, either to cover myself or slip between my legs, but I still know I mustn't. So I just stand there, arms hanging down uselessly at my sides. I can't face Valentino's intense scrutiny so I drop my gaze to the carpet and the polished toes of his expensive shoes.

'About time,' he murmurs coolly, 'a slave should always be modest, and adopt a submissive posture and a lowered gaze. I would have thought you would have realised that by now, but obviously not.'

'I – I'm sorry.'

'"I'm sorry, master",' he prompts.

'I'm sorry, master,' I parrot.

'And next time, do not speak until you're spoken to.'

'I'm sorry, master.'

He shakes his dark head and tuts, and even though I still daren't look up, I imagine that there's a glint of amusement, and what just might be kindness in his eyes.

'You're learning,' he says amiably, and then he leans across, and suddenly he's kissing me.

He kisses me hard, using his tongue a lot, really stamping his authority on me and gripping the back of my head with both his hands. I want to lift my arms and wind them around him, but I know that's something I mustn't do either. I have to be passive, submissive and receptive. But it's difficult, almost like torture. He's so beautiful that I want to be active and glory in him.

Eventually, he's had enough of my mouth and he steps back again, leaving me with a slightly aching jaw. I know I'm not supposed to look at him, but I risk it and am rewarded by the sight of his lips, which are slightly reddened and kiss-stung. They're probably nowhere near as red and swollen as mine, but it warms me to know that he's not unaffected by what's happening.

Thoughts of how else he might be affected compel my eyes downwards, and, sure enough, a distinct bulge deforms the line of his elegant trousers.

'Have a care, Annie,' he says softly and when I glance up again I see that he's monitoring my every move, my every response, his eyes narrowed and glinting ominously behind his glasses.

I cast my penitent gaze down again, shivering inside. What have I done? What will my rash and undisciplined behaviour have brought down on my novice head?

'My arousal is no concern of yours, slave,' he announces, obviously enjoying himself immensely. 'It's yours that we're interested in at the moment and I believe we will have to conduct a little inspection to see what your condition is.'

We? Who's this 'we'? Does being a part-time drag queen convey the royal prerogative on him?

As an object of sexual interest to him, I don't seem to have any say in the matter at all. Not that I'm complaining. My condition is that of a column of excitement, whirling and juddering inside while remaining superficially still. I feel as I did the other night, in the woodland glade. Only now I understand more, so the thrill is greater. My nipples stiffen inside my bra, pushing hard against the silky enclosing lace.

Valentino is moving again. I hear the sleek rustle of expensive fabric and, out of the corner of my eye, I see him hang his jacket over the back of a straight chair. Obviously he's stripping for some kind of action, and that reminds me of Robert Stone in the garden. These big men love their preparations and rituals – and don't they just hate making a mess of their pretty jackets.

What he does next, though, makes a deep, gouging shudder ripple through me. A primal gut reaction that makes my blood surge.

Valentino pulls open a drawer in the dressing table, and draws out a pair of very fine latex gloves of the type used by surgeons or forensic investigators. My clitoris pulses involuntarily as he snaps them on, one after the other.

'Shush,' he admonishes me, and it's only then that I realise I've moaned aloud.

Valentino advances upon me like fate itself, and I shudder like a willow when he reaches out and draws one latex-clad finger over the upper slope of my right breast, just above the edge of the lace. The rubber drags against my curve, creating a slight friction and rumpling the skin. I gasp, but this time I manage to keep it silent and inward. And I force myself not look at him – even though I'd give anything to see his expression.

A moment later I can't contain a gasp. With a neat twist of the wrist, Valentino thrusts his hand roughly inside my bra, and squeezes my breast, rolling the weight of it in his gloved palm.

'*Molto bene*,' he murmurs again, bouncing my flesh against his fingertips, then gripping my nipple between his first and middle one. When he twists it, I rise on my toes, wanting to dance, wanting to weave. I'll do anything to alleviate the ache in my breast and in my sex.

With his free hand, he lifts my face, one finger under my chin, forcing me to look into his eyes while he continues to manipulate me. His expression is calm, cool and curious, like a scientist monitoring the results of an experiment.

'Don't hide your feelings, Annie. Don't suppress them. Give me everything.' He twists again and I gulp, my eyes filling with tears again. My only distress, though, is that I want more, more, more.

'That's good,' he murmurs, then releases my nipple and deftly flips down the strap of my bra. He lifts my breast free of the cup, and lets it rest on the bunched-up lace. For a moment, I think he's going to leave me lopsided, one in, one out, but then he exposes my other breast too, arranging my bosom like two juicy peaches on a plate.

I can barely believe what's happening to me. It's like nothing I've done before. Like nothing I've ever imagined. It seems impossible that I'd want it, but I do, oh I do!

'Let's proceed.' Valentino sounds mightily pleased with himself. He even chuckles softly as he takes hold of me bodily and bends me face down over his arm. A second later, and without warning, he pushes his long thumb into my sex. I'm wet, swimmingly, slitheringly wet, and it slides in like the proverbial knife into butter. At the same time, his forefinger and middle finger find my clitoris.

I come immediately, shouting and kicking and wriggling. Valentino holds me effortlessly against him, his grip around my middle unyielding, and his thumb and fingers a merciless pleasuring pincer.

He flexes his wrist, thrusting harder and deeper.

My body flexes, coming harder and deeper.

'Oh, you're so weak and wanton,' he purrs, curving over me. 'I never gave you permission to come, Annie. Why are you coming?'

'I can't help myself!'

The words are a strangled squeal, high and strange sounding, not a bit like me.

He laughs happily, even as my sex pulses and flutters. 'Oh, *tesoro mio*, you'll suffer for this.' He pauses and his two fingers delicately pinch me, making me howl. 'And for other crimes.'

I know I've sinned, but I don't care. If I'm going to be punished, I might as well make it worth our whiles. My dangling hands grope around and caress his body, pawing at his legs, his thighs and even his tight male arse through the cloth of his trousers.

'Wicked girl,' he admonishes me, still chuckling, 'wicked, wicked girl.'

Supposedly to begin my punishment, he cocks his rubber-clad thumb inside me, doing demonic things to bundles of nerves I never knew existed. I lurch and flutter even more, my clitoris beating like a heart between his flanking fingertips.

Hanging over his arm, I throb and sweat and whimper until my crisis is over and I'm left panting like a clapped-out racehorse. When my breathing finally settles, Valentino swings me up on to my feet again and sets me in front of him.

For a moment he stares into my eyes, feeding on the remnants of my pleasure, and then he rips off his gloves as if he's a superstar surgeon who's just completed a radical new operation. He flings them into the chintz-decorated waste bin, then crosses his arms in front of him, and taps his long fingers slowly and ominously against his shirt-clad upper arm, playing at 'pondering' again.

'You know that I have to punish you now, don't you?'

I nod, and then lower my eyes, the perfect submissive.

'And do you know why?'

Because I came too soon, and without permission?

'You may speak.'

'I have to be punished because I'm weak and I came without your permission.'

'And what else?'

What else? I don't know . . . just because he wants to punish me. That's the most likely reason, I guess. I steal a little glance up at him, and find him watching my expression closely. I open my mouth to enlarge on my answer, but he holds up a hand. With the other, he fishes in his trouser pocket and pulls out a tiny slim-line digital recorder.

When he presses 'play', a voice issues from the speaker – it's small and tinny, but perfectly recognisable. 'He's just pretty beefcake. Eye candy. He probably doesn't have two brain cells to rub together. A guy like that probably just gets by on the size of his dick.'

When the recording is over, he flings the pocket memo away across the room, where it lands on the bed, then just regards me steadily, his dark head cocked on one side.

'I . . . I'm sorry.' I'm not really, though. Much as I adore him, he's an arrogant so and so and he does need reminding of it, even now when I'm so deeply in his thrall.

'Good. You're learning fast. Now, let's prepare ourselves.' He's all business now, and he sounds brisk and focused. 'Take a pillow from the bed, set it at the edge, and then lie over it. I want your bottom perfectly presented and available.'

Taking a step back, he nods and allows me to get on with my task. In just my shoes and stockings and my pushed-down bra I feel vulnerable, exposed and slightly foolish. But I suppose that's the whole point of the exercise. I'm rapidly coming to realise that in this half-stripped state I'm psychologically far more naked than I am without any clothes at all.

The pillow is huge and fluffy and smells subtly of a lily-of-the-valley fabric softener. Under Valentino's watchful eye, I lay it on the bed, parallel to the edge, primping it carefully into place in order not to commit any further transgressions. When I'm satisfied with the positioning, I cast a quick look his way, and he nods his approval.

'Excellent. Now you may assume the position.'

My heart thuds and thuds, and, even though I'm not quite sure what the position is in this case, I assume one anyway. I lie face down over the pillow, with my rear end up in the air, and, in an artistic touch, I shuffle forward on my toes, elevating myself higher.

'Very nice. Very creative,' Valentino observes, suddenly very close to me. He settles a warm, firm hand on my right buttock and gives it a vigorous, assessing squeeze, just as he did my breast. In a still, small part of my mind, I imagine that he's the very devil choosing fruit in the supermarket.

I can't believe this is happening. Will I wake up in a minute, back in my bed with my hand between my legs in the middle of a dream or a half-dream? I was barely aware that people did such things to each other until I moved in next door to Robert and Maria.

But the heat in Valentino's skin against mine is probably the most vivid, and the most 'real' sensation I've ever experienced in my life.

I *am* here. I *am* face down over a pillow. I *am* about to receive my first ever punishment.

'Just five, I think, as this is your first time,' Valentino

murmurs, then pauses, as if in contemplation. In my mind I can see him tilt his shining head on one side again, as he thinks and plans. 'If indeed it *is* your first time...' His fingers tighten on my bottom cheek, almost pinching, but not quite. 'You may answer me. Have you ever been punished before?'

'No, master, never.'

'Good. Very good,' he pronounces happily. 'There's nothing quite like a fresh virgin bottom for getting the sweetest reaction.'

He takes a step back, then what sounds like a half-step forwards, as if finding the perfect distance. I tense up the muscles of my backside, even though I don't know whether that will make things better or worse.

Eagle-eyed, Valentino obviously spots this.

'Relax,' he says, smoothing the flat of his hand over my agitated cheeks. 'Relax and you'll enjoy the sensation more.'

Enjoy?

I'm just about to be rash, and ask if I am supposed to enjoy it when, with no further ado, there's an explosion of heat in my right bottom cheek.

'Bloody hell!' I shriek, grabbing at myself involuntarily and rubbing at the burning place.

What in God's name did he use on me? It hurts like nothing on earth! Surely he can't have hurt me like this just with his bare hand?

But it seems he has, because there's nothing else around.

'Remove your hands,' he says firmly, and I realise I'm still massaging the target zone.

Reluctantly I obey, only to find that they want to fly to another place. Right between my legs. The fires that I thought he'd assuaged with his rubber-gloved fingers are suddenly raging again, and my clitoris is throbbing in time to the blood beat in my bottom cheek.

I slide my hands under my thighs, palms against the skin, and edge the tips of my fingers towards my sex.

'Uh oh,' warns Valentino. 'Place your arms across the bed, beside your head, hands stretched out. Playing with yourself during punishment is strictly forbidden.'

I stretch out my arms, and this *does* seem to make things ten times worse. Or is that better? My backside is burning, my clitoris is swollen and aching, and my hardened nipples are pressing against the bedspread. My body is tormented in every place that matters, and yet somehow I feel alive and alert in a mind-bending new way. It's as if all my senses have been retuned to a higher level.

When Valentino smacks me again, and the blow is even more powerful and painful than before, the sensation speeds through my body like liquid silver. I cry out again, knowing I shouldn't, but he doesn't admonish me.

He's being forbearing with a novice, I realise, in his own dark and twisted way. But suddenly I don't want any special privileges. I start to move provocatively on the bed, first rubbing my pelvis against the duvet in order to get a little bit of pleasure for my beleaguered sex, and then I lift my bottom towards his hand, enticing the next blow.

This induces one of his low evil, seductive chuckles, and the reward of a particularly keen spank that catches me right on the underhang of my left bottom cheek and makes me squeal like a stuck pig it stings so much.

How many is that? Two? Three? Twenty-three? I've completely lost the ability to count. And I lose the ability to remember my own name when more blows come, speedily following.

Slap! Another, on the other underhang.

Slap! This time right across the vent of my bottom,

impacting so hard that it strikes me squarely on the anus and makes me shout an obscenity I didn't even know I knew.

And then it's over and I'm lying here, in shock, fighting for breath and suddenly blubbering like a little child even while my very, very grown-up woman's body screams for the release of an orgasm.

How the hell does this happen? I don't understand the mechanism, but I know what it feels like. My bottom feels ten times its normal size, and my sex seems to yawn like a crevasse, pulsating with the need for ... for ... just about anything. His hand, his cock ... oh, dear Lord, his *mouth* ... What would that feel like? I don't think I'm going to get it, but simply the idea of it makes me groan even more noisily.

'There, there, calm yourself.' Valentino's voice is strangely sweet, despite a rough edge that I guess is desire. He's a polished and experienced master, but he wouldn't do it if it didn't turn him on, would he? He rests his hand on my simmering bottom, in a way I'm sure he knows stirs up the spanking, despite the thoughtfulness of his words.

I manage to stop snivelling, but I can't stop wriggling. Especially when his fingers curve around the inslope of my buttock, and nearly touch my pounding sex. He lets his hand rest there a moment. I squirm harder.

He heaves an exaggerated sigh. 'Ah, well, I suppose I'll just have to service you then, won't I, slave? You're very demanding for a novice. I fear I'll have to be harsher with you next time.'

The word 'harsher' turns me to jelly, but even so I can't help laughing inside at his mock weary voice. Out of the corner of my eye, I've just stolen a glance at his crotch, and the expensive fabric of his trousers is hugely tented.

Should I move? Or just roll over and open my legs? He anticipates my query.

'Stay there. Don't move.' I hear him cross to the bedside table, open the drawer. He's getting a condom, obviously, and that's confirmed when I hear the tiny familiar sounds of the packet being ripped, and him unzipping himself. A second later there's the very faintest intimation of a sigh or a gasp as he enrobes his dick in latex just as he enrobed his fingers a little while ago.

But just as he's about to move towards me again, and my greedy sex is almost pouting to welcome him, the bedside phone rings, and I groan in frustration. Valentino says something I suspect is deeply profane in Italian, and picks up the cordless handset.

'*Pronto?*' he says crisply, then, to my astonishment, he steps in behind me, summarily kicks my ankles apart and, with his free hand, rummages in my sex, opening me in readiness, whilst listening intently to a long spiel at the other end of the line. 'Very well, put her through,' he says with genuine exasperation and, while he waits for the connection, he positions his cock at my entrance then shoves hard with his powerful hips.

'Hello, Mrs Stevenson,' he says, all charm as I bite the bedspread under the impact of his magnificent cock reaming into me, and his clothing brushing against my tender bottom as he gets in close. 'I'm so sorry about the mix-up,' he goes on, then falls silent, presumably listening to some complaint or other.

Me, I want to complain too. Scream, shout, whimper and generally carry on alarming. Valentino feels enormous inside me, bigger even than the other night. Holding the phone in one hand, he continues his conversation, making solicitous comments every now and again, while with his other hand he steadies my body against his onslaughts.

I continue to chew the bedding. He's thrusting hard, really slamming into me, in an effort to offset the frustration he's experiencing with what sounds like a particularly awkward, and completely 'straight' hotel patron. His hand grips my hip ferociously, thumb digging right into the sore edge of my bottom.

The pleasure, when it comes, is like nothing on earth.

My sex grabs at him, momentarily stilling him in his tracks as my inner muscles contract and caress him. I slide my hand under my belly, and scrabble around to press hard on my juddering clitoris to sweeten my release. I know he can't remonstrate with me because not only is he on the phone, he's also so close to losing control himself.

My legs kick and flail – catching him on the shins – and with my other hand I reach around behind and grab at him, holding his clenching buttock.

'Yes,' he says quite abruptly, 'yes, of course ... I'll arrange that for you. It would be my pleasure.' His aura of civility and polish is being tested to the limit, but the distant Mrs Stevenson seems completely unaware of it. 'I'll return you to Saskia now, and I look forward to seeing you here next week. *Ciao!*'

The phone hits the carpet and then both hands are on my hips, thumbs gouging like talons. My pleasure flares, spiralling again because of the pain, and the relentless jackhammer action of Valentino's hips.

He lets out a loud, ragged and not very civil shout, and then flattens me against the bed, emptying himself into me.

I lose it too, seeing explosions of stars as my throbbing body grips and grips at him. I feel his shirt against my back and his breath against my ear and, reaching back blindly and awkwardly, I caress his muscular thighs.

We lie in a heap for several minutes, both panting like marathon runners with our bodies still joined. I can feel the thud, thud, thud of Valentino's heartbeat against my naked back, and its rhythm is a perfect match for mine. I'm unable to move, barely even think, but I feel his hand slide against my thigh, seeking mine, and, when he finds it, he laces our fingers together and squeezes with an almost heartbreaking tenderness.

'*Tesoro*,' he murmurs again, his lips like thistledown against my throat and the side of my face, kisses flitting against my skin with exquisite delicacy. Soft Italian words accompany the sweet reverent contact and, even though I don't speak his language, I seem to understand him, and the import of the communication makes me swoon anew. I can't believe what my soul seems to be telling me – it's impossible – yet on some deep level it shines and resonates with terrifying truth.

What's happened here? What's happened to me? To us?

I squeeze his fingers, hoping he understands my answer – if indeed there was even a question.

Pleasure and pain and orgasm have blown me away, and I sense that they've almost shattered him too.

But maybe it's just the shock of it all, and the influence of the *petit mort*? Perhaps I'm imagining things, reading too much into something that's nothing more than post-coital politeness and the effects of an intense release.

And we can't stay like this forever. With the supposedly poised and confident Signor Guidetti, stretched out and gasping across the back of an almost naked woman, his perfect sartorial elegance ruffled and disarranged. The real world seems to call us away from dishevelment and that dangerous realm of intimacy.

With a muttered Italian curse, Valentino pulls himself off me and out of me, and, a moment later, there's a tiny plop as the used condom lands in the bin, followed by a smooth rasp as he does up his zipper. Next thing, as I turn over to watch him, he's straightening his glasses, shrugging into his jacket again and smoothing at it carefully, dusting specks of invisible lint off it and his trousers.

I suppose I should be hurt that he's suddenly much more concerned with his appearance than with how I feel, but the sight of the Italian peacock male preening is both fascinating and strangely touching. He clicks his tongue reprovingly against his teeth as he moves to the mirror and discovers that several strands of his silky black hair have broken free of his pony-tail. I observe, becoming more and more entranced as he first removes his spectacles, and then leans forwards, close to the mirror, and undoes the clip that holds his hair. Quickly and deftly, he runs a comb from the dressing table through it to reincorporate the errant locks and then scoops and smoothes the whole raven mass. When he's refastened the clip, he dons his glasses again, and nods in approval now that immaculate perfection is restored to his coiffeur.

'Yes, I know I'm irredeemably vain,' he says with a wry smile, still admiring himself.

I'm not sure how he knows that I've been watching him, but it doesn't surprise me in the slightest that he senses it.

'You've got plenty to be vain about.'

I try to sit up, but it's an effort. I feel as if I've had all the air knocked out of me by a pneumatic press. Rolling around on the bed, I wince as my sore bottom rubs against the duvet, and then just lie there like a beached flounder, wondering where my knickers are.

Valentino tracks me and, using that extra sense of his, correctly deduces what I'm thinking about. He taps his jacket pocket. 'I have them. I'll keep them as a souvenir, if I may?'

'Whatever,' I mutter, suddenly far too weary to be bothered.

I suppose that it's post-orgasmic ennui that I'm feeling, but deep down, in my gut, I know there's more to it.

I love him.

A little frown puckers his smooth peaked brow, and my stomach drops. Has he read that thought? I don't know how he could have, but nothing about Valentino would surprise me. His face still a little troubled, he crosses quickly to the bed, and looms over me, looking more like the dark count than ever. When he swoops down to kiss my cheek, I almost flinch away, half expecting a bite on the neck instead.

'Are you all right?' His voice is gentle, and his accent sounds somehow more pronounced. He suddenly seems a lot more real and normal – less of a perverted god and more of an actual caring man who's worried about my welfare. My heart contracts with that strange, quiet, universally recognisable emotion that's a million miles away from kinky sexual thrills

'I'm fine. Just a bit sore and a bit shagged out, but OK really' I give him a reassuring smile. 'It's all been a bit of an event, you know? Not the sort of thing that usually happens to me ... Well, until the other night, obviously.'

Despite the fact that I can sense a sudden feeling of retreat in him, Valentino smiles too and, as ever, it's breathtaking. His dark eyes gleam ambiguously, and his white, ever so slightly uneven teeth seem to twinkle in the net-softened light from the window. My born-again girlish heart flips. He really is the most beautiful man on the face of the earth, and I'm reminded that it has to be counted as quite a coup that a gorgeously exotic creature like him seems to find a straight middle-aged widow like me desirable enough to tease and fuck and spank.

He might not feel what I feel but he does feel something.

'Why not have a rest?' His solicitous concern sounds, and feels, astonishingly genuine. 'The suite isn't booked, you could stay here, sleep a while, order some room service, maybe go down and have a sauna later?' He pauses, and his expression lightens with a familiar wickedness. 'You could stay the night here, and perhaps we could take your education a little further?'

Temptation lures me like a three-layer box of champagne truffles and I want to dive in and gorge myself stupid. But, even if Valentino thinks I'm ready to progress, I know I'm not. I need to get back to my own space and regroup sometime soon, so I trot out the first excuse I can think of – which just happens to be a perfectly valid one.

'It's very tempting, but I can't stay overnight. I have to leave soon. I have to get back home for my cat.'

Expecting the thinly veiled annoyance I'd get from someone like Charles, I'm confounded by Valentino's response. He smiles. And his eyes light up in a way that's so normal and uncomplicated it's almost scary.

'I would expect nothing else of you. I'm very fond of cats; I haven't had one since I lived in Italy, but before long I shall go to a local shelter and adopt a stray. What is your little *gatto* called?'

I almost tumble off the bed in surprise. The lord of kink and perversity is a cat lover just like the most average person in the street!

'He's called Boy. He's black and white. A bit of a mongrel, but I love him all the same.'

'I look forward to meeting him soon,' Valentino announces cheerfully, then, almost immediately, there's a tiny beeping and he frowns again, and consults a slender but magnificent wristwatch that I have a feeling might be very, very expensive. He grits his teeth in annoyance.

'Alas, *tesoro*, I have to go now. I have meetings with bankers for the rest of the day, which I should really have been preparing for. Very tedious but necessary, I'm afraid...' With a sigh, he reaches for a soft cashmere throw that's folded at the bottom of the bed, flicks it open and then carefully drapes it over me. 'I'd much rather stay here with you,' he says in a soft, rather odd voice and my heart starts to flutter as we stray into perilous territory again.

I stare at him, like the proverbial rabbit in the headlights, hypnotised by the strange play of emotions in his eyes, and by the way that – just for the second – he snags his lush lower lip with his teeth. The sight of the slightly crooked one imbues his face with a strange sweet vulnerability.

He reaches out, presumably to touch my face, and then suddenly snatches back his hand in the first instance of gracelessness I've ever seen in him. It's as if he's shocked himself again, and he needs to back-pedal. My silent heart screams 'go on!' but he's already regained control, and the moment is gone.

'Is there something wrong?' The words are out before I can stop them.

Valentino gives me a frustratingly veiled look and then shrugs his shoulders in a uniquely continental way. 'I don't suppose you're looking to add an interest in a rather unusual hotel to your portfolio, are you?' He smiles wearily. 'Perhaps not, though. It's not a particularly safe investment. Hotels are always risky.'

I'm all fuzzed from sex, and even without that my mind is whirling from the sudden revelation of how I really feel about this man ... but there's a little bit of my brain going tick, tick, tick. A truly appalling thought occurs to me, and it must show on my face, because Valentino suddenly takes me by the shoulders and makes me sit up and look at him.

'Never ever think that I would stoop so low as to pursue you sexually in order to get this hotel out of a hole.' He sounds quite angry, but some previously unknown genius of deep intuition tells me that his anger is directed inwards, not at me at all. Somewhere along the line, the thought of bamboozling me with pleasure in order to tap into my financial resources *has* crossed his mind, and he hates himself for it.

Which I suppose is a form of honesty that I can admire. At least Valentino accepts that he might be a scheming weasel, and tries *not* to give into those urges. Whereas Charles, I suspect, has no such qualms.

'If I thought that was the case, I'd tell you to take a running jump,' I say quietly, keeping my eyes locked on his, despite feeling dizzy again at the intensity of his look. 'Once bitten, twice shy.' It's my turn to shrug now. He knows, of course, about my dealings with Charles, from watching the 'live feed', and probably from 'little birds' like Maria and her Robert.

'Good. I'm glad we understand each other,' he says, bristling a little less. 'I'm interested in you for *you*, Annie, not your bank balance. I –' He swallows and his coppery eyes widen behind his glasses, almost as if he's aware that he very nearly said something that went way beyond his boundaries. 'I think you're an exciting and imaginative woman, and you have immense physical potential.'

It's not quite what the silly irrational dreamer in me wanted to hear, but, even so, I feel a foolish flattered glow. And I get an astonishing kick out of being called 'exciting' and 'imaginative'.

'Do you believe me?' he insists, still holding my shoulders, his fingers warm against my skin.

'Yes, I do.' A happy fluttery feeling envelops me when Valentino inclines forwards and kisses me very lightly on the lips. There's almost no sex whatsoever in it, but somehow that delights me even more.

But, when our lips part, Valentino releases me and gets immediately to his feet. 'And now I must go. I don't want to, but I must.' His hooded eyes narrow behind his spectacles. 'But you should stay a while, chill out, just lie here imagining what I might be doing to you if I wasn't called upon to wrangle with tedious financiers.' He seems about to walk away, but his hand flicks out almost faster than the eye can follow, and he cups my breast in a last quick light squeeze.

And then he walks away. Cool. Elegant. Focused. Like any man, already moving on to the next order of business, no matter how tender or intimate the moment he's just left behind.

But at the door he turns, and flashes me the whitest most blatantly sexy smile. 'If the need for me becomes too great, you'll find a substitute for me, albeit inadequate, in the bedside drawer.' He kisses his fingertips to me, and calls out, '*Ciao, bella donna*. Give my regards to Boy. He's a very fortunate pussy cat to have a sweet mistress like you.' He hesitates, his lips part as if he's about to say more, perhaps admit more, but he simply smiles again, murmurs, 'Call me later,' and then he's gone.

Bella donna ... Sweet mistress.

I shake my head, unable to suppress a smile. Of all the men I've ever met, not one of them has been able to make over-the-top compliments and bullshit sound as genuine and heartfelt as he does.

But he's done his disappearing act again, leaving me wanting him, wanting his body, and much, much more.

9 Trophy

The substitute is inadequate, just as Valentino said it would be.

It's a vibrator, and it's possible I might need it later, so I slip it into my bag as a trophy.

I suppose I could play with it here and now, in Suite Seventeen. I suspect that's what Valentino wants me to do. But I'm not in the mood to put on a show, regardless of whether the cameras are on or off.

I need to think. I need to plan. I need to be back in my own space. So I decide to bolt for home where I can take stock and clear my thoughts.

I dress in the bathroom. A gut feeling tells me there's no live feed in there. Perverts they might be at the Waverley, but I suspect that they do respect *some* boundaries and the bathroom is a private refuge for time-outs.

But it's just a feeling. So I spend a quick penny and throw on my clothes just as fast as I can without buttoning everything up wrong. I doubt if a Chanel suit was ever treated quite so casually.

And then I run for it, racing along the corridor and down the stairs as quickly as I can without breaking into an undignified trot. I slam on the brakes in the lobby, and then drag in a deep breath before I reach the reception desk. Maria is actually on duty now, and dispensing help and a sunny smile to an elderly couple who I suspect won't be in the market for Suite Seventeen.

Although you never know . . .

The smile she gives me is less about customer service and more about burning curiosity.

'So? All sorted?'

I give her an old-fashioned look. There are people all around and I can't really launch into a blow-by-blow account of what's just happened – either in a figurative or literal sense.

'OK, obviously now isn't the time,' she acknowledges equally. Her blue eyes narrow and cloud with concern. 'Are you OK, Annie? You look a bit shaken.'

Shaken? You could say that, although I can't think of a less adequate word to describe my feelings. I think my whole life just changed – and I'm not strictly sure whether it's for better or for worse. I could be in the most serious trouble I've ever been in. I've fallen in love with a man who'll probably never be able to love me in return. Even if he still wants to play with me.

'Don't worry, I'm fine!' I plaster on a smile. 'Just a bit tingly, you know?'

Maria's brows fly up and she leans forwards. 'Really?' She snags her rosy lip. 'Whereabouts?'

'Maria!'

'OK, OK, OK, but really, how was it? At least you can let me know if you enjoyed it.'

I pause. Did I enjoy it?

Oh, God, yes I did! In spite of everything, I'd never go back and undo what he and I did together.

'I *think* I did . . . you of all people should know how hard it is to tell with these things.'

She beams at me, and makes as if to lean in closer, incorrigibly desperate for some salacious titbits, but, just at that moment, a gaggle of new guests enter the lobby and begin making purposefully for the desk with a mountain of luggage in tow.

'Uh oh, duty calls.' She exchanges her look of divine mischief for one of quiet discretion. 'Is there anything else I can do for you? Any message for Signor Guidetti?' she enquires smoothly as the newcomers reach us.

Against all the odds, my brain clicks a cog, and I make a decision. 'No message at the moment, but there is something you can do, actually. There's a portfolio of documents of mine in the hotel safe. It's Charles's investment stuff. Do you think you could take them home with you and show them to Robert? I'd like his opinion before I decide how to proceed.'

'Of course, I'll make sure he sees those files, Mrs Conroy. Will there be anything else?' Her face is straight, but her twinkling eyes are suggesting all sorts of delicious services she'd like to offer me.

'No, that's all for now, Maria. I've got to be going.' I give her a firm look, but temper it with a wink. 'But I'll talk to you tomorrow, eh?'

'I look forward to it, Mrs Conroy.'

With that, she turns to her new customers, who are starting to mutter, and I walk as calmly as I can out of the hotel, my heart thudding and my thoughts winging towards its dark mysterious manager.

The drive back from the Waverley was a bit of a blur, with thoughts and images parading through my head in a confusing procession. Against all odds, though, I didn't have an accident and now I'm back at Lavender Court in one piece.

And I'm ready to start thinking and planning – as well as wondering how soon I dare turn one of my phones back on and call Valentino. Obviously, his financial meetings will last a while, but that's not the only thing that keeps me from reaching for the phone.

Much as I long to hear his voice, I don't want to come across like a sad and needy middle-aged woman.

So I wait, even though the strain of it makes my

head spin and my nerves jump. As a distraction, I concentrate on simple comforts. *Brief Encounter* is on the telly. I've opened a bottle of wine. And, instead of room service in Suite Seventeen, I've got a brand new box of Hotel Chocolat from their Tasting Club. Not exactly a nutritionally balanced lunch, but who cares? Boy is on my knee, purring like a motorboat and the soft thrum from his furry body is gently hypnotic.

Needing to start somewhere, I prepare a mental checklist.

Item one – I love Valentino.

Which is completely absurd and I can hardly believe it myself. I've only known him for three days, and I've already met three different versions of him.

Valentina, the drag queen.

Valentino, the stud.

Signor Guidetti, the sleek metrosexual hotel manager.

Which one of these do I actually love? All of them? I think so.

But how the hell could I have fallen so quickly? Stan and I courted for a year, and we were friends for a long time before we ever thought of marriage. We were sure of each other.

But, in the case of Valentino, it's impossible to know what he feels for me ... and part of me fears him as much as I worship and adore him.

Item two, and slightly less serious but just as radical – I'm kinky!

Reaching around under my robe, and getting a look of protest from Boy for almost dislodging him, I carefully palpate my bottom. It's not sore. Not really. I think there might be a kind of afterglow there, but I can't be sure whether that's just my imagination. It's very clear to me that I was in the hands of an artist when

Valentino spanked me. He's a consummate master who knows exactly how to create maximum sensation at the time and yet do it without leaving any hint of lasting injury.

It's quite a privilege really, and the thought makes me shudder. My cat looks up at me and gives me a stern feline glance before washing his whiskers in a way that seems slightly disapproving.

I reach for my glass and swig down a large gulp of wine without consideration for its bouquet or other nuances.

And, as if it wasn't enough falling for a deeply perverted man I barely know, who has 'older woman' issues, there's still the question of the Waverley and its need for funding. I shall have to find out in detail what the situation is. Either from Maria and Robert, or some other source. Saskia perhaps? And I shall have to do it quickly.

I suspect that the investments Charles wants me to pursue are probably bona fide, even if he is taking a very large commission. But the moment Valentino and I entered into our prickly interchange about 'investing in the hotel', I knew that was exactly what I was going to do – whether or not he and I become more deeply involved or not. Which we probably won't, given his history with older women who have money.

But, despite all this, I can't risk the Waverley having to close, or maybe even worse, being taken over by some faceless chain or conglomerate and turned into yet another chi-chi, oh so respectable retreat for the tedious status-conscious golfing set I was once a part of.

I want it to stay independent and kinky, just like me!

Is there a way to do that and still have a chance with its beautiful and even kinkier manager?

I stare at the screen and the high-minded almost-adulterers and wonder what they'd think of all this. Celia Johnson would probably consider me an awfully common person and prefer to throw herself under the boat train rather than sit with me in the buffet.

'Your mummy's turning into a very bad and a very crazy old woman, isn't she, Boy?' I observe to my cat as I pop two chocolates into my mouth, one after the other, with no effort whatsoever to pace myself. I notice that I'm choosing all the challenging flavours today too, like 'Bombe de Grappa' and 'Cherry soaked in Kirsch and Brandy'. Anything that's an assault on the senses seems to be my preference at the moment ... I wonder why?

Boy gives a little 'huff' and then tucks in his head even more neatly and battens down for sleep again. He clearly thinks I'm demented, but, comfortingly, he still seems to love me.

I end up watching two old movies, and then two episodes of my favourite cop show, while still trying to work out whether it's too soon to call Valentino or not.

Now it's way after midnight, and I've just come back to bed after plugging my home phone back into the socket and turning my mobile on. Of course, it's too late to call Valentino now, and I could kick myself. But at least there's little likelihood of getting a call from Charles at this hour. He might be desperate to contact me, but he'll not call after midnight.

There are multiple messages and texts from him. Most of them smooth and flattering and with lots to say about how fantastic he thought the sex was, but, towards the end, one or two sound decidedly less fulsome.

Not that I really care. Because there's another message on the answerphone. A silent one. And I know exactly whom it's from. I never gave him my number, but he'll have had no problem prising it out of Maria, that's for certain.

So, strangely, *he's* the needy one.

Before I can stop myself, I stab at a button to return the call.

'*Pronto?*' says the voice I expected, sleepily.

What have I done? I'd barely know what to say to him if it was a sensible time of day, never mind in the middle of the night. 'I – I'm sorry. I pressed the button by mistake. I didn't mean to wake you. I'm sorry, forget it. Good –'

'I wasn't asleep, Annie. I've been waiting for your call.'

Now I've got him on the line, what do I say to him? What can I talk to him about? *Everything*, that's what I want, but I can't tell him that. I only wish he were right here in bed with me. Then he could spank me or fuck me or do whatever he wanted to me. There would be no need for words as long as I could reach out and touch his perfect skin.

'I'm sorry it's so late. I don't know why I left it this late,' I lie. 'I've no idea what to say now. This is just mad.'

'No, not mad.' Even if he wasn't asleep, he still sounds vaguely weary. Yet, despite that, his voice is warm and gentle and very, very Italian. As intimate as it was when he was stretched across my back in Suite Seventeen, whispering sweet sexed-out nothings in my ear. 'Your call is late, *tesoro*, but welcome. Definitely welcome.'

'Is something wrong? You sound worried.' An odd, wistful, and what can only be described as maternal instinct wells up in me. I hate that he's worried. I hate that he's stressed.

'I'm fine, Annie. It's nothing, just hotel stuff. Very tedious. Let's not speak of it now.'

It's the money, isn't it? At least I hope it is. I open my mouth to ask if perhaps there's something else, but then I close it again. Why force issues that are better left alone for now? Why spoil the fact that I'm lying in bed, in the midnight hour, talking to one of the sexiest men alive?

'What happened today, it was amazing. I've never done anything like that before. I never even knew I wanted to . . . but it was incredible.'

Oh, Annie, don't gush! I admonish myself. But even so, I sense Valentino's spirits lifting. And as the bond between us metamorphoses in that strange alchemical way it has a habit of doing, I wonder if that's all that's on the rise. I try to imagine what he's wearing and whether or not he's actually in bed, or up and roaming around the hotel, or the grounds even. In an instant of grotesque jealousy, it crosses my mind he might be with someone. A spectacular and sexually voracious man like him must have no shortage of willing bed-mates, and I can't see him denying himself just because he's become mildly intrigued by a middle-aged widow with a nascent erotic curiosity to satisfy.

And yet instinct tells me that I'd *know* if he had company.

'For me too,' he says softly, and the three simple words pour over me like honey. And confirm that his mind is off his money worries.

'Oh, come on,' I tease. 'Let's face it, I don't know one end of a sex game from another. I'm a total novice and I haven't the faintest idea what I'm doing. I can't be all that spectacular.'

'Naughty, naughty,' he purrs, and I imagine I hear the rustling of bed-linen. Is he naked? 'Fishing for compliments, Annie, don't you realise that that's a punishable offence?'

'I'm sorry.' I hesitate. I don't want to call him 'master'. It doesn't seem like that sort of situation. I feel more or less his equal right now, even though I freely admit to myself that I adore him. 'I'm sorry, Valentino, that is rather pathetic of me, isn't it?'

There a long pause and I seem to see his lips. Smiling.

'Some people think they know it all, Annie, yet they understand nothing,' he murmurs cryptically. 'You do have much to learn, it's true. More than you realise. But your spirit already knows the things that matter.'

'Oh, very New Age.' I can't help poking fun, but, even so, his belief in me makes me feel all fluttery. And he's right. I think.

'Are you mocking me, Annie?' He's not stern or cross. I can almost hear the laughter in his voice.

'Perish the thought.' I giggle. What is he doing to me? I'm reverting into a giddy teenager.

But the mood has definitely lightened now. I feel flirty.

'Are you in bed, Valentino? I suppose you are. Most people are at this time.'

He indulges me. 'Yes, I'm in bed. Here at the hotel. I have a little flat, very small, but all my own.'

'That's nice.' I hesitate again, gnawing at my lip, trying to summon up the courage to ask the question that's just killing me. I suddenly feel very, very hot under the duvet, and I throw it off my legs. Fortunately, Boy isn't with me any more, having skipped off the bed an hour ago.

'Do you wear pyjamas, Valentino?'

He laughs loud now, his high amusement tangible even through the tiny speaker of my phone. 'No, my dear Annie, I always sleep in the nude.'

Nude? The word suddenly sounds much ruder than

its alternative *naked*. It's got an indecent, almost sleazy resonance, and suddenly I'm presented with a stunning mental image of a nude Valentino, so vivid I almost reach out to touch him

He has tanned Mediterranean skin, and on his chest and limbs it's smooth and hairless, a colour as rich and tempting as melted butterscotch against the backdrop of his pristine white bedding. His thighs are sleek and powerful, and from the cradle of his loins there rises the magnificent cock that I've twice had inside me.

'Are you painting the picture, Annie?' The mind-reader's voice is oh so silky.

'Sort of.'

'That's good, but don't you think that you owe me the opportunity to do the same?'

I glance down at my legs stretched out on the bed and allow myself a wry grin. Admittedly, it's not nearly as tempting a prospect as a nude and gleaming Valentino – but it's not too bad. 'Yes, I suppose so.'

'Well then, what are you wearing in bed, Annie?'

Should I lie? Should I weave some seductive Marilyn Monroe fantasy of sleeping naked apart from Chanel Number Five? Or maybe I should describe some luxurious lace cobweb of a slinky negligee or G-string?

No, better not. This man has seven senses. He'd see through my lie even if couldn't see my body.

'Nothing very sexy, I'm afraid. Just a pair of men's flannel pyjamas. They're cream with navy blue and burgundy stripes and they're about ten sizes too big for me. Quite voluminous, actually. I'm swamped by them.'

'Bravo! They sound charming. I wish I could see you in them.'

My God, will this man ever stop surprising me? 'I thought you'd be disappointed. I thought you'd prefer me to have nothing on, or be wearing something glamorous and skimpy in lace or satin.'

'I look forward to seeing you in luxurious lingerie in the not too distant future, *tesoro*, but you know me and my fondness for playing games with gender and clothing. I find the idea of you in a man's pyjamas irresistible.' He pauses, and I hear his breath catch. 'It makes me hard.'

And now it's my turn to ponder on things that are irresistible. Things that are *big* and irresistible. Is he playing with himself with his free hand even as we speak?

'Yes, I am,' he says, one step ahead, as always.

'I beg your pardon?'

'Yes, I'm masturbating. That is what you fell silent to think about, isn't it?' He chuckles again.

'OK, yes, I was thinking about that. It's not a crime, is it?'

'Oh no, far from it. Knowing that you're thinking about my dick makes the pleasure more intense. I just wish I was there to bestow the benefits of it upon you.'

It's my turn to laugh again now. Valentino really is the living end. He thinks his big Italian package is the answer to any maiden's prayer, and also to the prayers of those who haven't been maidens for many a year.

He makes a soft sharp sound that I can barely hear over the phone. But I can tell it's not one of exasperation. It's as if my laughter is just as much a turn-on as the idea of my pyjama-clad body is.

'But perhaps you don't need me,' he suggests, 'you have a substitute, don't you, I believe? A small trophy that you stole from my hotel this afternoon?'

I'd forgotten about the vibrator, but suddenly it's as if the sex toy has a voice too, and is calling to me irresistibly from the drawer.

'I don't know what you're talking about,' I prevaricate, switching the phone to my other hand, and sliding the drawer open as quietly as I can. Once I've taken out the item in question, and popped it on the mattress beside me, I take the opportunity to place the phone in its cradle and press the button for 'hands free'.

'Oh, I think you do,' responds Valentino, his voice rich and clear, almost filling the room and making me very pleased with myself at having invested in a high-end telephone. 'I think you know very well what I'm talking about, and I think that you have your stolen toy right there in your hand, even as we speak.'

Wrong, Signor Clever Clogs! Although only technically. The stolen toy is just about two inches from my pyjama-clad thigh, lying there on the sheet, all pink and rude as sin. There's no way on earth it could be classed as an adequate substitute for the real flesh and blood phallus that Valentino is currently fondling, but even so it's a very naughty object.

'Well, shows how much you know. I have nothing in my hands at all!'

'Your voice sounds different. Am I on speakerphone?' There's a click on the line, and for a moment my heart contracts at the thought he might have hung up on me, but a second later, I hear him again. 'There that's better.'

Ah hah! We both have two free hands now.

'So, are you not going to play with your stolen toy?'

'I might. I'm not sure if I'm in the mood.'

'Oh, Annie, Annie, Why are you trying so hard to provoke me? Your voice says you *are* in the mood. Why lie?'

How does he know? How can he tell? I only have to think about him and I'm ready. I slip my hand into my pyjama bottoms and here's the evidence, gleaming on my fingertips as I pull them out again. I'm swimming down there and I haven't even turned the vibrator on yet.

I pick it up. It's quite weighty and very, very smooth

with a dense, almost glassy texture, even though it isn't actual glass. There's not much similarity between it and a real cock and it lacks a real cock's most redeeming quality, mainly having a real sexy man on the end of it. Sighing, I wish it were Valentino's majestic cock I have in my hand, but alas that sensational monster is several miles away. Still, it seems that my dark prince wants me to play with this inadequate replica in his stead, so I give its bevelled end a cautious twist.

The noise is far more muted than I expected. The only vibrator I ever owned in the past was deafeningly loud, so much so that I rarely used it because the noise was too distracting. Not to mention that it put me in constant fear of being caught out, because, in those days, the idea of using a sex toy was a very private thing.

Not so now, though.

'Stop teasing me!' commands Valentino. 'Tell me what you're doing, tell me how it feels. Does it give you pleasure?'

'Can't you tell? I thought you had special powers of ESP?'

He laughs and it's a beautiful, joyous sound. 'I'm a man, *tesoro*, not a magician. A man who would very much like to share his woman's pleasure.'

His woman? I ought to be livid at his arrogant, chauvinistic assumptions, but I'm not. The notion of being Valentino's 'woman' makes me so weak at the knees that I'd be a heap on the floor if I wasn't lying on the bed.

'Surely you've used a vibrator before?'

'Of course I have.' I twist the bevel again, and slip the vibe into my pyjama trousers, resting it lightly against my belly. The purring sensation ripples through my gut and my sexual quick, insidiously stimulating my clitoris without going anywhere near it. I realise that, despite its unprepossessing appearance and relative quietness, my stolen silicone trophy packs an unexpected punch.

'Then use it now. Pleasure yourself, Annie. Do it for me.'

I obey, as ever, sliding the buzzing tip towards the hot zone. Slithering down on to my back, I stare at the ceiling, making it a screen on which to project the image of a golden-skinned man writhing against a white sheet, his black silk hair tossing against the pillows as he pleasures himself slowly and with languorous relish. The sensation of the vibrator against my flesh bears no resemblance to the beautiful breathless things this man can do to me, but, in his absence, my stolen trophy will have to do.

As Valentino groans unmistakeably, his perfect English deforming into shattered Italian that rips at my soul, I too go for broke and reach the zenith. Just at the very same moment he does.

I'm a slave coming dutifully for her master. I'm a woman coming willingly for her man.

I might be a trophy too, but the man I'm coming for is the prize.

10 **Attitude Adjustments**

Afterwards, for several moments, we lie in silence, the only sound, at both ends of the line, our synchronised heavy breathing.

I feel replete, yet unsatisfied. Happy, yet also sad. Pleased with myself for the fine, naughty thing I've just done, but somehow also uneasy.

Irrationally, the sight of the pink faux cock still clutched in my hand irritates me intensely, so I fling it away and watch with a frown as it bounces and rolls across the carpet.

Needless to say, though, the small noise it makes doesn't escape the attention of my keen-eared lover, even though he's over five miles away as the crow flies.

'Is everything all right, *tesoro*?' His voice is blurred by his recent pleasure and perhaps by sleepiness too, but there's a distinct note of worry, and the fact that he is worried about me clears my negativity.

'I'm fine, no worries. That was just the vibrator falling off the bed, not me. But I don't think I'll be able to move for another half an hour to pick it up.'

Valentino laughs softly. 'I feel much the same, but I think I will be able to sleep soon now, thanks to you.'

'Did I make you forget your hotel stuff?'

It just comes out on impulse and I could kick myself. Really, I am so stupid sometimes. Now I've mentioned the 'hotel stuff', it'll be back in his mind again, won't it?

'Yes ... yes, you did ... until you just mentioned it again,' he points out, confirming my fears, although happily he still sounds mellow.

'I'm sorry.'

'Don't be sorry, Annie. Never apologise ... unless we're playing, of course.'

My heart and my sex seem to twist suddenly. Are we going to go again?

But, when he speaks again, his voice is edgier. I might be imagining things, but I can almost hear him frowning all of a sudden. 'In the real world, a woman like you should never apologise for anything. You don't have to – you hold all the cards.'

I scoot myself up against the pillows, almost as if sitting straight might help me to think more clearly. 'I don't know what you mean – a woman like me. What cards do I hold, Valentino?'

There's another long loaded pause, but eventually he speaks, the words low and intense. 'All of them, Annie. You're intelligent and beautiful. Supremely innocent yet also knowing. I know you're inexperienced in certain areas. But, in every way that matters, you're complete. Grown-up. Gorgeous ...'

My eyes start to prickle and overflow. I'm glad he can't see it. There's nothing particularly gorgeous about me at the moment.

'But I'm not, Valentino. I'm just an ordinary, very middle-aged woman who's extremely naïve. You're the one who's gorgeous!'

Now, I've really done it. So much for his belief that I'm intelligent and grown-up. I've nullified that by gushing like the most gauche and lovestruck teenager. Another long silence only confirms the fact that I've made an idiot of myself.

Ah well, it was fun while it lasted. He'll be back to his lush, young beauties tomorrow, and I'll be forgotten

... or maybe just remembered vaguely as a diversion, or a close escape.

'Tut tut, that's either false modesty again, *tesoro*,' he says at last, a strange, almost wondering quality in his voice. 'Or you need some kind of an attitude adjustment.' There's another pause, and I get the most vivid picture of him snagging his soft red lower lip with his white but ever so slightly crooked teeth. 'Maybe we both do?'

'How so? There's nothing wrong with you. You're the most fascinating, self assured, amazingly imaginative man I've ever met.'

I've done it again! Why does this keep happening? Falling in love with a sexy younger man seems to have had a mushing effect on my brain. I've *got* to start behaving like that grown-up he says I am.

All the same, I laugh ... and so does Valentino.

'I'm shallow, vain, greedy and a hedonist at the expense of other, perhaps more worthy, pursuits. I also hide behind any number of masks to avoid facing the truths of my own insecurities.' There's a rustle of bedding, and I'd give every last penny of my financial portfolio to see what he's doing. 'There, does that make the playing field more even for you, Annie?'

'Yes, I suppose it does, but I'd love to know why you feel insecure. Can you tell me?'

He draws in a deep breath, and in my mind I see that broad smooth, hairless chest rise. 'Perhaps another time. Soon ... Although I suspect you're shrewd enough to guess from things I've said, and what Maria might have told you.' He lets out his breath again. 'You, above all the other women I've known in the last decade, might be the one to force me to face my demons ... and grow up at last.'

I daren't believe it. I daren't hope. But my heart is

flying, soaring, shooting upwards towards heaven knows what, attitude adjusted.

I pinch my thigh through my pyjama bottom, wondering if I've actually fallen asleep. Or whether I'm just imagining things or making something out of nothing.

'Fair enough.' I keep my voice light, cautious. I feel like a rather inept horse whisperer trying to gain the trust of a wild gypsy stallion. Where do these images come from? I suppose it must be Valentino's long black mane.

'You're an insightful woman, Annie Conroy. A lesser one would be making demands now. Insisting on information.'

'You don't know how close I am to that,' I snip back at him, subconsciously wanting him to see it as a prompt to give me exactly what I want, which is the knowledge of all that's in his heart.

'Oh, I think I do,' he answers, his voice teasing. It's almost a relief to hear the lighter more relaxed note.

'I'd love to play again,' he goes on, and I hear more small sounds of a large powerful body settling itself to comfort, 'but I have to go to London tomorrow on hotel business. I'm afraid my negotiations this afternoon were less than successful.'

I can't imagine how anyone – man or woman – could refuse him anything when he turns on the charisma, but it seems more than ever that my help is needed.

'What is it? Is the hotel losing money? Are you looking for backers?'

Is there a new chill in the air? Have I done it after all?

When he speaks again, though, his voice is more resigned than vexed. 'Backers ... after a fashion. What I need is sufficient funds to effect a management buyout. The Waverley is privately owned, and our owner is an elderly gentleman, who's had an offer from a large chain of country hotels. His accountants are advising him to accept, and soon. And I'm trying to come up with an alternative bid in order that the hotel will be able to retain its somewhat ... "special" character.'

'You mean as in Suite Seventeen?'

'Yes, the Suite is the focus of our activities, but what I'd really like is to develop the Waverley even more as ...' He pauses, and I sense him smiling now. 'Well ... a pervert-friendly venue. In a discreet sense, of course. The hotel would still continue to function as a perfectly normal luxurious country retreat, just with added extras for those in the know.'

'Sounds wonderful!'

'It could be ...'

'I could help. You know that, don't you?' I hold my breath and dig my nails into my thigh again. I've taken a chance, but I would have to have done it sooner or later.

'Yes, I do know that.'

The ether between us seems to reverberate with a thousand unspoken words, and I can almost feel him wrangling with those inner demons of his.

I want to say that the money I'm prepared to invest doesn't have anything to do with 'us', but the idea of there being an 'us' is still too delicate and friable.

'Look, why don't we discuss this when you get back? No use getting into it now. You might come back with bags of money, and then everything will be fine.'

'A beautifully positive attitude, *tesoro*. Most commendable.' He's teasing, but it's warm. It's easy. It's comfortable. 'And I do have one asset of my own that I can dispose of in order to bring in a tidy sum.'

I'm curious, but I've pushed enough already. 'What, you're not going to sell your gorgeous body, are you?' I want to keep things light and playful, but I suddenly wonder if I've blundered all over again.

But it seems not, because he laughs and, when he speaks again, I recognise an entirely different Valentino at the end of the line.

'Oh no, I've done enough parading of my flesh for the delectation of others. Maybe we should sell yours instead. That would bring in the funds, wouldn't it?' I imagine him licking his lips, his tongue red and devilish.

'Imagine it, a line of horny men queuing up outside Suite Seventeen, and you inside, my beautiful slave tied to the bed, legs wide open to receive them.'

Slave again? My heart flips and trembles.

'But I'm *your* property, master,' I gasp, as the image sears my brain and makes everything that had been dormant and sated spring to life again. In real life, I can't imagine wanting to service other men any more, but this is fantasy, fantasy...

'But it would please me, slave, and each time you come, you would be looking into my eyes. And giving your orgasm to me ... and *only* me.'

'Yes, master.'

Something in my voice must reveal that I'm not exactly taking this all totally seriously, because he comes back at me, half stern, half laughing. 'This is no joke. And if you treat it as such, you'll be punished.'

He pauses for a moment, and I hear a faint movement. Is he getting comfortable, so he can play with himself again while we talk? I hope so.

'Describe your bed to me. What is it like? Is it spacious ... with room to manoeuvre?'

'Yes, it's a big king size with a brass-railed frame. A bit like the bed in Suite Seventeen but with no canopy and no chintz.'

'Do you not care for chintz then?'

Is this a trick question? With no wrong or right answer, so I can't win and thus end up getting punished? My heart pitter-patters, hoping so.

'It's all right. It's just a bit ... um ... traditional.'

'In many ways, the Waverley is a very traditional hotel, slave. We conform to rules and standards and rituals. Surely you realise that?'

I nod, even though he can't see me.

'Do you understand?' he prompts, his voice so knowing, so thrilling.

It's as if he's already playing arpeggios of sensation across my flesh. Pain? Pleasure? It doesn't seem to make any difference.

'Yes, master.' Just the words make me melt and churn inside.

'I like the sound of your bed ... I hope we can play together there soon. I'd like to tie your hands to that so useful brass head rail, and perhaps also your feet, to the foot rail. I'd like you to be helpless and immobilised, totally open and available to me so I can make free with you in any way I choose. Would you accept that?'

'Of course, master.' I'm panting now, my voice thin.

'Grip the head rails ... part your legs. Try to imagine it.'

I reach back behind me, holding the rails in some kind of ersatz bondage. I'm dying to touch myself, but I want to understand what it would feel like not to be able to. I spread my legs as if they were shackled to the foot rail, one ankle at each corner.

'Mmmm...' He almost purrs, as if he can see what I'm doing. 'I'd like to put things into you, slave ... Fill you up, in every orifice ... With devices that stimulate, stretch and invade. Imagine your pleasure stoppered inside you. Your mouth, your cunt and your beautiful

British arse – all possessed by me.' He's warming to his theme now, and I can hear him moving. 'Close your eyes. Imagine a blindfold.'

Unable to see, the gathering, swirling torment is worse. My clitoris begins to pulse softly between my legs, and even though my fingers tingle and twitch, longing to fly to it, I just grip harder on to the rail. My pelvis feels as if it's filled with electrical energy. I want to twist and turn, scissor my thighs together for stimulation, but, instead, I bite down hard on my lip and resist.

'What a delicious sight,' he croons. 'Breasts, belly, thighs, cunt. What shall I do to you, slave? What shall I do?'

Anything. *Everything* . . .

I don't speak the words because, in our fantasy, I'm gagged. But I don't need to speak, he knows it all already.

'Your tits are beautiful. I want to play with them, plunge myself between them. But first, oh yes, a refinement . . . Have you ever worn nipple clamps, slave?'

The me of here and now in this bedroom is permitted to answer. Permitted to . . . to experiment.

'No, never.'

I let go of the rail with my right hand and take my nipple between my finger and my thumb. A little pressure doesn't feel so bad, but it does diabolical things between my legs. It's like a wireless network installed throughout my body. There's no physical contact, but the message still gets through.

I press harder, and now I can't keep still, no matter how I try. I shift my thighs about. I clench my buttocks. I clench my sex. My clitoris shimmers like a diamond.

'I know what you're doing, slave.' Valentino laughs silkily and I seem to feel it in my belly and my heart. His metallic eyes glitter in my mind.

'Pinch yourself. Pinch hard ... test your limits. Imagine that I'm with you. Show me what you're made of.'

But you *are* here. It's your fingers that are pinching and tweaking at my teat, making it hurt and burn and throb. It's your voice, lush as a swathe of velvet, stroking across my clitoris, up and down, up and down, teasing and stimulating but not granting release.

I clench again. I want to scream. I want him to be here, invading me, pushing into my body, and taking me however he pleases. Laying waste to me simply to gratify himself.

I'd allow all this. Invite all this. Endure all this ... just for one infinitesimal little flick against my clitoris. The casual touch of his divine hand to bring me off.

As I pinch harder, twisting and pulling, drawing out my soft breast like a cone, he speaks again. 'Do it now, *tesoro*, do it now ... for my pleasure.'

As I touch my aching flesh, I come immediately and shout his name.

I have a lot to do while Valentino is away, and I make a start by retrieving the vibrator from the floor, where I flung it last night.

On closer inspection of it, I find the words *Black Gardenia PLC* inscribed on the top of the bevel, and a swift Google, before I've even washed or dressed, brings up the website of an unexpectedly high-class sex-toy emporium. No cheap and cheerful ten-quid vibes here, I soon discover. All the merchandise is pricey and, as far as I can tell, well put together. And, if the testimonials are to be believed, they hit all the sweet spots too. I browse page after page, and, while some of the items I can barely credit even the most transgressive of perverts being interested in, and some, quite frankly, just make my jaw drop, there are plenty of goodies I think I'd like to sample.

By the time Boy sashays into the room, noisily demanding his breakfast, I've spent several hundred pounds, including express next-day delivery.

'Mummy is very silly, isn't she?' I say to him as he winds his tail around my bare leg to make sure that I'm getting his message, and, when I look down, his furry, expressive face says that he agrees.

After breakfast, it'll be time to start making phone calls in preparation for doing something that's a hundred times sillier and many, many thousands of times more expensive.

'Well, as I outlined, there's nothing bogus about this portfolio he has lined up for you. They're all sound investments, pretty safe, but not too static. The commission he's levying is a tad high, but no worse than a lot of consultants.' Robert Stone smiles at me from the other end of the settee, and shrugs, tilting his large head on one side. 'I'd probably ask for a similar rate myself if I were in the private sector.'

Suddenly, I feel terribly embarrassed and for once, lately, it's not about sex. 'Oh, God, you must think I'm terribly cheeky, expecting you to go over all this for nothing. Do, please, draw up a bill and I'll write you a cheque.'

He laughs, a deep masculine rumbling sound, and his rather broad face lights up merrily and looks extraordinarily boyish. 'I wouldn't dream of it, Annie,' he murmurs, leaning back against the upholstery and surveying me with a puckish twinkle. 'All I ask is that you stay and have a drink with us. We should have invited you over long ago, and now seems like as good a time as any.'

It sounds innocent enough, but suddenly the hairs on the back of my neck start to prickle. And, judging by the way Robert's grin widens, the expression on my face must be semaphoring my misgivings.

'Don't worry! It's just a drink. Nothing more than a neighbourly glass of wine. I know that you don't quite share our proclivities, Annie.'

Now I feel as if I'm coming across like a tight-arsed prude all of a sudden, which is ridiculous, given the events of the last few days.

'I ... er ... well, I'm new to all this, Robert. I'm still finding my way. It's not that I'm not flattered, you know. It's just ...' I can feel blood rushing into my face and I just hope that he doesn't think that I'm going all menopausal or something.

'What's the matter, Annie, is he propositioning you?'

Maria slinks in with a tray, a bottle of Cabernet Shiraz and three glasses. Her arrival should have defused the atmosphere in the room, but somehow it just hypes it up even more. The fact that she's wearing a very short robe, and most likely nothing else, seems to be at the root of the trouble. She's obviously fresh from the shower because her blonde hair is wet and tousled, and her skin has a delicious rosy glow.

She looks utterly adorable, and the expression on Robert's face paints an unmistakable picture. He's as madly in love and lust with her as she is with him.

My heart twists with wistful yearning at the sight of them. I want what they have ... with Valentino. But I have a horrible feeling that I might not be able to get it, and, at the same time, help save the Waverley from the mediocrity of becoming part of a hotel chain.

'No, not at all,' I reply belatedly, slightly distracted from my speculations by the sight of the curve of Maria's bottom as she leans over to pour the wine. Unsurprisingly, she doesn't seem to be wearing any underwear, although, if I was living with a sexy man like Robert Stone, I probably wouldn't either. 'Robert is a perfect gentleman,' I add, deciding as I say it that I sound like a half-wit.

For all my prim shilly-shallying, I can't deny that being around these two is a stimulation to the senses. Sexual mischief seems to pour out from them in waves.

Maria hands me a glass of wine, showing a generous proportion of her cleavage this time, as she leans forwards, then passes a glass to Robert. Settling down between us on the long sofa, she reaches for her own.

'A perfect gentleman? *Him*?' She reaches across and lays the back of her free hand gently against her lover's brow. 'Not sickening for something are you, hon?'

Robert sips his wine, giving her an avuncular but ever so slightly lascivious glance over the rim of his glass.

'So, is Charles trying to cheat you then?' Maria nods to the documents still spread out on the coffee table.

'No, it seems not.' I take a quick sip of my wine. It's gorgeous, and rather strong, so I put the glass down on the table for the time being. 'But I don't think I'll be following his advice.'

'So, what are you going to do? Just keep all your dosh under the mattress ... or invest it in the Waverley?'

'Maria!' Robert says sternly, narrowing his eyes at her.

She just laughs. 'Well, it's the obvious thing, isn't it? Annie's got money to invest ... and Valentino needs money to help with his buy-out. It isn't rocket science, Bobby. It makes perfect sense.'

Which it does.

I glance between Maria and Robert, and it's as if I can see electricity arcing between them. The longing for what they have tweaks at me again, and I decide that it's time to leave them alone together to make the most of it.

'She's right ... and ... er ... I must go.' I swig down my wine far too fast, and just about manage not to sway when I get up from the sofa. 'Thank you again, Robert, for everything you've done. If you won't let me pay you, you must let me take the two of you out to dinner sometime. At the Waverley, maybe? What's the restaurant like? I've eaten in the bar and that was pretty good.'

'It's fantastic! Anton is a fabulous chef. All the more reason to invest.' Maria springs to her feet alongside me, flashing glimpses of her breasts and her crotch as her thin robe flutters. 'Do you really have to go, Annie? Won't you have another drink?'

'Thanks, but maybe some other time. I've lots to think about, you know?'

Maria's bright face looks suddenly more serious, and her blue eyes are full of perception and sympathy. Under her flirty exterior, she's a very wise young woman.

'Yes, I guess you must have, but it'll all work out, believe me, Annie,' she says, taking my arm and giving it an encouraging squeeze as she escorts me to the door. 'And then we will all get together soon. That dinner sounds like a smashing idea.'

Robert accompanies us, and gives me a brotherly peck on the cheek as we all say our goodnights on the porch. When I look back at the two of them, I see his strong arm slide around Maria's slender waist and draw her to him in a way that's far more than sexual.

As she leans against him, her body fitting comfortably against his, I envy them their warm shared bed tonight.

11 **Prep**

For two nights in a row, my bed has felt as big as a football field and even emptier than it did in the earliest days after Stan's death. And Boy, bless his heart, has been sleeping at my feet in a way he never normally does, almost as if he senses that I really need some company.

Basically, I'm missing Valentino. Something that's quite bizarre, given that I've only known him a few days and our relationship is so unorthodox. But I can't deny it. And, at my age, I recognise 'the real thing'.

I keep thinking about Maria and Robert cuddled up together next door, sleeping the sleep of the blissfully satisfied after making love.

I want that. And I want it with the last man on earth who's likely to want it himself.

And now, even Boy's deserted me. His substantial body makes a soft thud as he leaps off the bed, and hurries out of the bedroom, heading for the cat-flap and, beyond that, the hunt.

But, just as the flap clatters down below, my phone starts to ring. I glance at the clock, see the time and my heart goes ballistic.

Only one person would ring as late as this.

'Good evening, Annie,' says the familiar voice as I lift the receiver. Evening was over long since, but I'm not splitting hairs.

'Hello,' I offer cautiously, aware that last time we spoke, it ended in an orgasm. 'I . . . um . . . How are you?'

My conversational skills seem to take a nosedive

every time we speak on the phone, and I curse myself for not being able to segue straight into sophisticated sex talk. But it's all becoming too intense, and too deep, and too important to me. I want to connect with him, and I want to do it face to face.

'I'm well, *tesoro*, but travelling, and that's tedious. I wanted to hear your voice to make the miles flow by faster.'

Now I listen more closely, I can tell he's on the move. Beneath his voice there is the most astonishing, growling engine roar. What on earth is he driving?

'Yes, you're obviously on the road. What's all that noise? Have you hitched a ride in a Eurofighter or something?'

'Something like it.' He laughs, the sound as rich and wild and thrilling as the sound of that powerful engine. 'Boys and their toys, you know. None of us can resist the lure of horsepower. It's in the blood.'

'Tell me about it. Stan always loved his Jags. He had quite a few over the years, but I'm not a great driver so I never kept the last one.'

I'm not sure what induced me to start talking about my late husband to my lover, but it doesn't produce the kind of response I might have expected.

'Tell me about Stan. Tell me about your life together. Do you miss him?'

What follows is strange and deeply painful at times, but also cleansing. It's a cliché to describe a great weight being lifted away from you when you finally manage to open up about an emotional pain, but it's a true experience. And it's what happens while I tell Valentino my story.

As he drives his powerful car through the night, and I talk and talk, I realise that it's not the grief of loss that hurts the most, but the guilt. Guilt at not feeling *more* grief. Guilt at how easy it's been for me to reach out and embrace life again – even though that lust for life is exactly what my kind and easy-going Stan would have wanted for me.

I couldn't tell my far-flung family about this guilt. I couldn't tell any of the friends from our mutual social set about it either, even if I saw them nowadays. I can't even properly tell my new confidante Maria about it.

No, it's only to mysterious and dangerous Valentino that I finally reveal my secret. And his quiet acceptance of it sets me free to move beyond it.

'But you were faithful to him? You supported him? You never revealed your secret dissatisfaction?'

'No, I'd never do that. He thought I was happy ... and most of the time I suppose I thought I was too. It would have destroyed him to know that our life wasn't enough for me.'

'Then you have nothing to reproach yourself for, Annie.' His voice is gentle and I can hear the sweet reassurance in it, even over the booming engine noise. 'You were a good wife. Your Stan could not have asked for better. He was a lucky man and I'm sure he knew that.'

Eventually, I'm all talked out and I find myself stifling a yawn. What the hell is the matter with me? I've just poured my heart out to the most exciting, glamorous and sexy man on the face of the earth and now I'm falling asleep.

A situation Valentino easily detects.

'You should rest now, Annie. Get some sleep. I'll be back tomorrow and we'll talk then.'

'Where are you?'

'I'm approaching Manchester, *tesoro*. I have meetings there in the morning, although I don't hold out much hope for their success.'

'And in London? Any luck there?'

'Alas no. There are no investors who I would trust to

approve of the Waverley's special facilities.' He says it with a smile, but I can detect the worry beneath.

'I *can* help, Valentino, you know that, don't you? I know you've got ... um ... issues. But we can work around them, I'm sure of it. Believe me.'

Oh no! I've put my foot in it! We were so close, moments ago. Closer than I could ever have hoped for, and now I've spoilt it by prodding at the one thing that's most divisive between us.

But to my shock, Valentino laughs softly, and his voice is low and tranquil. 'You are as generous as you are beautiful, Annie, and yes, we'll talk of it. But tomorrow. Now you need rest, and I need to find my hotel and begin preparing for my meeting.'

I'm so surprised and confused that I don't know what to say. Except ... 'OK then. Goodnight. Drive carefully.'

Valentino laughs again, a gentle, indulgent sound. 'Sleep well, my delicious Annie. I'll call again tomorrow.'

I reach out to close the connection, but, almost as I do, he speaks again, just a few words, something whispered and sweet in Italian that's barely audible above the powerful engine's roar.

I've no idea what he said, and whether he even meant it, but, as the phone clicks off, my heart begins to sing.

My sense of liberation is still with me when I rise, early the next morning. And, as I get into the day, I don't even fret for Valentino's phone call. It'll come when it comes, and not before, and in the meantime I have a full and busy programme.

I make several phone calls of my own, and one turns out to be pretty eventful and almost hilarious in an ironic twisted way.

I plan. A lot.

I dream and fantasise. I even masturbate, in stolen breathless moments. As I'm slicking myself to a hasty climax in the confines of my downstairs bathroom, it dawns on me – with a sense of surprise that almost but not quite steals my orgasm – that last night, talking to Valentino, there was no sex.

How peculiar.

But, even so, that conversation has freed me in more ways than one. I realise now that, before it, the brakes were still on in the recesses of my mind. There was still a sense of unfinished business, unfinished grieving, holding me back.

But that's not there any more. Thanks to Valentino, I'm truly free now, and there's nothing I daren't reach out for, try or do.

I ring the number Valentino called me from last night, but, unsurprisingly, it's on voicemail, so I leave a message, asking him to dinner tonight. At Lavender Court. At eight o'clock.

A short while later, the phone rings.

'Oh, hello, Mrs Conroy, it's Maria Lewis from the Waverley Grange Hotel here.' Maria sounds outrageously formal, but I can just tell she's laughing her head off and up to mischief. 'I have Signor Guidetti, the manager, here for you. May I pass you over to him?'

'Of course, please do,' I say, unable to keep the answering smirk out of my own voice.

I can hear noise at the other end of the line. Someone enquiring about a reservation, so I guess she must be speaking from the hotel lobby. Valentino's very businesslike 'Good afternoon, Mrs Conroy,' seems to confirm that, but, when he speaks again, I hear a softer note. 'How are you today?' This is the Valentino of last night, the sympathetic confidante.

'I'm fine, Signor Guidetti, absolutely fine.'

I don't know what it is with the two of us and phones, but silent messages wing to and fro in the brief hiatus. I am fine. Thanks to him. And he's glad about that. Now let's play on.

'It's so nice to speak to you again, Mrs Conroy, and thank you for your kind invitation. I'm sorry I didn't call to accept earlier, but my phone was turned off and I've just returned to the hotel after a business trip.'

I drag in a deep breath, and press my hand to my chest, trying to still my heart. Just those few measured and mock sociable words make the crazy woman inside me stir again. We're communicating on a dozen different levels, and the disparity between the businesslike and the intimate is deliciously exhilarating.

Who will speak next, I wonder. The suave hotel manager? The wicked, provocative master? The sensitive, perceptive friend?

'I'm so glad you're able to accept, Signor Guidetti,' I answer pertly. 'I'm looking forward to entertaining you in my own home.'

'*Really*?' He answers, managing to make the single word sound lusciously indecent. 'In that case, I'm doubly glad to be invited.' The timbre of the sounds in the background alters, and I can tell that Valentino has moved away from the desk. Something twists in the quick of my sex, anticipating what he might say when he can't be overheard. 'Is there anything you'd like me to bring? Perhaps some items that might, perhaps, spice up the evening a little?'

'Well, that would be wonderful, but actually, I do have one or two spicy items of my own on the menu.' I think of the parcel that arrived this morning, full of what are probably the silliest of foibles to an accomplished sexual connoisseur like him. But so what? They're *my* toys, and *my* choice.

'Well, that does sound intriguing. I look forward to

sampling them. Perhaps I could bring wine instead? We do have some rather fine bottles in the cellar here.'

'That sounds wonderful. Wine would be lovely.' But not half as lovely as you, I nearly add, only just managing to hold my tongue.

When he speaks again, his voice is low and intent. As beautiful as ever, but also so scary that it makes the hairs on the back of my neck prickle and induces a slow honeyed stirring down below. 'Wine it is then,' he says with precise and seductive warmth. 'I'll bring something I know you'll like.' He pauses and I can almost see that slow delectable smile of his. 'You do realise that you're encouraging me to have certain expectations, don't you? Expectations that you'll have to live up to when I get there.'

'Wh-what expectations?' I can't believe that he can make me stammer and flutter like this.

'You're questioning me?' He laughs softly. It's a sweet sound, but still carries weight. I get the impression that we've ascended to the next level of the game. And we haven't even seen each other yet.

'I – I didn't mean to.'

Silence again, and the moments drag out as if they're on elastic.

'I shall want to touch you tonight, Annie. Whenever it pleases me to do so. And I shan't expect to find any underwear to obstruct my examination. Do you understand me?'

My head feels as if it's floating and, as always seems to happen, I nod stupidly, and then remember he can't see me. 'Yes, I understand.'

'But will you obey?'

'Yes. Yes, I will.' Even as I answer, I'm conscious that I'm lying. Telling fibs and already speculating on their consequences.

'Eight o'clock then?'

'Oh ... er ... yes, eight o'clock,' I whisper, suddenly aware that I haven't actually done any shopping yet for this grand dinner party scheme, other than purchasing a selection of ridiculous sex toys. 'But it's not formal or anything. Just turn up when you can.'

'I will be there at eight,' he answers crisply, making me feel something lax and slovenly and deserving of punishment for being so casual about timekeeping. 'I look forward to seeing you again, Mrs Conroy.' He sounds more normal again now, whatever that is for him. I guess he's returned to the desk and Maria's beside him again.

'Er ... yes ... me too. It's a date then.' Suddenly I've come over all dizzy and excited, like an over-hormoned teenager making the arrangements for her first date with a boy she's got a huge crush on. 'Right, I'll see you tonight then. I've got tons to do. Can you just tell Maria that I'll see her later, or maybe tomorrow?'

'Of course.' He sounds grave, and decorous, and at the same time infinitely amused at my nervousness. I'm just about to ring off and curse myself six ways to Sunday for being a blithering idiot, when his voice drops again and he murmurs, '*Ciao*, Annie, I'll see you soon.'

And, with that, the line goes stone dead, and I'm left feeling as if I want to faint, ring back, dance about the room like a lunatic, or just simply masturbate myself into insensibility at the sheer thought of his beauty.

In the cloakroom again, moments later, I give in to that last feeling, shouting Valentino's name as I slither down the flower-print-papered walls and curl into a heap with my body pulsing in time to his steady distant heartbeat.

If I'm hosting a dinner party tonight, I need to get myself to Asda, and look sharp about it. I'm cutting it very fine if I'm to have everything ready in time.

Supermarket shopping has never been my favourite activity, but today I hit the aisles with enthusiasm. I scrutinise fruit and vegetables with new eyes, admiring their gloss and plump juiciness. Fresh meat seems primitive and vaguely obscene, and as for luxury ice-cream, premium coffee, extra thick cream ... Why have they all become so provocative all of a sudden? It's as if I've just beamed in from another world and everything here is unexpected, novel and exotic, and experienced with senses that have been radically enhanced. I glance around at mothers shopping with squalling kids, old folks frowning over prices, and young bright things buying low-fat, low-salt, low-flavour this and that.

None of you has any idea, do you? You couldn't possibly understand what's happened to me, even if I could explain it.

I've decided to go with a traditional English roast dinner. It's tried and true, I can prep a lot of it in advance, and I'd feel a complete fool trying to serve any of my usual Italian favourites to a real Italian. Heaven knows what he'd do to me if it didn't measure up.

I suddenly imagine myself bent over the end of my own dining table, being thrashed for my culinary deficiencies. The trouble is, the minute I think about that, I'm almost tempted to go for it. I think of the most elaborate Italian menu in my repertoire, and what the best way is to make a total hash of it. I even get as far as selecting a large packet of dried pasta while I imagine myself face down, naked rear end up, presenting myself to Valentino for his pleasure.

I drag in a breath, staring at the cellophane packet but not actually seeing it. My bottom suddenly seems to itch and glow inside my knickers and I have to bite my lip, as that phantom hand of his seems to stroke it with a slow measuring touch.

'Are you all right, Annie?' a voice asks, and I spin round, dropping the packet back on the shelf.

It's Barbara, a friend, of sorts, from the golf club and the Townswomen's Guild. It's only a few weeks since I last saw her, for a cup of designer coffee and a biscotti when we met while shopping, but it seems like a million years ago now, and in an entirely different world.

'Yes, I'm fine, just doing a bit of grocery shopping. Something for a dinner party. It's all a bit last minute.'

She gives me a cool disdainful look as if to say, who the devil are you giving dinner parties for? You're a singleton now, you should be sitting waiting for invitations and being jolly grateful when you get them.

A strange emotion passes through me. I feel sort of cross, but pitying at the same time. She's so boringly straight, so hung up on what people think and what their presumed status is. Even if I had a week to explain it to her, she'd never understand that there's a different way to live.

Before she has time to actually make a comment though, I breeze on airily, the very devil-spirit of Valentino controlling my tongue. 'It's for a new man I'm involved with.' I give her my best cat-got-the-cream smile. 'He's Italian. Fabulous looking ... A bit younger than me, but hey, who cares? He's got a body to die for and he's sensational in bed! Really experimental, you know?' I turn the smile on to full beam, feeling like that oversexed teenager again, and aware that I haven't actually been in a bed with Valentino yet. But I think it might be just a bit *too* much to tell Barbara that he's actually sensational when he's fucking me from behind after he's just spanked my bottom.

Barbara's mouth drops open, and she seems incapable of speech for a moment.

'Ah well, must get on. I've masses to do!' I give her

another cheery smile, shove some pasta in my trolley anyway, and start to push it along the aisle. 'I'll give you a bell sometime. We'll have coffee, eh? Maybe lunch?' I speed away as if I'm in *Supermarket Sweep*, not stopping to look back, but I'll just bet that her mouth is *still* hanging open.

With my trolley wobbly-wheeled and groaning with food and wine, I trundle into the clothing section. This is unnecessary, because I have plenty of outfits in my wardrobe that would be perfect for a casual summer dinner. Yet somehow, I'm compelled to seek out something different. Something for the new me that Valentino won't expect.

A little cotton top in soft turquoise takes my eye. It's sleeveless, with a low round neckline and fastens all the way up the front with tiny buttons, rather like a camisole. It has a pretty trim of fine pin-tucking and, even though it's not particularly well made, I can clearly imagine myself in it. There's a long, swirling, wrap-around skirt that goes with it too, and, as the whole ensemble has a slightly hippy-dippy Eastern feel to it and as I'm into peace and love and mind-expanding experiences at the moment, I toss both items on to the top of my trolley.

With my outfit supposedly sorted, I linger, as if in a trance, in front of the lingerie section. A little more than an hour ago, I was instructed *not* to wear underclothes tonight, and here I am, eyeing up bras and thongs and suspender belts. I feel a prickle down the back of my neck, and spin around, causing an overweight girl frowning over sports bras to jump in surprise.

But there's no tall dark, glorious, vampire-like figure behind me, scrutinising my purchases. The aisle is empty. Even the sports-bra girl has scuttled away. And, as there's no way on earth for the store's surveillance cameras to be hooked up to the Waverley's live feed, I reach out for the items I've taken a fancy to.

The white bra is pretty, feminine and distinctly girl-ish, trimmed with broderie anglais and little appliqué flowers in peach. As with the skirt and top, I have far better-made and probably much better-fitting bras at home, but, damn it, I just *want* the thing. And I want it for tonight, and to hell with the consequences.

I pop the bra and its tiny matching thong on top of my other purchases, and stride off with purpose towards the checkouts, before I can change my mind.

For a few seconds, old non-liberated Annie mutters and remonstrates with me, telling me I'm crazy. She even tells me to abandon all my shopping, get in my car and get as far away from the borough as I can. She whispers at me to take a holiday, perhaps, and just hang out on my own somewhere safe and conven-tional, where people are normal and don't spank each other and give incomprehensible orders that they fully expect will be defied ... and they certainly don't fall in love overnight with completely impossible men!

But then I smile, and tell old Annie to take a running jump.

By eight o'clock, my nerves are jangling like bells on a line, but I resist the urge to pour a calming drink. I want to be sharp tonight, unfuzzed and receptive, with the gates of my consciousness wide open.

As I hover in the hall, checking and rechecking my appearance, Boy mills around my ankles, chirping occasionally as if in approval. Or maybe he's just trying to reassure me. When my half grandfather clock strikes eight, I nearly leap out of my skin, then do some deep measured breathing, reminding myself that nobody is likely to actually arrive bang on time, not even Valentino.

Especially not Valentino.

But, thirty seconds after the last sonorous 'boing', Boy shoots off down the passage, and bashes out through his cat-flap, spooked not by the sound of the clock, but by the most astonishing noise coming from out front.

Engine roar. The booming, rasping growl of a performance automobile driven by someone who revels in its power. It's Valentino's supercar, the one he spoke to me from the road in.

'Breathe,' I tell myself again and smooth down my skirt as I walk to the front door.

But when I throw it open I almost laugh and my tension shatters.

What a cliché. I can barely believe it. My lips curve into a smile. Valentino, the very quintessence of a Latin lover, has the perfect Latin lover's car.

I'm no petrol-head, but I know a Ferrari when I see one. And this one's a stunner. Vintage, collectable – an object of desire and of beauty with its long low, aggressive lines and suggestive power bulge. And, naturally, it's red.

I put aside thoughts of how Valentino came by such an obvious collectable when the man himself pops the door and unwinds his tall long-limbed form out of the low racing cockpit.

My smile widens. I can't help myself.

This is Valentino version four, another unashamed cliché – the continental gigolo, or perhaps the retired porn star.

Hanging loose and untucked, his black short-sleeved silk shirt flutters lightly as he moves, making the red dragon motifs on the front panels seem to prance and menace. Beneath this pimp's dream, he's wearing black leather trousers of all things, tight as sin as they cling to his muscular thighs. His gorgeous hair is unbound and shimmers like watered satin, freshly washed.

As he stands beside his ferocious Ferrari, he stares at me, eyes inscrutable behind a pair of equally pimpish shades, and for the first time in my life I truly understand the phenomenon of one's knees turning to jelly.

Except that, in my case, my whole body seems to have turned to jelly, and, as I stare back at him, I can't define what it is I actually want from him right at this moment . . . other than absolutely everything.

Then, as he tosses his sunglasses back into the Ferrari, his slow white smile tells me he's fully aware of the effect he's having on me. Revealed, his eyes glitter with challenge, as if he's daring me to laugh out loud at his own preposterousness.

'*Buena notte*, Annie, you look very beautiful this evening,' he murmurs, sliding comfortably into Lothario mode and bending over my hand as he brings it to his lips. His mouth is as smooth and soft as velvet.

His eyes cruise my body as he straightens up, and my skin prickles as the rays of his extra-sensory perception or whatever it is reveal my secrets. His gaze flicks to my breasts and then to my crotch and that slight quirky smile of his tells me in no uncertain terms that he's aware of my disobedience.

A sudden intense weakness sluices through me when he releases my trembling fingers. Why can't we play the game now? Forget the roast beef and the trifle, the only thing I've got an appetite for is him.

And he knows it. He knows it as surely as he knows that I'm wearing a bra and a thong despite his orders.

The palms of my hand are moist and sweaty as I fight the compulsion to lift my skirt and reveal my sins.

Right here in full view of the street.

Our glances lock. His elegant head tilts in silent communication, making his hair ripple. I half expect him to confirm that he's read my mind, and then command me to do exactly what I've been imagining.

'Hello, nice to see you. Glad you could come,' I say belatedly, rendered inane and gauche by the power of my feelings. Is cocktail-party chit-chat all I'm going to be able to manage? 'I love your car. It's a Ferrari, isn't it?' I sound like a moron, but my brain cells are scrambled.

'Indeed it is.' Taking my damp hand again, he leads me back towards the cherry-red beauty, and I see a strange look of wistfulness in his eyes. He adores his car, that's clear. But his feelings about it are mixed. His free hand drifts along the bonnet, caressing it so slowly and lovingly that I actually feel jealous.

My sex clenches in a sudden sharp pang of longing, as if calling 'touch me, touch me' to those long exploring fingers.

Then the moment is gone, and he visibly braces up. It's almost weird to watch, as if someone's poured steel down his spine. The odd melancholic expression on his face disappears, only to be replaced by a look of measured calculation.

'Won't you come through to the patio?' I gesture back towards the door with an arm that still doesn't quite know how to follow my brain's instructions.

'One moment.' Valentino smiles now, but it's still hooded and knowing and alive with sly macho mirth.

As if he's thrown down a gauntlet, my spirit rebels, even if my body and my senses are still enthralled. My chin comes up and I want to demand that he just brings it all on. Come on, big boy! Let's start now and stop shilly-shallying about!

'I have some things for you.' From the Ferrari's passenger seat, he draws out an exquisitely prepared sheaf of roses in shades of white, peach and yellow.

The ground almost seems to shift under me, as if

kicked aside by the beauty of the flowers and the greater beauty of the gesture. The very essence of romance stings me on the raw and my eyes start to prickle. Ever so gently, Valentino puts the roses into my hands, then reaches out gently to stroke my cheeks.

'Hey, *bella Anna*.' His thumb curves and caresses my chin, the gesture slow and so sensual that my sudden *tristesse* is obliterated and every nerve in my body retunes to sex again. Valentino's eyes glitter as he registers the metamorphosis.

'Are you all right?'

'I'm fine,' I gasp, even though only parts of me are fine and most of me is a whirling chaos of hormones and emotion. 'These are glorious, Valentino. Truly beautiful. Thank you.' To hide my absurd girlish flutter, I lower my face to the heads of the roses and find that they smell just as intoxicating as they look.

'My pleasure,' he replies, soft and low, his voice both tender and suggestive. Then he turns away, back towards the car. 'I have the wine too.'

He retrieves a couple of bottles of awesomely good champagne, and quirks his dark eyebrows wickedly at me.

In the kitchen, I shuffle items around in the fridge, and make space for the wine. It's quite cool already so it won't need much chilling. Then I find a vase to accommodate my roses.

Still all over the place, I don't know whether to offer him a drink first, or do the flowers. All my usual hostess skills seem to have gone overboard with the launch of this brand-new me.

Without further ado, Valentino takes both the vase and the roses from me. 'Allow me,' he murmurs, placing them on an area of worktop not involved in food preparation. He lifts a rose, and sniffs it appreciatively just as I did. 'I'm good at this.' Then, with deftness and precision that would put most of the WI to shame, he begins placing the gorgeous blooms in the vase.

Whatever next? Will he decide he wants to help with the cooking too?

I check the beef, relieved to find it's right on schedule, but, at the same time, I can't help but marvel at the exotic phenomenon now inhabiting my familiar kitchen. I steal a sly glance as I close the oven door.

Valentino is intent on his task, his face cool and grave, his fingers disposing the flowers with confidence and delicacy.

'Something smells good,' he comments, not pausing in his task.

'It's a joint of beef, pot roasted. I used a recipe from a Delia Smith book.'

'I look forward to tasting it.' He gives me a slanted look, pausing for a moment, one long stem caught between his fingers. The sparkle in his eyes is devastating, and I'm not sure he's talking about the meat.

I'm gripped by that lingering lack of belief again. What have I done to deserve the attentions of a man so glamorous and beautiful that he's a living fantasy, the wet dream of any red-blooded woman? What on earth is he doing here? What on earth is he doing here for *me*?

I pinch myself through the thin cloth of my skirt, just to make sure I'm not dreaming.

But just as the sharp nip registers in the flesh of my thigh, Valentino spins around. Accentuated by the gloss of his contact lenses, his copper-coloured eyes look metallic and almost alien, and I'm convinced that he knows what I've just done. He doesn't say anything, but his crooked smile speaks volumes.

'Shall we have a drink, perhaps?' Valentino suggests when he's deployed the flowers to pride of place in the hall.

I head for the fridge and his champagne. But, before I can crack the champers, he lights upon an opened bottle of supermarket red, missing one glass that I drank yesterday. 'This will do.' He takes a couple of my ordinary glasses from the drainer, dries them off and half fills them.

Leaning on the edge of the counter, he holds out one to me, compelling me to cross the room to him. As I approach, he fixes that soul-stripping gaze and watches my mouth as I take the wine from him and gulp down a sip.

He tilts his glass in my direction and tastes his own, shrugging his approval.

'So, have you obeyed me, Annie?'

Suddenly, I need more than an indifferent red wine to fortify me. A hefty belt of gin would be better. My head goes so light that I seem to be floating towards the ceiling. Everything until now seems to have been all in my imagination, and only this moment of erotic connection is reality. I blink at him, imagining that I can see an invisible, silvery link between the two of us, forged by the strange interplay of an ever-tilting power balance.

I lower my head, staring into my glass, and twisting at the folds of my skirt between fingers that are a hot sticky echo of far stickier zones.

'No, No, I haven't.' My voice comes out tinny and nervous, echoing around the kitchen as if we're in a cathedral.

When I risk looking up again, Valentino's sculpted face is a picture. He's perfectly stern and his carved elegant features are formed into the cool lines of a wise mentor who's mildly disappointed with an increasingly hopeless pupil.

But his eyes, oh, his eyes are luminous. They're as dark as sin, yet brilliant with joy and anticipation. Despite the façade that form demands of him, I know he's elated by my answer.

He takes a measured sip of his unremarkable wine, still watching me. A past master of ratcheting up tension without any apparent effort, he makes me wait, for what seems like an age, before he answers.

'Now why does that not surprise me?' His voice is quiet and conversational and I doubt if a casual acquaintance would notice anything untoward about it.

But I do. To me it's as if he's just made the most obscene and explicit suggestion, and I blush so hard that I swear I can hear my ears sizzling.

'I – I'm sorry.'

'Don't be. I'm not.' He allows himself a smile now, and suddenly my heart turns over.

Again, the stark simple truth is hammered home to me, even as his dark eyebrows lift in provocation. I love him. And my heart twists with bitter-sweet joy as I watch his glorious face straighten in an obvious effort to get back on track again. He's no solemn, serious, po-faced master who's hung up on rituals. This is all fun to him. A sweet life-enriching game. And he wants to share it with me and enrich my life too.

'Lift your skirt,' he orders quietly. 'Show me the evidence.'

Abandoning my glass, I ease up the crinkled turquoise folds of my cheap skirt, feeling sweat break out all over my skin as it rises. He's seen every bit of my body, and sampled it as both a lover and a master, but every time I reveal myself to him has all the impact of the first time. My face heats up like an embarrassed teenage virgin's who's showing herself to a boy she's crazy about. Clumsily, I bunch my skirt around my waist.

'Come here. I'd like a closer view.'

I take a step towards him, but he halts me.

'Bring your drink.'

Skirt in one hand, wine in the other, I walk towards him, feeling strange and disorientated. Holding the glass somehow makes the exposure of my barely covered crotch a hundred times ruder. When I reach him, I hang my head, unable to face the brilliance in his eyes. I'm a penitent. A miscreant. Deserving of punishment, not the beneficence of wine.

He reaches out, lifts my chin and makes me look at him, ignoring my exposed crotch and the incriminating thong, and concentrating solely upon my eyes.

He heaves a mock sigh, clinks his glass to mine, and takes another sip from his. 'Drink up,' he murmurs, then he switches his glass to his right hand and, with his left, he pushes my flimsy underwear aside and dives two long fingers magisterially between my sex-lips.

It doesn't come as a surprise to me that I'm sopping wet and, when he strokes me, I groan out loud, unable to stop myself.

'Your wine, Annie,' he prompts, and I raise the glass to my lips, terrified I'll choke.

But I don't. I swallow the rich fruity fluid, savouring its slightly rough bite as Valentino's fingers glide back and forth, and my hips weave like a trollop's, working in sync with him.

He licks a droplet of wine from his lush lower lip, still watching my face as he flicks rudely at my clitoris.

'Delicious.' His head tilts a little and his tongue sweeps again, back and forth, caressing his lip as his finger caresses me.

I can't take it any more. I shove my glass down precariously on the counter, and clasp my fingers over his in defiance. My skirt drops down to cover our hands and I close my eyes to shield them from his gaze.

He wants evidence, does he? Well, he shall have it! Evidence of what he does to me, and how I feel. I cup my own breast with my free hand and pluck at my nipple. My hips weave even faster, rocking my sex against his touch and against mine.

I hear the clink of Valentino's glass joining mine on the counter. Then, a second later, he's rummaging amongst my skirts, his large warm hand closing on my bottom cheek for a moment, then sliding onwards, to cup my hip and pull my pelvis and our hands against his hips.

He's hot and hard and huge and I can distinguish the outline of his cock through the leather and the crumpled cloth that separate it from the back of my hand. He makes a low sound of pleasure, and his breath against my face is scented with wine.

'Delicious,' he whispers again, his parted lips settling against the side of my face as his clever fingers work beneath my own.

I rock against him, orgasm gathering like a summer storm deep in my loins. I'm almost there, and my hips start to jerk faster, when suddenly he whips both our hands away from between my legs, and locks them together at the small of my back. My crotch is still pressed against his, but I can't quite get the pressure I need. I whimper in protest, my body screaming for release, but he stifles my voice with the pressure of his mouth.

The kiss is total, almost brutal, and I wiggle and wriggle in his grip, trying to get off purely by friction. But he controls me totally, even though I'm grabbing at his leather-clad bottom trying to force our bodies together.

When we finally break apart, we're both panting.

'You're a greedy woman, Annie.' He laughs, but not unkindly. His fabulous metallic eyes blaze down at me, burning with a raw sexual greed that more than matches my own. 'You want me to give you pleasure ... and you haven't even served dinner yet. What kind of hostessing skills are those, *tesoro*? Surely you should feed your guest, and put his needs before your own?'

He's a wicked tease, and my sex almost flutters to fulfilment on the sheer devilment and joy in his handsome face. But not quite ... My clitoris aches for his touch again, but I know the rules of the game now. I can't come until I've given him his dinner.

'Let's eat then. What are we waiting for?' I fling at him, almost seeing sparks as I look up into his face with all the insolence I can muster when my mind is a mess of lust.

'Indeed,' he purrs, suddenly releasing me. He pauses for a beat, and then lifts the fingers that have touched me to his lips. One by one, he sucks them slowly, letting me know he finds my arousal to his taste.

'Let's eat,' he agrees, dropping me an outrageous wink as he slips his long forefinger lasciviously back between his lips.

12 **Feast**

I'm a good plain cook and, despite all the distractions, the meal is a minor feast.

The beef is tender, the potatoes aren't burnt and the veg are all perfectly *al dente*. Valentino, clearly a gourmet as well as an erotic connoisseur, is impressed and eats with obvious enjoyment. Champagne isn't the classic accompaniment to red meat, but it slips down a treat, all the same.

And we don't talk about sex in the beginning. Despite the fact it's all that I can think about.

Valentino admires my house, and my garden. It's a mellow balmy evening and we're dining on the patio, almost enacting a pure romantic idyll. Apart from the fact that every time I look at his mouth, I imagine him tasting me and, every time I look at his fingers, I feel them moving between my legs. If he's turned on, he's not letting it interfere with his performance as the perfect dinner guest.

'So, what do you do when you're not gardening or tending to your house? What are your hobbies? How do you fill your time?'

Lounging back in his chair, he twirls the stem of his glass between his fingers, making me shudder and want to squirm. Beneath the tablecloth, I press the palm of my hand against the vee of my crotch and sit down hard in my chair, pressing myself open.

'Hobbies?' I'm having difficulty framing thoughts. I can't stop myself trembling. The sight of his long tanned hands, his strong shoulders beneath his black silk shirt and the way his hair shines in the lowering sun – they all seem more real to me than my life of golf and charity lunches ever did. My years with Stan seem to belong to another woman.

Valentino's black brows quirk with amusement, but he waits for my answer, taking a sip of champagne.

'Well ... I used to meet friends for lunch, help plan charity events, attend the Townswomen's Guild, that sort of thing.' What the hell *did* I do with my time? It all seems like a strange dream to me now. Not a bad one, just one lived by an entirely different woman. 'And I used to play golf, sometimes, although very, very badly.'

Valentino chuckles to himself.

'What's wrong with that?'

'Nothing at all. In fact, I'm in negotiations with the golf club about a reciprocal arrangement with respect to facilities.' His gorgeous mouth curves mischievously. 'It's just that I'm trying to imagine you in a canary-yellow jacquard sweater with a matching kilt and a sun visor ... and no underwear.'

I laugh, but I'm one step ahead of him. In my imagination we're in the rough, rolling around, fucking like bunnies.

'So, we've covered hobbies,' he continues, reaching over to pour more wine into my glass, 'now what about lovers? What about your handsome financial adviser, Charles? You seemed to enjoy him ... are you planning to fuck him again?'

'No!' The word's out without even a second thought.

'Why not? You looked magnificent when you were putting him in his place ... and he certainly seemed to knuckle under to your dominance.'

'That was a one-off. I'm not sure I could do it again. In fact, I think I need to give him a bit of breathing space from me.'

Valentino's eyes narrow. 'Why so?'

'Well, when I rang him to decline his suggestions for my portfolio –' I pause, aware that we're straying into choppy territory now '– he broke down and told me he loved me and he wanted to marry me!'

Valentino puts his glass down with an audible clunk and for once seems genuinely non-plussed.

Which is more or less what I was, too, when Charles suddenly blurted out his declaration. It was the last thing I was expecting and, the moment he'd uttered the words, I could tell that he knew he'd gone too far. A few moments later, we were both agreeing never to speak of it again. Which is a good thing, especially as Charles also sheepishly admitted that he has a steady girlfriend!

I may never marry again and, if I do, it won't be anyone like Charles. Mainly because of the man sitting in front of me.

'The man is a fool to let a jewel like you slip through his grasp,' Valentino observes dryly. His eyes lock on mine, shining and dark and utterly serious. 'What was your answer?'

'No. A definite "no". I may retain him to handle certain investments, but from now on I'll only deal with him in a professional capacity, and perhaps, eventually, as a friend.'

Now would be the moment to bring up the matter of the Waverley, and its future, and how my money might affect that future – but I feel far too fluttery at being called a 'jewel' and too desperate to touch Valentino and be touched by him.

'Good,' he says at length, 'one should always have *friends*.'

He places heavy emphasis on the word, and there's an odd glitter in his eyes. Good God, is he jealous? This man who is so sexually unfettered and believes in sharing lovers and encouraging his women to fuck other men?

He reaches for his glass again, and then seems to change his mind. In a slow considered gesture, he lifts his arms, smoothing his thick black hair back with his hands and letting it swing forwards again. As it settles into place again, like a sheet of heavy silk, he says softly, 'Come here.'

My heart goes thud, thud, thud in my chest as I rise to my feet and crumple my table napkin on to my seat. I seem to fly towards him, yet at the same time it's difficult to move, as if my blood is too heavy in my veins.

Valentino's eyes narrow, expressing his disapproval of my tardiness, and I speed up, walking around the table, trying to project grace and poise when all I feel is an almost maniacal excitement.

It seems strange to be above him as I stand just inches from his leather-clad knees. I'm looking down into his face, but somehow he still seems to loom over me and dominate me. Especially when he snakes out an arm, catches me by the waist and pulls me between his open thighs.

My arms hang limp at my sides. I know I have to be compliant. But my fingers itch to reach out and touch his silky hair. It's so thick, so vital and lustrous. I can almost imagine some of the wispy-headed menopausal matrons at the golf club wanting to garrotte him in envy of such a magnificent mane.

'What is it, slave? You want something, don't you?' He gives me a sly heavy-lidded look, challenging me to deny his mind-reading talents.

'It's your hair, master. It's so beautiful. I want to touch it.'

'And, if I let you touch it, what would you give in return?'

My stomach trembles and my sex clenches hard with longing.

'Everything, master.'

I gaze down at his hand, resting loosely on his thigh, against the leather. I no longer dare look at his glorious face.

'*Bene, molto bene*,' he murmurs and, even as I watch, those elegant fingers flex, and his hand seeks mine to bring it up and press it to the side of his face and his dark shimmering hair.

My own fingers curve and flex too, digging in amongst the richly shiny strands, loving their beautiful texture. Unable to prevent myself, I incline forwards and breathe in the scent of a spicy woodsy shampoo and the faint odour of his clean male scalp beneath it, then draw a hank towards my lips and press it against them.

Valentino's face is close to my breasts and, once again, I feel that strange piercingly sweet, almost maternal yearning. He's younger than me, but he's not *that* much younger. Perhaps ten, fifteen years. But, for just a moment, I want to cherish and care for and nurture him.

And then the balance tips completely, and he gently puts me apart from him, draws my hand back down to my side and looks up at me like the very devil incarnate. 'Time to pay, slave.'

His voice is low and thrilling and, in a quick deft movement, he locates the fastening of my wrap-around skirt and unties it, then undoes the inner button. Like a matador executing a dramatic *veronica*, he swirls the garment away from my body altogether and sends it floating like a turquoise cloud across the patio.

My thong is very tiny, very flimsy, and rather soggy now, from my aroused, excited flow. I'm also aware again that I should have had that bikini wax. But I didn't, and now my flossy pubic hair is peeking out naughtily from either side of the microscopic triangle of white cotton that doesn't anywhere near cover my mound.

'Very pretty,' Valentino comments, his eyes zeroing in on my less than immaculate personal grooming. He reaches out and coils a single curl around his fingertip. When he tugs lightly, it's as if he's tugging on every nerve-end in my sex.

'I should have waxed. I look like a gorilla-woman, er, master.' I remember my role at the very last minute. It's hard to concentrate with that gentle little pulling and teasing action going on down there.

'Sshhh. I prefer you this way. Natural. Womanly.' He smoothes his fingers over the soft curls and fluffs them a little. For a moment, I think he's going to whisk my thong clean off, but, instead, his large warm hand slides around my hip and curves possessively around my right bottom cheek. He squeezes my flesh as if assessing it like a choice cut of meat. He's testing its resilience, revisiting old territory. Suddenly I wish he'd slap me. The skin there seems to cry out for impact, and my sex moistens anew in anticipation.

'Exquisite,' he whispers, then grasps me by the back of the head, bringing my face down to his for a searching kiss. At the same time, his fingers crook and curve, pressing against my anal furrow and my sex lips as his tongue marauds my mouth, tasting and probing.

I groan, the sound muffled by his lips, grunting and panting as his fingers flick, explore and fondle. I feel as if I want to struggle against it, yet at the same time succumb completely in total surrender. He tweaks on the thin cotton string of my thong, where it bisects my buttocks, and induced friction seems to violate me more than his fingers did. The thong is inanimate, and unfeeling, yet it stimulates me furiously as it rubs my clitoris, my vaginal entrance and my anus.

As I lean forwards, chained by his hand and his savage kiss, my naked bottom is thrust out rudely. For a moment I imagine a thousand eyes leering at my bare rounded shape, men and women aroused by the way I'm moving and twisting involuntarily, dancing lewdly to Valentino's wicked tune.

Once again, I'm excited by the idea of being watched, just as I was in Suite Seventeen. My body tingles as if lewd gazes are licking over it like flames, and I smile beneath Valentino's mouth as I realise that I might even be being watched in reality, not just in my mind.

If I can see into Robert Stone's garden to watch his and Maria's high jinks, the couple next door can most certainly see back into mine. I writhe even more enthusiastically, hips twisting and weaving like a belly dancer's, and I lift my hands to caress my own breasts. I haven't been given permission to do this, but I don't care. So he punishes me? It's what I want, isn't it?

In fact, this whole thrilling interlude is about what *I* want, really.

I am a queen. I am a goddess. I am in charge.

As Valentino's finger pushes rudely at my anal cleft, and I feel a silky rush of lubrication trickle down my naked thigh, I realise that, even though, superficially, I'm the subservient here, in actuality I have the upper hand.

This is my choice. My pleasure. And this complex beautiful, exotic man is here at my behest, and servicing my newly discovered and deliciously twisted needs.

I'm acting like his sex toy and yet I've never felt more powerful.

I rock against his fingers, I swirl the engorged tips of my breasts between my fingers, the friction heightened by the cotton of my bra, and twine my tongue around his, like a serpent's, inside my mouth.

I am supreme. I'm an empress of sex. I'm having the time of my life and, if my horny neighbours are watching me, all the better. Let them watch!

Valentino pulls away from me, his copper-coloured eyes almost flashing real sparks. He smiles, his face alight with pleasure as if he's read my exultant thoughts and they delight him. 'You are a wicked, licentious woman, slave,' he accuses me mockingly, his fingertip still poking lewdly at my bottom while he saws the side of his other hand slowly back and forth up and down my sex cleft. The thin cotton of my thong abrades my clitoris.

'Yes, I am,' I concur, bending my knees a little, opening myself even further for him, working myself reciprocally against the action of his hands.

'You know you have to be punished for your forwardness, don't you?'

'Yes, master,' I answer, my voice cracking as my sex flutters and I come in a quick light orgasm that's not really satisfying, but just an appetiser for more. Unable to help myself, I thrust my body forwards rubbing my breasts against his chest and my crotch against his hands as my head tilts back and a mew of pleasure escapes my lips.

'Wicked ... wicked ... wicked ...' he whispers, but he allows me my moment and even sweetens it with a kiss against my throat as my sex gently pulses.

My greedy wanton climax is over all too quickly though and, grasping me firmly by the arms, Valentino sets me away from him by just one pace. His darkened gaze roves over my flushed face, my sex-reddened chest and my bare belly and thighs. His elegant nose wrinkles as he breathes in what I'm breathing in – the odour of my arousal which is more pungent than the garden flowers or the lingering aromas of the meat and wine we've consumed.

Helplessly, I reach out to touch him, but he puts my hands down by my sides. He's gentle, but purposeful, not to be gainsaid. His mock stern look forces me to lower my eyes, and watch as he unbuttons the front of my camisole to expose my rounded breasts cradled in the white cotton lace of my bra.

'This needs to go,' he says casually, and, from the pocket in his leather jeans, he produces a slim silver-coloured cylinder. He presses a tiny stud on the side of it, and the mysterious object is revealed to be a small switchblade.

In three swift strokes, he slices the straps of my bra and the material between the cups. I feel the wind of the cuts, but not the travel of the blade, and, before I know it, he's flicked away the tatters of my supermarket brassière and flung it across the patio to join my abandoned skirt.

Two more lightning, but accurate slashes and my G-string follows. I pluck at the pin-tucked front of my camisole, but he says, 'No, leave it.'

So I do.

The blade disappears. The little knife is set aside. And Valentino takes hold of my breasts, cupping one in each hand.

His fingers are strong, the skin of his palms smooth, and he hefts the weight of my breasts, assessing them for firmness and resilience just as he did my bottom. His thumbs glide across my nipples as he examines me, each stroke seeming to slither across my clitoris too, as if my entire body is a subtle wireless network.

'Your body is delicious, Annie,' he murmurs, pinching my nipples a little now. The pressure is tantalising, hyping up the swiftly reviving excitement between my legs. But somehow it's not the physical stimulation that begins my rise again, but Valentino's sudden use of my name. It's humanising. Intimate. It seems to set our game on a new course that's closer and more meaningful. I don't know how, but I sense that we're in new territory somehow, in a zone that Valentino's never entered before.

'You are beautiful and lush,' he continues, leaning towards me. As his tongue settles on a hot patch of skin in the hollow of my throat, he licks away the sweat there as he plucks and twists the puckered and aroused tips of my breasts, 'Everything about you is real ... and ripe for the taking.' His tongue moves slowly, lapping again. 'I want to play with you, Annie. I want to explore every inch of you. Handle your breasts. Your cunt ... Your arse ...'

His tongue meanders again, licking at my chest, then along the upper slopes of my breasts. He pulls at a nipple, bringing it up to his lips, and then sucks it into his mouth, teeth closing lightly on the stiffened crest.

My hips roll again as he nips and bites. He doesn't do it hard, just nibbling really, but the effect it has between my legs is monumental. I start moaning again as he switches to the other breast, keeping up the pressure on the first with his fingers as his satin hair swings against my burning skin.

The torment lasts as much as a minute, or maybe more, as he mouths and taunts me. My sex seems to yawn wide with arousal, even though it's only a short while since I last came. He seems determined to drive me crazy with thwarted lust, again and again.

Eventually, though, he lifts his face again and smiles at me, slowly and wickedly.

'Where are your sex toys, Annie? Those "spicy items" that you mentioned?' His tongue snakes out, and he licks his lips as if still savouring the taste of my nipples. 'I think it's time we had a little fun with them.'

'They're in my bedside drawer. I – I haven't tried any of them yet.'

Even as I'm speaking, Valentino rises to his feet, making me step back. His hands are round my buttocks in a flash, and he steps forwards to fit our bodies flush against each other. The bulge in his leather jeans is breathtaking, hot and hard against my naked belly.

'Let's not wait then,' he says, and gives me one swift hard kiss on the mouth, before turning me and propelling me towards the house, his hands lightly clasping my bare bottom as we walk.

There's something very rude and demeaning about our progress and being 'driven' by a man's hands upon my arse, and yet, somehow, I can't help but glory in it. I love the way he squeezes and plays with me, his fingertips forever straying into the cleft. When we reach the stairs, I want to run ahead, up them, then kneel and present myself to him, cheeks parted so he can see everything more clearly. As it is, I sway my hips as I ascend the staircase, and he laughs softly because he knows exactly what I'm doing.

As I push open the door to my bedroom, I'm struck by a vague similarity in the layout of this room to the topography of Suite Seventeen. There's no chintz here, the furnishings are mostly in solid muted colours, but the brass-railed bed is much like the one at the Waverley, and the amount of floor space and general distribution of furniture is similar. I even have a television, but alas there's no special sex channel, just the ordinary ones.

Daringly, I turn around and find Valentino smiling.

'A veritable home from home,' he observes, his dark head cocked on one side as he scans the room and echoes my thoughts. 'I especially like your bed.' He nods approvingly and his hair swishes and dances. 'Brass head and foot rails allow for interesting possibilities.' He gives me a narrow look, his eyes dark and naughty.

I'll just bet they do.

Now we're here though, I start to feel a little nervous, and unsure of what to do next. Should I kneel? Take off the last of my clothes – my little camisole – and my sandals? Should I abase myself face down and kiss the toes of his polished black boots?

Instead of all of these, I meet his gaze with a foolhardy boldness that astonishes me as much as it clearly amuses him.

We move forwards into the room, and he back-heels the door shut behind us. It closes with a soft click that seems to echo and echo, signifying the sealing of our pact, our private world.

'Well, here we are, Annie. Are you ready?'

Am I? I suppose ... No, I *know* that I am! Part of me has been ready and waiting for Valentino all my life.

Unbidden, I kneel before him. I want to show perfect submissiveness and humility, but somehow I end up hugging him around his narrow hips and pressing my face against the prominent leather-clad swell of his erection. I rub my cheek against it in a slow adoring greeting.

Valentino allows me my moment of self-indulgence. He even makes a low sound of approval, and bucks his hips towards me. But almost as quickly, he takes me by the shoulders and puts me away from him.

'You're wilful, Annie. You're getting ahead of yourself. Your chance will come, but we have stages to pass through.'

I bow my head, but my mouth is watering at the thought of what lies beneath that leather.

'So, does this little cache of toys of yours include a slave collar, I wonder?'

'Yes, sort of ...'

'"Sort of?"' He sounds amused, and I hope he'll remain that way when he sees my little collection.

'I don't think it's a proper one. I just liked the look of it.'

'Indeed? Well, I'm sure that if you like it, *tesoro*, I'll like it too.'

With that, he strides to the bedside unit and slides open the drawer. I sneak a look at his face as he peers inside, and watch his beautiful mouth quirk into an entertained smile.

'*Molto bene*,' he pronounces, reaching in and plucking out an item. 'I think we shall do very well with your choices –' He coils the collar between his long fingers as if assessing its suitability, '– although I'm not sure about the colour of *this*!' With the buckle between his finger and thumb, he lets the strip of pink leather dangle and swing. 'And they don't usually have writing on them either, but never mind. It looks serviceable enough.'

He advances to where I'm kneeling, and stands above me, making a small performance of reading the word picked out in silver on the narrow pink strip.

S. L. U. T.

'Very droll,' he murmurs, reaching down and buckling it around my neck, then positioning my 'title' neatly towards the front.

It's such a simple act, and such a jokey mundane object, but, somehow, the very act of marking me out with the symbol of servitude makes me tremble with a delicious spine-melting yearning. My head goes light again and I almost sway where I kneel it's so intense. The urge to submit myself to him is now so complete that I can't stop myself doing what I fantasised about. I pitch forwards and press my mouth hungrily against the black leather of his boot.

For several long moments, I crouch there, shaking,

my mouth open against the smooth hide. I can feel him looking down at me, his eyes moving slowly over my hair, my shoulders, my back and my rudely bared bottom. Then I feel the touch of his hand on the back of my head as he says, 'Get up now.'

I feel clumsy and shaky as I get up, but he still seems pleased. He pats my cheek, and smoothes back my hair, then deftly slips the camisole off my shoulders and divests me of it. He tosses it aside, and then nods to me to step out of my sandals.

I obey and, a second later, I'm standing before him nude, apart from my collar, with my hands neatly at my sides.

'*Que bella*,' he murmurs approvingly, then slips his hand quickly between my legs to test my wetness. While I'm still gasping, he brings the shining evidence of my helpless lust to his nose and draws in a deep breath. Satisfied with my odour, he holds out his fingers for me to lick clean of my own juices.

I'm not sure what I was expecting, but my own taste is strangely bland, just a little salty more than anything. It smells more than it tastes, and like a dutiful slave I suck every last trace of it off his skin.

'Good girl,' he says with a smile, inspecting my handiwork. 'Now lie down on the bed, arms above your head.'

It seems very odd to be lying on my own bed, on top of the covers, with no clothes on, and I feel very self-conscious when Valentino lights the bedside lamp and begins to sift through the items in my 'toy drawer'. Every so often, he'll lift something out for closer inspection, then quirk his dark brows at me as if highly amused by my naïve choices. He places one or two items on the top of the bedside unit, and then casually fondles my nipples as if they need his attentions to stay erect.

'More pink,' he says with a chuckle, lifting a pair of faux-fur-covered handcuffs on a long chain, 'and fluffy too. Is this your idea of romantic bondage?'

He's mocking me, but I don't care because his voice is warm, almost kind. He knows that I'm new to this and I hope he finds my inexperience piquant – and arousing.

A glance towards his groin shows that my hopes are fulfilled. He's hugely rampant.

'I just thought they were pretty, master,' I answer, even though I'm not sure I was supposed to.

'Indeed they are ... and more so once they're around your wrists, my love.'

My love?

13 **Painted Love**

My heart thuds. Was that a slip of the tongue? Do Italians even call each other 'love' in the way we British folk do?

I'm shaking like a leaf as he threads the long chain round one of the bed rails, clips the cuffs around my wrists and then snaps their simple 'play' fastenings in place.

'Hey, relax,' he says, smoothing his fingertips over my cheek and my brow, 'this is just a game, for our pleasure ... no need to worry.' He presses his lips against the corner of my eyes, and then my mouth. 'If you don't want to go on, you only have to say so.'

'I'm fine, master. I want to go on.' My very soul seems to twist when he smiles his approval.

'Good girl,' he breathes, his tongue sliding along the line of my jaw as he kisses his way downwards, towards my breast, where he takes my nipple between his lips again and nips it playfully.

I'm glad he can't see my face because, despite the silvery jolt of pleasure his mouth on my breast gives me, I can't help but grin at being called a 'girl' ... mainly because I *feel* like a girl when I'm with him.

For a few minutes he plays with my nipples, experimenting with his fingers and with his lips, contrasting sweet, soft caressing pressure with intense pinching, twisting and tweaking. By the time he sits back, surveying the stiff, reddened peaks, I'm gripping the bed-head, writhing involuntarily and there's a damp sticky patch beneath me where I've been seeping onto the duvet cover.

'Exquisite, but they need adornment.'

He reaches into the drawer, and brings out the little silvery nipple clamps that are part of my toy haul. They're only play clamps, nothing like the real thing, I'm sure, but they still nip sharply when he closes them on the tips of my breasts. I swallow hard, fighting not to cry out, and my hips roll against the mattress.

He stands up, dark head tilting as he seems to study the effect. Brushing his hair away from his brow, he smiles, and then, satisfied, he glances around the room. Then, leaving me to my wriggling and chain rattling, he starts to wander around my bedroom, studying my furnishings, my décor and my possessions.

He lifts a dress that's hanging on the front of the wardrobe, and checks the label. It's one I was half considering wearing tonight, before I chose my cheap Asda outfit, and it's quite a high-end garment, if not especially revealing or sexy. Valentino holds it against him, and turns this way and that in front of the mirror. The sight of him posing reminds me – with a low kick of arousal – that this is a man who sometimes likes to dress as a woman, and 'Valentina' seems to like my frock, even though I rejected it.

After replacing the dress, he turns to the dressing table and sits down, his large frame strangely graceful on the delicate girly stool. He lifts the cap on my scent, sniffs and purrs appreciatively, then moves on to my cosmetics that are still scattered across the surface.

For a moment, my physical torments and pleasures are almost forgotten, as I watch him, rapt.

He picks up a soft kohl pencil, leans towards the mirror and proceeds to outline his glittering eyes, almost as I would do mine, even to the smudging of the line for a smoky effect. Mascara next, two coats on lashes that are already so long they're just unfair. As a finishing touch, he uncaps a few lipsticks, considers and rejects them, and finally settles on a new innovation of mine, something from the Avon lady, a subtle but long-lasting lip-tint in the form of a felt-tip pen.

'What an ingenious idea,' he comments, as if genuinely intrigued. A moment later, he's colouring his lips with all the deftness of practice, then muting the intensity with a swift tissue blot.

If I was turned on before, I'm almost out of my mind with it now. Valentino turns to me, inviting me to admire the exotic effect. He looks more beautiful, dangerous and perplexing than ever and yet still completely a man.

'What do you think?'

'I – I think it looks wonderful ... much better on you than on me.'

'Now, now, that's false modesty again, *tesoro*. You know that you're a supremely beautiful woman. You must learn to glory in that, and demand homage for it.'

'Homage?'

He laughs, which makes his painted face a tantalising enigma. 'Yes, homage. Do you not think that I'm paying homage to your beauty right now? Playing with your body is just a perverse way of honouring it, Annie. I test your senses because I admire you ... because I –'

He stops and blinks, his long lashes fluttering, then almost storms across the room to kiss me again, brutally and possessively, his rose-pink lips crushing mine as if the pressure might clarify a burning inner confusion.

I know what he was going to say. And I know that part of him knows the truth of it, despite the fact that the man who was hurt in the past will fight to deny it. But the near admission makes me long to be free and hold him.

I struggle in my bonds, yanking on the long chain to try and caress him as he kisses me. It's not quite lengthy enough for me to reach his body, but I bury my hands in his lush hair as our bodies twist together and the little clips on my nipples are knocked and tweak me cruelly. I don't care though. The pain is like a backwash, flowing straight to my aching sex and my clitoris. I jerk my hips against him, struggling for stimulation. My hands dig into his scalp, and I must be hurting him too, but he seems not to notice.

'You're hot ... so hot,' he growls against my lips, his hands starting to rove all over my body, testing my limits.

He pulls at the nipple clamps, making me hiss for breath.

He presses a finger into my navel in a way that compels my hips to lift and jerk.

Sitting back, sliding from my limited reach, he presses open my knees, spreading my sex lewdly before his eyes, and then lightly pinches my clitoris between his fingertips.

'Oh, God! Oh, God!' I cry out, then to my horror the most uncouth gurgles of response tumble from my lips as he manipulates me. My sex begins to flutter again, and fresh slipperiness oozes out of me, coating the inner slopes of my buttocks.

'Homage, *bella mia*, homage,' he breathes, fingers still delicately tugging. His beautiful face leans over mine, like an androgynous Satan.

I'm just on the point of coming when he lets go, and sits up straight, his eyes arch and teasing.

'Oh no, not yet. There are toys yet to be played with before we resolve this. Don't you want to try them?'

Defiance, frustration, desire and impatience on a dozen different levels well up in me. 'No! I want to come! I want you to fuck me!' I shout, wrenching at my bonds.

'In good time, all in good time,' he murmurs and,

unfazed by my outburst, he rises from the bed and glances around the room.

A silk scarf slung carelessly over the back of a chair catches his eye, and he walks over, picks it up and returns to the bed.

'It would be rather nice to silence your protests with my cock in your mouth, Annie, but somehow I think that would mean things would be over far too quickly . . . I think this will do the job very well instead though.'

With the practice of long experience, he gags me, knotting the silk scarf twice in the middle then making sure that the knot is pressing down firmly on my tongue when he ties the ends around the back of my head.

'There, that's better. Now I can go to work without petulant interruptions.'

He seems to have slipped into some sort of erotic tutor or mentor mode now. The wise experienced professor working patiently on the impetuous impatient postulant. It's true though, and the reality of it makes me sweat and squirm even harder.

Valentino shakes his head, clicks his teeth and, when he's laid out a few wicked goodies beside me on the duvet, he kicks off his boots and climbs into position on the bed, between my outstretched legs. Kneeling in front of me, he compels me to remain spread wide open.

I start to salivate profusely into my gag. His bulging crotch is directly in my eye-line and, as if displaying himself to me, he wafts his hips forwards, once, twice . . . then teasingly, like the male porn star he once was, he starts to disrobe.

Button by button, he unfastens his dragon shirt at a leisurely pace, and then shimmies out of it, twisting his broad shoulders. Off across the room it flies, and then slowly and with evidence of utter enjoyment, he runs his hands over his smooth chest and classically ripped torso.

You want this, don't you? his fingertips seem to say as they explore. *You want this perfect body to pleasure yours.*

And I do, oh God, I do!

My shackled hands itch to follow the same sensuous tracks as Valentino's do. I want to feel the heat of him, and not only with my fingertips, but with the whole of my body. I want to feel that chest, hard and warm and strangely comforting against me as he fucks me. It dawns on me suddenly that we've never done it face to face, and, right now, it's the thing I most want in the world. To be under him, while he's in me, and see the evidence of genuine emotion in his eyes as he looks down at me while we're *making love* … not just fucking.

Will it ever happen?

The realist in me tells me not to be silly and spoil the feast of sensation spread out before me. Valentino may not have quite those finer feelings for me and, even if he does, he may never be able to acknowledge them … but at least he still gives me what he can.

His long fingers strumming at his nipple, Valentino looks down at me, right into my eyes. For a moment, he's all about pleasure, display, self-indulgence … then there's a flicker somewhere deep in those copper depths and he frowns slightly, cocking his dark head on one side, making his hair shimmer.

I almost hear the words *I know*, and for an instant he looks confused, as if he's trying to understand not me, but himself. But then he smiles again and shrugs, as if accepting the reality of our situation, just as I have.

Leaning over me, he settles his hands on my hips, and then spreads his fingers on my belly. Slowly, slowly, they start to travel …

He fondles my adorned breasts, making me gasp and gobble obscenely behind my gag. He touches my armpits, the hollow of my throat and the shallow curve of my waist. He exerts a demonic pressure, with the heel of his hand, over my pubic bone, which seems to touch my clitoris somehow from the inside, and has me scrabbling with my heels and trying to lift my bottom from the bed, despite the awkwardness of my widely spread legs.

With his free hand, he slaps me hard on the inner thigh, just once, then says, very quietly, 'Be still.'

When I obey, he reaches for a thick stubby dildo, slathers a huge amount of silky lubricant over it and, before I've time to draw breath, he pushes it into me, dripping, without a pause or by your leave. It's not a huge thing, but it seems to feel enormous simply because it's inanimate. I clamp down on it with inner muscles whose sudden strength astonishes me, and in an instant I've stolen a climax right from under him.

'Wicked, wicked, wicked,' he chants but, despite my misdemeanour, he sweetens the pleasure with a firm pressure on my clitoris.

The noises I make sound more like an animal than a woman, but they seem to delight Valentino, who laughs exultantly. He pitches forwards and kisses and sucks at my neck, next to my pink slave collar, and whispers, 'Oh yes, you are such a slut, such a horny slut, aren't you?'

Yes, I am! I want to shout, but of course, I can't. Instead, I just weave my hips in deliberate licentiousness, rubbing the sore place on my thigh against his leather-clad hip.

'You're asking for trouble, you know.' His lips move slowly down my chest, and he presses open-mouthed kisses against the slopes of my breasts. 'I'm going to have to punish you.'

I twist my pelvis, pushing my crotch against him as best I can, in encouragement.

'Wicked,' he murmurs again and, when he sits up, he suddenly reaches out and plucks the clamp off one of my nipples.

I shout behind my gag, lurching up off the bed as if I've been electrocuted. The tip of my breast feels as if it's been dipped in molten lava.

'It stings, doesn't it?'

A second later I almost forget my own discomfort when Valentino attaches the clamp to his own nipple, biting down on his rosy lip, and rolling his eyes as he lets it dangle.

My hips lift again and my sex weeps, anointing the dildo. My clitoris flutters again, almost as if he's touched it.

'Tut-tut,' he chides, and then reaches amongst the little haul of toys on the bed. The high flush on his slanted cheekbones says he's not immune to the pain he's just inflicted on himself.

A moment later I'm jangling my chain as he runs a small leather slapper – complete with an inlaid pink heart on it – slowly up and down the insides of my thighs. He's taunting me with the gentle stroke, teasing me and hinting what a proper blow might feel like. I've only experienced his hand so far, and something tells me that the taste of leather is very different.

While I'm still wondering what it might feel like, I discover the truth.

I shriek, making ugly sounds beneath the knotted silk again.

For a split second it's just shock, and then it's hot white fire, a bit like the blood rushing into my squashed nipple, but somehow different and worse. I wrench at my chain, longing to clasp at the sizzling place, but, before I can complete that thought, there's another place, and another and another.

Valentino works his way up and down my thighs with strokes that a detached observer would know are really quite light and circumspect out of consideration for my inexperience. But the decidedly attached penitent, submissive, masochist or whatever just knows that the blows hurt like hell and that they're turning my skin to flame.

Punishment to the fronts and insides of my thighs like this makes me feel utterly open and vulnerable in a way a bottom spanking didn't.

I can see the crimson surge of blood beneath the surface. I can see the dildo poking out of my body. I can see – and smell – the slick silkiness of arousal gathering amongst my pubic hair, especially so when he pushes my heels up towards my buttocks a little way and then starts to work the blows in and around the inner sides of my thighs.

Pausing to survey his handiwork, he cocks his head on one side intently. It seems as if there's some pattern he's following, some standard he has to observe. He even nods to himself, as if he's pleased, and then he looks up and into my eyes. His eyes are almost black with lust, and beneath the leather of his trousers, his erection is pushing hard against his fly.

I can't read his mind, the way he seems to be able to read mine, but I can read his body, and it's telling me he's ready to take his pleasure.

He flings the slapper away and starts stroking his fingertips and his nails against my welts. I struggle and surge, wrenching against the toy restraints in a way that might snap them at any minute. They hold fast, though, even when Valentino starts to touch me in a decidedly more sensuous way. He slides forwards, lifting me, opening me wider as my legs spread across his thighs, and starts to finger my sex and the groove and in-slope of my bottom.

I start to protest and squirm as his forefinger paddles against my anus, playing there in the slipperiness of my arousal that's seeped and slithered down into my groove.

'Yes, oh yes,' he purrs, his painted eyes almost slitted like a cat's, 'I'd like to take you there ... oh yes, I'd really, really like to ...'

He pushes harder and I moan, low in my throat. Whether from fear or hyper-arousal, I really do not know. I suspect it's both and one is feeding off the other.

I've never done what he's suggesting. Never. Ever. What he wants from me is an entirely new virginity.

And I want to give it to him, but I'm very, very scared.

His fingers grow still, and he leans forwards; his hair swings softly against my face and throat as he kisses my mouth at the edge of the silk scarf.

'I want to fuck you here.' He exerts just a little extra pressure with a single fingertip. It's so light it's barely there, but it speaks volumes. 'I want it a lot ... but you have to want it too.'

He rubs his face against mine, almost the way a cat would, and the scent of his shampoo is as intoxicating as the way he's touching me.

I nod my head, and he pulls back, looking into my eyes. He doesn't speak, but his own eyes ask the question.

I nod again, and with hurried, not quite steady fingers, he reaches around behind my head, unfastens the scarf and draws it out from between my lips.

'Are you sure? Answer me. You have to want it as much as me.'

'I want it.' Denied speech so long, my voice comes out all light and breathy, but still also resolute.

'*Bella Anna*,' he whispers, kissing my face again, peppering it with small kisses this time. Quick. Hurried. Excited.

I feel him reaching for the catches on the handcuffs and, suddenly, I find myself saying, 'No! Leave them!'

He rears back a little, his eyes dancing. '*Bravissima!* You are a bold woman, *tesoro.*' Then he's kissing me again, deep and hard, his tongue in my mouth.

What have I done? What have I committed to? I'm still afraid, but I'm hungry. I want it. And I want it now. With this man I want to try anything. *Everything*.

I twist beneath him, rubbing my bare hip against him, pressing my bare bottom against his thigh. The simmering heat in my thighs flares again, but the feel of it only goads me on, making me shimmy and wriggle harder. Even when he detaches the nipple clamp and removes the dildo, it doesn't deter me. New layers of sensation only make me undulate more lewdly and groan aloud like a wanton.

Valentino laughs, his hands roaming quickly over me as he treats me to what sounds like a poem of praise in fast and husky Italian. He lifts me bodily and, as there's plenty of play in my chain, he's able to put me on my front, my face amongst the pillows. He gasps and curses as he removes his own nipple clamp and I hear it chink as he tosses it away.

Heat surges through me and I feel rude and frisky, so I come up on my knees and elbows, presenting my bottom to him like a mare in season. He crows with delight and handles my buttocks vigorously. A moment later, he's tipping lubricant into the cleft of my bottom, more and more, more and more, until I'm swimming.

Unable to resist, I turn round and look over my shoulder at him as he unzips.

It dawns on me now that this is the first time I've actually seen his cock fully erect in the flesh. I've felt it, but not *seen* it this hard, other than in that porn film I watched in Suite Seventeen.

And it's magnificent. Big and thick and rosy and veined. Smoothly circumcised, with a fat tempting glans.

And he's going to put that thing inside my bottom?

Fear wells up again, but gets short-circuited somehow into overpowering lust. I flirt my hips at him again. Inviting . . . no, demanding.

He calls me something that just might be 'dirty little bitch' very affectionately in his native tongue, then reaches for a condom from amongst the cache of sex toys. For a moment, I wish I was unshackled, so I could help him roll it on, but he performs the task far quicker and more efficiently than I ever could, so I just promise myself I'd do it for him some other time.

And now it's time. The moment of truth. We're right on the point of my new deflowering.

I bow my head, feeling deeply submissive, almost sacrificial, as he moves in behind me, positioning the head of his cock carefully between my bottom cheeks.

My heart thuds and I moan involuntarily.

'I'll stop if you want to,' he says, his voice so tight with arousal that I know it'll cost him if he has to. I feel a great weakening and melting inside that has nothing to do with sex, and I grasp the bed rail and push back against him encouragingly.

'You don't have to, Valentino, you don't have to.'

'*Amore mio.*'

And then he's pressing, pressing, pressing and it's like nothing I've ever felt before, so strange and confusing that I've no idea whether I'm aroused or horrified. I only know I'm being laid open in a way that's entirely new.

Dark messages surge along unexplored nerve pathways, and I start to shudder wildly and sweat breaks out in my armpits, my groin and at the nape of my neck. I bite the pillow, stifling my moans of automatic protest against the infernal sensations.

Valentino pauses, one hand on my hip, the other curving round to cup my crotch gently. He asks me a question – in Italian – and, even though I don't get the words, I comprehend the meaning.

'No, go on! Go on!' I urge him, working myself backwards again, ignoring the perverse and dangerous signals, and welcoming the bloom of a very new and peculiar form of pleasure. One that Valentino enhances by gently stroking my clitoris.

And he moves. Slowly at first, then faster, and all the time coaxing, crooning, praising, cursing, exhorting, talking at me in Italian, the beautiful crazy words flowing into one incredible poem of distorted communication.

Not that I'm quiet either. I too yell, moan and make noises I've never heard come out of my throat, while sensations I've never felt in my body before beat and crash like a riptide in spring.

At last, of course, it's all too much, and pleasure blooms like a mushroom cloud and I can't tell if I'm feeling it in my sex, my arse, in the tips of my toes and fingers . . . or whether it's happening in another dimension to another version of me.

I start to black out. Shadows rush in from the four corners of my consciousness, and the last thing I feel is a slow deep, sweet pulsation inside of me as Valentino comes too, and I think I hear the faint words, '*Ti amo.*'

My first thought as I come to is that I've never actually passed out from pleasure before, but I suppose there's a first time for everything.

Stirring, I realise several things at once. I'm

unchained. I'm wrapped haphazardly in the duvet. And Valentino isn't in or on the bed with me, but I can hear him talking softly somewhere in the room. In Italian again.

His voice is so gentle and tender and playful that a huge bitter rush of savage jealousy washes through me.

How dare he talk to another girlfriend on his phone, here in my bedroom, after the cataclysmic thing that's just happened between *us*?

But, as I heave my thunderstruck exhausted body up off the bed and the pillows a bit, and glance across to the doorway, a smile of pure sappy happiness curves my lips.

Valentino is all zipped up and wearing his shirt again, and he's hunkered his tall frame right down so that he can have a conversation with my cat.

Boy is purring like a well-tuned motorboat and rubbing his head blissfully against any bit of Valentino he can reach. Valentino in turn is stroking Boy and chuntering on to him in the way only a devoted cat lover would do.

Amazingly, Boy now seems to speak Italian – something I wasn't previously aware of.

'Your cat is a very splendid fellow indeed,' says Valentino, turning to me. 'We seem to have struck up a friendship.'

Am I imagining things, or does he sound just a little wary? He smiles, and for him it looks almost sheepish. My heart lurches a little. Too much, too soon, that's it.

I try to keep calm. OK, I love him, that's a given, but I can't expect it to be reciprocal, even if he might have said so, albeit in a language I don't understand, in the heat of the moment.

Valentino is a sexually omnivorous deviant and dominant, and a ladies' man of long standing. He obviously doesn't want to get involved too deeply, and almost overnight, with an older woman who might turn out to be clingy.

I *want* to cling, but I need to be circumspect. If I'm to have any of him, and any kind of future with him, it needs to be on his terms ... at least for the moment.

'You're very honoured,' I say lightly, and I'm charmed, despite my emotional turmoil by the sweet sight of my cat and a man who might be mine if only in an unconventional sense. 'He's usually very picky about who he makes up to, and he's not fond of strangers ... but he does seem to have made an exception for you.'

Boy accepts a last stroke, and then does his tail flick thing that means he's off again for the moment. We both watch him sashay away in the direction of the stairs.

Valentino stands where he is. He's definitely not quite his normal super-confident self, although he gives me a quirky little smile.

'Could you open a window?' I ask, for something to say. Actually it does smell very strongly of sex in here, and suddenly I'd love some fresh air to clear my head.

'Of course.'

He draws back the curtains a little, pausing, then quietly opens the window. He frowns again as he stares out, and down, and then a look of almost wistful envy passes across his cool sculpted face, and is gone again almost as soon as it appeared.

'I have to go now,' he says, returning to the bed and looking down on me. He gives me a smile, quite a tender one, and then leans to kiss me on the cheek.

It's a fight not to wind my arms around his neck and pull him down on to the bed. It's a fight not to tell him – beg him – never to leave and just stay here in this room with me forever.

But I know I mustn't, so I don't. I just accept the

touch of his velvety lips against my skin. I daren't say anything for fear of saying something stupid that'll screw things up for good.

'I have a busy day tomorrow, but come to the hotel tomorrow night. For dinner, perhaps? We need to discuss certain issues, don't we?'

'Yes, I think we do,' I intone, and he must catch the note of tension in my voice.

'Don't worry, *tesoro*,' he says softly, kissing me again, 'we'll work something out . . . for the hotel and for us.'

My heart leaps. At least there is an 'us'!

'OK, yes. What time is good?' I ask, amazing myself with my calm easy-sounding reply when really I feel more like rolling around on the bed, kicking my heels and shouting 'Yes!' over what really is the tiniest flame of hope.

'Around eight? In the bar?'

'And will you be the one in the dress? I've only ever seen "Valentina" in the bar, not Valentino or Signor Guidetti.'

He laughs, tossing his head slightly and making his beautiful hair sway. 'Probably not. I'll just be me, Annie, just me.'

'That's enough.'

He tucks the duvet around my neck as if I'm a child with a chill and he's my nurse, and then, after stroking my hair away from my face, he strides to the door, murmurs, '*Ciao*,' and he's gone.

I guess that he'll latch the door after him, so I could, theoretically, just lie here and doze off . . . if I could.

But I can't do either and, as soon as I hear the door close downstairs, I'm capering through the house to the front bedroom, dragging the duvet along with me, just so I can watch him leave.

He's just sliding into the Ferrari as I reach the window and, a second later, there's a burst of noise as he starts it up. He keeps it to a minimum, though – no boy-racer revving. He just backs out neatly into the close, and then straightens up, and he's away.

Just like that.

I feel empty. Lost.

I wander back to my bedroom, and look out of the window at whatever Valentino looked at.

My neighbours are out in their garden again, but not, this time, up to anything strange or kinky, or in any way naughty or sexy.

Maria and Robert are just lounging in a couple of garden chairs, eating slices of pizza, straight from the box, and washing them down with bottled beer.

It's strange. I've seen them fucking, playing spanking games, doing all manner of things pervy and transgressive down there in that garden, but somehow this quiet al fresco meal is the most intimate exchange so far.

They don't even speak much, just the odd comment, the occasional soft laugh and smile. They don't need to speak. They're completely in tune with each other.

'Oh, Valentino,' I whisper as I pad back to bed and throw myself on it, still tangled up in my crumpled duvet, and wishing he and I could share such perfect communion.

14 **In The Dark**

It's been a long day. I've spent most of it fighting not to ring Valentino, just so that I can listen to his voice.

Oh dear, I've got it bad.

I fluff my hair, check my face and wonder whether to paint another slick of lip stain on top of the first. Using the same pen that he did last night.

I feel a slow twist of desire, low in my groin. Instead of my own face, I see his. Chiselled, male, dominant ... and painted.

Oh, God, I can't wait any more! I grab my bag and clatter down the stairs, pausing only to dive into the kitchen to make sure Boy has something to eat, before I'm out of the door, slamming it shut, and racing for my car.

It's lucky that there aren't any speed cameras on the way to the Waverley, because I drive far faster than I usually do, which is foolhardy for someone who isn't particularly accomplished behind the wheel.

As I'm leaving town, my phone rings.

Shall I be even more foolhardy and answer it while I'm driving? I'm in a stream of fast-moving traffic. I suppose I could pull over, but it's almost as if I'm being drawn inexorably by a powerful magnet towards the hotel, and I can't withstand the pull of it enough to slow down. I put my foot down, mentally crossing my fingers and hoping – and praying – that it's not Valentino, cancelling our dinner.

I don't want to think about what we might discuss over the meal. It'll be issues, and I don't want to deal with issues. I just want to love him. And yet the experience of my years tells me these things have to be faced so we can move on.

My phone rings again but, even when I reach the Waverley, I don't stop to check it. I stride straight into the lobby, my heart surging at the thought that he might be there, waiting for me. Glad to see me.

I don't even stop to worry what I look like, despite the fact that I've taken great care in choosing my clothes. In black trousers, silky top in rich magenta and cool mannish jacket, I look good. Not too young, but not an old fuddy-duddy either. Just elegant, grown-up and a little bit sexy.

My assertive entrance causes a few heads to turn in the lobby. It's the cocktail hour and people are drifting between the Lawns Bar and the restaurant, most of them, I guess, completely oblivious to the Waverley's secret sexual underbelly. Although there's one woman in a leather dress and fuck-me heels who I suspect might be in the know.

'Good evening, Mrs Conroy. How are you? We've been trying to get in touch with you,' is Saskia the Assistant Manager's greeting. 'I'm afraid Signor Guidetti won't be able to dine with you tonight after all. He's been trying to let you know. He's indisposed, but he would like to invite you to dinner tomorrow instead . . . or perhaps lunch? Whichever suits you?'

Right now, I couldn't eat anyway. My head whirls, I can't think straight. I'm torn between desperate worry for him and a horrid, horrid suspicion that I hate myself for. I love him. I should believe him. But I'm a woman . . . and he's a man. And sometimes they're sneaky, even when they really do care.

'Indisposed? What does that mean?' I'm aware that I'm being abrupt, but I can't help it.

'It means he's got a migraine and he's making a major drama out of it,' a familiar voice says from behind me. 'Instead of taking an Imigran and just getting on with life the way a woman would.'

I spin to find Maria, dressed in her receptionist suit, presumably coming to take over from Saskia. 'Robert's just the same,' she says cheerfully as she slides behind the counter. 'One twinge and it's a brain tumour – you know how men are.'

I have to smile. She's so right. Even a sex god is governed by the foibles of his gender.

'Perhaps you'd like to slip up to his apartment and look in on him?' suggests Saskia with a slight smile, as if she too feels her boss might be making a meal out of something a woman would simply deal with. 'I'm sure he'd appreciate seeing you, if only for a few moments.'

'Yes, go up and see him, Annie love,' encourages Maria, her eyes twinkling. 'I'm sure he'll make a miracle recovery as soon as he sees you. You look gorgeous tonight.'

'Er ... thanks. I think I will go up. Could you tell me where to go?'

A few minutes later, I'm pushing open a door marked 'Private' on the third floor and letting myself into the manager's flat.

The lamp-lit sitting room isn't the haven of perversity that I was half expecting. In fact, it's unexpectedly snug and chintzy like Suite Seventeen, only with a much more lived-in and slightly shabby feel to it. Obviously the staff quarters are furnished with bits and pieces that are no longer smart enough for the public rooms.

Only the same eclectic mix of magazines on the coffee table reveals its occupant's preferences.

Skin Two. Bizarre. Marquis. Along with a couple of industry publications, *Private Eye* and, on a mundane note, the latest *Radio Times*.

No sign of the flat's occupant, so I call out, 'Valentino? Are you there?' very softly. If his migraine is one of the absolute stinkers I get now and again, the last thing he'll want is somebody shouting at the top of their voice anywhere near him.

I'm answered by the sound of a muffled groan. It comes from the doorway to a darkened room beyond, so I follow it and squeeze through the small gap. A sudden shaft of light won't be very welcome either.

'Valentino?' I whisper, heeling off my shoes and padding towards the shadowed bed, and the generally man-sized hump beneath the quilt. The huddled figure has the covers over his head, but his long black hair is visible draped across the pillow. 'Are you all right?'

Silly question. He obviously isn't.

'*Me dispiace, bella Anna.* I tried to call you. I have *una emicrania* ... a migraine. *Me dispiace.*'

Poor baby, his voice is thin and reedy and he does sound genuinely poorly. I sink to my knees and, peering through the gloom, I locate one long hand protruding from the quilt and reach for it. His fingers lace with mine almost desperately, as if the grip were a lifeline.

'You poor thing,' I breathe, experiencing the most agonising yearning to lurch forwards and enfold him in my arms so I can draw the pain out of him by osmosis. 'I get them sometimes and they're a nightmare. Have you taken anything? Is there something I can get you? A glass of water? A cup of tea?'

Oh so British – the panacea for all ills, a cup of tea. But the Italians probably have their own preferred remedies.

'Tea? Oh *dio*, yes! I'd kill for a cup of tea ... and another pill.'

'OK, I'll make some for us.'

I try to rise, but Valentino doesn't seem to want to let go of my hand, and his fingers tighten.

'But you'll have to let me go.'

He mutters something that my pounding heart seems to interpret as 'never', but despite that his fingers reluctantly unfurl.

I rise, but, as I do so, part of his head emerges from under the covers, and I see his eyes. They're dull and dark with pain, yet still, bizarrely happy. 'Thank you for coming, *tesoro*. I left a message, telling you not to come, because I couldn't bear you to see me so pathetic.' A little more of his peaked but still glorious face comes into view, revealing a wan smile. 'But all the time I was really praying that you *would* come. It was all that I wanted. All I've been thinking about since the headache started.'

'Oh, don't say *I* gave you the headache,' I say lightly, trying to cover the way I'm being buffeted by the most astonishing whirl of emotion. I've got to stay practical and calm, and care for my patient.

'No, not you . . . never you. Just my own foolishness.' It seems as if he's going to say more, but then he gives a little groan and retreats. 'I'd love that tea now.'

I smile to myself. Men, they're all the same – well, at times like these. They're all drama queens when they think that they're poorly. And, if anyone knows how to play the big production, it's Valentino more than most.

Valentino's tiny kitchen yields up not exotic continental tisanes but that old stand-by Twining's English Breakfast. I make a pot and stick it on a tray with mugs and milk and sugar.

The Italian patient has crawled out from under the covers again on my return, although he still has his face buried in the pillow. I do my Florence Nightingale act for a few minutes, fussing over milk and sugar, and helping him sit up to drink water and take more pills. He does seem genuinely fragile, but manages to remain upright, leaning amongst his pillows to sip his tea.

A strangely comfortable silence settles over us. I pull up a chair, drink my tea and just observe my bedraggled hero as best I can in the low shadowy light.

Valentino is a mess, but infuriatingly sexy all the same. I know that in his place I'd look an absolute crone, but he manages to make lank tousled hair, a drawn face and pasty lips seem exotic and dissolute. His chest is bare, and for all I know the rest of him is too, and there's a slightly wolfish smell of perspiration emanating from his clammy-looking skin. I decide that it's far more perverse of me to fancy him while he looks so god awful and frankly ill than it is to want to play any kind of bondage games. I should be ashamed of myself, but I desperately want to fuck him.

'There's so much I wanted to say to you.' His voice is flat and tired and, as he sets his cup aside, the effort of moving seems to cost him. I'm sure *some* of this is over acting, but most of it's genuine. 'But my brain is refusing to work.' He covers his eyes with his hand, but his mouth quirks as if there's some life in him. 'And even my body is letting me down for once. Having you in this close a proximity to a bed should render me insatiably rampant, but, alas, nothing doing.'

He uncovers his eyes and gives me a forlorn smile. 'I'm sorry, *tesoro*. After last night, I was hungry to drown us in pleasure all over again.'

I reach and touch his hand, which is hot as if he's running a temperature. 'Don't worry, we can drown tomorrow, when you're feeling better. You can chain me up and do unspeakable things to me to your heart's content.'

His hand remains inert under mine, as if any kind of response is too much of an effort.

'But for now you need to rest. I'll phone you in the morning and see how you are.'

I make as if to rise, but suddenly it's as if he's galvanised into action, and he laces his fingers tightly with mine. 'Stay! Please stay! I know I'm no good to you right now, but I need your company, Annie, I really do.' Then, as if the exertion was too great, he collapses amongst the pillows, then turns on his side and curls up foetally, still holding on to my hand, tighter than ever.

It pains me to see him laid so low, but, even so, my spirits sing. Of course I'll stay, but there's something I must do first.

'It's all right, Valentino, I'll stay. Just let me have my fingers back for a minute, eh?'

He releases me, and I pad into the other room and make a quick phone call down to Reception, telling Maria where to find my spare key, my alarm code and the location of the cat food so she can feed Boy if I don't return home before morning.

'I knew he'd make a miracle recovery when he saw you,' she says smugly.

'Well, it's something like that.'

After a quick trip to the bathroom, I return to the bedroom and find Valentino huddled under the covers again. He's breathing deeply and evenly, and, astonishingly, despite his pain, he seems to be sleeping.

'Great!' I mutter, and then I slip off my jacket, trousers and top.

Only one thing to do. Gingerly, I lift the quilt at the other side of the queen-sized bed, and slide beneath it. As I expected, Valentino is naked and his body does feel feverish. He's facing away from me, so I just curl up against his back the best I can, hoping that, somewhere in the depths of his migraine-addled dreams, the presence of another human body beside him is comforting.

245

And as for my own dream?

I guard it in my heart like a little golden flame, and turn it over and over again as I fall asleep.

My dream seems to be about Dracula, only the seductive count has Valentino's face, and I can actually see him in the mirror as he stands behind me. But, as his hands come around my body to caress my breasts and his uncharacteristically warm mouth settles on my neck, I wake up.

I don't know how long we've been in bed, but somewhere along the line, we've both turned over and now Valentino has me cradled spoon-style against him. Just as Drac was doing, he's kissing my neck and fondling my breasts though my bra, but the phenomenal erection that's prodding my bottom is very much from the land of the hot-blooded living.

When I open my eyes, I discover light in the room. It's muted and smoky somehow, but the fact that it's there at all is significant.

'Is your head feeling better now?' I back up my question with a little wriggle that indicates I'm well aware of his improved condition in other areas.

'Much better now, thanks to you.' He mouths my neck hungrily and, as I feel the touch of his tongue, he pushes my bra aside and begins to play with a nipple. After a bit of shimmying around, he shifts our position slightly and slides his other hand into my knickers and searches through my pubic hair to find my clitoris.

Oh bliss! This is my reward for my kindly nursemaid act. I sigh and wriggle again as he fondles me, strumming my nipple gently and touching my sex with a slow comfortable yet infinitely delicious precision. No pleasure-pain games now, just glorious mind-melting sensations and a sweet generosity of touch. I hook my feet around his ankles and arch like a bow, as a soft glimmering climax gently blooms. I clasp my hands over his as I hit the peak.

'There, are *you* feeling better now?' he purrs as I come back down to earth.

'Considerably, but I think there's still a small matter to deal with before we have a conversation.'

'Small?' His voice is full of mock outrage as he grinds his erection into the groove between my buttocks, the rolling pressure exciting me all over again. I'm not quite sure if I want to go down that route right now, but I probably won't take much persuading.

'Well, a *big* one then ... I was only speaking figuratively.'

Valentino chuckles, gives my erogenous zones one last affectionate squeeze, and then rolls away from me, presumably for one of the condoms he keeps stashed in his bedroom drawer.

I roll too, squirming out of my bra, knickers and my trouser socks as I go.

The lamp is draped in a dark silky scarf, which explains the subdued lighting. But even with its glow tamped down, I can see that Valentino appears 100 per cent better. His handsome face has lost that pinched look, and his skin shines again with the soft honeyed glow of relaxed health. It's disgustingly easy how a young fit man recovers.

'Let me,' I insist as he turns back to me, foil packet in hand.

Valentino throws back the quilt to give me room, and I find my fingers shaking in anticipation as I roll the rubber down over his marvellous cock. He's beautiful, sumptuous, utter temptation – and for a moment I toy with the idea of scooting down the bed and taking him in my mouth. But my sex flutters and clenches imperiously, demanding attention.

Mindful of my lover's preferences, I roll over, ready to offer him access from the rear.

'No, *amore mio*, not this time.' His hand on my shoulder is unequivocal, and strong. He puts me on my back and looms over me, his eyes huge and dark in the soft light. 'Face to face now, Annie. I want to see your eyes and your beautiful face as you climax.'

Emotion surges through me like a sea fret driven by a great and significant change. I sense we're at the beginning of a very special journey and, maddeningly, my eyes fill with tears at the importance of it.

Valentino says nothing, but his own eyes gleam revealingly, and he gently blots away the moisture with his fingertips.

And then he begins to kiss me as he moves between my thighs.

He pushes in firmly, adjusting with his hips as he goes, and my body yields as if accepting an old friend. Odd how sweet and familiar this moment is, despite the fact that we've only ever fucked three times before, and one of them was last night, and perversely different. The action is slow and easy, and he rocks his pelvis with a fluid undulating swing. I imagine us dancing, which is an odd fantasy to indulge at a moment like this, yet strangely it seems full of erotic power. Valentino moves with such grace that he must be a demon on the dance floor.

Arching his spine, Valentino pulls back from our kiss and looks down into my eyes just as he said he would. His black hair swings around our faces, and in the dark metallic depths of his gaze there seems to process a series of questions and also their answers.

He and I are different, in so many ways, but we have the power to resolve every issue that stands between us. Knowledge passes through us, and as one we smile, then kiss again.

But stately leisurely fucking can't last forever, much as part of me would love it to. Seductive friction soon begins to up the ante.

Valentino fucks like a fury, his cock pounding me and impacting on a million singing nerve-ends. I feel orgasm speeding towards me like a fireball, and determined to snare it for me he reaches between our bodies and strokes my clitoris to bring me home.

I shout something. I think it's 'I love you', but I can't be certain of the exact words. His hips moving like a jackhammer, Valentino cries out too, and I've a suspicion he's said more or less the same. I don't speak Italian, but who needs to when the heart translates the meaning.

'I won't take no for an answer over the money, you know.' Our hands are laced as we lie beside one another in the soft light, and I squeeze Valentino's fingers in an effort to press my point. 'I'm not going to let this hotel turn into part of a bland characterless chain just because you've got issues about feeling obligated to older women.'

Valentino laughs. But it's a relaxed laugh, indulgent and admiring, and I'm not worried. '*Brava, bella ragazza!*' he murmurs, his eyes gleaming at me as I turn to him. 'I didn't expect you to. And I've decided to stop being a total fool anyway. If you want to invest in the Waverley, you are welcome to with all my heart, believe me.'

He draws my hand to his lips and kisses it, at first in tribute, and then slightly more salaciously, turning it over to press his tongue against my palm.

'You've changed your tune, Signor Guidetti.'

'It's time to let go of the past and embrace the future, Annie.' Exerting gentle pressure, he pulls me to him again, and kisses my lips instead of my hand. 'And anyway, with what I'll get for the Ferrari, we'll both have a considerable stake in the hotel's future.'

'You're selling your beautiful car?'

'Yes. It's part of the past, but I can see it simply as an asset now. I've discovered things far more precious that I want to hang on to.' He smiles slowly, mischief dancing in his eyes and around his mouth. 'And I don't just mean the bricks and mortar of this place either.'

I wrap my arms around him, grabbing him, holding him, needing to know that his warm body is real and I'm not just in the middle of some middle-aged woman's fantasy.

'Don't shake, *tesoro*,' he whispers in my ear, his hands smoothing up and down my back and my buttocks. 'I know this seems strange, and fast, and unexpected, but, believe me, it's real. It's real.' He kisses me again. Little ones. Soft ones. Deeper ones. On my lips. My neck. My jaw. My brow. All the time murmuring words in Italian, words even I can't mistake.

Eventually, I calm down, and I stop shaking. I feel something inside me rise and I know it's the belief I always knew was there all along.

I am a queen. I am a goddess. I am in charge ... and I am loved.

I can say anything now.

'It's not just an ordinary Ferrari, is it?'

'No indeed, it's a very special one,' he replies, sounding momentarily wistful, 'It's a classic GTO from the Sixties. There were only around forty ever made and I've just had it valued.' He whispers a figure in my ears that astounds me.

'Bloody hell!'

'And yes, you're going to ask how a provincial hotel manager who lives in a tiny flat on the premises comes to own and run such a collectable car.'

'Your other older woman?'

He sounds calm now, at ease, as if his past is no longer a source of unease. 'It was Sofia's parting gift to me; she's even been funding the insurance for it from her Swiss account.' His hand moves gently on my back again, as if stressing my reality. 'It's her pay-off, I suppose. I shouldn't have taken it, but I was young, and I'm Italian . . . and it's a Ferrari. I was weak.'

'In your place, I think I would have been weak too.'

His arm tightens around me again and, in a strangely asexual gesture, he rests his hand against my sex.

'You could never be weak, Annie. You are strong and brave and magnificent.'

Part of me accepts that I just might be that, but there's still a tiny bit of the old me that attempts to raise doubts. 'Oh, come on, Valentino. I'm just –'

His mouth crushes mine hard, and his tongue subdues the doubts in a way that leaves me breathless. 'All it needs is for you to accept what you are, my love . . . a goddess.'

I laugh because it's so much like my mantra.

Valentino laughs too, in between more devouring kisses.

'And let's have no more nonsense about older women, shall we?' he says archly, folding his fingers around my breast and beginning to strum my nipple in a way that makes me feel as young as spring itself. 'Either from me or you.'

I whisper my years into his ear, revealing the birthday I'll be scoring in a month or two.

'*Dio*, woman, there isn't all that much between us anyway! What're twelve insignificant years?' His hand slides silkily from my breast, to my crotch again, and then around my hip to my bottom, 'You're plenty young enough to be spanked for being a naughty, wilful girl, you know.' He squeezes the rounded cheek, testing its firmness ... which is pretty good, and would be even if I were a sweet young thing.

My body clenches in longing, and – wilfully – I grab at his hardening cock. I know I'm being naughty, but we've had our tender almost sacramental lovemaking session, and now it's time to explore the flipside of our relationship and the wicked pleasures that I'm rapidly becoming addicted to.

'Uh oh,' he warns, but I fondle him anyway. 'If you don't stop that, Signora Conroy, I will be forced to put you across my knee, redden your bottom, and then torture you with pleasure until you scream.'

'I'll take my chances, *Signor* Guidetti.' Flinging off the covers, I scoot around until I'm kneeling against him, looking down at the astonishing erection I still have between my fingers. 'But there's something I've just got to get out of the way first.'

Inclining over his groin, I part my lips and slide them over him.

Epilogue

I stare up at the ceiling, and for a moment I can't remember where I am.

Then I see the ornate mouldings and the mini chandelier and it comes back to me. I'm in Suite Seventeen at the Waverley Grange Hotel.

My hotel.

Well, at least partly my hotel. Between us, my lover and I are the majority shareholders, but there are others with stakes – larger or smaller – in its future.

Tonight is the night of the party when we celebrate that future. And not only that, it's my birthday into the bargain. Which is what the little shadow-play we just went through is all about.

A scenario. A performance. My treat.

A chance to get my mind blown before the shared festivities start.

But, for the moment, I don't think I've the energy for dancing and carousing, not even with all the high-spirited, oversexed and frankly pervy friends I've made in the last couple of months.

Right now, I just need to recover – and enjoy the various delicious glows in my mind and body.

A large warm hand settles on my breast and cups it possessively. A long thumb slowly flicks at my nipple and, amazingly, tingles of sensation begin to flare again between my thighs. I've come ... and come and come ... but there still seems to be plenty more life in me. Something he knows well, familiar as he's become with my every last response.

'You're a greedy, sinful man, Signor Guidetti. Stop fiddling with my tit or we'll never get to the party.'

'It's not time yet,' he murmurs, his voice like velvet and loaded with sexual wickedness.

When I turn to him, the likelihood of getting downstairs to greet the guests any time soon recedes significantly. How could any woman with red blood in her veins resist a delicious sight like that?

Valentino is lounging on the bed beside me, his clothing in at least as much disarray as mine. My bra and blouse are twisted all over the place and not covering anything, and although I'm still wearing my hold-up stockings, one's at half-mast and the other's around my ankle. Valentino does at least still have his leather jeans on, but they're unzipped and his glorious cock is hanging rudely out of his fly.

Semi-erect again already, I notice.

'Still, we ought to be there to do the meet and greet,' I protest without any real conviction.

The way he's tweaking my nipple is making it very necessary for me to writhe against the mattress now. I can't stop shifting my hips to and fro, and he knows that. He also knows that the way I'm moving is stirring the residual heat in my freshly spanked bottom. As he continues to play with my breast, I bring my knees up, lifting my haunches off the bed so I can stroke the simmering fires of my punishment and reignite the hot sensations between my legs.

'*You're* a wicked woman, *tesoro*. Stop that! I haven't given you permission.'

'I don't need it. *I* choose now ... and I'm taking what I want.'

Sometime in the last few moments, we reached a tipping point. I don't have to do what he says any more. The balance of our deliciously mutable relationship has tilted again, and I can do what I want now, with myself – and with him.

And I choose to wiggle and jiggle against the duvet, rubbing my reddened bottom against the crisp cotton while I slip my fingers between my legs and play with myself.

Valentino growls something I have no doubt is perfectly blasphemous and obscene in Italian, and, when I turn my head for a better view of him, I find that he's got his cock in his free hand and he's pumping it vigorously.

'Did I say you could do that?'

His hand stills and he grins at me. His teeth gleam whitely in the soft lighting, that one imperfection in his otherwise perfect appearance – his slightly crooked front tooth – as ever strangely endearing. Then he gives me a mischievous wink, and a ridiculously feigned naughty puppy-dog look, and starts to stroke himself all over again.

'Fuck you, Valentino,' I reprimand him cheerfully.

'I wish you would.' He jerks his narrow hips at me, making his fabulous cock dance in his fingers.

It's too much. *He's* too much. I almost fly up off the mattress to position myself over him, my glowingly pink thighs tense as they hold me aloft, just inches from the tip of his cock. I slide down, rubbing my pubic hair against his shaft, wickedly tickling him.

He curses again, but he's laughing at the same time. I continue to tantalise and tease him, all the time enjoying the view.

I still can't believe that I've managed to snag myself such a marvel. A tall, dark and handsome Latin stud. Sex on two legs. A wickedly imaginative and depravedly kinky younger man.

Not that he really seems that way any more. I feel

younger than springtime. He's finally grown up and shaken off the shadows of his past. And we've met somewhere in the middle as perfect equals.

I press closer, parting my bush with my fingers, pressing myself intimately against the long hot column of his cock. Valentino murmurs something else outrageously filthy in Italian, with great affection, and then reaches around to grab my sore bottom cheeks so he can increase the pressure.

I call him something rather filthy in English in return.

'Enough of this nonsense,' he replies. Somewhat imperiously, I think, given that I'm the one who's supposed to be in charge now. 'Let's fuck again, *Signora* Conroy. Get me a condom.'

I narrow my eyes at him, but somehow it turns into a big beaming smile and I blow him a kiss as I reach across to the bedside drawer and tug it open. Fishing around inside, I find something unexpected sitting on top of the protection.

It's a small square velvet-covered jewellery box.

Valentino's hands tighten on my buttocks as I bring it out, but I don't notice the soreness. When I flip open the top of the little box, there's a ring inside.

My heart flutters. I feel scared as hell, and, for a moment, I want to leap up and run to some still quiet place where I can think.

But a second later, I'm not looking at the ring, but into a pair of still, strong copper-coloured eyes, filled with such emotion that my last doubts evaporate.

I take out Valentino's birthday gift, which just might be something else too, and admire it happily. It's antique, pretty and not big or flash, but exactly what I'd have chosen for myself. And, as I stare at it, longer and stronger fingers than mine take it from me and hold it against a significant fingertip.

He cocks his head enquiringly on one side, and for a moment there's total vulnerability in his eyes.

I nod, his eyes flare, and he slides it into place.

This is the craziest thing I've ever done in my life. Even crazier than fucking a perfect stranger on the first night I ever set eyes on him. And even crazier than spending all the money that would have kept me comfy in my old age on a wildly unorthodox country hotel. But I've never been surer of any choice than I am at this moment.

'Happy Birthday, Signora Conroy,' Valentino says quietly, a few moments later, when I've enrobed him in latex and I'm sliding down upon his cock, 'and thank you.'

'Thank you too, Signor Guidetti,' I answer, and it's not just for the ring or his adorable flesh inside me ... but for everything.

Will we ever get out of Suite Seventeen in time to attend our own party? I wonder as we begin to rock together and touch and kiss each other.

But do you know, as I start to come, I just don't care!

Read on for an extract from

THE ACCIDENTAL
CALL GIRL

The first book in the delicious 'Accidental' trilogy,

Also by Portia Da Costa

BLACK
LACE

THE ACCIDENTAL CALL GIRL

by Portia Da Costa

It's the ultimate fantasy:
When Lizzie meets an attractive older man in the bar of a luxury hotel, he mistakes her for a high class call girl on the look-out for a wealthy client.

With a man she can't resist...
Lizzie finds herself following him to his hotel room for an unforgettable night where she learns the pleasures of submitting to the hands of a master. But what will happen when John discovers that Lizzie is far more than she seems...?

A sexy, thrilling erotic romance for every woman who has ever had a *Pretty Woman* fantasy. Part One of the 'Accidental' Trilogy.

1

Meeting Mr Smith

He looked like a god, the man sitting at the end of the bar did. Really. The glow from the down-lighter just above him made his blond hair look like a halo, and it was the most breath-taking effect. Lizzie just couldn't stop staring.

Oops, oh no, he suddenly looked her way. Unable to face his sharp eyes, she focused on her glass. It contained tonic, a bit dull really, but safe. She'd done some mad things in her time, both under the influence and sober, and she was alone now, and squarely in the 'mad things' zone. She'd felt like a fish out of water at the birthday party she was supposed to be at in the Waverley Grange Hotel's function room with her house-mates Brent and Shelley and a few other friends. It was for a vaguely posh girl who she didn't really know that well; someone in her year at uni, who she couldn't actually remember being all that pally with at the time. Surrounded by women who seemed to be looking at her and wondering why she was there, and men giving her the eye with a view to chatting her up, Lizzie had snuck out of the party and wandered into the bar, drawn by its strangely unsettling yet latent with 'something' atmosphere.

To look again or not to look again, that was the question. She wanted to. The man was so very hot, although not her usual type. Whatever *that* was. Slowly, slowly, she turned her head a few centimetres, straining her eyes in order to see the god, or angel guy, out of their corners.

Fuck! Damn! He wasn't looking now. He was chatting to the barman, favouring him with a killer smile, almost as if he fancied *him*, not any of the women at the bar. Was he gay? It didn't really matter, though, did it? She was only supposed to be enjoying the view, after all, and he really was a sight for sore eyes.

With his attention momentarily distracted, she grabbed a feast of him.

Not young, definitely. Possibly forty, maybe a bit more? Dark gold-blond, curling hair, thick and a bit longer than one would have expected for his age, but not straggling. Gorgeous face, even though his features, in analysis, could almost have been called average. Put together, however, there was something extra, something indefinable about him that induced a 'wow'. Perhaps it was his eyes? They were very bright, and very piercing. Yes, it *was* the eyes, probably. Even from a distance, Lizzie could tell they were a clear, beautiful, almost jewel-like blue.

Or maybe it was his mouth too? His lips were mobile, and they had a plush, almost sumptuous look to them that could have looked ambiguous on a man, but somehow not on him. The smile he gave the lucky barman was almost sunny, and when he suddenly snagged his lower lip between his teeth, something went 'Oof!' in Lizzie's mid-section. And lower down too.

What's his body like?

Hard to tell, with the curve of the bar, and other people

sitting between them, but if his general demeanour and the elegant shape of his hand as he lifted his glass to his lips were anything to go by, he was lean and fit. But, that could be wishful thinking, she admitted. He might actually be some podgy middle-aged guy who just happened to have a fallen angel's face and a very well-cut suit.

Just enjoy the bits you can see, you fool. That's all you'll ever get to look at. You're not here on the pull.

With that, as if he'd heard her thoughts, Fallen Angel snapped his head around and looked directly at her. No pretence, no hesitation, he stared her down, his eyes frank and intent, his velvet lips curved in a tricky, subtle quirk of a smile. As if showcasing himself, he shifted slightly on his stool, and she was able to see a little more of him.

She'd been exactly right. He *was* lean and fit, and the sleek way his clothes hung on him clearly suggested how he might look when those clothes were flung haphazardly on the floor.

The temptation to look away was like a living force, as if she were staring at the sun and its brilliance was a fatal peril. But Lizzie resisted the craven urge, and held his gaze. She didn't yield a smile. She just tried to eyeball him as challengingly as he was doing her, and her reward was more of that sun on the lips and in the eyes, and a little nod of acknowledgement.

'For you, miss.'

The voice from just inches away nearly made her fall off her stool. She actually teetered a bit, cursing inside as she dragged her attention from the blue-eyed devil-angel at the end of the bar to the rather toothsome young barman standing right in front of her.

'Er . . . yes, thanks. But I didn't order anything.'

There was no need to ask who'd sent the drink that had

been placed before her, in a plain low glass, set on a white napkin. It was about an inch and a half of clear fluid, no ice, no lemon, no nothing. Just what she realised *he* was drinking.

She stared at it as the barman retreated, smiling to himself. He must go through this dance about a million times every evening in a busy, softly lit bar like this. With its faintly recherché ambience it was the ideal venue for advances and retreats, games of 'Do you dare?' over glasses of fluids various.

What the hell was that stuff? Lighter fluid? Drain cleaner? A poisoned chalice?

She put it to her lips and took a hit, catching her breath. It was neat gin, not the vodka she'd half expected. It seemed a weird drink for a man, but perhaps he was a weird man? Taking a very cautious sip this time, she placed the glass back carefully and turned towards him.

Of course, he was watching, and he did a thing with his sandy eyebrows that seemed to ask if she liked his gift. Lizzie wasn't sure that she did, but she nodded at him, took up the glass again and toasted him.

The dazzling grin gained yet more wattage, and he matched the toast. Then, with another elegant piece of body language, a tilt of the head, and a lift of the shoulders, he indicated she should join him. More blatantly, he patted an empty stool beside him.

Here, Rover! Just like an alpha dog, he was summoning a bitch to his side.

Up yours!

Before she could stop herself, or even really think what she was doing, Lizzie mirrored his little pantomime.

Here, Fido! Come!

There was an infinitesimal pause. The man's exceptional eyes widened, and she saw surprise and admiration. Then he slid gracefully off his stool, caught up his drink and headed her way.

Oh God, now what have I done?

She'd come in here, away from the party, primarily to avoid getting hit on, and now what had she done? Invited a man she'd never set eyes on before to hit on her. What should her strategy be? Yes or no? Run or stay? Encourage or play it cool? The choices whirled in her head for what seemed like far longer than it took for a man with a long, smooth, confident stride to reach her.

In the end, she smiled. What woman wouldn't? Up close, he was what she could only inadequately describe as a stunner. All the things that had got her hot from a distance were turned up by a degree of about a thousand in proximity.

'Hello . . . I'll join you then, shall I?' He hitched himself easily onto the stool at her side, his long legs making the action easy, effortless and elegant.

'Hi,' she answered, trying to breathe deeply without appearing to.

Don't let him see that he's already made you into a crazy woman. Just play it cool, Lizzie, for God's sake.

She waited for some gambit or other, but he just smiled at her, his eyes steady, yet also full of amusement, in fact downright merriment. He was having a whale of a time already, and she realised she was too, dangerous as he seemed. This wasn't the kind of man she could handle in the way she usually handled men.

'Thank you for the drink,' she blurted out, unable to take the pressure of his smile and his gently mocking eyes. 'It wasn't what I expected, to be honest.' She glanced at his identical glass. 'It doesn't seem like a man's drink . . . neat gin. Not really.'

Still not speaking, he reached for his glass, and nodded that she take up hers. They clinked them together, and he took a long swallow from his. Lizzie watched the slow undulation of his throat. He was wearing a three-piece suit, a very good one in an expensive shade of washed-out grey-blue. His shirt was light blue and open at the neck.

The little triangle of exposed flesh at his throat seemed to invite the tongue. What would his skin taste like? Not as sharp as gin, no doubt, but just as much of a challenge and ten times as heady.

'Well, I am a man, as you can see.' He set down his glass again, and turned more to face her, doing that showcasing, 'look at the goods' thing again. 'But I'm happy to give you more proof, if you like?'

Lizzie took a quick sip of her own drink, to steady herself. The silvery, balsamic taste braced her up.

'That won't be necessary.' She paused, feeling the gin sizzle in her blood. 'Not right here at least.'

He shook his head and laughed softly, the light from above dancing on his curls, turning soft ash-blond into molten gold. 'That's what I like. Straight to the point. Now we're talking.' Reaching into his jacket pocket, he drew out a black leather wallet and peeled out a banknote, a fifty by the look of it, and dropped it beside his glass as he slipped off the stool again. Reaching for her arm, he said, 'Let's go up to my room. I hate wasting time.'

Oh bloody hell! Oh, bloody, bloody hell! He's either as direct as a very direct thing and he's dead set on a quickie . . . or . . .

Good grief, does he think I'm an escort?

The thought plummeted into the space between them like a great Acme anvil. It was possible. Definitely possible. And it would explain the 'eyes across a bar, nodding and buying drinks' dance. Lizzie had already twigged that the Lawns bar was a place likely to be rife with that sort of thing, and it wasn't as if she didn't *know* anything about escorting. One of her dearest friends had been one, if only part time and not lately, and Brent would most certainly be alarmed that she'd fallen so naively into this pickle of all pickles. She imagined telling him about this afterwards, perhaps making a big comical thing out of her near escape, and hopefully raising some of the old, wickedly droll humour that fate and loss had knocked out of her beloved house-mate.

Trying to think as fast as she could, Lizzie balked, staying put on the stool. Escort or casual pick-up, she still needed a moment to catch her breath and stall long enough to decide whether or not to do something completely mental. 'I think I'd rather like to finish my drink. Seems a shame to waste good gin.'

If her companion was vexed, or impatient, he didn't show it. In a beautiful roll of the shoulders, he shrugged and slipped back onto his stool. 'Quite right. It *is* good gin. Cheers!' He toasted her again.

What am I going to do? What the hell am I going to do? This is dangerous.

It was. It was very dangerous. But in a flash of dazzling honesty, she knew that the gin wasn't the only thing that was too good to waste. The only question was, if he *did* think she was a call girl, did she tell him the truth now, or play along for a bit? She'd never done anything like this before, but, suddenly, she wanted to. She really wanted to. Perhaps because the only man she knew from the wretched party she'd left, other than Brent and some other friends from the pub, was a guy she'd dated once and who'd called her uptight and frigid when she'd rebuffed a grope that'd come too soon.

No use looking like a pin-up and behaving like a dried-up nun, he'd said nastily when she'd told him to clear off.

But this man, well, there wasn't an atom in her body that wanted to rebuff *him*!

What would it be like to dance on the edge? Play a game? Have an adventure that was about as far from her daily humdrum routine of office temping as it was possible to get?

What would it be like to have this jaw-droppingly stunning man, who was so unlike her usual type? She usually went for guys her own age, and Fallen Angel here certainly wasn't that. She was twenty-four and, up close, she could see her estimate of mid-forties was probably accurate. A perfectly seasoned, well-kept, prime specimen of mid-forties man, but still with at least twenty more years of life under his belt than she had.

And if she explained his mistake, he might well just smile that glorious smile at her, shake her hand, and walk away. Goodnight, Vienna.

'Cheers!' she answered.

He didn't speak but his eyes gleamed a response.

I bet you know what to do with a woman, you devil, paid for or otherwise.

Yes, she'd put any amount of money, earned on one's back or by any other means, that when Fallen Angel was with an escort, it was no hardship to be that working girl.

And she couldn't keep calling him Fallen Angel!

On the spur of the moment, she made a decision. This was a game, and she needed a handle. A name, an avatar that she could hide behind and discard when she needed to.

Looking her companion directly in the eye, and trying

not to melt, she set down her glass, held out her hand and said, 'I'm Bettie. Bettie with an "ie". What's your name, Gin-Drinking Man?'

Apparently ignoring the offered handshake, he just laughed, a free, happy, hugely amused, proper laugh. 'Yes, obviously, you *are* Bettie.' Looking her up and down, his laser-blue eyes seemed to catalogue her every asset; her black hair with its full fringe, her pale skin, her lips tinted with vivid bombshell red, her pretty decent but unfashionable figure in a fitted dress with an angora cardigan over it. When she went out, especially to a party, she liked to riff on her superficial resemblance to Bettie Page, the notorious glamour model of the 1950s. And being an Elizabeth, Bettie was a natural alternate name too.

Having subjected her to his inspection, he did reach for her hand then, grip it, and give it a firm shake with both of his clasped around it. 'Delighted to meet you, Bettie. I'm John Smith.'

It was Lizzie's turn to laugh out loud, and 'John' grinned at her. 'Of course you are, John. How could you possibly be anyone else?' The classic punter's name. Even she knew that.

He rocked on the stool, giving his blond head another little shake, still holding on to her. 'But it's my name, Bettie. Cross my heart . . . Honestly.'

The way he held her hand was firm and no nonsense, yet there was a tricky quality to the way his fingertip lay across her wrist, touching the pulse point. She could almost imagine he was monitoring her somehow, but the moment she thought that, he released her.

'OK, I believe you, Mr John Smith. Now may I finish my drink?'

'Of course.' He gave her the glittering smile again, laced

with a sultry edge. 'Forgive me, I'm being a graceless boor. No woman should be rushed . . .' There was a pause, which might have included the rider, *even a prostitute*. 'But once I know I'm going to get a treat, I'm like a kid, Bettie. When I want something, I tend to want it now.'

So do I.

Lizzie tossed back the remainder of her gin, amazed that her throat didn't rebel at its silvery ferociousness. But she didn't cough, and she set the glass down with a purposeful 'clop' on the counter, and slid off her stool.

'There, all finished. Shall we go?'

John simply beamed, settled lightly on his feet and took her elbow, steering her from the crowded bar and into the foyer quite quickly, but not fast enough to make anyone think they were hurrying.

The lift cab was small, and felt smaller, filled by her new friend's presence. Standing, he was medium tall, but not towering or hulking, and his body was every bit as good as her preliminary inspection in the bar had promised. As was his suit. It looked breathtakingly high end, making her wonder why, if he was looking for an escort, he didn't just put in a call to an exclusive agency for a breath-takingly high-end woman to go with it? Rather than pick up an unknown quantity, on spec, in a hotel bar. Leaning against the lift's wall, though, he eyed her up too as the doors slid closed, looking satisfied enough with his random choice. Was he trying to estimate her price?

'So, do we do the "elevator" scene?' he suggested, making no move towards her, except with his bright blue eyes.

Oh yeah, in all those scenes in films and sexy stories, it always happened. The hot couple slammed together in the lift like ravenous dogs and kissed the hell out of each other.

'I don't know. You're in charge.'

'I most certainly am,' he said roundly, 'but let's pretend and savour the anticipation, shall we? The uncertainty. Even though I do know that you're the surest of sure things.'

Bingo! He does *think I'm an escort.*

Confirming her suspicions like that, his words should have sounded crass and crude, but instead they were provocative, exciting her. Especially the bit about him being 'in charge'. Brent had always said it was the whore who was really in charge during a booking, because he or she could just dump the money, say 'No way!' and walk out. But somehow Lizzie didn't think it'd be that way with Mr John Smith, regardless of whether or not he believed she was a call girl.

This is so dangerous.

But she could no sooner have turned back now than ceased to breathe.

'And anyway, here we are.' As he doors sprang open again, he ushered her out, his fingertips just touching her back. It was a light contact, but seemed powerful out of all proportion, and Lizzie found herself almost trotting as they hurried along the short corridor to John's room.

As he let her in, she smiled. She'd not really taken much note of their surroundings as they'd walked, but the room itself was notable. Spacious, but strangely old-fashioned in some ways, almost kitsch. The linens were in chintz, with warm red notes, and the carpet was the colour of vin rouge. It was a bizarre look, compared to the spare lines and neutrals of most modern hotels, but, then, the Waverley Grange Hotel *was* a strange place, both exclusive and with a frisky, whispered reputation. Lizzie had been to functions here before, but had never seen the accommodation, although she'd heard about the legendary chintz-clad love-nests of the Waverley from Brent's taller tales.

'Quite something, isn't it?' John grinned, indicating the deliciously blowsy décor with an open hand.

'Well, *I* like it.' Perhaps it was best to let him think she'd been in rooms like this before; seen clients and fucked them under or on top of the fluffy chintz duvets.

'So do I . . . it's refreshingly retro. I like old-fashioned things.' His blue eyes flicked to her 'Bettie' hair, her pencil skirt and her angora.

Lizzie realised she was hanging back, barely through the doorway. Now *that* wasn't confidence; she'd better shape up. She sashayed forward to the bed, and sat down on it, trying to project sangfroid. 'That's good to know.' Her own voice sounded odd to her, and she could hardly hear it over the pounding of her heart and the rush of blood in her veins.

John paused by the wardrobe, slipping off his jacket and putting it on a hanger. So normal, so everyday. 'Aren't you going to phone your agency? That's what girls usually do about now. They always slip off to the bathroom and I hear them muttering.'

Oops, she was giving herself away. He'd suss her out any moment, if he hadn't already. 'I'm . . . I'm an independent.' She flashed through her brain, trying to remember things Brent had told her, and stuff from *Secret Diary of a Call Girl* on the telly. 'But I think I will call someone, if you don't mind.' Springing up again, she headed for the other door in the room. It had to lead to the bathroom.

'Of course . . . but aren't you forgetting something?'

Oh God, yes, the money!

'Three hundred.' It was a wild guess; it sounded right.

Sandy eyebrows quirked. 'Very reasonable. I was happy to pay five, at least.'

'That's my basic,' she said, still thinking, thinking. 'If you find you want something fancier, we can renegotiate.'

Why the hell had she said that? Why? Why? Why? What if he wanted something kinky? Something nasty? He didn't look that way, but who knew?

'Fancy, eh? I'll give it some thought. But in the meantime, let's start with the basic.' Reaching into his jacket pocket, he slipped out the black wallet again, and peeled off fifties. 'There,' he said, placing the notes on the top of the sideboard.

Lizzie scooped them up as she passed, heading for the bathroom, but John stayed her with a hand on her arm, light but implacable.

'Do you kiss? I know some girls don't.'

She looked at his mouth, especially his beautiful lower lip, so velvety yet determined.

'Yes, I kiss.'

'Well, then, I'll kiss you when you come back. Now make your call.'

2

Something Fancy

Well, well, then, 'Bettie Page', what on earth did I do to receive a gift like you? A beautiful, feisty, retro girl who's suddenly appeared to me like an angel from 1950s heaven?

John Smith considered having another drink from the mini bar, but, after a moment, he decided he didn't need one. He was intoxicated enough already, after the barely more than a mouthful of gin he'd drunk downstairs. Far more excited than he'd been by a woman in a long time, and certainly more turned on than he'd ever been with an escort before. Not that he'd been with a professional woman in a while. Not that he'd been with a lot of them anyway.

It was interesting, though, to pretend to Bettie that he had.

Sinking into one of the big chintz armchairs, he took a breath and centred himself, marshalling his feelings. Yes, this was a crazy situation, but he was having fun, so why deny it? And she was too, this unusual young woman with her vintage style and her emotions all over her face. That challenging smile was unmistakeable.

'Bettie, eh?'

Not her real name, he was sure, but perhaps near to it.

She looked the part for Bettie Page, though. She had the same combination of innocence, yet overflowing sensuality. Naughtiness. Yes, that was perfect for her. But *how* naughty? As an escort she probably took most things, everything, in her stride. Surely she wouldn't balk at his favoured activities? And yet, despite her profession, there was that strangely untouched quality to her, just like the legendary Bettie. A sweet freshness. A wholesomeness, idiotic as that sounded.

How long had she been in the game, he wondered. What if she was new to this? She was certainly far younger than his usual preference. His choice was normally for sleek, groomed, experienced women in their thirties, courtesans rather than call girls, ladies of the world. There might be a good deal of pleasure, though, in giving something to *her* in return for her services, something more than simply the money. Satisfaction, something new . . . a little adventure, more than just the job.

Now there was the real trick, the deeper game. And with any luck, a working girl who styled herself as 'Bettie' and who was prepared to take a client on the fly, after barely five minutes' chat, was bold enough to play it.

Suddenly he wasn't as bored with life and business as he'd been half an hour ago. Suddenly, his gathering unease about the paths he'd chosen, the insidious phantoms of loss and guilt, and the horrid, circling feeling that his life was ultimately empty, all slipped away from him. Suddenly he felt as if he were a young man again, full of dreams. A player; excited, hopeful, potent.

When he touched his cock it was as hard as stone, risen and eager.

'Come on, Bettie,' he whispered to himself, smiling as his

heart rose too, with anticipation. 'Hurry up, because if you don't, I'll come in there and get you.'

When Lizzie emerged from the bathroom the first thing she saw was another small pile of banknotes on the dresser.

'Just in case I have a hankering for "fancy",' said John amiably. He was lounging on the bed, still fully dressed, although his shoes were lying on their sides on the carpet where he'd obviously kicked them off.

'Oh, right . . . OK.'

Fancy? What did fancy mean? A bit of bondage? Spanking? Nothing too weird, she hoped. But it might mean they needed 'accessories' and she had none. You don't take plastic spanking paddles and fluffy handcuffs to the posher kind of birthday party, which was what she was supposed to be at.

'I don't have any toys with me. Just these.' The words came out on a breath she hadn't realised she was holding, and louder than she'd meant to. She opened her palm to reveal the couple of condoms she'd had stashed in the bottom of her bag. 'I wasn't originally planning to work tonight, but the event I was at was a bit tedious, so I thought I'd take a chance in the bar . . . you know, waste not, want not.'

What the hell am I babbling about?

John grinned from his position of comfort and relaxation. A tricky grin, as sunny as before, but with an edge. He was in charge, and he knew it. Maybe that was the 'fancy'?

Something slow and snaky and honeyed rolled in her belly. A delicious sensation, scary but making her blood tingle. His blue eyes narrowed as if he were monitoring her physical responses remotely, and the surge of desire swelled again, and grew.

She'd played jokey little dominance and submission games with a couple of her boyfriends. Just a bit of fun, something to spice things up. But it had never quite lived up to her expectations. Never delivered. Mainly because they'd always wanted her to play the dominatrix for them, wear some cheap black vinyl tat and call them 'naughty boys'. It'd been a laugh, she supposed, but it hadn't done much for her, and when one had hinted at turning the tables, she'd said goodnight and goodbye to the relationship. He'd been a nice enough guy, but somehow, in a way she couldn't define, not 'good' enough to be her master and make her bow down.

But golden John Smith, a gin-drinking man of forty-something, with laughter lines and a look of beautiful world-weariness . . . well, he *was* 'good' enough. Her belly trembled and silky fluid pooled in her sex, shocking and quick.

Now was the moment to stop being a fake, if she could. Maybe explain, and then perhaps even go on with a new game? And yet she could barely speak. He wasn't speaking either, just looking at her with those eyes that seemed to see all. With a little tilt of his head, he told her not to explain or question or break the spell.

But just when she thought she might break down and scream from the tension, he did speak.

'Toys aren't always necessary, Bettie. You of all people should know that.'

Had she blown it? Maybe . . . maybe not. Schooling herself not to falter, she shrugged and moved towards him. When she reached the bed, she dropped her rather inadequate stash of condoms on the side table and said, 'Of course . . . you're so right. And I love to improvise, don't you?'

Slowly, he sat up, and swivelled around, letting his legs swing down and his feet settle on the floor. 'Good girl . . .

good girl . . .' He reached out and laid a hand on her hip, fingers curving, just touching the slope of her bottom cheek. The touch became a squeeze, the tips of his four fingers digging into her flesh, not cruelly but with assertion, owning her.

With his other hand, he drew her nearer, right in between his spread thighs. She was looking down at him but it was as if he were looking down at her, from a great and dominant height. Her heart tripped again, knowing he could give her what she wanted.

But what was *his* price? Could she afford to pay?

He squeezed her bottom harder, as if assessing the resilience of her flesh, his fingertips closer to her pussy now, pushing the cloth of her skirt into the edge of her cleft. With a will of its own, her body started moving, rocking, pushing against his hold. Her sex was heavy, agitated, in need of some attention, and yet they'd barely done anything thus far. She lifted her hands to put them on his shoulders and draw the two of them closer.

'Uh oh.' The slightest tilt of the head, and a narrowing of his eyes was all the command she needed. She let her hands drop . . . while his free hand rose to her breast, fingers grazing her nipple. Her bra was underwired, but not padded so there was little to dull his touch. With finger and thumb, he took hold of her nipple and pinched it lightly through her clothing, smiling when she let out a gasp, sensation shooting from the contact to her swollen folds, and her clit.

Squeeze. Pinch. Squeeze. Pinch. Nothing like the sex she was used to, but wonderful. Odd. Infinitely arousing. The wetness between her labia welled again, slippery and almost alarming, saturating the thin strip of cloth between her legs.

'I'm going to make you come,' said John in a strangely normal voice, 'and I mean a real one, no faking. I think you can do it for me. You seem like an honest girl, and I think you like the way I'm touching you . . . even if it *is* business.'

Lizzie swallowed. For a moment there she'd forgotten she was supposed to be a professional. She'd just been a lucky girl with a really hot man who probably wouldn't have to do all that much to get her off.

'Will you be honest for me?' His blue eyes were like the whole world, and unable to get away from. 'Will you give me what I want? What I've paid for?'

'Yes, I think I can do that. Shouldn't be too difficult.'

Finger and thumb closed hard on her nipple. It really hurt and she let out a moan from the pain and from other sensations. 'Honesty, remember?' His tongue, soft and pink slid along his lower lip and she had to hold in a moan at the sight of that too.

She nodded, unable to speak, the pressure on the tip of her breast consuming her. How could this be happening? It hurt but it was next to nothing really.

Then he released her. 'Take off your cardigan and your dress, nothing else.'

Shaking, but hoping he couldn't detect the fine tremors, Lizzie shucked off her cardigan and dropped it on the floor beside her, then she reached behind her, for her zip.

'Let me.' John turned her like a big doll, whizzed the zip down, and then turned her back again, leaving her to slip the dress off. He put out a hand, though, to steady her, as she stepped out of it.

She hadn't really been planning to seduce anyone tonight, so she hadn't put on her fanciest underwear, just a nice but fairly unfussy set, a plain white bra and panties with a little edge of rosy pink lace.

'Nice. Prim. I like it,' said John with a pleased smile. Lizzie almost fainted when he hitched himself a little sideways on the bed, reached down and casually adjusted himself in his trousers. As his hand slid away, she could see he was huge, madly erect.

Oh, yummy.

He laughed out loud. He'd seen her checking him out. 'Not too bad, eh?' He shrugged, still with that golden but vaguely unnerving grin. 'I guess you see all shapes and sizes.'

'True,' she replied, wanting to reach out and touch the not too bad item, but knowing instinctively it was forbidden to do so for the moment. 'And most of them are rather small . . . but you seem to be OK, though, from where I'm standing.'

'Cheeky minx. I should punish you for that.' He laid a hand on her thigh, just above the top of her hold-up stocking. He didn't slap her, though perversely she'd hoped he might, just so she could see what one felt like from him. 'Maybe I will in a bit.' He stroked her skin, just at the edge of her panties, then drew back.

'You're very beautiful, you know,' he went on, leaning back on his elbows for a moment. 'I expect you're very popular. Are you? Do you do well?'

'Not too badly.' It seemed a bland enough answer, not an exact lie. She had the occasional boyfriend, nothing special. She wasn't promiscuous, but she had sex now and again.

John nodded. She wasn't sure what he meant by it, but she didn't stop to worry. The way he was lying showed off that gorgeous erection. 'Do you actually, really like your job, then?' He glanced down to where she was looking, unashamed.

'Yes, I do. And I often come too. The things you see on the telly. Documentaries and stuff . . . They all try to tell people that we don't enjoy it. But some of us do.' It seemed safer to cover herself. If she didn't have a real orgasm soon, she might go mad. He'd barely touched her but her clit was aching, aching, aching.

'Show me, then. Pull down the top of your bra. Show me your tits. They look very nice but I'd like to see a bit more of them.'

Peeling down her straps, Lizzie pushed the cups of her bra down too, easing each breast out and letting it settle on the bunched fabric of the cup. It looked rude and naughty, as if she were presenting two juicy fruits to him on a tray, and it made her just nicely sized breasts look bigger, more opulent.

'Lovely. Now play with your nipples. Make them really come up for me.'

Tentatively, Lizzie cupped herself, first one breast, then the other. 'I thought you were going to make me come? I'm doing all the work here.' A shudder ran down her spine; her nipples were already acutely sensitive, dark and perky.

'Shush. You talk too much. Just do as you're told.' The words were soft, almost friendly, but she listened for an undertone, even if there wasn't one there.

Closing her eyes, she went about her task, wondering what he was thinking. Touching her breasts made her want to touch herself elsewhere too. It always did. It was putting electricity into a system and getting an overload in a different location. Her clit felt enormous, charged, desperate. As she ran her thumbs across her nipples, tantalising herself, she wanted to pant with excitement.

And all because this strange man was looking at her. She could feel the weight of his blue stare, even if she couldn't see

284 THE ACCIDENTAL CALL GIRL

him. Were his lips parted just as hers were? Was he hungering just as she did? Did he want a taste of her?

Swaying her hips, she slid a hand down from her breast to her belly, skirting the edge of her knickers, ready to dive inside.

'No, not there. I'll deal with that.'

Lizzie's eyes snapped open. John was watching her closely, as she'd expected, his gaze hooded. Gosh, his eyelashes were long. She suddenly noticed them, so surprisingly dark compared to his wheat-gold hair.

In a swift, shocking move, he sat up again and grasped the errant hand, then its mate, pushing them behind her, and then hooking both of them together behind her back. Her wrists were narrow and easily contained by his bigger hand. He was right up against her now, his breath hot on her breasts.

Bondage. Was this one of his fancy things? Her heart thrilled. Her pussy quivered. Yes. Yes. Yes. He held her firmly, his arm around her, securing her. She tried not to tremble but it was difficult to avoid it. Difficult to stop herself pressing her body as close to his as she could and trying to get off by rubbing her crotch against whatever part of him she could reach.

'Keep still. Keep very still. No movement unless I say so.' Inclining forward, he put out his tongue and licked her nipple, long, slowly and lasciviously, once, twice, three times.

'Oh God . . . oh God . . .'

His mouth was hot and his tongue nimble, flexible. He furled it to a point and dabbed at the very point of her, then lashed hard, flicking the bud. Lizzie imagined she was floating, buoyed up by the simple, focused pleasure, yet tethered by the weight of lust between her thighs.

'Hush . . . be quiet.' The words flowed over the skin of her breast. 'Try not to make any noises. Contain everything inside you.'

It was hard, so hard . . . and impossible when he took her nipple between his teeth and tugged on it hard. The pressure was oh so measured, but threatening, and his tongue still worked, right on the very tip.

Forbidden noises came out of her mouth. Her pelvis wafted in a dance proscribed. A tear formed at the corner of her eye. He dabbed and dabbed at her imprisoned nipple with his tongue, and when she looked down on him, she could see a demon looking back up at her, laughter dark and merry in his eyes.

He thinks he's getting the better of me. He thinks he's getting to a woman who's supposedly anaesthetised to pleasure, and making her excited.

Hard suction pulled at her nipple and her hips undulated in reply.

I don't know who the hell this woman is, but the bastard's making me *crazy!*

Lizzie had never believed that a woman could get off just from having her breasts played with. And maybe that still was so . . . But with her tit in John Smith's mouth she was only a hair's breadth from it. Maybe if she jerked her hips hard enough, it'd happen. Maybe she'd climax from sheer momentum.

'Stop that,' he ordered quietly, then with his free palm, he reached around and slapped her hard on the buttock, right next to her immobilised hands. It was like a thunderclap through the cotton of her panties.

'Ow!'

The pain was fierce and sudden, with strange powers. Her

skin burnt, but in her cleft, her clit pulsed and leapt. Had she come? She couldn't even tell, the signals were so mixed.

'What's the matter, little escort girl? Are you getting off?' He mouthed her nipple again, licking, sucking. Her clit jerked again, tightening.

'Could be,' she gasped, surprised she could still be so bold when her senses were whirling, 'I'm not sure.'

'Well, let's make certain then, eh?' Manhandling her, he turned her a little between his thighs. 'Arms around my shoulders. Hold on tight.'

'But . . .'

'This is what I've paid you for, Bettie' His blue eyes flashed. 'My pleasure is your compliance. That's the name of the game.'

She put her hands on him, obeying. The muscles of his neck and shoulders felt strong, unyielding, through the fine cotton of his shirt and the silk of his waistcoat lining, and this close, a wave of his cologne rose up, filling her head like an exotic potion, lime and spices, underscored by just a whiff of a foxier scent, fresh sweat. He was as excited as she, for all his apparent tranquillity, and that made her dizzier than ever. This was all mad, like no sex she'd ever really had before, although right here, right now, she was hard pressed to remember anything she'd done with other men.

'Oh Bettie, Bettie, you're really rather delightful,' he crooned, pushing a hand into her knickers from the front, making her pitch over, pressing her face against the side of his. His hair smelt good too, but fainter and with a greener note. He was a pot-pourri of delicious male odours.

'Oh, oh, God.' Burrowing in with determined fingers, he'd found her clit, and he took possession of it in a hard little rub. Her sex gathered itself, heat massing in her belly she was so ready from all the forays and tantalising gambits he'd put her through.

'If you have an orgasm before I give you permission, I'll slap your bottom, Bettie.' His voice was low, barely more than a breath. 'And if you come again . . . I'll slap you again.'

'But why punish me? If you want me to come?' She could barely speak, but something compelled her to. Maybe just the act of forming words gave her some control. Over herself at least.

'Because it's my will to do it, Bettie. Because I want you to come, and spanking your bottom makes me hard.' He twisted his neck, and pressed a kiss against her throat, a long, indecent licking kiss, messy and animal. 'Surely you understand how we men sometimes are?'

'Yes . . . yes, of course I do . . . Men are perverts,' she panted, bearing down on his relentless fingertip that was rocking now. 'At least the fun ones mostly are, in my experience.'

'Oh brava! Bravissima! That's my girl . . .' Latching his mouth on to her earlobe in a wicked nip, he circled his finger, working her clit like a bearing, rolling and pushing.

As his teeth closed tighter, just for an instant, he overcame her. She shouted, something incoherent, orgasming hard in sharp, intense waves, her flesh rippling.

The waves were still rolling when he slapped again, with his fully open hand, right across her bottom cheek.

'Ow! Oh God!'

John nuzzled her neck, still making magic with his finger, and torment with his hand, more and more slaps. Her body was a maelstrom, her nerves not sure what was happening, pain and pleasure whipping together in a froth. She gripped him hard, holding on, dimly aware that she might be hurting him too with her vice-like hold.

'Oh please . . . time out,' she begged after what could have been moments, or much longer.

The slaps stopped, and he curved his whole hand around her crotch, the gesture vaguely protective . . . or perhaps possessive?

'Not used to coming when you're "on duty"?' His voice was silky and provocative, but good-humoured. 'It's nice to know I managed to make you lose it. Seems that I've not lost my touch.' He pressed a kiss to her neck, snaking his arm around her back, supporting her.

Lizzie blinked, feeling odd, unsorted. She hadn't expected to feel quite this much with him. It had all started as a lark, a bit of fun, testing herself to see if she could get away with her pretence. She still didn't know if she'd achieved that, and she wasn't sure John Smith would give her a straight answer if she found a way to ask him.

Either way, he'd touched her more than just physically. He'd put heat in her bottom, and confusion in her soul.

For a few moments, she just let herself be held, trying not to think. She was half draped across the body of a man she barely knew, with several hundred pounds of his money in her bag and on the dresser. His hand was still tucked inside her panties, cradling her pussy, wet with her silk.

'You're very wet down there, sweetheart,' he said, as if he'd read her thoughts again. He sounded pleased with himself, which, she supposed he should be if he really believed she was an escort and he'd got her as dripping wet as this. 'And real, too . . . not out of a tube.' He dabbled in her pond.

'It's not unknown, John. I told you that . . . Some of us enjoy our profession very much. We make the most of our more attractive clients.'

'Flatterer,' he said, but she detected a pleased note in his voice. He was a man and only human. They all liked to be praised for their prowess. His hand closed a little tighter on her sex, finger flexing. 'Do you think you could oblige this attractive client with a fuck now? Nothing fancy this time. Just a bit of doggy style, if you don't mind.'

In spite of everything, Lizzie laughed out loud. He was a sexy, possibly very devious character, but she also sensed he was a bit of a caution too, a man with whom one could have good fun without sex ever being involved.

'I'd be glad to,' she replied, impetuously kissing him on the cheek, wondering if that was right for her role. Straightening up, she moved onto the bed, feeling his hand slide out of her underwear. 'Like this?' She went up on her knees on the mattress, close to the edge, reaching around to tug at her knickers and make way for him.

'Delightful . . . Hold that thought. I'll be right with you.'

Over her shoulder, Lizzie watched him boldly, eager to see if his cock was as good as it had felt through his clothes.

Swiftly, John unbuttoned his washed-slate-blue waistcoat, and then his trousers, but he didn't remove them. Instead, he fished amongst his shirt-tails and his linen, pushing them aside and freeing his cock without undressing.

He was a good size, hard and high, ruddy with defined, vigorous veining. He frisked himself two or three times, as if he doubted his erection, but Lizzie had no such doubts. He looked as solid as if he'd been carved from tropical wood.

'OK for you?' Jiggling himself again, he challenged her with a lift of his dark blond eyebrows.

'Very fair. Very fair indeed.' She wiggled her bottom enticingly. 'Much better than I usually get.'

'Glad to hear it.' He reached for a condom, and in a few quick, deft movements enrobed himself. A latex coating didn't diminish the temptation.

Taking hold of her hips, he moved her closer to the edge of the bed in a brisk, businesslike fashion, then peeled off her panties, tugging them off over her shoes and tossing them away.

'Very fair. Very fair indeed,' he teased, running his hands greedily over her buttocks and making the slight tingle from where he'd spanked her flare and surge. 'I'd like to spank you again, but not tonight.' Reaching between her legs, he played with her labia and her clit, reawakening sensations there too. 'I just want to be in you for the moment, but another time, well, I'd like to get fancier then, if you're amenable.'

'I . . . I think that could be arranged,' she answered, panting. He was touching her just the way she loved. How could he do that? If he kept on, she'd be agreeing to madness. Wanting to say more, she could only let out a moan and rock her body to entice him.

'Good, very good.' With some kind of magician-like twist of the wrist, he thrust a finger inside her, as if testing her condition. 'I'll pay extra, of course. I don't like to mark women, but you never know. I'll recompense you for any income lost, don't worry.'

What was he talking about? She could barely think. He was pumping her now. Not touching her clit, just thrusting his finger in and out of her in a smooth, relentless rhythm. And when her sensitive flesh seemed about to flutter into glorious orgasm, he pushed in a second finger too, beside the first. As she wriggled and rode them, she felt his cock brushing her thigh.

'Are you ready for me?' The redundant question was like a breeze sighing in her ear, so soft as he leant over her, clothing and rubber-clad erection pressed against her.

'What do you think?' she said on a hard gasp, almost coming, her entire body sizzling with sensation.

'Ready, willing and able, it seems.' He buried his face in her hair, and nuzzled her almost fondly. 'You're a remarkable woman, Bettie.'

And then she was empty, trembling, waiting . . . but not for long. Blunt and hot, his penis found her entrance, nudging, pushing, entering as he clasped her hip hard for purchase and seemed to fling himself at her in a ruthless shove.

'Oof!' His momentum knocked the breath out of her, sending her pitching forward, the side of her face hitting the mattress, her heart thrilling to the sheer primitive power of him. She felt him brace himself with a hand set beside her, while the fingers of his other hand tightened on her body like a vice, securing his grip. His thrusts were so powerful she had to hold on herself, grabbing hunks of the bedding to stop herself sliding.

'Hell. Yes!' His voice was fierce, ferocious, not like him. Where were his playful amused tones now? He sounded like a wild beast, voracious and alpha. He fucked like one too, pounding away at her. 'God, you're so tight . . . so *tight*!' There was surprise in the wildness too.

Squirming against the mattress, riding it as John rode her, Lizzie realised something. Of course, he had no idea he was taking a road with her that not too many men had travelled. She'd had sex, yes, and boyfriends. And enjoyed them immensely. But not all that many of them, throughout her years as a woman. Fewer than many of her friends, and hundreds fewer than an experienced escort.

But such thoughts dissolved. Who could think, being possessed like this? How could a man of nice but normal dimensions feel like a gigantic force of nature inside her, knocking against nerve-endings she couldn't remember ever being knocked before, stroking against exquisitely sensitive spots and making her gasp and howl, yes, howl!

Pleasure bloomed, red, white heat inside her, bathing her sex, her belly, making her clit sing. Her mouth was open against the duvet; good God, she was drooling too. Her hips jerked, as if trying to hammer back against John Smith as hard as he was hammering into her.

'Yes . . . that's good . . . oh . . .' His voice degraded again, foul, mindless blasphemy pouring from those beautiful lips as he ploughed her. Blue, filthy words that soared like a holy litany. 'Yes, oh God . . . now touch yourself, you gorgeous slut . . . rub your clit while I fuck you. I want you to be coming when I do. I want to feel it around me, your cunt, grabbing my dick.'

She barely needed the stimulus; the words alone set up the reality. The ripple of her flesh against his became hard, deep, grabbing clenches, the waves of pleasure so high and keen she could see white splodges in front of her eyes, as if she were swooning under him, even as she rubbed her clit with her fingers.

As she went limp, almost losing consciousness, a weird cry almost split the room. It was high, odd, broken, almost a sob as John's hips jerked like some ancient pneumatic device of both flesh and iron, pumping his seed into the thin rubber membrane lodged inside her.

He collapsed on her. She was collapsed already. It seemed as if the high wind that had swept the room had suddenly died. Her lover, both John and *a* John lay upon her, substantial, but not a heavy man really. His weight, though, seemed real, in a state of dreams.

After a minute, or perhaps two or three, he levered himself off her, standing. She felt the brush of his fingers sliding down her flank in a soft caress, then came his voice.

'Sorry about calling you a "slut" . . . and the other stuff. I expect you've heard a lot worse in this line of work, but still . . . You know us men, we talk a lot of bloody filthy nonsense when we're getting our ends away. You don't mind, do you?'

'No . . . not at all. I rather like it, actually.' Rolling onto her side, then her back, she discovered him knotting the condom, then tossing it into the nearby waste bin. His cock was deflating, naturally, but still had a certain majesty about it, even as he tucked it away and sorted out his shirt-tails and his zip.

'God, you look gorgeous like that.' His blue eyes blazed, as if his spirit might be willing again even if his flesh was currently shagged out. 'I'd love to have you again, but I think I've been a bit of pig and I'll be *hors de combat* for a little while now.'

You do say some quaint things, John Smith . . . But I like it.
I like you.

'Perhaps we could go again? When you've had a rest?' She glanced across at the second pile of notes on the dresser. It looked quite a lot. 'I'm not sure you've had full value for your money.'

John's eyes narrowed, amused, and he gave her an odd, boyish little grin.

'Oh, I think I've had plenty. You . . . you've been very good, beautiful Bettie. Just what I needed.' He sat down beside her, having swooped to pick up her panties, then pressed the little cotton bundle into her hands. 'I haven't been sleeping too well lately, love. But I think I'll sleep tonight now. Thank you.'

A lump came to Lizzie's throat. This wasn't sexual game playing, just honest words, honest thanks. He seemed younger suddenly, perhaps a little vulnerable. She wanted to stay, not for sex, but to just hug him, and hold him.

'Are you OK?'

'Yes, I'm fine,' he said, touching her cheek. 'But it's time for you to go. I've had what I've paid for, and more, sweet girl. I'd think I'd like to sleep now, and you should be home to your bed too. You don't have any more appointments tonight, do you?'

'No . . . nothing else.' Something very strange twisted in her mid-section. Yes, she should go now. Before she did or said something very silly. 'I'm done for the night.' She got up, wriggled into her knickers as gracefully as she could, then accepted her other things from John's hands. He'd picked them up for her. 'I'll just need a moment in your bathroom, then I'll leave you to your sleep.'

She skittered away, sensing him reaching for her. Not sure she could cope with his touch again, at least not in gentleness.

John stared at the door to the bathroom, smiling to himself, but perplexed.

You haven't been working very long, have you, beautiful Bettie?

How new was she to the game, he wondered. She didn't have that gloss, that slightly authoritative edge that he could always detect in an experienced escort. She was a sensual, lovely woman, and she seemed unafraid, but her responses were raw, unfiltered, as if she'd not yet learned to wear a mask and keep a bit of herself back. The working girls he'd been with had always been flatteringly responsive, accomplished, a massage to his ego. But there'd always been a tiny trickle of an edge that told him he was really just a job to them, even if they did genuinely seem to enjoy themselves.

But Bettie seemed completely unfettered by all that. She was full throttle. There was no way she could have fabricated her enjoyment of the sex; there was no way she could have faked the unprocessed excitement she'd exhibited, the response when he'd spanked her luscious bottom.

She loved it, and maybe that was the explanation. Most whores encountered clients who wanted to take the punishment, not dish it out. Maybe she wasn't all that experienced in being on the receiving end of BDSM? But she was a natural, and he needed a natural right now. Someone fresh, and vigorous, and enthusiastic. Unschooled, but with a deep, innate understanding of the mysteries.

He *had* to see her again. And see her soon.

3

Gorgeous

'Are you out of your mind, you idiot? Just because it's called "being on the game" that doesn't mean it *is* a game. You can't just play at it, Lizzie!'

Brent was furious. Lizzie got that. Her male house-mate had been an escort himself, on and off, and her wild escapade with John Smith must seem like a bit of an insult to him, and to men and women who lived the life and took it seriously.

She looked from one of her companions to the other, hoping for some support from Shelley, the third house-sharer. But Shelley was just gawping at her as if she was a space alien, as if a pod person had overtaken her normally moderately sensible friend.

'I meant to tell him, really I did. But things got a bit passionate, and there didn't seem to be the right moment.' Their black tailless cat, Mulder, leapt up onto her lap and automatically Lizzie began to stroke her. The rhythmic action, and the little feline's soft purr, settled and centred her. 'Also, it was patently obvious he *wanted* an escort. Not a one-night stand. No complications, know what I mean? If I'd told him he was mistaken, it might have been, "Oops, sorry, thank you and goodnight" . . . and he was far too gorgeous for that.'

Gorgeous was too small a word, though. Too simple. John Smith had a plain name but her instincts told her he was a complicated man. Very complicated.

'Ooh, I wish I'd nipped into the bar and seen him.' Shelley finally found her voice. 'The party was OK . . . but there wasn't much talent, and what there was seemed to be taken already. Same old story.'

Guilt tweaked at Lizzie. Not about John, but about abandoning her friends. If she'd stayed with them, they'd all have found a way to have a laugh, dud party or no dud party. Between them, she and Shelley might even have coaxed the old Brent out of hiding. The one who'd always had them in stitches with snarky remarks and razor-sharp observations.

But Brent was still frowning, his black brows low. They all three were sitting in the kitchen together, the morning after the night before, touching base. There had been no chance to talk in the taxi home from the Waverley because the driver had been the nosy, garrulous kind, asking questions in a slightly seedy way about their evening. Lizzie had feigned an exhaustion that hadn't been entirely faux, and once they'd got home, to the house they shared in a quiet suburban road, not too far out of town, Lizzie had scuttled to her room with yawned apologies to Shelley and Brent, not wanting to do anything but think about John Smith.

And she'd done nothing but think of him all night. Despite her tiredness, she'd lain awake, imagining herself still lying under him, being pounded. She could still feel him now, as if his flesh had imprinted itself upon her, as if his cock was there inside her still. As if his strong, deft fingertip was still on her clit as he spanked her.

Lizzie! Get a grip! Stop being a sex fiend!

But hell, yes, that spanking. She kept coming back to it, again and again.

And now, both Shelley and Brent were still staring at her. Shelley looked a bit lost in admiration, to be honest, but their handsome flatmate was cross. Lizzie knew why. He was worried about her welfare, and knowing what he knew about the life of an escort, she could easily see why he'd be concerned.

'I think you'd have liked him. You're a good judge of character. If you'd met him, you'd have known he was pukka.'

Brent's expression softened. 'I'm not that great a judge . . . not always.' He gave a shrug of his lean shoulders, and swept his dark hair out of his eyes. Eyes that could flash with wicked humour, but also show a terrible, terrible sadness. 'But still, this John Smith of yours . . . I mean, "John Smith", what the hell kind of name is that? At least he could have chosen something a bit more imaginative.'

Lizzie fished a card out of her robe pocket. A business card, plain white, with a name and a mobile number in a sharp, no-nonsense font and a tiny logo, an entwined J & S in the corner.

'It's his name. Really.' As Shelley craned for a look, she handed over the card to Brent, remembering her bark of astonished laughter.

'It really is my name,' he'd reiterated, smiling as she'd emerged from the bathroom, her clothing set to rights, even if her mind and her senses were still in turmoil. He'd changed into a long, dark blue silk robe, and the idea of his naked body beneath the thin, light cloth had almost made her beg him to let her stay.

But she hadn't. He didn't want that. He'd calmly and

composedly explained that all he wanted for the duration of his stay in the area – business stuff, looking over properties, acquisitions – was a beautiful and experienced woman to have sex with, someone who'd be comfortable with his 'preferences', and game for a bit of the 'fancy'. He was willing to pay, and pay well, particularly if she were to make herself available exclusively to him for the duration. He'd make sure that she was well compensated for any income lost by not seeing other clients.

Brent turned the card over in his fingers as Lizzie outlined all this to him, and Shelley listened, all ears.

'Ooh, just like *Pretty Woman* . . . You lucky bitch!' She grinned, and though Lizzie sensed a bit of genuine envy in her friend, she knew it was good-natured. 'Trust you to score a freaking millionaire or whatever, you jammy thing.'

'Well . . . on the face of it, it sounds like the ideal gig,' observed Brent. 'A high-roller with not too many strings attached, and hopefully not too weird. He doesn't want the girlfriend experience, then? No all-nighters?'

'Nope, just evenings. He's busy with what sounds like high-powered "tycoon" type stuff during the day, and at night he prefers to sleep alone.' Ignoring the word *weird* for the time being, she nevertheless experienced a pang. It was daft to want it, but the idea of actually curling up for sleep with John was suddenly infinitely appealing. Almost as much as fucking him, or feeling his hand strike her bottom. She could still smell the clean scent of him, and imagine cuddling against his warm skin, dozing off.

No, no, no . . . don't go there. This is what it is.

And that thing was a slightly crazy lark and a chance to broaden her sexual horizons with an interesting and very desirable man. A chance to be someone other than Lizzie

Aitchison, ordinary girl bored to death with office temping, and in a limbo of not quite having figured out what to do with her life, even at twenty-four.

'Probably for the best. You're playing with fire, my girl, and the less time you have the matches in your hand, the better.' Brent shrugged sagely.

Mulder the cat wriggled out of her arms, as if sensing her unease, and trotted off out of the room. While Shelley made 'Don't listen to him . . . tell me more!' faces behind his back, Lizzie eyed Brent, who'd got up to fetch the teapot and top up their mugs. It was easier to talk to his narrow shoulders about certain matters.

'Er . . . what do you know about BDSM? John seems to be into that sort of thing. He said he'd like to . . . well . . . experiment more next time.'

'BDSM? Yikes!' Shelley edged forward. She looked like a wide-eyed, slightly prurient pixie, with smudges of last night's mascara and her cap of ash blonde hair standing up in morning tufts.

Brent rolled his eyes as he set down the teapot on its mat in the middle of the table. 'Oh, please don't tell me he wants you to spank him? It's much harder than it looks in the films and on the telly. It's an art, and you can really hurt someone if you don't know what you're doing. Which, unless I know less about your previous adventures than you've told me, you don't.'

Eyes narrowed, he poured the tea, waiting; while Shelley seemed beside herself with excited anticipation.

'No, actually, it's the other way round. He wants to spank me . . . Um . . . to spank me again.'

'Oh my, we are already in deep, aren't we?' Brent studied her over the rim of his mug, his pale blue eyes worried. But

he also looking vaguely admiring, as if she'd impressed him
somehow. All three of the house-mates shared quite intimate
confidences, but she and Brent were especially close, both
emotionally and about their sex lives. Lizzie hoped it could
stay that way. She couldn't bear to think they'd just hit a
barrier with him when he needed both her and Shelley so
much.

'Deepish . . . although I don't think he's a vicious sadist
or anything. It's just a pain and pleasure thing with him.' She
stared into her mug, imagining it was a glass of gin, crystal
clear and with answers swimming in it.

'Do you even know what a sadist is? Or a dominant?
They're a bit different, you know.' Brent's voice was sharp.

'Yes, I sort of get the gist . . . but it's all theoretical, from
sexy stories and what have you. I've never had any practice,
really, other than a bit of horsing around that didn't account
to anything and ended up just getting rather embarrassing.'

'Er . . . what horsing around? You've never told me about
this?' Shelley demanded.

Lizzie felt rather hot all of a sudden. It was OK talking to
one or other of her friends about personal topics, one on one,
but this was turning into something suspiciously like a being
grilled by the panel situation. 'Er . . . don't you have a special
gig this morning?' she asked Shelley, grasping a welcome
straw that had just occurred to her. The two of them temped
for the same secretarial agency, and she knew the other girl
had something booked in for today, even though it was a
Saturday. Double rate was always welcome.

'Oh shit! Fuck! Yes, I have and I'm going to be buggering
well late!' Shelley flung herself off her stool, spilling tea in
the process. Abandoning her mug, and grabbing a banana
from the fruit bowl for a travelling breakfast, she made for

the door. 'I want all the gruesome details later! I mean it! Promise?' she flung over her shoulder before disappearing out of the door and thundering up the stairs to her room.

'Promise,' said Lizzie, returning her attention to Brent now they were alone.

'You do need to be careful, love.' Worry was winning the battle in his eyes. 'You need to set firm limits beforehand. Establish a safe word. Especially if you're supposed to be an escort . . . Most don't tend to "sub" because they can't risk getting bruised and looking a mess for the next client. I've often been asked to dispense it, though. You know, women, and men too . . . when they read the latest hot book and they want to know what it feels like.'

Lizzie explained the general outline of John's proposition, and how he'd offered to compensate her on that score.

'Well, in that case, if you promise to stay safe, and keep your phone handy with my number at the ready . . . Maybe you should go for it, if only for one more date. Are you supposed to see this gorgeous, gin-drinking dominant of yours tonight, then? How are you communicating with him? You haven't given him your normal phone number, have you?' He glanced across at the twin electrical socket in the corner, with his personal iPhone, and his 'working' iPhone, both currently charging. He hadn't been on any appointments in a long, long time, but he still kept the phone charged out of habit. 'Escorts always have a separate phone, solely for "business".'

Lizzie reached for a biscuit, but took two, then another. She'd expended a lot of calories last night in all that writhing about and squirming in pleasure. 'Ah, I thought of that. I told him I'd just had my phone stolen, and that I wasn't officially working last night. I gave him my "Bettie" Gmail address so he could contact me . . . and I was going to nip to the phone shop today and get a cheap second phone.'

Brent looked admiring again. 'Well, at least part of your brain wasn't completely softened by lust. Shall we make a day of it? I'm not due in until the four-to-eight stint. We could have lunch, then hit the O2 shop? To spend some of your ill-gotten gains?' Brent sometimes worked on Saturdays too, in a garden centre, a job he'd dismissed as menial when he'd first grudgingly accepted it as a stop gap, but now seemed to have taken to.

'Absolutely. Unlike you two, I've got absolutely no work of any kind today, and I'd love to do lunch.' Lizzie's heart lightened, seeing something of the old Brent twinkle coming back. 'I need some new undies as well . . . something a bit more deluxe.' She paused again, and felt her blush intensify. 'And maybe a little detour into the Anne Summers shop . . . for a few, um, accessories. And a lot of condoms, of course.'

'Of course.' Brent looked solemn, but he was fighting not to laugh. 'One must be prepared for anything.' He reached across the table. 'If you're going to do this bonkers thing, you might as well do it right . . . and enjoy yourself. Especially if he's as gorgeous as you say.'

'Oh, he is . . . he is . . .'

'I'll make some breakfast, then we'll make plans.' Brent rose, lithe and handsome as he crossed the room. Lizzie still found him attractive, but in a detached sort of way. The two of them had enjoyed a fling very briefly, a year or two ago, but had soon realised they liked each other much better as friends, partly because Brent's true emotional preference was for men.

'Incidentally, how much did you charge?' he flung over his shoulder, rummaging in the fridge.

Lizzie named her price, and the bonus John had given her.

'Good grief, woman, you must have been good! That's as much as I'd have charged for an all-nighter. I can't believe you pulled down that amount of dosh for something you'd have done for nothing anyway. There's no justice in this world, you acquisitive little bitch,' he finished amiably.

'Well, I shan't keep it all. Just enough for the undies and stuff, and some for the rent and bills pot.' She remembered her guilt, not over the sex and the subterfuge, just about the money. 'I'm going to put the rest in an envelope and slip it through the letterbox at the Cats' Protection shop. Either that or keep it all and give it back to him when he goes.'

Brent shook his head. 'If you're going to do this thing, do it properly. He's obviously loaded and the money means nothing to him. So spend the money on yourself and on the lucky kitty cats, if you must.'

Maybe I will . . . Maybe I will . . .

But why did she somehow feel that she was the one who ought to be paying John Smith for her pleasure, rather than the other way around?

Don't look anywhere but where you're going, Belle had said in *The Secret Diary of a Call Girl*. Swan straight into a place as if you're meant to be there, head up, gaze forward, looking fabulous.

Well, yes, that probably worked beautifully in a huge cosmopolitan hotel in a big city, but the Waverley Grange was just a modest-sized country house hotel, and the staff on reception probably knew precisely who all their guests were, and who was or wasn't supposed to be in the building. Lizzie's heart thudded, and not from the delirious excitement of seeing John again. No, it was the fear of being called to account by someone that had her pulse hammering.

'I shouldn't worry, love,' Brent had said. 'The Waverley is a rum sort of place and they won't turn a hair over a guest sending out for an escort. They have regular fetish nights, and the bar is known as an upmarket pick-up spot. Hell, I've done appointments there myself, in the past.'

Still, Lizzie's nerves jumped when she forgot her resolutions and glanced at the reception desk. A tall, dark, slightly Latin looking man with long black hair was behind the desk. He wore a superb suit, something she might imagine John wearing, but just a tad flashier. The manager, she thought, and he doesn't half fancy himself. Dark eyes behind metal-framed spectacles appraised her, and he smiled slightly, but his barely perceptible nod seemed to be her pass to the hotel's interior.

In the lift, she tried to slow down her breathing, and checked her look in the mirror on the back wall. She'd gone for a businesslike vibe with a smart, navy blue suit she'd once got for a big interview, worn with a crisp white blouse. She hadn't got the job – there were a hundred people up for it – but she knew she'd looked fantastic on the day. Her hair was shining black, easily guided into its almost natural 'Bettie' style, her shoes were her highest heels, and she carried her most humungous bag that could still be termed a handbag rather than a tote. She didn't like to think what would have happened if the hotel manager had insisted on a security check, although if what Brent said about the Waverley was true, maybe almost everybody marched into the place with bags full of condoms, sex toys, spare lingerie, lubricants and goodness knew what else.

Reaching John's floor in moments, she drew in a big

breath and stepped out, remembering last night. She'd been with him, his hand at the small of her back, guiding her. Now she had to proceed under her own steam, with the choice to chicken out entirely at her disposal. She fingered the new phone in her bag, with John already listed as a 'favourite', along with Brent and Shelley. It would be so easy to call or text, politely declining. Brent would probably even know an alternative girl who'd be happy to take the gig.

No way!

At his door, she rapped firmly before second thoughts could grip her.

'Bettie! So glad you made it.'

Ah, she hadn't dreamed him. John Smith was just as handsome as she remembered, just as real. It seemed like a week since she'd seen him, a long week in which she'd spent most of her waking moments wanting him again, but really it was just twenty-four hours.

As he conducted her into the room, she wondered if he'd been aware of her doubts. Something quizzical in his expression seemed to suggest so, as if he were privy to her most intimate thoughts . . . and perhaps the depth of her deception? 'Nice to see you again, John,' she said, masking it all, and leaning in towards him, to kiss his cheek. Her lips brushed a faint hint of stubble, and he was dressed for business, apart from his abandoned jacket. Had he been hard at work doing whatever it was he did, even far into the evening?

'You look perfectly delicious, woman. That's a great outfit. Do you always dress for business when you're doing business?' He winked at her, his expression puckish and provocative.

'Doesn't do to look too obvious in my line of work. Keep

the goodies in a plain brown wrapper, so to speak.' She winked back at him.

'Speaking of business . . .' John crossed to the dresser and came back with a plump envelope. The cash sum, she presumed, that they'd agreed when she'd emailed her new phone number.

Knowing it was crass to count it in front of him, she said, 'Might I powder my nose before we . . . we get started?'

'Of course.' His blue eyes glittered. Had he heard the little hesitation? She still couldn't be sure he didn't suspect. He seemed to be almost humming with thoughts and secrets all the time, his smile open like the sun, yet hiding Lord alone knew what shadows and deceptions of his own.

In the bathroom, she counted the cash – all there – then texted Brent to say everything was OK and he mustn't worry. After a few deep centring breaths, she spent a penny, rinsed her hands, and refreshed her lip gloss.

Ready as I'll ever be. Now or never and all that . . .

She pushed open the door.

John was sipping a small drink. Gin, she supposed. She could detect a faint hint of its balsamic tang as he came close to her. 'Drink?' he enquired.

'I'll just have some water, please, if I may?'

'You are businesslike tonight, aren't you?' His grin was tricky as he opened a bottle and poured for her.

'Well, I'm in a service industry. I like to stay sharp and give value for money.'

'Admirable . . . admirable . . .' he murmured, watching her like a raptor as she took a few sips, then put aside the drink.

Another deep breath. 'So, John . . . what's it to be?'

His beautiful mouth quirked, then for just an instant, he snagged his plush lower lip between his teeth. Then even though there was barely any visible sign of it, she sensed him turn to steel in front of her. It was as if he grew an inch or two, at least in aura, radiating power. She imagined him as a demon, a bastard of the negotiating table, getting everything he ever wanted with barely any effort.

'Well . . . first, indulge me, beautiful Bettie . . . Call me "master".'

It was like being back in the lift again, but with the cable cut. The word sent her plunging wildly, perhaps not down a lift shaft but a hurtling roller-coaster plunge, a thrill of terror ride. This was it. The game. She could play, or just give him his money back and flee.

Never!

'Yes, master,' she said. Her voice was soft; he'd taken her breath away.

He took her face between his two smooth hands and looked into her eyes, the intensity of his scrutiny stripping her. Still fully clothed she felt more than naked, all her hopes and fears revealed. Then he kissed her, gently at first, then more powerfully. Thrilling to her submissive role, she kept her lips still, and pliant, receptive, passive. Her arms hung by her sides as he ravished her with his lips and tongue, tasting the soft interior of her mouth, subduing her, filling her to the brim with the kiss.

'Good,' he said abstractedly, releasing her lips. 'Very good.' Sliding his thumb across her face, he pushed that into her mouth like a pacifier. 'Suck it.' As she obeyed, he let his other hand glide down her body, over breast, flank and thigh, then, tugging at her skirt, he hauled it up ruthlessly and cupped her bottom cheek in a rough, rude grip. Her flesh was dough to him, he kneaded it, fingertips digging in. After a second or two, he pushed his fingers into her anal groove, rubbing her there, teasing, pressing, his other thumb dragging at the corner of her mouth as she gasped, breathing hard.

'Such a delicious little strumpet,' he whispered, hard up against her, his breath wafting her hair as he massaged her anus through her knickers. 'Dirty little minx . . . You like this, don't you?' He probed her, pushing, pushing. 'I bet you'd like a cock in there, wouldn't you? Or a plug? A big fat black plug?'

Heat surged through every cell in her body. Goddammit, she was sweating, despite her industrial strength deodorant. Her head filled with visions of herself kneeling on the chintz covered bed, her bottom well up, heavily lubricated, while John pushed obscenely inside her rectum. Swaying, she was weak at the knees at the very thought of it.

'Answer me.' His thumb slid out of her mouth.

'Yes . . . yes . . . I'd like that.'

'Cock or plug?'

'Either . . . if it pleases you.'

He laughed happily, sounding almost boyish. 'Perfect answer, my darling.' He kissed her again, softer this time. 'We'll do that . . . play those games. Maybe not tonight, but soon.'

His lips plundered hers again, more rough kisses as he fingered her rear portal.

'Lovely girl,' he said at length, freeing her, setting her from him and looking her up and down again as her skirt slid back into place. 'And lovely suit too . . .' He touched her breast fleetingly through the crisp jacket. 'I think I'd like you to keep it on for a while.'

As she stood there waiting, he retrieved his drink and sipped a small mouthful before putting it aside. 'Will you bring that chair from over there into the centre of the room?'

He nodded to a very plain wooden upright chair that she'd never noticed before. Had it been there last night? She didn't think so. Had he requested it specially, for his devious purposes?

She set the chair in the centre of the room, a few feet from the bed, facing it.

'Now sit down, please.'

Trembling a bit, Lizzie took her place, arms resting on her thighs. John moved to stand directly in front of her, looking down. She tried to keep her eyes respectfully lowered, but she couldn't stop herself staring at his crotch. His erection was massive already.

'Naughty, naughty . . . you mustn't look at that. You can't have that for a while yet, much as I know you're wet for it.'

She was. She really was. Perspiration wasn't the half of it. Her expensive new knickers were already saturated with silky arousal. There wouldn't be any necessity for her to fake her enthusiasm with lube, no way.

'Sit very still. Eyes lowered. No peeking.'

He strode away, towards the dresser, and opened a drawer. Curiosity boiled. She wanted to see what he was taking out, but she managed to keep her eyes downcast, only stealing an oblique glance when he threw a few items on the bed. It looked like a handful of silk scarves, the substantial, men's kind, and perhaps some ties.

Bondage now? Well, she'd expected it.

Trailing a scarf, he came and stood behind her, and with no warning, drew first one of her arms then the other behind the chair-back. In quick, precise movements, he tied her wrists. The knot was firm, though not painfully restricting, but the positioning of her hands made her chest lift, and her breasts press against the fabric of her jacket and blouse. She was breathing hard as he went away, and then brought back another scarf.

This, he fastened around her eyes. It was a black scarf, in a tight weave. She could no longer see a single thing. As he adjusted it, he stroked her hair, tidying and smoothing.

What now? What now?

She could hear him moving about. She could almost hear him thinking, although not the actual thoughts. He was plotting, scheming.

He was close.

Strong hands settled on her thighs and she realised he was actually kneeling in front of her. Surely that was wrong? He shouldn't kneel to her; he was the master here. Then she had a flash of what he was up to, the second before he did it.

He pushed up her skirt, saying, 'Hup!' to make her lift her bottom from the seat so he could bunch the fabric around her waist, back and front. Next, he slid his thumbs in the elastic of her knickers and skinned them down in a brisk, ruthless action. The waft of his shirtsleeved arm seemed to suggest him tossing them away across the room.

'Sublime.'

Steps away again, then he was back at her, and with more scarves, he secured her ankles to the front legs of the chair, immobilising her with her crotch on show and her bare bottom and her pussy pressed to the wooden seat.

Oh God, oh God, oh God!

A sensation of light-headedness engulfed her, powerlessness and extreme excitement. It was like being very young again, right on the sexual threshold, and about to go all the way for the first time. Her heart thundered, and she almost wanted to cry, but in a good way. The very best way.

'Pretty as a picture,' said John roundly. She could sense

him still very close, crouching in front of her as if he were staring intently at her exposed bush. There was absolute silence for a moment, apart from his breathing and hers, which was far more rapid and fluttering, then she felt it.

A fingertip slid in amongst her pubic curls, parting her labia, to settle right on the tip of her clit in the very lightest ghost of a contact. Her hips jerked, pushing her forward, chasing pressure, but the touch was gone again as suddenly as it had occurred, and she sensed John rise to his feet in front of her.

'And now, I think I'll take a shower.' His footsteps receded away from her. 'Be a good girl while I'm away, won't you?'

Then the bathroom door opened, and closed, and she was alone.